VIRAL MISERY

Book One

THOMAS A WATSON
TINA D WATSON

Credits

EDITED BY SABRINA JEAN
www.fasttrackediting.com

COVER ART BY NICHOLAS A WATSON

Characters

^Arthur Steele (poppa) - 44

^Wendy Steele - 43

Joseph Steele - 24 Naval pilot

Kit(M) and Kat - Black labs.

Donald and Daisy - Rottweilers.

Mickey and Minnie - Persian cats

Gloria - Wendy's baby sister

Alicia - Wendy's friend

^Shawn (14) & **Beth** Byrd (5) **Lucas** (4mo) - neighbor of Shawn

^Kirk (10), **Pat** (8), **Jim** (6) Willis -had older sister and younger brother.

^Andrea Fox (dirty blonde) 18 **Shelia** Meyer (red head) 13 **Betty** Owens 10 **Tony** Johnson 11

^Nicole Bryant (blue eyes, very blonde) 2 months first with Arthur

Tammy & Ted- Sara's parents

^Vicki (10 Little Momma) **Jodi** (7) **Robin** (brown hair) (2) ^**Pam** (6mo)

^Joann & ^**Sally** Payne (8) twins

^Ryan (7 months) Wendy pulls info sheet in nursery

^Noah- (2) Wendy finds searching houses.

All kids: 8 Boys - *Tony (11) *Kirk(10) *Pat(8) Jim(6) *Shawn(14) Noah(2) Lucas (6mo) Ryan(7 mo)

11 Girls- *Andrea(18) *Shelia(13) *Betty(10) Beth(5) Joann & Sally(8) Nicole(2mo) *Vicki(10) Jodi (7) Robin (2) Pam (6mo)

Rudy - neighbor

Starlie & Jack Wright - closest neighbors

^Dr. Scott Sutton - CDC assistant director

Winston Vander- secretary of commerce

Surgeon General - Jackson

Secretary of Defense - Kenner

Secretary of Treasury - Temple

Secretary of Labor - Kasich

Secretary Homeland- Paterson

Secretary of HHS- Ginger Stringer

Director CDC - Ernie Ostimer

Leading Virologist- ^Dr. Richard Skannish.

^Sarah- intern assigned to Sutton.

Kercher Farm- where they hide road

Logan Lancaster LL-

Dean-16yo evil kid that tried to join

Title Page

Copyright

Credits

Cast of Characters

Dedication/Acknowledgements

Chapter 1 1

Chapter 2....................................8

Chapter 3....................................13

Chapter 4....................................20

Chapter 5....................................27

Chapter 6....................................34

Chapter 7....................................43

Chapter 8....................................52

Chapter 9....................................61

Chapter 10..................................68

Chapter 11..................................84

Chapter 12..................................90

Chapter 13..................................96

Chapter 14..................................105

Chapter 15..................................118

Chapter 16..................................129

Chapter 17..................................135

Chapter 18..................................144

Chapter 19..................................158

Chapter 20..................................169

Chapter 21..................................185

Chapter 22..................................196

Chapter 23..................................206

Chapter 24..................................217

Chapter 25..................................226

Chapter 26..................................240

Chapter 27..................................247

Chapter 28..................................258

Chapter 29..................................267

Chapter 30..................................276

Chapter 31..................................283

Chapter 32..................................290

Chapter 33..................................302

Chapter 34..................................310

Chapter 35..................................315

Chapter 36..................................332

Dedicated to the Memory Of

This book is dedicated in memory of Larry O. Watson and Starlie Dyer. The world is a little darker without these two in it.

Acknowledgements

Thank you to all of you that helped with this one: Dana Rice, Sabrina Jean, Leslie Bryant, Yalonda Butler, Denise Keef, William Beedie, Jim Broach, Leora Kipmio, William Allen, Deb Serres and Cora Burke. Tina has helped with all my books in one way or the other, this one we did together. I'm so proud of her.

Chapter One
Unleashed

March 27

Climbing out of his BMW over a hundred miles north of Hong Kong, Zhang Wei smiled to see his father walking out of the small farm house he'd grown up in. Zhang was under no illusions. He knew how much his parents had sacrificed for him to go to school. Walking over, Zhang noticed his father's eyes were red. "Hello, father," Zhang said, tilting his head and then engulfing his father in a hug.

His father, Lei, pushed back, "No, son, I just came from the fields and your suit is too nice," his father said, dragging his forearm across his nose. Looking hard at his son's gray suit, Lei grinned. "Silk, very nice."

Reaching in his suit, Zhang pulled out an envelope. "Here is money for the family; don't tell mom," Zhang said, shoving the envelope into his father's hands.

Trying to push the envelope back, "No, son, you keep this," Lei said, but Zhang pulled his hands away.

"Father, I got the promotion," Zhang cried out with a big grin.

Lei froze, holding the thick envelope. Slowly, a smile filled his face as he lunged forward and hugged his son tight. "We are so proud of you," Lei said, fighting back tears. Realizing he was dirty and hugging his son, Lei stepped back. "I don't want to get your suit dirty, sorry."

"Please," Zhang laughed. "I can afford more and now you can. The others can fix up the house."

Looking down at the envelope stuffed with money, Lei gave a sigh. "I always knew you would make it, son."

Looking at the ducks in the rice fields, Zhang nodded. "I learned everything I needed to know from you and mom on this farm."

"Let's go tell your mom," Lei said and Zhang put his arm over his father's shoulders.

When his father tried to pull away, Zhang held him tight. "I know you love to farm, but now you can do it as a hobby," Zhang said, watching his father wipe his nose again with his wrist but paid it no mind.

Working in the rice paddies with the ducks, Lei had contracted a visitor. From the loving embrace of his father, one of the deadliest viruses ever dreamed of had latched onto Zhang's hand. This invisible killer was known to science, but had never been transmitted human to human. But like viruses do, a small change had occurred to HAPI A (H5N1) or in other terms, Highly Pathogenic Avian Influenza Virus Type A H5N1. All the right changes had been made to the small piece of genetic material that would unleash misery on the world as never seen or dreamed of before.

Lei would find several of his chickens and ducks dead the next day, but would brush it off. As the virus multiplied slowly in his body overloading his symptoms, Lei would continue to work and interact with his family and neighbors. It would be over a week until he felt sick. When Lei started coughing on the eighth day after getting infected, he would be dead before the sun rose on the ninth day.

Neither father nor son knew of this killer in their midst as they walked into the small farm house to share the joyous news.

On the other side of the globe in Arkansas

Wendy Steele stepped out the back door, giving a sigh. "He made another trip," she mumbled, looking at her husband's pickup truck. The bed was loaded with junk to her. To her husband, Arthur, it was free work material. She could see half a dozen computer towers and then, a stack of laptops. Then in two neat rows were electric motors of various sizes.

Since they had bought the land they were living on over eighteen years ago, Arthur made one trip a week to the landfill near Clarksville, over twenty miles to the south. "He could just buy the stuff," she groaned but knew it was a lost cause.

Arthur was a tinker. He loved to build stuff and that's what had gotten him several patents. None of the patents were earth shattering, but the royalties let them live in reasonable comfort.

She had met Arthur at a party when she'd been in high school. One of her friends had snuck a group of them into a college party at the University of Arkansas and Wendy had fallen head over heels for Arthur. At the time, Arthur had been in his first year of nursing school.

When she'd graduated high school in the fall, Wendy had enrolled in nursing school and the two were married a year later. They had only worked as nurses for a few years before Arthur had filed his patents and sold them to industries. They'd moved from Little Rock to the land they lived on now for almost two decades.

Walking around the swimming pool, Wendy heard music coming from Arthur's shop. Coming to a stop, Wendy looked around at the wooded backyard. Oak and cedar trees dotted the area behind the house with the only real clearing around the swimming pool. The house was set on a steep almost one hundred-foot cliff, overlooking the valley floor and in front of a saddle between two small hills that barely rose fifty feet. Arthur's shop was dug into the hill on the right, or west side.

Originally, they had bought three hundred acres but four years ago, they had bought two hundred and fifty more acres that bordered their property to the south. The first property had come with a two-bedroom house that now served as Wendy's studio and office. The second had come with a bigger brick house, but nobody had lived there in thirty years so Arthur had torn it down, salvaging everything he could. Now, they had pallets of bricks.

Also on that property was another barn. It had been overgrown, but they'd cleaned it out and rebuilt it. That barn was where they did a lot of their textile work. They produced silk, hemp cloth, cotton, and wool. Not in large scale, but the quality was very good. In truth, the farm produced for them a nice living by itself, but they had to carefully itemize so the government didn't take everything that they loved to do.

They had lived in the small two-bedroom house as Arthur, over two years, had built their dream home where they lived now. Granted, it was much bigger than they needed, but they were hinting to their son that they had room for grandkids; even though Joseph had only been twelve when they'd moved into it.

Thinking about their son, Joseph, Wendy smiled. He was twenty-four now and in the Navy flying transport planes, waiting for his chance to fly jet fighters off aircraft carriers. Joseph had been ten when they had moved and the hills, creeks, and ponds on the land had become his playground. Many times, Wendy had had to send Arthur out to collect Joseph for supper. And long ago they quit counting how many times he 'fell' into the creeks on the property.

Glancing over to the east hill, she saw the windows of the greenhouse that was buried in the hill. That greenhouse was their year-round garden. There were two more greenhouses that were massive just behind the two small hills, but those were more orchards. "That man can build anything," Wendy chuckled, then turned back to the swimming pool. When Joseph had been in junior high, Wendy had told Arthur she wanted a swimming pool, since Joseph was constantly swimming in the creeks and ponds.

She'd handed Arthur a sketch of what she wanted and in three months, it was done and only the concrete had been bought. Everything else had been salvaged by Arthur. The pool was kidney-shaped with a hot tub near the shallow end where water flowed out over rocks and into the pool.

In truth, Wendy didn't mind the 'salvage' because it had saved them tons of money and Arthur always kept the land neat. She could almost set her watch that by tomorrow, the truck bed would be empty and all the junk neatly stored in bins in the shop until needed.

The whole reason they had moved to the middle of nowhere was that they hated being raped by the government. What the government called taxes, they called rape. They made more money now than they had when both were nurses full time, but when working as nurses the feds had taken over forty percent of their earnings.

Now, with Arthur's royalties from his patents and the books he had written, her crafts and selling vegetables at the farmers markets, and other goods grown on the farm they were using an accountant that had them paying thirty percent taxes. Granted, they didn't like that, but it was better than forty plus. Of course, there were many times they forgot to file cash payments. Their whole goal of moving here was to see just how self-sufficient they could become and so far, they were doing pretty damn good.

They generated their own power, made their own material for clothing, and grew their own food. It had taken awhile, but they had achieved their dream: becoming totally self-sufficient. The only thing they had ever wanted more of, were kids. But that wasn't in their deck of cards. When Joseph was born, Wendy's uterus had ruptured and she and Joseph were lucky to be alive. That had been the end of her childbearing years.

When Joseph was in high school they had tried to adopt, but were turned down the first time because there were guns in the house. It made no difference that all the guns were in safes. Arthur loved guns and Wendy loved shooting guns with him, so they'd given up. Then three years later, they had tried again and were turned down because they lived too rural.

Walking into the bay door of the shop, Wendy saw Arthur in his metallic suit, guiding a four-foot sheet of steel with long tongs that were glowing red. This was one of the first things Arthur had built, an induction furnace to melt metal.

When the sheet of metal hit a bar on the rollers, Arthur pulled a lever to shut the flow of metal off and hit a button. She could hear the hum of hydraulics as a thick metal blade slowly extended, cutting the glowing metal. Moving down the conveyor roller line, Arthur lifted the stop and pushed the glowing sheet down the line rollers on the table until it hit another line of rollers that moved perpendicular to the first.

As Arthur moved back up to the furnace, Wendy looked at the three sheets of glowing metal and was guessing it was half an inch thick. She knew it was four-foot-wide and eight-foot-long. "If he builds a tank, I'm going to throw a fit," Wendy vowed.

Looking at the far wall, she saw the entrance into the machine shop. Glancing back and seeing Arthur rolling out another sheet of metal, Wendy moved over to the door walking past the metal sheets and felt the heat radiating off the glowing sheets. Stepping into the shop, she grinned at seeing the rows of shelves that held the assorted junk, or as Arthur had put it, 'merchandise we can get for nothing'.

Everything was neatly organized in bins around the machine shop. Glad to see the machines silent, she moved down and passed the small area Arthur had set up to work on electrical components. The last room was his woodworking area and was sealed off from the machine shop by a door. Two years ago, Arthur had put a small bay door in for the wood shop because he was tired of wood dust getting into the machine area.

Again, glad to see the wood area not set up to do work, Wendy moved back to the furnace room and closed the door to the machine shop. The only reason she could stand in the room was two huge fans that were sucking the hot air out. Seeing Arthur cutting the sheet and then move back to the furnace, Wendy knew the vat was near empty.

Confirming her guess, Arthur opened a slot and the molten metal poured out like syrup into a stone cistern. Grabbing his tongs, Arthur guided the sheet of metal down the line as Wendy saw the flow of metal slowly stop several inches from the top of the cistern. "One day, he's going to miscalculate," Wendy mumbled as Arthur turned around, taking the helmet off.

Wendy couldn't help but smile as Arthur grinned at her. Even at forty-four, he still looked good, making her heart skip a beat. "You done?" she yelled over the vent fans.

Not hearing her but reading her lips, Arthur nodded and pointed out the bay door. Taking the silver fire jacket off as he headed for the door, Arthur hung it up as Wendy stepped outside beside another building and when she glanced at it, couldn't help but laugh.

Inside that building was the largest saltwater battery Arthur had ever built. The reason she laughed was his first try had been in the power house fifty yards from the house. The battery Arthur had built was six feet tall, seven feet wide, and ten feet long and when he had filled it with water, the two-inch slab he had poured busted. Wendy had chuckled for a week, but never when Arthur was around because she had told him that was going to happen.

The battery he'd built for the machine area was twice the size of those for the house. When he had set up the power building for his shop, Arthur had poured a ten-inch floor. "What'cha got, gorgeous?" Arthur asked, coming out of the shop. He looked Wendy's five-foot-six body over with a grin.

Turning around, Wendy laughed to see the mischief on Arthur's face. "Daniel called to make sure we were coming to wire up the new fellowship hall," Wendy said in-between chuckles.

Reaching back and pulling his sweat-soaked ponytail off his neck, "I told the pastor, my ass was going to be there at noon, it's not even nine," Arthur huffed.

"Hun, everyone we know has come to realize when you get into a project, you forget the time," Wendy said, watching Arthur wipe his hand over his sweat-soaked brown hair.

Dropping his hand to his beard and stroking it, "Not when I give my fucking word," Arthur mumbled.

Giving a long sigh, Wendy overlooked the only flaw she had with Arthur. He was a potty mouth no matter who was around. "So, we are still going?" Wendy asked.

Pointing past Wendy, "I have my stuff in the work truck," Arthur answered and Wendy glanced back, shaking her head.

The 'work truck' was a massive International 4300 that used to be owned by a power company. Arthur had bought it wrecked and even though it was over a decade old, it looked brand new. It had taken Arthur six months to rebuild it. Gone was the yellow paint job and it was now black. Painted on each door was a huge muscle-bound man, strangling a donkey in one hand and an elephant in the other. Below the painting in bold letters read, 'No Politics Construction'.

When Arthur had asked her to paint it, Wendy had laughed so hard she'd wet her pants. They loved their country, but not those that ran it. Wendy didn't consider herself an artist, even though she sold painting and crafts. All in all, they were over five different companies and hadn't made a profit, according to their books, in the last decade.

"So, we are taking that and not your pickup?" Wendy asked.

"Hell, yeah," Arthur sang out and started blabbering, explaining why.

Stepping over to him, Wendy raised her finger and put it over his mouth. "Hun, you're taking your Adderall today," she told him with a stern face.

Giving a groan, Arthur stepped back and stormed off toward the house. "I hate taking that shit!" he shouted.

"Then stop talking so damn fast and moving like the people in the Matrix!" Wendy shouted after him. "You make me tired when you do that!"

Wendy chuckled as Arthur held up his middle finger as he opened the back door and her black labs ran out. "Here, Kit. Here, Kat," she said, clapping her hands. Kit, the male reached her first and sat down. As Wendy started petting him, Kat, the female sat down.

"Were Don and Daisy bothering you?" Wendy asked, petting Kat. Don and Daisy were Arthur's Rottweilers.

Taking off at a jog, "Come on," Wendy said over her shoulder and the labs took off after her, beating her to the back door. Walking in, Wendy found Arthur at the sink drinking a glass of water. Seeing a medicine bottle on the counter, she grinned and walked over to wrap her arms around him.

"How about we go to the bedroom and you make me feel like a woman before we leave," Wendy purred.

The next thing she knew, she was scooped up in Arthur's arms as he carried her in a run to the bedroom.

Chapter Two
Life is good

April 2

Looking around the boardroom, Zhang gave a grin at seeing the other thirty senior executives from Tong Shipping, the largest seafaring freight shipping company in the world. Every office was represented from Rome to Los Angeles, thirty-four in all. The most senior of the outlying executives was James Taylor, over from the London office.

When the senior vice president called for a break, Zhang stood up and turned to James. "So, will you be joining us tonight?" Zhang asked, rubbing his nose with the back of his hand.

"Are you kidding?" James laughed. "I haven't missed a gathering after a meeting since I've been with the company, and that's over ten years."

"I'm glad tomorrow's meeting starts at noon," Zhang laughed.

Glancing at Zhang's tag, "Zhang, that's why they start the next three days late," James laughed.

Tilting his head to James, "If you don't mind, can I stay near you?" Zhang asked in a low voice. "I don't know how to act in an executive gathering."

Holding his hand out, "Mate, if you don't have a blast, I won't ever attend another gathering," James bet.

Shaking James's hand with relief, "Thank you," Zhang said relieved. "I don't want to be noticed as the new guy."

"You'll have a blast," James laughed as everyone moved over to a table filled with refreshments. Running a finger around his collar, James wiped his forehead with his hand. "Grab me a cup of coffee if you wouldn't mind, Zhang. I'm going to find the thermostat and turn on some air."

"Yes, it is a bit warm," Zhang chuckled, even though he thought it felt nice in the boardroom.

As James walked away, a visitor he didn't want had embedded in his nasal passage. The unwanted visitor had a communicability level of over ninety percent, so anyone close to Zhang would receive the slow, deadly visitor. James just got it faster.

Arkansas

Riding on the tractor, Arthur looked behind him at the plow. He looked ahead and slowed as he neared the fence. The garden was on the east side past the fish pond and was ten acres, surrounded by ten-foot deer netting. They had found out last year that the netting worked on elk as well. However, Arthur had still had to put up an electric fence to keep the black bears out of the beehives they had put in the garden.

That was a lesson he had learned seven years ago, when he'd started keeping beehives. One bear had decimated his four starter hives in one night. Then two days later, the bear had gotten into the chicken coop. Unfortunately, that same bear had come back a week later after Arthur had brought four more beehives home, and had died suddenly of lead poisoning.

Not satisfied with a normal electric fence, Arthur had made his own controllers for his electric fences. He'd only forgotten one time when he'd bumped into the electric fence he had put around the chicken coop. When he'd woken up a few minutes later lying on the ground, Arthur had hung engineering ribbons on the fences, so he wouldn't do that again. After that, he'd never had bear problems again.

That couldn't be said about raccoons. He had always heard they were smart, but he had gotten a lesson those first few years. After losing half his chickens to the bear, Arthur had lost the rest to coons in the same week. Buying more chickens, Arthur had put a game camera up and watched in awe as a raccoon had climbed the chicken wire up to the door handle and opened the door.

As the ringleader had climbed down, Arthur watched two other adults and four smaller coons waltz right in and have a feast. That was how the coon war started for Arthur, and it would last full bore for the next five years.

The first thing he'd done was put a deadbolt on the door and then bought traps. There were casualties on both sides. Arthur lost chickens and cats, but the coons were losing numbers. Over five years, Arthur had trapped, stalked, ambushed, and hunted thirty-four raccoons in the war.

Last year a ninja coon showed up, but a veteran now, Arthur had dispatched him with only losing one cat and one chicken. The cats around the barn weren't really pets. Arthur let them live there as long as he didn't have mice. Not only did the cats help keep the mice down, but they did a fair job on the squirrels, gophers and wild rabbits. Only able to guess, Arthur thought about a dozen or so cats lived on the property.

The only cats he claimed were the two Persian cats that lived in the house; Mickey and Minnie. They were inside cats and as far as Arthur was concerned lazy as hell and got hair everywhere, but Wendy loved them so he kept his mouth shut. If he fed an animal, that animal better show him respect. That's why Arthur didn't like cats.

Lifting the plow up, Arthur turned the tractor around and started another set of rows. Glancing over, he saw Wendy driving her four-wheeler down the rows he had already made, planting seeds. It'd only taken him four years to convince her to use the four-wheeler, instead of planting the rows by hand.

Walking ten acres back and forth to him was wasteful, but Wendy had put up a fight until the first time Arthur had let Joseph use a four-wheeler to plant. After she'd watched how fast their son had planted, her four-wheeler had better be set up for planting or she would let him know about it.

When he was done, Arthur pulled the tractor out and turned it off. He climbed out and checked the sprinkler system as Wendy finished. Hearing the four-wheeler turn off, Arthur turned around and saw Wendy walking over to him. "Don't say it," she said, holding up a gloved hand.

"I would never say that you were hardheaded about using technology," Arthur gasped in fake shock.

Chuckling, Wendy turned to look at the neat rows. "We should've planted two weeks ago," she sighed.

Standing up, "We only have one shift a month as nurses and someone volunteered us to help build the new fellowship hall at church," Arthur chided.

Punching Arthur lightly in his arm, "You said it was okay," Wendy popped off.

Laughing, Arthur put his arm around her and turned to the north. The house he had built was sitting a hundred feet over the valley below. The hundred acres below them were all fields, divided into twenty acre sections so they could alternate the cows, horses, and sheep. Their property stopped at Pine Creek, but Arthur thought it should've been called Little Pine River.

The creek on the east side of the property that he used for hydropower was a creek. There was another creek to the west, plus three ponds. Only the valley floor they owned was fields, the rest of the land was covered in trees and most were hardwood. They had orchards of mulberry and peach trees. But Arthur loved his oak and pecan trees.

At the very back edge of the field below the steep rise was a massive red barn, then further to the east was the original two bedroom house. Looking at the small house, Arthur was proud of how far they had come with all the work. "Ready to go work in the greenhouse?" he asked.

"I get stung by a bee today, I won't be happy," Wendy sighed. "I like working in the greenhouse when they are in the hive."

Shrugging, "We can go swimming and do the greenhouse this evening," Arthur offered.

Looking behind her, Wendy saw the eight-hundred-square-foot building that housed their gym beside the pool. On the outside, Arthur had put a shower and people could use the bathroom in the gym without tracking water into the house. "Okay," Wendy said, heading for the swimming pool.

"Skinny dipping only!" Arthur sang out, running past her for the swimming pool.

"Then we aren't getting in the hot tub because you'll fall asleep," Wendy shouted, breaking into a run. Their closest neighbor was over half a mile away up the valley. Within five miles of the house, there were only six other houses and all of them were up the valley. Their land sat at the end of the valley, so they had isolation.

In fact, they had to drive twenty miles just to reach a small gas station. Clarksville was just over twenty-eight miles away, but they had to drive almost fifty miles to get there. As Arthur liked to point out, they lived at the ass end of nowhere and that was fine with them.

Both stripped as they ran and were soon joined by the dogs. "If your dogs take off running with my bra again, they get shot," Wendy shouted as Arthur skidded to a stop and pulled off his cowboy boots.

"They haven't done that since they were puppies," Arthur snapped, dropping his boot.

Watching Arthur dive in, Wendy put her right boot at the back of her left and pulled her left foot out as she started unbuckling her jeans. "One day, someone is going to drive up here while we are acting like teenagers," she laughed as Arthur tread water.

"My dogs know how to attack because the gate up here is locked. Everyone we know calls before showing up," Arthur told her, watching Wendy strip. He loved their lifestyle. Their job was here and they laughed and played just like they had when they'd met.

Thinking of the other families they knew, Arthur really felt sorry for them running the rat race. They made almost everything they needed. Hell, they pumped so much extra power back into the grid, they made good money.

When the government had offered to pay for half of any solar setup years ago up to twenty grand, Arthur had taken them up on it. Near the small house were fifty panels, and working with the hydro, wind turbine, and sterling power plant, Arthur was sure the power company hated them. Every quarter, a large check had to be mailed out to Arthur and Wendy.

Watching Wendy dive in, Arthur swam over to her as she broke the surface. "I'm going to work on my next book tomorrow," Arthur told her.

"The fantasy one?" Wendy asked, wrapping her arms around his neck.

Nodding, "Yeah, I'm getting e-mails from people wanting the next book," Arthur said. He had four hobby project books out, along with two fantasy series. With the stuff they sold from the farm and with his patents and books, they only worked a few nursing shifts to keep their licenses. Truth be told, they worked as nurses so the IRS bandits would leave them alone. Everything they earned as nurses was turned over to the government.

That was their whole idea of this land they'd bought. Become self-sufficient, so they didn't have to buy and pay in taxes. So far, it was paying off and was only getting better. Not only were Arthur and Wendy married, they were best friends.

Chapter Three

The world is really a small place now

April 8

Relaxing in first class, James grinned, just thinking about the fun times they'd had every night. It'd been the second night that Zhang had finally loosened up and had a blast. On the last night, Zhang couldn't stop sneezing until he'd drunk five shots. "The company picks up the dime, you have fun," he mumbled, remembering the VP handing over a credit card for the first bar tab of ten grand.

They had spent money like they were mad at it.

Feeling his nose itch, James rubbed it with the back of his hand while feeling the airplane level out. "Care for a pillow, sir?" the attendant asked beside him.

"Please," James smiled. When the attendant placed the pillow behind his head, James reached back and brushed her hand with his as he put the pillow where he wanted it.

"Care for a cocktail?" she asked, smiling.

Feeling his stomach inform him not to, James looked up. "You have any tea?" he asked.

"Certainly," the attendant smiled, leaving James.

Before his layover in Greece, James gave ten others on the flight an unwanted visitor, including the attendant. On his four-hour layover, James unwittingly infected over a dozen but also, touched an ATM and his armchair in the first class lounge. Those two surfaces alone delivered another eight unwanted guests. Not to mention the man who'd taken James's credit card to pay for his bill. Before flying out, James was able to enjoy his hobby.

Before he'd reached London, James had spread the invisible guest to over sixty people.

The problem was, out of the other thirty executives who had also been infected, James had infected on a scale none could ever imagine. Because of James, the visitor was spreading like wildfire across the globe, thanks to his hobby.

April 10

Hearing his cellphone ring, Zhang reached a hand out from under the covers, patting around his nightstand. Feeling his phone, he grabbed it and pulled it under the covers. "Hello," he mumbled, seeing it was only five a.m.

"Zhang, you must come home. Father is very sick," an elderly female voice cried out.

Jerking upright and sitting up in the bed, "Mom?" Zhang asked, blinking his eyes open and gave a hard sneeze.

"Yes," she sobbed. "Your father is coughing up blood."

"Take him to the doctor," Zhang shouted, jumping out of the bed and hearing his mother sneeze.

"You know we can't afford that."

"Mom, get the envelope I left and take dad to the hospital," Zhang ordered, grabbing a pair of pants. "I have to get someone to cover for me, but I should be on the road in an hour."

In the background, Zhang heard a violent, barking, hacky cough. "He is burning up," his mom wailed.

"Mom," Zhang barked in the phone, hoping to calm her down. "When did the coughing start?"

"Just after midnight and continuously getting worse," she answered.

Feeling relieved at that, Zhang slowed down in getting dressed. "Then the doctors can help him, mom. I'll meet you at the hospital."

"Son, he started passing blood before he started coughing."

Zhang stopped in pulling on his shirt, "Father peed blood?"

"No, out of his bottom," his mother sobbed.

"Mom, get dad to the hospital. We have money now," Zhang told her. "I will get there as fast as I can."

"Okay, I will get Chen next door to help me get your father in the truck," his mom said, sounding more relaxed and then sneezed. "Please hurry, so you can explain what the doctors say."

"I will, mom. See you in a few hours," Zhang said, hanging up and calling the office to tell them that he had an emergency.

Thirty minutes after hanging up with his mom, Zhang's father died on the way to the hospital.

April 16

Sitting on the front porch with Wendy and watching the sun set, Arthur heard the phone ring. Giving a sigh, he got up and jogged inside. Grabbing the cordless phone, he grinned to see Joseph's satellite phone number. "Hey, son," Arthur sang out, answering the phone.

"Hey, dad. How are you and mom?" Joseph asked.

"Doing good, and you?"

"I'm living the Navy dream, baby!" Joseph yelled out.

"That's good, so you are still coming home on leave?"

"Yeah, that's one reason I'm calling. Got my ticket and you can pick me up May first at 2300 at Little Rock," Joseph said. "Man, I can't wait to see the place! I miss those hills and trees. The guys think I'm crazy spending thirty-two days at home."

Grabbing a marker, Arthur made a note on the dry erase board beside the phone. "Well, the place misses you, but not as much as we do," Arthur said, dropping the marker. "You find a woman yet and start on some grandkids?"

Giving a long groan, "Dad, please," Joseph moaned. "I will give you some grandkids, I swear. I'm only twenty-four, I have plenty of time."

"What about us?" Arthur chuckled.

"I have a layover in Greece, I should just find a kid and bring them so you and mom will give me a breather," Joseph offered.

"Hey, we'll take it," Arthur laughed, walking back outside and Wendy turned. Seeing the happiness on Arthur's face, she knew who he was talking to.

"He find a girl yet?" Wendy asked in a low voice and Arthur shook his head. "He doesn't have to marry them. Just shack up with one, he's handsome enough," she cried out, throwing her hands up.

"Tell mom, I heard that," Joseph replied in a flat voice.

"Son," Arthur said. "You know damn well she wanted you to."

Busting out laughing, "Yeah, mom may not cuss much, but she damn sure doesn't mind letting others know how she feels," Joseph howled.

Getting serious, "Son, did you say one reason you called was to confirm your flight?" Arthur asked.

"Yep," Joseph shouted proudly. "When I report back for duty after I leave the farm, I report to Tampa on June second and learn to fly F-18s. I'm going to be a real Naval Aviator and not a delivery man."

"That's great!" Arthur said enthusiastically. He and Wendy didn't like Joseph in the service, but it was his life. If the military was used as it was supposed to, they would've liked it more, but they always supported Joseph no matter what he did. They understood the military was being used like a police force for the large corporations to make tons of money.

But that had been Joseph's dream, to be shot off a carrier in a fighter and then become a Navy SEAL. As Joseph's parents, be damned if they would stand in the way of his dreams.

"Is mom still going on the cruise?" Joseph asked.

"Yeah, twenty-one days through the Caribbean with her sister and the girls from church," Arthur answered. "She leaves April twenty-third and will be back on May fifteenth so you will get to spend half your leave with her."

"You tell her she'd better go," Joseph snapped. "The deal they got on tickets should be illegal."

Giving a curt chuckle, "I said the same thing," Arthur agreed.

"Let me talk to mom. I don't want to know how much you are paying for my sat phone," Joseph said.

"To talk to our boy, it's well worth it," Arthur told him. "You call if you need anything or think of something you want to do when you get here."

Giving a homesick sigh, "I just want to walk the land, dad. Then maybe fish in the ponds," Joseph answered.

"Love you, son. Here's your mom," Arthur said and handed the phone to Wendy.

"Hey, big man," Wendy sang out as Arthur sat down. Wendy talked to Joseph for half an hour and then said goodbye.

Setting the phone on the glass table between them, "I should cancel," she said.

"Babe," Arthur said, throwing up his hands. "You have been looking forward to this trip for eight months since you got the tickets."

"You were never going," Wendy said, reaching over and squeezing his hand.

"Babe, we can't leave the farm for that long anymore," Arthur said. At one time, they'd had a worker named Jason. He had started working for them soon after they'd bought the land but a year ago, he had died in a car crash and they didn't like anyone who'd applied for the job since.

"I know, but it's been a year and a half since I've seen my baby," Wendy pouted.

"You will get to spend over two weeks with him and I say, let's drive him to Tampa," Arthur suggested. "We would only be gone a few days and that's not a problem for the farm."

Raising her eyebrows, "Well," Wendy mumbled.

"Babe, this will give me and Joseph time to bond, walking around and farting and such," Arthur said in a serious voice.

Busting out laughing, Wendy almost slid out of her chair. "You two better have all that out before I get home," she howled, kicking the floor. "I can still remember having to run out of the house for a breath of fresh air."

As Wendy stopped laughing, Arthur shrugged his shoulders. "Besides, I used my chemistry set to cook up some date rape drugs. I'm going to drug Joseph and grab a hooker to rape his ass, then tie her up in the barn until she delivers."

"Arthur," Wendy snapped, making him turn to look at her. "You don't tie her up in the barn. Tie her up in the basement, so we can tend to her."

Nodding with a grin, "Yeah, that is a better place," Arthur said.

Wendy held his hand tight as she looked out over the rise. She had come from a large family, but Arthur had spent his life in foster homes until he'd graduated high school. That was the only thing she felt bad about in the marriage. She couldn't give Arthur more kids, but it showed her how much he loved her.

"He will give us grandkids," Wendy said in a serious voice. "But if he hasn't by the time he's thirty, we drug his ass."

Squeezing her hand as he chuckled, "It's not like we would have to pay a girl, Joseph is a nice-looking kid," Arthur said.

Nodding her head, "You know, I think I was the only mom who, when Joseph was in high school, wanted my son to knock a girl up," Wendy admitted.

"That would've killed his dream, though," Arthur sighed and Wendy sighed after him, agreeing. "I want you to promise me that you will have a good time."

Slowly turning to look at Arthur, "I will be stuck in the same room with my baby sister for twenty-one days and you want that guarantee?" Wendy scoffed.

"Gloria is a sweetheart," Arthur snapped.

"Shit, you didn't grow up with her ass," Wendy huffed. "I should steal some of her kids, she has four. She won't miss one."

"Nah, I hate to say it, but they are brats," Arthur said. "Every time they come to stay, I want to run and hide in the woods until they leave."

"Hun, Gloria was much worse, so I see them as an improvement."

Getting out of the chair, Arthur kneeled down in front of her. "Love, I want you to have fun. This will be the first vacation you've had without me up your ass in the twenty-six years we've been married."

"I would have more fun if you were there," Wendy mumbled.

A grin spread across Arthur's face. "I want you to come back with tan lines, so I can request light meat."

Throwing her arms around his neck, Wendy busted out laughing again. "You are so bad," she laughed. Wendy was spoiled and she knew it. For the last decade, Arthur had bought her a new BMW every two years. The only reason was when they were in college, Wendy had seen the rich kids driving them and had told Arthur she wanted one just to flaunt it.

Being Arthur, he'd taken it seriously and did buy her one after they graduated, but only after finances allowed. Then ten years ago, he had started buying her a new one every two years. No matter how much she bitched, Arthur still bought her a new one. To date, only Wendy had ever had a new car. Arthur bought used ones and fixed them up.

The one time she'd tried, Arthur had found her researching new pickup trucks on her laptop and holy shit did a fight ensue. Wendy did buy him a new tractor and Arthur was only mad for a week. Finally, he'd hugged her and said. "Babe, I like building them so if something breaks, I already know how to fix it."

So that was the only new thing she'd bought, except guns. Not even Arthur would bitch when she bought him a gun. The electric carts, four-wheelers, and side by sides they had, Wendy bought them used and helped Arthur and Joseph when he still lived with them, fix them up.

Even Joseph was corrupted on new cars. On his sixteenth birthday, he wanted a classic Camaro and he got a '67.

"I will have fun, but it's not fair that you don't get a vacation," Wendy said.

"I went to that six-day combat class in Arizona last year alone," Arthur reminded her as Wendy sat back.

With a flat expression and voice, "You shot guns in the desert," Wendy said. "We've been to those classes together and shoot all the time here."

Shrugging, "I know, but it was still fun," Arthur smiled. "You realize you won't be able to take your pistol, right?"

"Yeah," Wendy snapped. "I can't even take your damn dogs. I've never been unarmed that long."

"I like looking at you holding weapons," Arthur chuckled. "How about you put on a swimsuit and let me take some pictures?"

Standing up, Wendy grinned down at him. "How about nudes?"

She laughed as Arthur scooped her up in his arms and ran into the house.

Chapter Four
Disaster looming

April 19

Walking into the White House, Dr. Scott Sutton held up his ID to the Secret Service agent. "They're waiting for you, sir," the agent said and led Sutton through the halls. Sutton had been the assistant director of the CDC for over a year and this was the first time he'd had to give a report to the president.

The agent held open a door and, seeing the president and his cabinet sitting around the table, Sutton nodded at the agent as he walked in. "Mr. President," Sutton said, moving to the other end of the table.

Setting his briefcase down, Sutton opened it to take out bound reports. Passing a stack to each side, Sutton took one for himself and sat down while opening it up.

"Can I ask what is so important that I'm missing my tee-off time? I was feeling hot today," the President said, taking one of the bound reports.

"Mr. President, a lethal virus has sprung up in China," Sutton said and everyone around the table groaned. "We are basing our preliminary information on what the Chinese have researched on the virus. We are working on confirming this now."

"Dr. Sutton, you do realize China is on the other side of the globe, right?" Kenner, the Secretary of Defense said.

Stopping a smartass comment on the tip of his tongue, "Yes I do, but there is a confirmed case in London," Sutton replied and everyone became very interested. "The first death was on the fourteenth of this month and as of today, over fifty more from one village. We have a team on the ground and the report you are holding is what we have so far."

Opening his report, the president saw the map and where the village was at. "How did someone in London get infected from this little farming village?" the President asked.

"We are looking into that," Sutton answered as the others started reading.

"What's the lethality rate?" Jackson, the Surgeon General asked.

Clearing his throat, "So far, one hundred percent," Sutton answered and everyone dropped their reports and looked at him. "If everything continues to unfold the way we have all feared, H5N1 has learned to transmit human to human."

"Incubation period?" Jackson asked.

"Six to ten days after infection, but the victim shows no signs, with the exception of a slight runny nose, sneezing, and itching of the nose and eyes," Sutton said.

"Oh, come on, it's spring! Half the population has that now," Kenner shouted.

Ignoring Kenner, "When are they contagious?" Jackson asked in a trembling voice.

Nodding his head, "Thirty-six to forty-eight hours after infection, yet won't show signs for another week," Sutton said and Jackson rocked back in his chair, visibly shaken.

"Care to enlighten?" the President asked, looking at Sutton.

"Sir, those infected don't show signs of it until six to eight days later. The most prevalent is hard coughing as the lungs fill with fluid, but some patients pass blood in the bowels from a cytokine storm," Sutton said, looking at the president. "After the coughing starts, average time to death is twelve to twenty hours. Those put on ventilators manage to hang on for another day before dying."

Before the president could respond, "How are the anti-viral meds working?" Jackson asked.

Shaking his head, "The advance team report none are responding," Sutton answered. "Even Flu-X shows nothing."

"So," the President snapped, looking from Jackson to Sutton. "We developed a flu drug in secret, spending billions, and it doesn't work?"

"That's correct," Sutton answered with no shame.

"How about a vaccine?" the President asked.

Cringing and dropping his eyes to the report, "We should have a trial dose ready in ten months," Sutton finally said.

"We know anything about the case in London?" Jackson asked, grabbing a glass of water.

"Just that James Taylor left Hong Kong on the twelfth," Sutton said. "He's a senior executive for Tong Shipping, but MI6 is doing background."

"Can't they ask him?" Temple, the Secretary of the Treasury snapped.

"No, he's in a coma and they don't expect him to live much longer. He arrived at the hospital in a coma," Sutton snapped back, getting tired of feeling like he was responsible.

"What's the CDC recommendation?" the President asked.

"Total travel ban in and out of the US for two weeks," Sutton said and most of the table jumped up yelling.

Grabbing a cup, the president tapped the table to get the attention of those that were yelling. "Please!" the President shouted, looking at their chairs. "Surely that can't be all," the President said, leaning back in his seat.

Taking a deep breath, "Yes sir, Mr. President. We feel if a case is confirmed in the US, we need to declare a fourteen-day holiday and force people to stay at home," Sutton responded. This time, even the president jumped up, shouting with the others.

"Shut the fuck up!" the President bellowed at the others. The throng of cabinet members all froze, staring at the president in shock. "I'm the boss, so sit down," the President snapped and then looked down the table at Sutton. "Do you realize the impact to the economy those actions would bring?"

Nodding, "Yes sir, but if people start dying, then that would be worse because there wouldn't be anyone to work or spend money," Sutton answered as sweat beaded on his forehead.

Sitting back down, the president narrowed his eyes at Sutton. "So, the CDC is one hundred percent sure this will reach us?" the President asked.

"We believe it already has," Sutton replied. "We are waiting for confirmation on a case in Los Angeles."

Glancing around the table and stopping at the Secretary of Treasury, the President leaned back in his chair. "Temple, is there any way we could do a shorter holiday like Mexico did years ago?" the President asked.

Scoffing as he threw his hands up, "Mr. President, our economy is a thousand times bigger than Mexico's. Our economy generates over fifteen billion dollars a day, sir. You do the math," Temple huffed.

Sutton's eyes grew wide, hearing the numbers as the president looked over at the Secretary of Labor. "Kasich, is a minimal shutdown feasible from your area?" the President asked.

"Mr. President, unemployment is finally under four percent. Asking the companies to shut down, even for a short period, means they will have to lay off thousands," Kasich answered.

"Mr. President?" the Secretary of Homeland Security said, holding up his hand.

"Yes, Paterson," the President sighed.

"Reports over the last two decades indicate the average family only keeps three days' worth of food in the home," Paterson said, looking down at the report. "Even if we declare this holiday, people will have to get out to buy food or they will riot."

"Everyone," the President said, clearing his throat. "I want each of you to come up with fifty million dollars from your area by the end of the day and transfer it to the CDC. I want Homeland to allot seven billion," the President commanded, then looked at Sutton.

"You tell everyone at the CDC, nobody goes home until we have a vaccine. You will have the finances, now you should be able to put more people working on a vaccine with ten billion dollars," the President told him.

The Secretary of the Treasury gave a sigh of relief, pulling out his smartphone. "Mr. President, I'll make sure the CDC has that in the next few hours," Temple said with a lazy smile. "Hell, if need be, we can double that."

"Mr. President," Sutton said, feeling lightheaded with the way everyone casually tossed around the word 'billion' associated with money. "The finances will help, but research takes time and no matter how much we spend, we can't buy time."

"I beg to differ," Temple laughed out and most joined in, giving a chuckle.

Looking down at the end of the table to Sutton, the president leaned over the table and rested his arms. "Sutton, you head back and get your people to work and hire who you need. I expect a report in one week, right here."

"Mr. President," Kasich said in a low voice. "You will be in Texas next week."

Flopping back in his chair and giving a curt grunt, "No, I won't," the President chuckled. "I don't want to go there anyway, they didn't vote for me. I'll be here for Sutton to give me an update."

Everyone laughed as the Secretary of Defense handed out his own bound reports. "Mr. President, I'll see Dr. Sutton out," Jackson said, getting up.

"Thank you and will you read his report and explain it in English for me?" the President asked, picking up a pen and making notes on a pad.

Walking around the table, the Surgeon General waited as Sutton packed up his stuff. When Sutton stood up, instead of leading Sutton to the hall, Jackson led him out a back door into another room. Closing the door, Jackson turned to Sutton. "When will your team have a more detailed report on the virus?" Jackson asked.

"We only got a sample here two days ago, so in the next forty-eight hours we can confirm what the Chinese sent us," Sutton answered.

Looking at Sutton hard for a few seconds, "In your report, it said the virus could survive outside a host for five hours. You think that's right?" Jackson asked.

"No, that's what the Chinese stated," Sutton answered quickly and Jackson sighed in relief. "I think it can survive outside longer," Sutton replied and Jackson paled. "The virus is encapsulated, unlike any H5N1 we've ever seen, that I already know and was going to explain."

Closing his eyes, Jackson took a deep breath to steady his nerves and then opened his eyes, waving at the door to the meeting. "None in that room would understand, just like they don't understand research takes time," he sighed. "What about the other trial pre-pandemic vaccines we already have for H5N1?"

"The Chinese have the same vaccines we do and so far, none show an immune response in patients. But the real problem is the virus is highly lethal to chickens, more so than us. Most avian species show symptoms in twelve hours and die within five days but there are a few, seagulls for one, that last over a week," Sutton explained and Jackson stumbled back into a chair.

"Holy shit," Jackson gasped.

Glad to see Jackson understood what they were facing, Sutton put his briefcase down. "Just from what we know now, this is the virus that we have always worried about. It's airborne, can live on surfaces for hours, has a long contagious phase with the patient showing no symptoms, and is highly lethal," Sutton said and Jackson noticed Sutton was nervous.

Reaching in his pocket and pulling out a business card, "Call me if you need anything, and keep me updated," Jackson told Sutton as he took the card. "You think our H5N1 test kits that we have will work to identify people who are infected?"

Shaking his head, "No," Sutton answered and Jackson felt the weight of the world press down on him. "The Chinese reported that, but this virus has a hemagglutinin sequence we've never seen before. Several of the virologists that are working on it now said this virus shouldn't exist."

Reaching out and grabbing Sutton's arm, "They don't think it is a created bioweapon, do they?" Jackson gasped.

Shaking his head rapidly, "No, this is nature's creation. We are positive on that," Sutton answered confidently.

"Damn, a part of me was kind of hoping because that would mean a vaccine was already prepared," Jackson said, letting Sutton's arm go. "If it reaches our shores, I really feel this can turn into a doomsday scenario."

"Like our leading virologist Dr. Skannish told me, nature creates the ultimate viruses, not man," Sutton said. "Jackson, it already is a doomsday scenario unless we keep it off or contained early on this continent."

Nodding, "I'd have to agree with him on viruses, and you on that," Jackson said as a Secret Service agent opened the door behind them.

"Sirs, I should tell you, this room is recorded for security," the agent said in a serious voice. "I can show you a room where you can talk privately."

Jackson turned to the agent, "Have your supervisor mark this recording classified."

"Yes sir," the agent nodded. "The room across the hall is cleared."

Turning back to Sutton, "Keep me updated," Jackson said, holding out his hand.

"I will," Sutton promised, shaking his hand and grabbing his briefcase.

"We won't need the room," Jackson said, heading to the door that the agent was holding open.

Following Jackson out into the hall, "Will you talk to the President and explain that money will help, but action would do more?" Sutton almost begged.

Stopping at the door, Jackson glanced back at Sutton. "I'll try, but you have to realize that everyone in that room has been bought and paid for, and I'm not talking about the citizens of America," Jackson said and the agent snorted, trying to hide a grin. "They answer to corporations and banks. Sutton, you have to understand, that's who will be losing money and that's who will be calling the shots."

Giving a sigh, "Yeah, the director told me the same," Sutton sighed.

"Why isn't he here?" Jackson grinned.

"Visiting drug company executives and to be honest, I think his doctorate is honorary only," Sutton groaned. "He doesn't understand anything we talk about."

Laughing as he walked out into the hall, "That could be said for many here in Washington," Jackson said as the agent closed the door.

Following Jackson down the hall, "Aren't you going back in?" Sutton asked.

"What they're talking about now doesn't concern me," Jackson shrugged, leading Sutton out. "Besides it usually pisses me off, so I leave now and don't get stressed out."

Giving a curt nod, "I've never heard of money in the millions and billions talked about so casually," Sutton admitted.

"That's why I'm leaving," Jackson grinned.

As the two stepped outside they parted ways as the silent killer started picking up speed at a lightning pace and more people picked up unwanted guests as James Taylor's hobby flooded the world.

Chapter Five
A destroyer in the air

April 23

Sitting at the table and eating breakfast, Arthur looked over at Wendy and could tell she was excited about the trip. "You make sure to have fun," Arthur grinned after finishing his plate.

As Arthur got up, Wendy nodded. "I will and if you need help, you call Starlie and Jack," she said. Starlie and Jack Wright were their closest neighbors. They were both in their sixties but had an active ranch. To Arthur and Wendy's envy, they had six kids all grown now with kids of their own. The ranch they owned next to them up the valley used to be a hobby but now, Jack raised cattle full time after retiring from construction.

"Shit, Jack calls me once a week to do something for him, so I know he stays busy," Arthur said, rinsing his plate off and putting it in the dishwasher. He moved over to the back door and a large touchpad screen mounted on the wall. A list of daily chores was listed on the screen and Arthur started tapping the ones they had done, making them drop off the list. Because he was driving Wendy to the airport today, they had started earlier than they normally did.

"Well, you can always call Rudy," Wendy laughed out as she got up.

Tapping 'workout', Arthur watched it drop off the screen and then turned around as Wendy put her dishes in the dishwasher. "If I call Rudy, it will be to tell his bitch ass to bring back my shit," Arthur snapped.

Closing the dishwasher, "Do you even know what he has?" Wendy chuckled.

"Log splitter, chainsaw, riding mower, half inch electric drill, jig saw, shovel, and posthole diggers," Arthur answered, counting them off on his fingers.

Walking over and wrapping her arms around Arthur, "Yeah, he brings one thing back but borrows two other items," Wendy smiled. "I thought he was going to cry last week when you told him he couldn't borrow anything else until he brought everything back."

"Cocksucker tried to load the wheelbarrow up he'd brought back because I wouldn't let him use the plumbing snake," Arthur snapped. "If I didn't have duplicates of what he's borrowed, I'd go to his shack and stomp his ass."

Holding her arms around Arthur's waist, Wendy looked up at his face. "You wait till I get back if you do that, I want to watch this beat down."

"You going to help hide the body?"

"Oh, hell yeah," Wendy laughed, letting Arthur go. "Remember to take the two pies in the refrigerator to church on Sunday for the raffle."

Scoffing, "They might get one," Arthur mumbled. "I spent over a hundred hours building that fellowship hall and they are raffling stuff to pay for it."

"Arthur," Wendy snapped. "It's to buy the stuff they are putting in it, you know that."

Looking at Wendy with a grin, "Yeah, I know," he said. "Just like rousing your dander at times."

Laughing as she headed to the den where her luggage sat by the stairs, "Will you take the BMW?" she asked.

Letting out a long groan, "Oh, come on," Arthur whined. "Can't we take my truck?"

Turning around, Wendy stomped her foot. "I don't like riding for over an hour in your truck," she moaned. "My car rides a thousand times better."

"Fine," Arthur said, walking over and grabbing two suitcases. "I'll look like a fucking yuppie."

Grabbing the large rolling suitcase, "Hun, nobody would ever think you were a yuppie," Wendy told him. "You're wearing jeans, boots, and a long plaid shirt."

Heading for the front door, Arthur looked down at the thin blue plaid shirt. "I have to wear something to conceal my pistol," he said, setting down the suitcase in his right hand.

"Yes, and we all know the only shirts that do that are plaid," Wendy laughed out as Arthur opened the door and picked the suitcase back up.

"Just for that, I'm not feeding your damn silkworms," Arthur snarled jokingly.

"Fine, I have more in the fridge," Wendy shrugged as the dogs ran over. She stopped in the door and stood the rolling suitcase up as she leaned over loving on the dogs. "You four better leave the cats alone."

"Babe, they haven't chased Mickey or Minnie since they were puppies," Arthur said, walking off the porch and heading for the garage He stopped, looking at the two open doors. The first held Wendy's light gray BMW. The next held his 1984 Blazer. Parked outside the garage next to the house was his truck. A 1986 quad cab Chevy diesel that was jacked up six inches with monster forty-inch tires.

"I don't want to ride in that," Wendy sang out, seeing Arthur looking at the truck.

Letting out a long sigh, Arthur carried the suitcases to the BMW. "I like my big truck," Arthur mumbled, opening the trunk and putting the cases in.

"Oh, I like it, but not riding for long periods," Wendy said. "If you want, we can take the Blazer, it doesn't beat me to death as bad."

"Nah, my girl likes her Kraut car," Arthur sang out, turning around and grabbing the rolling suitcase to put it in the trunk.

As Arthur closed the trunk, Wendy leaned over and kissed his cheek. "I'm so spoiled," she whispered.

"Yeah, but you're worth it," Arthur laughed.

They climbed in and Arthur backed out, hitting the remote to close the garage doors. Driving down the driveway, Arthur got comfortable in his seat as he buckled his seatbelt. "Did you fix the gate camera yesterday? I still saw it on the list," Wendy asked as Arthur hit the remote to open the gate.

"Yeah, I fixed it but didn't put it up, so I didn't mark it off," Arthur answered, driving through the gate. There were cameras everywhere across their property. Like everything else, most were reclaimed by Arthur. The main reason for most cameras was to let them know if wildlife was on the property. Arthur was certain the raccoons were regrouping for a major counterattack any day.

There were cameras around the house, but they were to see if deer were eating the flower beds. The barns had cameras to watch for dreaded coons and opossums. All the greenhouses and gardens had cameras just because there were beehives inside them now and the bears really liked the honeybees. The only cameras that could be considered security cameras were the ones on Arthur's shop, the gate, and the root cellar that was behind the barn, buried into the rise.

Those had been added because of Rudy.

Glancing at the backseat, "How much luggage is Alicia bringing?" Arthur asked.

"I don't know," Wendy shrugged as Arthur honked the horn, waving at Jack and Starlie as they passed in front of their house. "Wonder where they are going?" Wendy asked, seeing Jack and Starlie climbing in Jack's truck.

"You know they shop at the end of the month," Arthur said, weaving around a deep pothole. "You see? They took *his* truck."

"I ride in your truck to town all the time," Wendy popped off and Arthur just glanced at her, grinning. "You going to shop since you're going to be in Little Rock?"

"Not in your car," Arthur chortled.

Rolling her eyes, "I should've known. You wanted to take your truck so you could've gone to the dump," Wendy groaned.

"Landfill," Arthur corrected. "Don't see what the problem is, we go to garage sales all the time. What people don't sell at their garage sales ends up in the landfill. I just skip paying them for it."

Reaching over and patting Arthur's leg, "Next time we go to the big city, you can go to the dump," Wendy snickered.

"I'm changing your ticket to one way," Arthur sighed.

"I don't care, I have credit cards and know my address," Wendy said, leaving her hand on Arthur's leg. Glancing out as they passed a small house, Wendy waved at a young couple on the porch, holding a small baby. "Make sure you take Joseph down to Tammy and Ted's," Wendy sighed, waving and saw both wave back. "Little Nicole is so precious."

Letting his right hand drop off the steering wheel, Arthur held her hand as he drove down the valley. Arthur smiled at the tiny bundle in Tammy's arms as they passed. "I offered to babysit," Arthur mumbled.

"Please," Wendy chuckled as Arthur turned at the Y at the end of the valley. "They are new parents and won't let that baby out of their sight until she's two." Ten miles later, they reached the small paved county road. Hearing a ring and buzz, Wendy pulled her hand from Arthur's lap and grabbed her cellphone.

Before looking at the screen, they both said, "It's Alicia."

"Hey, Alicia," Wendy answered the phone, never even looking at the screen.

"Are you on the way?" Arthur heard Alicia moan.

"Yes, we should be at your house in a few minutes," Wendy laughed.

"Okay, I'll be outside," Alicia cheered and then hung up.

Tapping her screen, "I hope Alicia finds herself a new husband soon," Wendy said, setting her phone down.

"As much as that woman bitches, she won't keep him for long," Arthur pointed out and Wendy reached over, popping his arm.

"She's not that bad," Wendy snapped and reached down to hold Arthur's hand again.

"Oh yeah," Arthur said. "There are four other women going from church, but we were the only ones stupid enough to agree to take Alicia."

"Okay, I'll go so far as to say Alicia can be annoying at times and she may not have a husband now, but she divorces nicely," Wendy chuckled.

Nodding with wide eyes, "If I ever had to pay that much in alimony, you would disappear, I'm just saying," Arthur said.

"Not able to argue against that," Wendy agreed.

Twenty minutes later, Arthur pulled up to a nice house and saw Alicia standing in her driveway next to three suitcases. In her late thirties, Alicia was a hefty woman with short brown hair. "Only three? I'm shocked," Arthur said, putting the car in park.

Opening the trunk as he climbed out, Arthur watched Alicia run around the car and jump in behind Wendy. "Sure, I'll get your suitcases," Arthur said as Alicia shut the door.

Only able to get two in the trunk, Arthur opened the back door putting the last one in the backseat and heard Alicia talking nine hundred miles an hour. "Oh, we are so listening to rock and roll when we hit the interstate," he mumbled, closing the door.

Climbing back in, Arthur tried to block Alicia's voice, but he figured he would have better luck turning lead into gold. "What do you think about that flu they are reporting in China?" Alicia asked, buckling up as Arthur started the car.

"All I've heard on the internet is it was a bird flu," Wendy answered as Arthur pulled out.

"I get my flu shot every year," Alicia announced like she deserved a cookie.

Wendy squeezed Arthur's hand wanting him to join the conversation, but Arthur just looked ahead as he drove. "You hear anything else, Hun?" Wendy finally asked, so Arthur would talk and Alicia wouldn't.

"Just what you and I've talked about," Arthur answered curtly and Alicia filled them in on what she had heard. Not about the flu, but all the gossip. Arthur sighed, convinced Alicia knew dirt on every person in the state of Arkansas.

When they reached the interstate, Arthur pulled on and held up his hand to stop Alicia's babbling; she hadn't stopped in the last half hour. "Sorry, but we are on the interstate and I have to have music," Arthur barked and turned on the radio.

"Yeah, I have to listen to music when I drive a long way also," Alicia shouted over the music.

Squeezing Arthur's hand, Wendy waited until he turned to her and she mouthed 'Thank you'. "Hey, you're going to be on a plane with her," Arthur mumbled, but Wendy read his lips.

"Why do you think I paid for first class?" Wendy snorted and Arthur barely heard her.

"Oh, you are so smart," Arthur grinned, but Wendy couldn't tell what he said and just looked out the window.

Reaching Little Rock, Arthur followed the directions on the navigator screen. If he'd thought Alicia would keep her mouth shut, he would've turned down the radio to listen to the directions. Having known Alicia for over five years, Arthur was convinced Alicia hated silence and loved the sound of her own voice.

When Arthur pulled up to the airport, Wendy turned the radio down. "Just pull up to the door," she said. "We have to check in and it's no use for you to pay and park."

Nodding, because Alicia had started talking as soon as Wendy finished, Arthur was thinking about having a cocktail when he got home. By the time he'd pulled up to the curb, Arthur was thinking about drinking a bottle.

Getting out, Arthur yanked the back door open and fought the urge to throw Alicia's suitcase on a passing car, in the hopes that she would chase it down. Opening the trunk, he put Alicia's suitcase on the curb and grabbed Wendy's suitcases. "I wish we were sharing a cabin," Alicia sang out as she and Wendy got out of the car.

"I would jump off the goddamn ship and tie bricks to my own ankles just so I couldn't be rescued," Arthur vowed, grabbing Alicia's two suitcases from the trunk.

"Sorry, but that's the only way I could get my sister to come," Wendy smiled, stacking one of her suitcases on her rolling case.

As Alicia fought with her luggage, Wendy stepped over to Arthur and wrapped her arms around him. "Miss you," she said and then kissed him.

"Miss you more," Arthur smiled, hugging her tight. "Call me and let me know you got there all right."

"I will," Wendy smiled and hugged Arthur again.

Letting her go, Arthur watched Wendy lead a babbling Alicia into the airport. None of them knew that lethal visitors were close. Arthur had even passed people with the virus in the city of Clarksville. In the large airport, there were many people that were disgorging the visitors. It was sheer luck, but Wendy and Alicia made their plane without picking up an unwanted visitor. But they would find it waiting on the cruise ship.

That evening as Arthur was having his second cocktail, still trying to get Alicia's voice out of his head, the visitor had made it to his valley. When his neighbor, Starlie, had grabbed a shopping cart at the store, the visitor had latched on.

Chapter Six

The unimportant masses don't need to know

April 24

Pulling up to the White House, Sutton jumped out of his car as a security officer came around the car. "They are waiting on you, Dr. Sutton," the guard said.

Reaching inside, Sutton grabbed a tote bag and handed it to the guard. "Hold this," he said, grabbing another one and his briefcase. Turning to the driver, "Go park and I'll call when this is done," Sutton said and the driver nodded.

No sooner had he closed his door, than the driver pulled off. Grabbing the tote bag from the guard, Sutton threw one on each shoulder and followed the guard through the doors. "Just put your bags on the scanner," the guard said.

Tossing the bags on the conveyor, Sutton walked through the metal detector only to hear it buzz. "Just let him through!" a voice shouted and Sutton turned and saw Paterson, the Secretary of Homeland, charging down the hall.

"Sir, we have to scan everyone," one of the guards said, pulling out a metal detecting wand.

"The day you wand me, by the next day you'll be taking orders at a drive-thru window," Paterson snapped, walking over and grabbing the bags off the conveyor belt. When the guards went to speak, Paterson raised his hand and stopped them. "Keep on, and the only job you will be able to get will be cleaning porta potties at a county fair."

Both guards clamped their mouths shut as Paterson handed Sutton his bags. "Come on," Paterson said, spinning around and walking briskly away. Keeping up with Paterson's power walk, Sutton almost had to jog.

Leading him to the conference room, Paterson nodded at agents standing outside the door and they held it open. When

Sutton walked in, he found the room was packed and almost every person was on a phone talking. Walking to the end of the table he sighed with relief, seeing Jackson, the Surgeon General was sitting next to him.

Dropping his bags, Sutton started pulling out bound reports and Paterson grabbed some and tossed them in front of people as he walked to his chair. "Yeah, they understand now," Jackson said, hanging up his phone. "Your team finish the last numbers?"

"Yeah," Sutton groaned, handing a stack of reports to Jackson who took one and passed it down. Grabbing the other tote, Sutton pulled out several folders to set at his spot and then pulled out a laptop.

"How much longer do you need, Dr. Sutton?" the President shouted out and Sutton looked down at the other end of the table to see the president holding his hand over the bottom of his phone.

"Just a few more minutes, Mr. President," Sutton answered, turning his computer on. As he sat down, Jackson plugged in a monitor cable to Sutton's laptop.

Arranging his stuff around his laptop, Sutton glanced up to see people ending calls and grabbing notepads. He was shocked to see several already reading the report he had just passed out. "Anytime you're ready, Dr. Sutton," the President said, hanging up his phone.

"Yes sir," Sutton said, tapping his keyboard. "As many of you are aware, we have confirmed cases in nineteen major cities inside the United States," Sutton reported.

"How many confirmed cases?" someone asked.

"As of nine this morning, we have one hundred and four here in the US," Sutton answered, looking up for who had spoken.

"That was from me," Temple, the Secretary of Treasury said and Sutton turned to him. "That seems like a low number, so we can stop worrying, right?"

"No, sir," Sutton huffed. "That's a terrifying number. We are still testing another three thousand, four hundred some odd samples. We are expecting another two thousand to be delivered today."

Everyone turned to look down the table at Sutton. "Let me clarify, we went from one in LA to sixteen the next day," Sutton said, tapping the keyboard and a map of the US popped up on screens around the room with the nineteen cities marked in red. "The next day, forty-seven and the day after that, two hundred and nine," Sutton said glumly.

"We can't keep a lid on this much longer," Paterson groaned, looking back down at the report.

"I'm surprised you have been able to keep it off the major news stations this long," Sutton admitted.

"How is a vaccine coming?" the President asked.

Sutton looked up with a long face. "Very slowly," he answered. "The virus is lethal to chickens, so we have to breed off chickens that are immune until we get some that can lay eggs that we can then use to develop a vaccine. Chickens have a higher mortality than we do at ninety-five percent, but they don't always pass that immunity on in their DNA."

"Whoa," a woman shouted out, holding up her hand. "What is the mortality for humans?" she asked, dropping her hand down and started flipping through the report.

"Ninety percent without medical help," Sutton informed her and there were many gasps around the table.

Leaning toward Sutton, "That's Ginger Stringer, Secretary of Health and Human Services," Jackson whispered, then turned to the table. "Everyone, let me clarify," Jackson said. "By 'medical help', everyone has to be placed on a ventilator to breathe for the patient. I've talked to several doctors who have and are currently caring for the patients, and they are telling me about pulling liters of fluid from the lungs of those infected in hours."

"So we are able to treat them?" the President asked.

Turning to Sutton, Jackson nodded. "Yes, we can treat them, Mr. President, but even with medical care over eighty percent still die. Medical care only improves your chance of survival slightly," Sutton reported and the president slumped down in his chair.

"Tell us what you can about this virus but please remember, we aren't doctors," the President sighed.

Tapping his keyboard, everyone saw dark rods on the screens around the room. "This is our killer, but it's not like any H5N1 we've ever seen. This one is designated A/duck/Hong Kong-China/RU-8/22(H5N1). When this is over I can tell you, there will be an H5α classification added," Sutton said, looking around the table. "I won't bore you with the details on the structure, but this is unlike any H5N1 anyone even dreamed of."

"We've traced it to a village 100km northeast of Hong Kong," Sutton said, looking down at his notes. "We thought a Lei Wei was patient zero, but he wasn't. There were six others in the village infected before him but it was Mr. Wei's son, Zhang Wei, who delivered it out of the small village. Zhang is a senior executive for Tong Shipping and there was an annual board meeting of the top thirty executives," Sutton stopped and tapped his keyboard. Everyone turned to the screens and saw cities around the world light up.

"These are where the executives came from and that is the outbreak points for each country. We have confirmed on...," Sutton paused, looking at his notes again. "Yes, Mr. James Taylor, who was mentioned at the last meeting was there, and we've tracked down people on his flight. By the time he reached London, Mr. Taylor infected over eighty people. But one day after returning from China, Mr. James Taylor flew to the US, Mexico, Brazil, and Spain in forty-eight hours and then returned back to London."

"How is it spread?"

Watching Sutton glance around the table for the speaker, the President spoke up. "If you haven't talked to Dr. Sutton before, announce who you are when you ask a question."

"Sorry," a man said. "Winston Vander, Secretary of Commerce."

Looking at Vander, "Airborne and droplets, or what most call contact," Sutton answered.

"I've heard all kinds of contagious periods, can you clarify?" Vander asked.

"Incubation is thirty to forty-eight hours after contact, but the problem is the host doesn't show any symptoms for seven to ten days with six days being the mean," Sutton answered and then sighed. "But in that time, they are spreading it."

"What are the symptoms?" Stringer asked.

"First is an itchy nose and sneezing. That usually shows up two days before onset of a very mild fever, followed by cough days later," Sutton said, taking a deep breath. "When the coughing starts, the patient's lungs start filling with fluid. Death usually occurs six to twenty-four hours later."

"Oh, fuck," someone cried out.

"I said a lot more than that," Sutton nodded, tapping his computer and the screens filled with equations. "These are all the mathematical models and I've explained them, starting on page seventy in the report I passed out."

Everyone started tearing open their report booklets as Sutton continued. "We will be in full pandemic levels in less than a month."

"Um, can you clarify 'pandemic levels'?" Paterson asked, looking at the report.

Thinking for a second, "Millions infected with hundreds of thousands dead," Sutton told him.

Paterson dropped the report on the table and then flopped back in his chair. "Dr. Sutton," the President called out and Sutton looked up the table at him. "Would those interventions you spoke of last time have made any difference?"

Taking a breath to respond, Sutton felt Jackson kick him under the table. "Mr. President, the virus was already here," Sutton said carefully as Jackson held his report over to Sutton.

At the bottom of the page Jackson had written, 'Be very general and don't place blame'.

"Sorry, Mr. President," Jackson said and then looked at Sutton. "Are these numbers right?" Jackson asked to cover his message.

"What numbers?" the President asked.

Looking down at his report, "On page seventy-seven in the report, they have found six cases in ducks in New York City," Jackson said. "The equation on that page is showing how fast we can expect the virus to spread into the bird population here in the states, but the numbers seem skewed."

Everyone started flipping pages as Sutton looked into Jackson's eyes and saw Jackson barely shake his head and point to the word 'blame' he had written. Sutton gave a nod and turned back to the president who was looking at the equation or more correctly, the paragraphs on the next page that explained it. "So, none of the recommendations would have made a difference?" the President asked.

"No sir, it was already here," Sutton replied quickly and the president gave a contented sigh. "The best we could've hoped for was to buy time, but it would've only been days."

"How long until we have a vaccine?" the president asked.

"We are currently working on a culture vaccine until we have a poultry reservoir to use. We expect to have results and start testing batches in six months," Sutton told him.

With most still reading, everyone groaned. "Even with the extra money we allotted to the CDC?" Temple cried out.

"Without that money, it would've been a year easy before we could've tested batches," Sutton answered. "Culture vaccines are much harder to develop and can only be produced in small scale."

"How much more funding do you need?" the President asked, grabbing a glass of water.

"It's not about funding now, Mr. President, it's about time," Sutton explained. "It takes time to grow cultures and test them."

"Mr. President," Jackson said, glancing up the table. "I asked Sutton's team to come up with a few ideas that we can go over to try and halt the spread of the virus."

"Oh, by all means," the President sighed with relief, waving a hand at Sutton for him to continue as he put the glass down.

"First and foremost is to limit panic," Sutton started, tapping his screen. "The more people move, the faster this will spread. We are recommending all top government personnel be placed in isolation ASAP. Next, we need to start shutting down all nuclear power plants."

"They only provide about twenty percent of the nation's power," Paterson pointed out.

"Right, but if too many get sick, there won't be anyone to shut them down properly," Sutton responded as several grabbed pens and started making notes. "Second, when panic hits we need to shut down power to stop people from moving around."

"But it's in the bird population," the President said.

"Yes sir, but stopping people from moving around will buy us time to save more lives," Sutton explained. "There needs to be a way to slow down international travel and travel out of cities that have high infection rates."

"I'll come up with something," Paterson offered as he wrote.

"When panic starts, the first thing we need to tell people is to avoid others. Large crowds will spread the virus really fast and I asked one of our docs who is also a psychologist, and he agreed that will stop many from rioting," Sutton said, then looked down at his notes. "Next, when we reach pandemic levels in a few days, keep the jails locked down, period. Not just prisons, but anyone in jail needs to stay there until we get a vaccine into production."

"Why? They are isolated," Paterson asked, looking up.

"They are, but the guards aren't and the other people who work or visit there aren't. One of our positive samples came from a prison in New York. I can guarantee you, every one of those inmates is infected now," Sutton explained.

Turning to the president, "We need to call our troops home," Paterson said.

"I would lock down the bases first and have all Navy ships put out and those that are out now, should have no contact with anyone from land," Sutton told him.

"I want you to do the press conference in the next few days," the President said, looking at Sutton.

"Sir," Sutton said, holding up a hand. "I may be an assistant director, but I'm a scientist first. My director has said he will be more than happy to give the briefings. His exact words were, 'Scott, I'll talk to the press because you may give too much. I can say the words but don't know what they mean and I can tell them I will get back to them. You may try to explain and give something we don't want out'."

The President chuckled, "That sounds just like Ernie. I agree, we'll let him give the briefings."

"Where is he?" Temple asked.

"In Atlanta, drafting speeches and doing mock answer and question sessions," Sutton answered.

"That's Ernie," the President repeated, looking down at Sutton. "Worst case scenario, what can we expect the loss of life to be here in the states?"

Moving two of the folders beside his laptop, Sutton picked up one that had a bright red cover. He stood up and walked down the table and handed it to the president. "That's the only copy of our recommendations and projections, sir," Sutton said as the president took the thick report.

"I will read it, I assure you, but could you answer the question?" the President asked again.

"In three to five months, two hundred and fifty million dead in the US," Sutton answered, staring at the president.

The president's mouth fell open in shock, then he snapped it closed and turned around. Looking back at a young female aide standing behind him, "Sarah, tell the joint chiefs I want to meet with them in the situation room in four hours," the President said and the aide left the room.

Everyone else was panting after hearing that number. "This virus is that lethal? It's going to kill three quarters of our population?" Paterson mumbled.

Walking back to his chair, "Not alone," Sutton replied and then sat down, looking at the president. "Mr. President, how much do you want me to give out here? I'm under orders from the director, this is for your ears only."

Glancing around the room, "Whatever you tell me, they can hear," the President answered.

Taking a deep breath, Sutton turned to Paterson. "If it goes all out, we are predicting only seven to twenty million people will be alive by this time next year in the continental United States," Sutton answered remorsefully and Stringer of HHS slid out of her chair, crashing to the floor as she passed out.

"You said the virus only kills eighty to ninety percent!" Paterson shouted.

"It does, but there will be other diseases to pick apart those that are left. People don't know how to live without the modern world," Sutton told him as several people went to check on Stringer. "Mr. President, we've already locked down the labs and all personnel in Atlanta. I suggest you do the same."

"You just tell us what you need," the President mumbled. Suddenly, he looked up. "What about the rest of the world?"

"Less than a hundred million," Sutton answered.

"How many people here in the US, do the CDC think are infected now?" Jackson asked.

Tapping his keyboard, Sutton looked up at his screen and everyone numbly looked at the screens around them. They saw a box graph with the days at the bottom, 'Projected Infected' in bold letters at the top. April twenty-fourth, today's date: 8,764,357 was in the box. The numbers increased the next two days and then exploded on the twenty-sixth to a staggering 96,627,951. "As you can see, every three days, the numbers skyrocket as more new infected are brought in," Sutton sighed, rubbing his face.

"Our current projections are that by the end of May, over ninety percent of the population will be exposed," Sutton said, dropping his hands.

"So, you can't use a person's blood who has recovered to make a vaccine?" Temple asked.

"No, but as of right now, *we* haven't had one survive yet," Sutton answered. "The Chinese have a few and found two that have been exposed but not infected."

"Dr. Sutton, I would like you to stay here and keep me updated daily," the President ordered, opening the red report book.

"Um, Mr. President, I'm on one of the vaccine teams, the leading team in fact," Sutton said and everyone turned to look at him in shock. "It's safe," he cried out. "I work with lethal viruses all the time."

"You mean, you actually work in the labs?" Temple asked, stunned that a lowly worker was in the room.

"Yeah, I graduated at the top of my class and spent twenty years working in this field. My team is credited with mapping eleven new viruses and developing treatments for nine other viruses. Just because I sit behind a desk, I wasn't going to become a useless piece of shit," Sutton barked, glaring at Temple.

"Mr. President," Paterson said in a low voice. "Let's get Dr. Sutton set up at Mount Weather."

Nodding and liking that idea, "Dr. Sutton, gather your team and report back here tomorrow," the President commanded. "You can continue your work and also keep us updated."

"Mr. President, you don't have level four research centers like we do in Atlanta," Sutton cried out.

"Yes, we do," Paterson said, closing the report.

"Dr. Sutton, I assure you that you can continue your work, but if you find out you need something, let us know and it will be there in hours," the President said, then pointed around the room at select people. "Meet in the situation room."

Jackson stayed with Sutton as he packed his stuff up and the president walked down to them. "You have family, Dr. Sutton?" the president asked.

"No, sir, none close. Haven't talked to my sister in years," Sutton answered, closing his laptop. "My research is my family."

"Well, any that you put on your team, we'll make room for their immediate family," the President said and Sutton looked up at him in shock. "Choose who you'll need and I'm making arrangements to have the facility in Atlanta stocked and guarded."

"Is there video conference set up where you want us?" Sutton asked.

Nodding, "Yes, and Jackson, bring him up to speed," the president said, leaving.

When the president was gone, Jackson leaned over close to Sutton's ear. "You played that very well. Don't try to place blame because you may have an accident," Jackson whispered, then leaned back.

"Thought that was what you were trying to get across," Sutton said, packing his stuff.

"I'll meet you at the Pentagon tomorrow," Jackson said and saw Sutton look up. "I guarantee you, Sutton, you will be happy with this lab."

"You need to tell them to start limiting contacts because I can guarantee you, the virus is in Washington by now," Sutton told him, nodding toward the door everyone had left through. When Jackson nodded, Sutton slung his bags on his shoulders and headed out while calling his driver.

Chapter Seven
We know what is good for you

April 27

Arthur glanced at the clock and moved to the den and sat down, turning on the large flat screen TV. He laughed to himself as he sat down in his chair because he'd bought the TV for ten dollars because the man had said it didn't work and when Arthur got it home, he found out a tiny fuse had blown. Replacing a ten-cent fuse, Arthur had gotten a seven grand TV for ten dollars and ten cents.

He turned it to a major network, something he hadn't done in years, and waited. The director of the CDC was to come on at five and give a report of the flu virus that was breaking out. He'd made a few calls to the hospitals he worked at and none of them said they were getting stockpiled with any treatment drugs.

On the websites he visited, there were talks of deaths from the flu but they were mostly from Mexico City. Hospitals in major cities were filling up, but weren't reporting deaths. To be honest, if Wendy had been at home, he wouldn't have been concerned.

As the commercial ended, the screen cut to a podium with CDC in glass letters stuck on the front. A man that looked to be in his mid-thirties stepped up to the podium. "Good evening, for those that don't know, I'm Ernie Ostimer, Director of the CDC.

I'm speaking to you this evening about the flu that arrived in our country a few weeks back. First, yes, there have been deaths, but as I hope everyone knows, the flu still kills. The latest death was an eighty-two-year-old in Rhode Island."

Ernie looked down at the teleprompter and then down at his notes before turning back to the cameras. "The CDC is recommending that everyone use standard precautions and make an appointment with your primary care physician to receive your flu shot early this year. We are working with manufacturers to get the first batches out soon."

Arthur leaned the recliner back, "This is the same shit you fuckers say every year," he mumbled. He may not watch TV, but he still had to read the handouts the CDC sent to the hospitals. For twenty minutes, Arthur listened and swore Ernie was just babbling. When he'd finished his speech, Ernie started taking questions and Arthur shook his head.

"My god, is this guy even a doctor?" he mumbled as Mickey jumped up in his lap. "Oh, come on, I don't want your hair all over me," he said, picking the cat up and putting it on the couch.

As Ernie finished talking after the last question, because he sure wasn't answering them, a reporter yelled out. "What about the deaths we are hearing about in Mexico?"

Arthur turned to the screen as Ernie turned toward the reporter with a remorseful smile. "I'm sorry to say, there are more deaths in Mexico than here like there always is but I hate to say it, Mexico doesn't have our health care system. They don't have the vaccination programs we have, so I hope you can understand why they have more deaths," Ernie replied, ending in a sigh.

"This idiot doesn't know and isn't saying shit about what he does know. He talked for half an hour and never gave any information," Arthur gasped in awe. "He's going to be president one day."

As Ernie took another question, the local news came on and a male anchor filled the screen. "We will bring you the highlights of the rest of the press conference at the CDC during our ten o'clock program tonight," the anchor smiled at the screen. "We have your news and weather now."

Raising the remote, Arthur turned the channel to the Science channel. "You ain't bringing me shit, numb nuts," Arthur popped off. "At least when you had the hot redhead, I could look at hooters."

When the phone rang Arthur leaned over, grabbing the cordless and saw an international number. "Hello," he answered.

"Hey, hun," Wendy said.

"Hey, babe, how are you?" Arthur said, sitting up in his chair.

"About to go eat," Wendy answered. "Did you watch the CDC press conference?"

"Yeah, and it was so boring that the local station cut it off and will play the highlights tonight at ten."

"Did they say anything?" Wendy asked.

"Just what we always get in the pamphlets at the hospitals," Arthur laughed. "Oh, and the director of the CDC is the male version of Alicia. He can talk forever and not say one damn thing."

The phone was silent and Arthur looked to make sure he hadn't lost the call. "We have to make sure they never meet," Wendy declared.

"So, is Alicia being her normal self?"

"Eww-ah," Wendy warbled as she suppressed a shiver. "Hun, she's wearing a two-piece bikini and the bottoms are thongs."

Pole-vaulting out of his chair, "What?!" Arthur shouted and the cats took off running. "She's seventy pounds overweight! Don't they have, like, fashion police on the ship? I know there has to be kids, that could scare some people."

"You're being generous with her weight," Wendy said, shivering again. "Alicia is an inch shorter than me and weighs well over two fifty; closer to three hundred."

Forcing the images out of his mind, "So are you and your sister getting along?" Arthur asked, wanting his mind sidetracked.

"Oh, Gloria is having a blast and I have to say, I'm enjoying rooming with her," Wendy laughed. "You having any trouble?"

"Trouble?" Arthur scoffed. "I'm getting yours and my tasks knocked out before eleven."

"Well, I might just see if I can take a longer cruise," Wendy snickered.

"You can, but your cats won't be here," Arthur replied. "We need to look at using their fur to make sweaters. You brush the angora rabbits out, I'm sure you can make sweaters from your cats."

"Arthur, you better be nice to Mickey and Minnie," Wendy snapped. "And for your information, you can do that."

Cradling the phone into his shoulder as a used car commercial came on blaring loudly, Arthur grabbed the remote to turn the volume down on the TV. "I am being nice to them."

"Please don't start shearing the sheep until I get back," Wendy begged.

"Babe, I can shave stupid ass sheep," Arthur moaned.

"You shave them in patches."

"Wendy, they aren't silkworms. Their fur isn't one long thread," Arthur laughed.

"Will you wait?"

"Yes, I'll wait," Arthur promised.

"I heard you took the pies," Wendy said and he could tell she was beaming.

"Yep, they raffled off for fifty apiece," Arthur told her. "That's more than we get for a pound of coffee we grow. I think you need to concentrate on making pies."

"No," Wendy barked, then softened her voice. "So, you're not having any trouble?"

Laughing, "No. Oh, you wouldn't believe how many ducks were in the field the morning after you left," Arthur told her.

"Oh they wait till I leave," Wendy barked. She loved to duck hunt, that's why she had labs. Even though she was partial to ducks, Wendy loved bird hunting of any kind. "Have you worked on your book?"

"Sure have," Arthur smiled. "I stopped typing at three this morning."

"Don't you kill off the knight, I'm warning you."

"I won't," Arthur said.

"Hey, baby, they are ready," Wendy said quickly. "I love you and will call you at our next port stop. The satellite phones on the ship are expensive. Check your e-mail to keep in touch."

"Have fun, baby. I will," Arthur said. "Love you."

When he heard the dial tone, Arthur hung up the phone and put it in the docking station. Turning to the kitchen, he saw the cats sitting in the doorway and staring at him. "What? You have food, water, and your litter box is cleaned out," he shouted at the cats as they stared at him with indifference.

"You can wait till Wendy gets back because I'm not feeding you the canned cat food," Arthur huffed as Don and Daisy came down the stairs. He grinned, hearing the massive Rottweilers' thumping footsteps on the stairs.

Still returning the cats' stare, "Keep on, Mickey and Minnie and I'll let Donald and Daisy eat some pussy," Arthur laughed out.

Don and Daisy came over and he bent down and patted them. "Where did you leave Kit and Kat?"

The dogs just looked up at him, groaning with the pats. Standing up, Arthur headed to his office. Sitting down behind a massive desk, he pulled his chair up and tapped the keyboard to wake up his computer. Opening the daily roster, Arthur added, 'check the oil and other fluids in the tractor' to tomorrow's list.

Several things were on every day, like gather eggs and milk cows. Then depending on the season, more would get added. One thing Arthur loved was order and with this list, he and Wendy rarely forgot any chore that needed to get done. His only regret was that he hadn't thought of it back when Joseph was a kid. The computer replaced the dry erase board that used to hang by the back door.

Glancing at his list for tomorrow, Arthur put the computer to sleep and headed to the master bedroom located downstairs. There was another one upstairs, but that one was Joseph's. Upstairs, there were three more bedrooms, two bathrooms, and another room that he used for a library.

Walking into the bedroom, he found Kit and Kat sprawled out over the bed. As he stared at them, Don and Daisy jumped up on the bed. "I think I'm sleeping on the couch," Arthur said, heading to the bathroom to take a shower.

***

Hearing the alarm, Arthur cracked his eyes open and saw the four dogs on Wendy's side of the bed. "When momma gets back, she's going to kick your asses," Arthur groaned, sitting up and turning on the lamp on his nightstand. Don lifted his head off the bed and looked at Arthur and then looked up at Wendy's pillow.

Blinking the sleep out of his eyes, Arthur turned to Wendy's pillow to see the cats lying side by side. "Don, don't. You know Wendy lets the fur balls sleep in the bed."

Giving a groan, Don put his head back down as Arthur got up. "Up," he barked and the four dogs jumped up and bounced off the bed. Looking at the bedspread, he could see the dog hair. Like the cats, the dogs were brushed regularly, but they still shed. Unlike the dog hair, there was much more cat hair.

Turning to look at the four dogs sitting in a row and looking at him, "Hey, you know momma lets them sleep up there. I'm going to have to wash the bedspread to get your hair off," Arthur said, grabbing his workout clothes and heading to the bathroom. "Wish I could leave the cat hair, though."

Brushing his teeth and washing his face, Arthur grabbed a towel to dry his face when he heard, "Meow," at his feet. Since Mickey was a very dark grey, he knew it was Minnie, the light grey at his feet.

"I don't like you," Arthur stated, putting the towel back on the rack and Minnie rubbed past his leg, meowing. "Yeah, I let the dogs sleep on the bed and you can't tell momma," he teased, walking out of the bathroom.

Walking into the kitchen with all the animals following, he smelled the coffee. "Automatic coffee maker; definitely a top ten invention," Arthur said and felt both cats rubbing his legs. "What?" he cried out, pouring a cup of coffee.

The cats looked up at him and meowed. Stepping over, he looked at the cats' food bowl. Spinning around and glaring at the dogs, "Who ate the cat food?" he yelled.

All four dogs laid down on the floor, looking pitiful. "I know one of you ate it because these two haven't emptied their food bowl in the last year," Arthur snapped, walking over to the pantry and getting a scoop of cat food.

The cats charged him and then one went to each leg, walking in a circle and rubbing against him while meowing loudly. "So, you act like you love me only when you have no food?" Arthur accused, dumping the food in their bowl. Getting what they'd wanted, the two cats left Arthur and paid him no further attention.

Putting the scoop away and grabbing his coffee, Arthur turned around and saw each cat take two bites before walking off into the living room. "I hate cats," he mumbled, heading for the back door.

The dogs leapt up, running for the door as Arthur held it open. When the dogs ran out, Arthur closed the door and headed to the gym. All the gym equipment was reclaimed or bought from a gym going out of business. He wasn't a bodybuilder; Arthur just wanted to stay in shape.

It was Wendy who had started them on getting and staying in shape soon after Joseph had been born. They were both lean and well-built, looking much younger than their ages.

Working out and then swimming a few laps, Arthur climbed out of the pool to see the four dogs sitting at the back door, looking away from him. Grabbing his towel and drying off, Arthur headed for the door and saw one of the outside cats. The only one he kinda liked, but he wouldn't get close to the damn thing.

It was a short-haired yellow cat reminding him of Morris from the TV commercial. The only difference was the size. This was the only outside cat that had a name: Kong. He, nor Wendy had ever picked the cat up but he knew it weighed close to if not over, forty pounds. When Kong was sitting, his head was well over Arthur's knees.

The security camera at the barn several months ago had caught Kong fighting a raccoon and killing it. Searching the internet, Arthur couldn't find anyone that had proof that a cat could or had killed a full-grown raccoon.

Kong would follow him around and Arthur was expecting any day for the cat to look up at him and bark. There wasn't an animal on the farm that didn't give way to Kong. Even the bull moved away when Kong walked out of the barn.

Stopping at the dogs as he dried his hair, Arthur watched Kong lazily look around, paying the four dogs no attention at all. "Hey, I would let you in the house, but I know you would kill the cats and I'm worried you might kill me in my sleep," Arthur explained with no shame, letting the towel drape over his shoulders.

Turning his head slowly, Kong looked at him, blinking his eyes lazily. "Okay, I'll bring out some food when I'm dressed," Arthur offered, thinking he needed to start bringing his pistol outside when he worked out.

Walking in, he saw Mickey and Minnie at the dog's bowls. "Hey, get your ass out of there!" he shouted as the dogs charged their bowls. "I should let Kong in, to whoop your asses," Arthur mumbled as the cats just strolled off and he fixed a quick breakfast, then dressed.

Grabbing his 1911 and shoving it into his clip-on holster, Arthur stopped in the kitchen and grabbed a large sausage patty. Opening the back door, he saw Kong sitting on the patio, waiting on him. "Here," Arthur said, tossing the patty to the far side of the patio as the dogs came out. "Just keep away from me."

As Kong got up and slowly walked over to the patty, daring the dogs to run for it, Arthur closed the door. "Hey, the dogs aren't stupid," Arthur told Kong as he pulled his phone out to make sure it was charged.

Putting his phone away, Arthur looked over to see Kong lying down with the patty right in front of him. "Pussy, eat the sausage," he said, walking off the patio. Climbing on the electric cart he'd just built, Arthur unplugged it and hung the cord off the outdoor grill.

Turning the switch on, Arthur backed up and saw Kong watching the four dogs make a wide path around him. "Something's not right when Don and Daisy will attack a person but avoid that cat," Arthur noted, driving over to the shop.

Grabbing his tool belt and the camera for the gate, Arthur headed down the rise on a small path he had cut into the side of the rise with Jack's excavator. The cows were waiting for him at the door. He let them in as they walked into the stalls.

They had four cows and a bull, but were only milking two cows. At one time, they were selling raw whole milk, but the government had passed a law that said you had to have an expensive food license, pay for inspections, and had to follow a list of expensive regulations. To combat that, he and Wendy just stopped selling milk.

Pulling his gloves off, Arthur moved over and turned on the water hose. Washing the udders off and hooking up the automatic milking machine, Arthur turned them on and then poured a scoop of feed into each trough. That's why the cows wanted in. The two cows he wasn't milking had calves now and he would rotate them out, letting the other two rest and get pregnant.

Checking the milk tank, Arthur headed out after grabbing the egg basket and then headed to the chicken coop. They had over thirty chickens and they were all in the mobile coop, now that winter was over and the raccoons were leaving them alone. After gathering the eggs, Arthur put the basket on the buggy and then headed back in, turning off the milking machine.

After the cows headed back out to the field, he moved over to the other side of the barn and fed the horses and sheep. He laughed at the super fluffy sheep until he got to the two rams. Their large spiral horns jutted out from their heads as they looked at him with their demonic eyes. "I'm not scared of sheep and the last time a ram butted me, he got ate," Arthur informed them, moving among the sheep.

Finished in the barn, Arthur headed over to the tractor and looked out into the field. "How in the hell did you get out again?" he moaned, looking at a juvenile pig in the pasture. "Three days in a row, pig. Any more and you're going to be the first in line for bacon. That's where the chickens are going."

Grabbing a bucket of feed, Arthur walked out into the pasture tapping the bucket and the pig darted over to him, oinking loudly. Patting the pig as it tried to get the bucket, he led the pig back to the pig pen and saw the bottom lock on the gate hadn't been locked. "I know I locked that damn thing yesterday, just like the other three times," Arthur mumbled, tossing the bucket of feed into the trough and the pigs in the pen charged the trough, fighting for position.

Turning around to let the escape artist back in, Arthur stood spellbound as the pig forced his way in through the bottom of the gate. After the pig got back inside, Arthur locked the bottom of the gate. Hearing a piglet squealing, he climbed over the fence and spread the feed out in the trough.

Grinning at the pigs, Arthur reached over to pat the escape artist. The escape artist moved back and then rubbed his snotty snout on Arthur's hand. "Oh man, that's gross," Arthur snapped.

He climbed out and went back and cranked up the tractor, hooking up to the mobile chicken coop. Stopping before climbing on the tractor, Arthur saw where the escape artist pig had rooted around the chicken coop. He pulled it out into the field where the escape artist had been rooting around and several days ago, where a flock of ducks had been. Unknown to Arthur, he had a visitor in his body after he swatted away a fly from his face as he hooked up the chicken coop. But this visitor was different from the one going around the world.

Avian viruses can cross into swine and the escape artist had picked up the virus, but his body had altered it at one link in the chain of proteins. If there was ever a lottery one wanted to win, Arthur had won it, big time. The virus in his mucous membranes was now slowly shedding its shell to start replicating.

Arthur's prize, a much milder version of the virus, was in his system but would grant him immunity to the worst killer the planet had ever witnessed. And yet, Arthur would never know. The other lottery winners were the chickens he'd just parked over the spot where the escape artist had been rooting around. The pig had already infected them while rooting around their coop.

Chapter Eight
A thief discovered

April 28

Putting the tractor back in the barn, Arthur headed back to the electric buggy and put his work gloves on. After climbing in, Arthur headed to the main road that led to the house. Driving through the trees at the base of the rise until he reached the driveway, Arthur stopped and looked behind him to see the dogs. "You know, you let the pig escape again," he told the four. The four dogs stopped, looking at him like it wasn't their fault.

With the sun now well up, he turned the buggy and headed for the gate and the dogs ran past him. When he'd reached the gate, Arthur found the dogs waiting. "Oh, you thought I wanted to race?" he said, getting off. Putting on his tool belt, Arthur grabbed the camera. Using the heavy bar gate as a ladder, he climbed up to replace the camera on the ten-foot-tall pole that the heavy gate was mounted on.

Fifteen minutes later he was done and checked the camera on his smartphone, then headed back to the house. This time, he drove like a bat out of hell to beat the dogs. Pulling up to the back patio, Arthur gave a sigh of relief at not seeing Kong around. Walking in, he tapped off the daily chores and the camera.

Grabbing another cup of coffee, Arthur made a mental list of what else had to be done today. That was what he loved so much about their property; it was so diversified that there was always something to do. Granted, Wendy was by far better in the greenhouses and gardening than he was; Arthur had learned from her.

He had no problem working with the plants, but he wouldn't touch her silkworms unless Wendy was standing right beside him. Preferably, telling him what to do.

Carrying his coffee with him, Arthur headed to the garden and turned the irrigation system on. Finishing his cup, he headed to the greenhouse buried in the hillside. This greenhouse grew traditional crops using hydroponics. Of all the endeavors on the farm, the greenhouses used the most power, but with all the power generation on the farm, they still had enough to sell back to the power company.

The buried greenhouse had a wall of Plexiglas windows that ran the three-hundred-foot length. From the ground, the windows ran up and sloped back to give them a twenty-foot ceiling and snow couldn't build up, not that they had much snow, but Arthur had wanted to be sure. Just over thirty feet wide, they had over seven thousand square feet of hydroponics on the ground and a skywalk that had half that area.

Checking the beehives, he found the bees busy working and left them alone. Checking the pumps and readouts, Arthur made a few changes and then headed outside. As he headed to the patio to get the buggy, his cellphone chimed. He pulled it out and smiled, seeing the camera showing him the gate view.

Seeing a small semi on the screen, he tapped the screen as a man rolled down the window, sticking his head out. "Hey, Chuck," Arthur said, tapping the screen again to open the gate.

"Want me to pull up to the shop?" Chuck shouted over the diesel engine.

Turning the volume of the speaker mounted under the camera to maximum, "Yeah, that's good," Arthur said and saw Chuck cringe back inside the cab. "Oh, guess that was too loud," Arthur mumbled and turned the speaker back down.

He walked to the shop and saw the delivery semi pulling a short trailer with one large wooden crate and another half the size of the big one. When Chuck stopped, Arthur saw a delivery forklift mounted on the back of the trailer.

When Chuck turned the engine off, Arthur walked over. "Chuck, you didn't have to bring your forklift, we could've used the track steer," Arthur told him as Chuck climbed out.

"We have the thing, so I'm going to use it," Chuck laughed. "Hey, thanks for calling and telling me you had that big one coming and I could wait to deliver. Saved me some money, not having to make two trips."

"Sorry I took up some of your dock space for ten days," Arthur said, shaking Chuck's hand. Unfortunately for Chuck, he and Arthur had on gloves and Arthur had washed his hands and changed gloves, so Chuck didn't get the lottery winning visitor.

Waving his hand and brushing off the apology, "Where do you want 'em?" Chuck asked, taking the straps off the crates.

"Just set 'em off on the ground and I'll move them," Arthur answered, following Chuck to the back of the trailer.

"What did you get this time, if you don't mind me asking?"

Watching Chuck unlock the forklift, "The big one is a CNC machine I got from a government auction website. The small one is an industrial carder," Arthur told him.

Stopping the task of unlocking the forklift, "Is that like some kind of slot machine?" Chuck asked.

Laughing out, "No, a carder is a machine that combs out fibers to process into thread and yarn," Arthur told him.

"Damn, learn something every day," Chuck said, finishing unlocking the forklift. "Where's the other half?"

"She's on a cruise," Arthur answered, watching Chuck climb into the forklift and crank it up.

Giving a loud laugh, "So, you're living the bachelor's life for a little while," Chuck teased.

"Hardly," Arthur chuckled as Chuck lowered the forklift down. Chuck pointed at the ground near the shop and Arthur nodded.

As Chuck offloaded the crates, Arthur went inside and grabbed a flat of eggs from the fridge. Taking them outside, he saw Chuck was reloading the forklift. "Damn, that was fast," Arthur said, walking over.

When Chuck climbed off the forklift, Arthur handed over the flat of eggs. "Here's some eggs for you."

Taking the flat of eggs, Chuck grinned. "I almost brought your card machine just to get some eggs," Chuck admitted, setting the eggs on the trailer. "Can I see that 1911 again?"

Pulling his pistol out, Arthur ejected the magazine and racked the slide, ejecting the live round before handing it over. Chuck took the pistol tenderly. The metal finish looked like layered Damascus steel. "This is a work of art," Chuck said in awe.

"Yeah, it took me awhile to figure out how to make the rings like the pattern of Damascus steel," Arthur told him. Arthur did have guns that were bought, but his pride and joy were the ones he had made. He had made several pistols, half a dozen ARs, and two rifles. The only thing Arthur couldn't make were the super small springs. Large ones were no problem, but he still hadn't figured out how to make the tiny ones consistently.

"I saw one like this at a gun show a few years back and it had a price tag of twenty grand," Chuck said, turning the gun over in his hands.

"Hey, I thought about selling some. You can make your own gun as long as it follows all the BATF rules, but you can't sell them ever," Arthur said. "When I looked into making them to sell, I found out you had to suck fifty bureaucrats' dicks and let another twenty fuck you up the ass without lube. Since I don't like either option, I'll just make my own."

Chuck busted out laughing as he stared at the pistol. "Yeah, you have to have permission on something that's a given right under the constitution. How long did this take you?"

"I can mill out the frame and barrel in a day. It's the steel folding that is a pain in the ass. That takes me a few days."

Handing the gun back, "Will you let me know when you do another one? I would love to watch. Hell, if I could, I would buy one, just not for twenty grand," Chuck said.

"Tell you what, you find me a nice dozer for a good price and you can come out here when I'm making one. I'll hold your hands and show you what to do, so you can say you made it," Arthur offered.

The open mouth grin fell off Chuck's face. "What size dozer?" he gasped.

"Something around the size of a D4, but it has to have the six-way blade," Arthur answered and Chuck reached out, grabbing his arm.

"My dad left me a 1989 D5. It's got a six-way blade. All I do is crank it up every few months and move it around. It hasn't done any work in years."

Raising his eyebrows, "How much you want for it?" Arthur asked.

Pointing at the pistol in Arthur's hands, "You let me make one of those with your help and we can call it even," Chuck said.

"When will you have a few days off?"

With a content grin, Chuck leaned back on the trailer. "I have two weeks off at the first of June."

"Okay, let me know exact dates so I can gather up the steel."

"Some of the hydraulic hoses need replacing," Chuck told him.

Shrugging, "I can make hydraulic hoses," Arthur laughed.

"My vacation starts the first, how about I deliver the dozer on the third and I can make the gun?" Chuck asked.

When Arthur nodded, Chuck clapped his hands as Arthur told him, "Sounds good."

Shaking Arthur's hand, Chuck turned and grabbed the eggs. "Well, let me get back to work," Chuck said, heading for the cab.

Arthur headed to the patio as Chuck backed up and headed down the driveway. Pulling out his phone and tapping the screen, Arthur tapped the program for the front gate camera. When he saw Chuck drive through, he tapped the button to close the gate. "Momma will like the dozer," Arthur said, jumping on the buggy.

He checked the other greenhouses and finished the midday chores, then headed to the house to grab a bite to eat.

It was after one when he stepped out the back door and saw Kong sitting on the patio. "Why are you staying up here?" Arthur asked. "Go kill an elk."

Slowly standing up, Kong strutted away and Arthur kept an eye on him as he walked to the shop. Grabbing a crowbar and a cordless impact drill, Arthur went back outside and started uncrating the boxes. When he had the massive CNC open, he looked at it and was very surprised at the shape it was in.

"Well, I'll just have to hook it up and see how much work needs done," Arthur said, moving over to the smaller crate. The smaller crate was still seven feet long, four feet tall, and almost five feet wide. But compared to the massive CNC crate, it had looked tiny.

When he had one end open, his cellphone chimed again. Giving a groan, Arthur pulled his phone out. "Oh, hell no," he shouted, tapping the screen that showed an older pickup sitting at the gate. He turned the volume of the speaker back to max. "Rudy, what the hell do you want?"

A scruffy-looking man in his late twenties stuck his head out the window. "That speaker is loud as shit," Rudy said, looking at the camera. "I brought your stuff back."

Genuinely surprised, "Oh," Arthur said, turning the volume down on the speaker and opened the gate.

Putting his phone back, Arthur continued working to uncrate the machine. Minutes later, Rudy pulled up and Arthur looked over and saw the old riding lawn mower he'd let Rudy use. It was one of the first he'd rebuilt and since he had two more, he hadn't been in a hurry to get it back. The fact that Rudy had waited until Arthur had demanded Rudy return his stuff was what bothered Arthur.

Rudy got out and walked over while looking at the CNC. "That's one of those metal working machines, isn't it?"

"Yeah," Arthur answered and set down his crowbar. "You brought everything back?"

"Except for the posthole diggers," Rudy said. "I'm putting a fence in at Ms. McDonald's place. That's why I need to ask if I can borrow the augur."

Giving a sigh, Arthur nodded. Ms. McDonald was in her late seventies and went to his church. "Just bring the shit back," Arthur moaned and Rudy nodded.

Moving over, Arthur helped Rudy pull the ramp out and Rudy unloaded the mower, then stacked the rest of the stuff around and on the mower. Seeing that Rudy had more of his stuff than he'd known about, Arthur tried to remember when he'd let Rudy borrow everything. The fact it was his was undeniable, Arthur had engraved or welded his initials on all of his tools and equipment just for that reason.

"So, can I get the augur now?" Rudy asked.

Arthur didn't answer and just headed for the buggy with Rudy following. Driving down to the barn, Arthur still couldn't remember letting Rudy borrow a sander, air compressor, paint gun, or the electric jackhammer.

Stopping at the barn, he helped Rudy load up the augur in the buggy and headed back up to the house. "You need anything done around here?" Rudy asked.

"Nah, just keeping the place up," Arthur replied as the answer hit him.

"Anytime you need a hired hand, let me know," Rudy said as Arthur stopped by his truck.

"Will do," Arthur said with a false smile, then helped Rudy put the auger in his truck.

Rudy climbed in his truck and waved as he turned around and headed down the driveway. Pulling his phone out, Arthur saw Rudy drive out the gate and then tapped the phone, shutting the gate. Shoving his phone back in the holster, he jumped on the buggy and sped off.

He drove between the two knolls behind the house and the trees became thicker along the small dirt track he was on. The track had a gentle rising slope and Arthur rounded a curve and stopped at four shipping containers. All four containers were on a leveled brick platform, bolted together.

There were four other storage areas like this around the property and one refrigerated shipping container near the textile barn. They used it for a meat locker and processed meat in it. The groups of containers were just storage sheds and this group held tools and machines he had rebuilt.

Climbing off the buggy, Arthur looked at the last container, the only one that didn't have a lock. This one was left unlocked because it held small tools that they used a lot. Opening the doors, he reached inside and turned on the battery-operated lights. He walked down an aisle in the center and stopped, looking at another air compressor with an empty spot beside it.

"That motherfucker," Arthur growled and continued down and saw where the electric jackhammer used to hang on the wall. "He knew this one was unlocked and there are no cameras here."

Walking around, Arthur thought some more stuff was missing, but couldn't be sure until he inventoried. When he had several tools of the same type, he would sell some when the church had its swap meet twice a year. People came from all over and the church received ten percent of all sales.

Turning off the lights, Arthur closed the doors and then inspected the locks of the other three containers. The last container's lock was scratched up but looked intact. Walking back to the buggy, Arthur opened the glovebox and grabbed a key ring.

Using the key, he opened the container and looked in at the ATVs and a golf cart parked along one wall and several dirt bikes on the other. All these Arthur had gotten from the salvage yard or yard sales and had repaired them. These also got sold at the swap meet, but he and Wendy would pull some out when her family would come over.

"Well, time to put some more cameras up and lock that last container," Arthur mumbled, closing the door and relocking it.

Just to make sure, Arthur went and checked on the other container sites. They were placed around the property in different places, so it wouldn't look junky. All the containers had been repainted and looked brand new. When he had bought all the containers, the market had been flooded. All of them were the long forty footers and he couldn't build a metal container for what he'd bought them for.

Now, containers were selling for five grand a piece. He couldn't build one for that price, but it was getting close. Even though he poured his own metal and could make almost anything, Arthur always factored in his time in the cost.

Each area held certain items and Arthur started racking his brain to remember if Rudy had ever been inside the others. Visiting the three other storage areas around the property, Arthur jumped on the buggy. Driving up to the textile barn, Arthur could only remember Rudy looking inside three of the tool and machine containers.

The last group and the lone refrigerated container were behind the textile barn. Arthur knew for a fact that Rudy knew where all of the storage containers were located because he had hired him two years ago to help fence off the property.

Stopping at the meat locker container, Arthur saw the shiny lock untouched. Inside were several machines to process meat, but then Arthur remembered Rudy had seen inside that one just a few months ago. Wendy had been inside processing the chickens they had culled when Arthur had paid Rudy to help him paint the textile barn.

He drove over to the other four and stomped the brakes. "That motherless cocksucker," Arthur snarled, getting off the buggy. Two of the locks were twisted and beat to shit, but were still in place. These containers held the cloth, leather, thread, and yarn they produced.

What they made didn't compare to what a textile mill could do, but they could make their own clothes and even sell some specially woven cloth. The reason they weren't taxed was because they made it and sold it for cash. Cash; the item the government hated and loved to take away.

The textile barn had an alarm system Arthur had salvaged, but he and Wendy had wanted it only because it would tell them if there was a fire. The burglar alarm was just an afterthought. The house didn't even have a burglar alarm.

Unlocking the small door, Arthur walked in and turned off the alarm. All the machines to process fibers were on the right side and weaving looms were on the other side. This barn was just as massive as the livestock barn and Arthur had always wondered if the same people had built them. When they had rebuilt this barn, they'd closed it in and put in a ton of lighting and electrical sockets.

He went upstairs to check on Wendy's silk area. Seeing the three refrigerators that held her silkworm eggs, Arthur made sure the locks were still in place. Wendy kept them locked so the doors would stay closed without a doubt.

Turning around, he saw the rows of huge bins that they loaded with mulberry leaves to feed the silkworms. It had taken her awhile but Wendy had finally got her hands on one clutch of domesticated silk moths. Domesticated moths couldn't survive without human intervention. They had a few wild silk moths in the mulberry orchard, but even Arthur could tell the difference in the amount of silk they got from the wild silkworms and the domesticated ones.

"Momma will be back soon and you know she likes putting you guys to work during the summer," Arthur said. It just amazed him that Wendy could put the eggs in the fridge and pull them out when she was ready. The longest she had kept a batch cold was a year and they had survived just fine.

The lady who Wendy had gotten the eggs from had told them that she had kept a batch in the fridge for five years, but Wendy never wanted to try that long.

Finding everything all right, Arthur headed back out, turning the alarm on and locking the door. He stopped and looked at the dogs sitting in a line, looking up at him and panting. "Why didn't you tell me that Rudy stole some of our shit?" he huffed, putting his hands on his hips.

The dogs didn't move and just continued panting and looking up at him. "Well, I guess it's hard when you're inside," Arthur grinned and dove down, wrapping his arms around the dogs. The dogs started licking his face as he loved on them.

Getting up, Arthur headed for the buggy. "Well, time to put up cameras and some alarms," he said.

Chapter Nine

Get mom home, lies abound

April 30

Hearing a phone ringing, Arthur swatted over at the nightstand and felt his cellphone. Realizing it wasn't vibrating, he sat up and crawled over the cats and dogs to Wendy's nightstand. Grabbing the cordless phone, "Hello," he yawned.

"Hey, dad," Joseph said and Arthur came awake instantly, looking over at the clock.

"Son, did you leave early?" Arthur asked, seeing it was just after three a.m.

"No, dad, that's why I'm calling. My leave was cancelled and I have to fly out to Diego Garcia in an hour," Joseph told him and Arthur heard the disappointment.

"Son, what about your fighter school?"

"I've been assured that I will be reassigned there before the end of the year," Joseph sighed. "I told them if I wasn't, I'd be leaving the service."

"That's right! You're hot stuff and you make them give you what you want," Arthur snapped, even though a part of him had hoped Joseph wouldn't get the assignment. And that small part made Arthur feel terrible because that had always been Joseph's dream. "I'll call our congressman. Hell, I donate to him like I'm paying the mafia for protection, so that son of a bitch owes me!"

"My CO thinks he can get me in this class and I will just have to do some makeup work," Joseph said, sounding better at hearing his dad pissed off. "Please don't get the politicians involved yet."

"Hell, son, you want me to kick someone's ass?"

Joseph busted out laughing and Arthur relaxed at hearing the sound. "No, dad. The last time you did that, you and mom almost went to jail," Joseph howled out.

When Joseph stopped laughing, Arthur asked. "Why did they cancel your leave?"

"This flu thing," Joseph sighed. "Word's coming down the pipeline that it has gotten stronger and more people are dying."

"I've heard that, but they haven't said anything about numbers," Arthur said. "The hospital in Clarksville called yesterday and asked if I could come in."

"You didn't, did you?!" Joseph shouted.

Shocked at the outburst, Arthur climbed out of the bed. "No, son, I can't leave the farm. I just found out that Rudy is a punk-ass bitch and has been breaking into the storage containers."

"I never liked that cocksucker."

"Well, I've been putting in more cameras and even put in two alarm systems. One here and another at the office house," Arthur said. "I won't be done with that for several days. Besides, I don't have a shift at the hospital until June and that's fine with me."

"Um, you heard from mom?" Joseph asked.

"Yeah, she called yesterday, but son, you talk to her as much as I do on the computer."

"Dad, you think you can get mom to fly back at her next stop if there's an airport?" Joseph asked hesitantly.

Feeling his heart rate skyrocket, Arthur asked. "Son, is something wrong?"

Several seconds passed and Arthur could hear the phone moving around. "Dad," Joseph whispered. "It wasn't just my leave. All leave throughout the military was cancelled. They are putting all bases on lockdown, keeping all personnel on base."

"Whoa," Arthur mumbled.

"Yeah, but I talked to an Air Force pilot who flies heavy lifters and he said he was part of a large flight that just flew five thousand troops from South Korea back to the states."

"Son, when do you fly out?" Arthur asked.

"Wheels up in an hour."

"You get your ass on that island and call me when you can," Arthur told him. "Will you have internet there?"

"Yeah, I was there for a week last year."

"If I find out anything, I will e-mail it to you," Arthur told Joseph and heard jet engines in the background. "Son, where are you at?"

"I can't say, but it's isolated," Joseph chuckled. "I never knew we had a base here and neither did anyone in my flight."

"Son, you call if you need us. I know how to drive a boat."

Joseph swallowed a lump in his throat. "Dad, I'll be fine. I will be sitting in the middle of the Indian Ocean. It's you and mom I'm worried about."

"Love you, son," Arthur said.

"Hey, dad, my CO just waved at me. I have to go. Love you," Joseph said quickly and hung up.

Dropping into his chair, Arthur put the phone on his desk and grabbed the mouse. Taking a deep breath, Arthur hit the web. The first thing he noticed was the internet was moving very slowly. "I paid for high speed and I get syrup," he mumbled.

A few alternate news sites had articles on the flu and Arthur just started printing them because it took the pages so long to load. Then, he moved to two message boards he liked. When the first board's home page popped up, his mouth fell open.

The first discussion was, 'Dead bodies being taken from hospital in New York'. He clicked the link and the message board opened up and he saw pictures below a typed message. He clicked on the pictures and then moved them to his second screen as they slowly downloaded. Then, he started to read.

'Stone Hunter here. I live in NY and the hospitals are overflowing. I was walking around and saw this at the hospital near me, guys in hazmat suits loading body bags in vans. I went around front and a woman said her husband was flown to a treatment center in Arizona because the hospital was full. The kicker is; all airports up here only have about a quarter of the flights they normally have. The woman told me the next flight she could get on was ten days from now.

Walking around, I found several others that said they had family flown out to different parts of the country. The hospital told several they couldn't fly until they had a three-day course of Tamiflu because they had been exposed.

Well, I know a nurse at the hospital and went to talk to him. His exact words were, 'The CDC and Homeland were responsible for transporting patients to high care centers across the nation'. When I asked about the flu, he told me to avoid the top four floors at all costs. He had been on shift for twelve hours and they had lost nine patients.

Hearing that, I left, but I never asked about the body bags because there were National Guard there acting as security and they were wearing gas masks.

If anyone hears something, let me know. Peace out.'

Highlighting the message, Arthur printed it and then looked over and saw four of the five pictures were open and number five was still downloading. He hit print on the pictures, then clicked to go back to the board.

The next message read 'Rudolph Flu'. He clicked it and saw a very long post. He highlighted it and hit print. He clicked back to the message board and waited for the page to reload. All four pictures and the text were finished printing before the board filled the screen.

Moving to the next post, Arthur went to click it and the window went blank. "Fuck!" he yelled as a 'Site Unavailable' message filled the blank window. He clicked reload and got the same message. Turning to the other screen, he saw the last picture had never downloaded.

Closing them, he headed to the next board and found it unavailable. Heading to Google, he typed in Rudolph Flu and hit search. Watching the little hourglass turning as the page loaded, Arthur was tempted to call the cable company and scream at them.

'None Found' appeared in the blank window. There were no links to anything, not even advertisements. "I don't fucking believe it, I found something Google doesn't know?" Arthur cried out in shock.

A gray box popped up on his screen. 'Malware detected, leave this site immediately'.

Reaching down, Arthur turned the router off. "Holy shit fuck," he mumbled.

He tapped the gray box and it opened his virus program. He opened the partial file in view mode and saw it was a Trojan horse program. "Damn, I would like to see the rest of the program. I thought I could write a good program to fuck shit up, but this is first class."

He erased the file and then bleached it. Grabbing the stuff he had printed, Arthur got up and headed to the kitchen. Turning the timer on the coffee pot off since he was already up, Arthur turned the pot on and leaned back against the large kitchen island.

Studying the pictures, he could see stacks of body bags on a loading dock, but couldn't tell how many. There were two vans, one white and one black. Looking at another picture that was shot zoomed out, he could see people in hazmat suits holding M4s. Behind them were the two vans, but you couldn't tell what was going on.

Putting the pictures at the back of the stack, he read the 'Rudolph Flu' post.

'First, I'm not a health care provider, but this is what I've found out. Rudolph flu is named because the person has a red nose from all the rubbing they do because their nose is itchy, but this usually doesn't happen until around day eight with a mild fever.

The person is contagious around day three and shows no symptoms until ten days after infection. When the fever starts getting high, a bad cough shortly follows. Can't find any reference to what type of flu Rudolph is. I've found posts that say the death rates are between ten and thirty percent here. In Mexico, the rates are over forty.'

Setting the papers down, Arthur grabbed his coffee cup. "Well, if it's as high as thirty percent that would suck ass," he mumbled, filling his cup. Spooning in the creamer and sugar, Arthur shook his head. "I've never heard of any influenza with an incubation period that long."

Knowing his knowledge base was a long way from a virologist, Arthur picked his cup up to take a sip. Leaning over the bar, he read the other post as he sipped his coffee. Reading the post, Arthur could confirm the person had no medical background. "Coma, bloody stools, if it's the flu, it can't be H1N1 or anything I've studied in nursing school," he mumbled.

Not finding much else, Arthur looked away from the paper. He walked in the living room and turned on the TV to one of the 24-hour news station. The anchors were talking about the president in closed door sessions with the Security Council, talking about the war in the Middle East.

A grin filled Arthur's face as he lifted the remote and hit the guide button. "Three hundred channels and for the first time, I'm looking for that Mexico City news station. Been a while since I've spoken Spanish," he mumbled. Finding it, he hit the button to turn to the channel only to see 'Currently Unavailable' on the screen.

"Oh, this is bullshit!" he bellowed and tossed the remote on the couch. He heard the pounding footsteps of the dogs as they ran into the living room and looked at him. "Yeah, I'm pissed," Arthur told them, then headed back to the computer.

Turning the router back on, he sat back down. This time, he only went to the major news sites and besides telling him about the war in the Middle East, protests in Paris, and a Hollywood actress giving birth to a baby girl, he didn't learn shit.

Searching for an hour, Arthur finally gave up and tried his message boards and found they were still down. He opened his e-mail and typed 'Call home' and sent it to Wendy.

Getting another idea, Arthur typed the website of a hospital he used to work at in Little Rock that had ER wait times posted on the website. To him, that was the stupidest shit in the world. You only go to the ER for an emergency, but he was an ER nurse and knew eighty percent of who they saw could've been seen in a doctor's office.

When the site popped up, he leaned back in his chair. "Seventy-one hours and twenty minutes?!" Arthur gasped.

Knowing a few more hospitals that did that, he searched for their websites as his internet speed seemed to crawl. One in Dallas had a wait time of sixty hours and the other three were unavailable. "There is no fucking way any organization or government could blanket out this much information."

'Ring' sounded from the phone and Arthur jumped in the chair, spilling his coffee on his bare legs. "Fuck!" he shouted, putting his cup down and wiping the coffee off, then grabbed the phone and saw the international number.

"Hello," he answered.

"Hey, Hun, what 'cha need?" Wendy asked and he could hear music and cheering behind her.

"Have you heard anything about the flu?"

"Yeah, the captain came over the intercom yesterday and said a flu outbreak was in the states and China and if anyone felt sick, they should report to medical. Five or six people were taken off at the last stop at St. Kit and sent to the hospital," Wendy told him.

"What about when you went ashore?"

"Yeah, flights to Mexico City were cancelled at our last stop. The couple next to me and Gloria tried to fly home," Wendy told him. "They couldn't reach their family, but that's not unusual. I tried three times to get through to you this time."

"Wendy, you think you can catch a flight home at your next stop?"

There was a pause before Wendy spoke. "What's wrong?"

"I don't know, but this is weird. I can't find any information on this flu," Arthur said.

"Hun, there are long delays on airplanes. They are screening passengers to make sure they don't have this flu. The ship's doctor spoke last night at supper and said the information he got was that this was a nasty one, putting people in bed for over a week. He said many needed care while they were sick. That's why he offloaded the ones on the ship," Wendy explained.

"How are you feeling?"

"I feel great," Wendy laughed. "How are things there?"

"Just running the farm," Arthur said, not wanting her to worry about him. "But Joseph won't be coming home."

"What?" Wendy snapped.

"His leave was cancelled," Arthur said, then lowered his voice, "because of the flu."

He could hear Wendy's breathing increase into the phone. "Did he say anything else?" Wendy asked with a shaking voice.

"He couldn't," Arthur told her. "He's the one who told me to get you to fly home."

"Arthur, I would have to stay on the island to catch the plane and that's if the flight isn't cancelled. I really feel this boat will get me back the fastest way," Wendy confessed and Arthur noticed all the cheer was now out of her voice.

Giving a long groan, Arthur held the phone tight as he spoke. "Babe, you keep safe."

"I will, Arthur," Wendy said. "There is a line to use the sat phones but I got lucky, and you wouldn't believe what they charge the credit card!"

"I don't care. You need something or need to tell me something, you call."

"Arthur, I will, but the internet will be the fastest way for us to talk. I got your message when you sent it. I just had to wait in line for the phone for half an hour," Wendy told him.

"Okay, babe. You stay safe. I love you," Arthur said, feeling helpless.

"Love you too," Wendy told him and Arthur heard the phone click.

Looking at the phone with a sigh, he carried it back to the bedroom and put it back in the base on Wendy's side of the bed. He looked on her pillow to see the cats side-by-side like sphinx, ruling over their land. "I'm telling Wendy neither of you were worried about her," Arthur huffed and neither cat even cracked an eye open.

Grabbing his workout clothes, Arthur headed to the bathroom and just started the day ahead of schedule. Brushing his teeth, he said a prayer for Wendy and Joseph but even now, the visitor was slowly multiplying through Wendy's body.

Chapter Ten

Only those in charge need to be safe

May 2

Hearing a tap behind him, Dr. Sutton stepped back from the lab table and turned around. He saw Jackson at the view window overlooking the lab. Inside a pressurized lab suit, Sutton reached down and pressed the radio box connected to the outside intercom. "Yes?" he said and saw Jackson motioning with his hands. "Look to your left and you will see a communication box. Press the green button to talk."

Glancing to his left, Jackson stepped over and pressed the button. "Sutton, the president has arrived and wants an update," Jackson told him.

"I need ten minutes," Sutton snapped. "I'm almost finished with these dishes."

"I'll let him know and will be waiting outside the airlock," Jackson said, then walked away.

Moving back to the microscope, Sutton went back to work spreading the virus on the prepared culture medium. When he had the last one done, he grabbed the stack of petri dishes and carried them to an incubator. Looking over at his assistants, "Mark lot four in," he called out.

"The latest report is in from Atlanta," one of the assistants said and Sutton waved a thanks, then opened the pressurized door. Walking into the sealed chamber, he relocked the door and pressed the shower button.

Holding up his arms, Sutton let the bleach water wash over him as the UV lights came on. Turning in slow circles, Sutton let the water wash flow over him as two sprays started on the sides. For ten minutes, he continued the dance he had done too many times to count in his career. When the water shut off, steam erupted under his feet. This was new and he had only seen it in this new lab, and it scared the shit out of him.

He felt the heat inside the suit as visibility was lost in the cloud of steam. Then a hum sounded and the steam was sucked out. In front of him, a green light turned on and he opened the outer door and saw Jackson waiting in the changing area.

Sutton had to admit, he liked the Surgeon General. He had been in the Mt. Weather complex for four days and he was blown away at the size. He had been expecting a cave, but he'd found a small city buried under a mountain. "One of your people handed me this," Jackson said, holding a stack of papers.

"Latest reports," Sutton said, unzipping the suit and started the process of taking it off. It didn't take as long as putting it on. Putting it on, one knew it was your last line of defense while working with the most lethal killers of nature and you did it slowly and correctly. Even after decades at his job, Sutton took his time, triple checking everything.

"Yeah, I think the virus is moving faster than your team predicted," Jackson said.

Hanging his lab suit up, Sutton turned around to stare at Jackson. "Atlanta discovered two mutated viruses yesterday," Sutton told him.

"Please tell me one is less lethal," Jackson pleaded.

"Sorry," Sutton said, kicking his Crocs off and shoving his feet in his loafers. "I'm not putting on a suit and tie. I'm coming back here when I'm done."

"If anyone says anything, I'll take care of it," Jackson assured him, looking at Sutton who was wearing scrubs. "Remember, no blame on them."

Grabbing the stack of papers, Sutton gave a tired smile. "Thank you for helping me through the political waters."

"We need you and I'm not kidding. If they, the ones in charge, think someone will place blame on them, that person will disappear," Jackson said, holding the door open.

"The director told me, off the record of course," Sutton said, flipping the folder open. "Has the mountain been sealed?"

"It was after the president came in from Camp David. I put your laptop in my cart," Jackson grunted, opening the door out of the building. The door opened up to a cement road in a tunnel. Golf carts were parked in marked spaces like cars would be in front of the building buried in the side of the tunnel.

Following Jackson to a cart, Sutton climbed in the passenger side as Jackson jumped behind the steering wheel. "Thank you, I always forget my laptop," Sutton yawned. "If someone infected got in, then we are dead," Sutton said, looking at the folder. "I hope everyone has at least been mucosal screened."

Backing up and heading down the tunnel, "Yes, the nasal swab screen has been done on everyone before they entered," Jackson assured him.

"It still takes one day after infection to become positive," Sutton said, flipping through the papers.

Driving along, the tunnel opened up into a huge cavern but it didn't look like a cavern. A hundred feet up, huge lights blocked out the roof. There were shops, stores, and buildings on both sides and a large lake on the left with a small park. "You have everything you need?" Jackson asked, passing other golf carts as they approached a crossroad.

Looking up from the papers and turning to Jackson, "That lab is better than the one I had in Atlanta, and it was supposed to have the best equipment," Sutton snorted.

"So, you have everything?"

"Equipment wise, yes. But we have none of the chickens yet and I would like to get samples of the mutated viruses," Sutton said, not paying any attention to the wonders around him.

"I'm working on the chickens, but the flocks are being decimated and the Department of Agriculture is destroying any flock that shows infection. I should be able to get you the samples," Jackson said, approaching another crossroad and turned left. He honked the small horn on the cart as a man tried to walk across the road. Sutton looked up as the man jumped out of the way.

"Was that Senator Dayle?" Sutton asked.

Chuckling, "Yeah," Jackson smirked.

"Should've run his ass over, he cut our funding," Sutton grumbled, turning his attention back to the papers.

The buildings around them stopped and the walls closed in as they entered into a tunnel. Slowing down, Jackson stopped at a barrier gate like those in parking garages. But there were soldiers manning this one.

"They are expecting you," one of the guards said, waving at a booth and the yellow gate swung up and Jackson pulled through and the tunnel opened up to a smaller cavern.

Pulling up to another building, Jackson parked in one of the vacant spots and climbed out. Closing the folder, Sutton slowly got out and grabbed his laptop bag. "I hope they give me a few minutes so I can go over this," Sutton said, holding up the folder.

"They will," Jackson smiled. "Paterson came to see you yesterday and saw you working in the lab."

"What were they expecting me to be doing?"

Shaking his head as he opened the door, "It shocks them that people at the top do actual work," Jackson laughed.

"I didn't have a choice about taking the job as associate director," Sutton said, walking in. "The other man for the job could barely tie his shoes."

"Could almost say the same about some in the room we are about to be in," Jackson commented as they walked across a large room and a guard opened a set of double doors. Walking down the hall lined with doors, two guards were standing beside double doors.

Seeing the two coming, they opened the doors as Jackson held up his ID card. Reaching down, Sutton held up his ID card hanging on a lanyard around his neck.

The guards nodded as they walked into another room where a man wearing a suit sat beside another door. Not seeing the man, Sutton gave a cry of excitement at seeing a table loaded with food. He ran over as a Secret Service agent opened a door on the opposite wall. Jackson grinned as Sutton put his laptop and papers down and grabbed a plate, loading it with food.

"I take it, you haven't eaten?" Jackson laughed.

Glancing at his watch, "Fourteen hours ago," Sutton answered, grabbing a can of soda. "I really want this vaccine and I forget to eat when I'm working."

Hearing the word *'vaccine'*, the agent tilted his head to Sutton and then stepped over to grab Sutton's laptop and the folder with the stack of papers. "Thank you," Sutton said, smiling.

"Pleasure, sir," the agent said and followed them inside.

The room held a long table almost identical to the one at the White House and Sutton barely gave a glance as he started eating, heading to an open seat. Moving past Sutton, the agent pulled his chair out and set the folder and then his laptop bag down.

With his mouth full, Sutton gave the agent a funny grin and the agent just nodded with a smile. "Dr. Sutton, haven't they prepared you any food?" the President asked, sitting at the head of the table.

Holding up his hand as he chewed faster, Sutton opened the soda and took a drink to wash the food down. "Sorry, Mr. President," he said with a dry voice, then took another swig of soda. "I've been in the lab and when I took a nap at my desk, one of the guards brought me and my team some sandwiches."

"That was fourteen hours ago, Mr. President," Jackson said, sitting down beside Sutton.

Everyone at the table gave an impressed nod as the president snapped his fingers and the aide standing behind him stepped forward. "Sarah, I'm assigning you with Dr. Sutton twenty-four-seven. Your job is to make sure he and his team are fed and taken care of."

"Yes, Mr. President," the young lady said and stepped back to the wall.

"Where are we at, Mr. President?" Jackson asked. "I wanted to give him a chance to eat and read over what Atlanta sent because Dr. Sutton's already told me that he's headed back to the lab when we are done here."

Nodding his head, the President grinned as Sutton shoveled food in his mouth, reading a stack of papers in a folder. "The NSA is reporting that they are having problems keeping panic off the internet and several broadcasters are getting antsy about not reporting the deaths," the President answered.

"We have an actual death toll?" Jackson asked and Sarah ran from behind the president and down the table. Stopping beside Jackson, she handed him a bound report and put one beside Sutton, then ran back behind the president.

As Jackson opened the report, Paterson looked across the table. "As of this morning, over six million, four hundred, and twenty thousand," Paterson said glumly.

Not looking up, "Shit," Jackson gasped, looking at the printout in the report that listed areas of the nation. "It's growing exponentially like Dr. Sutton said, but it's every other day, not three, and these numbers are much higher."

"Fuck," Sutton mumbled with a mouthful and leaned down to grab his laptop out of his bag.

Jackson and everyone at the table turned to Sutton as he opened his laptop up. "Problem?" Jackson said and Sutton's chewing exaggerated as he turned on his laptop and held a hand up to Jackson. Grabbing his soda, Sutton shook it and gave a depressed sigh, hearing it was empty.

As Sutton pushed his chair back, the President pointed to the door and Sarah took off running. Jackson grabbed a water pitcher from the middle of the table and poured a glass, seeing Sutton needed anything wet so he could swallow.

Grabbing the cup, Sutton downed it and emptied his mouth. "Shit, I can't eat like that anymore," he grumbled, setting the glass down and looking at his laptop screen. "Oh, come on!" he cried out, reaching down and grabbing his power cord.

Jackson leaned over and saw the low battery shutdown warning on the screen. He grabbed the plug and stood up, plugging it into a power strip in the center of the table and Sutton plugged the supply into his laptop. "Mine does the same thing. When I need it the most, the battery dies," Jackson said and everyone around the table nodded and chuckled dryly, not liking the look on Sutton's face.

"That's why I bought this one, it has the largest battery available," Sutton huffed, waving his hand at the computer and then typed in his password.

As the computer came to life, Sarah came back with two cans of soda. Setting one unopened on the table, she opened the other one and set it beside Sutton. "Thank you," Sutton said, clicking the wireless connection. "The password is not the same here?" Sutton cried out.

Leaning over, Sarah pushed Sutton to the side and started typing on his laptop. When she hit enter, the screen showed access. "There you go," Sarah smiled.

Sutton looked up and saw Sarah was a young intern and couldn't be much over twenty-five. "Thank you again," Sutton grinned. "Sorry you had to get that close to me when I've been wearing a pressured lab suit for days on end."

"You haven't been shown your quarters?" Paterson cried out across the table.

"Oh, I threw my suitcases in there with my home computer, but then I went to the lab," Sutton replied, grabbing more food but putting smaller pieces in his mouth. "I may be senior in rank but not in the lab, and I hauled Dr. Skannish up here from Atlanta. He forgave me as soon as he got in the lab. We aren't slowing down until we make some headway."

"Thank you for eating smaller sizes, I don't want to do the Heimlich," Sarah smiled and moved back behind the president.

Sutton nodded at her, then turned to Paterson. "I had one of my assistants go and find some cots to put in our offices by the lab so we can grab a few winks. It took him over an hour and some major tried to arrest him for taking the cots," Sutton told him.

"You have the name?" Paterson asked and Jackson tapped Sutton with his foot.

"Sorry, but that was several viral sequences ago and to be honest, he wasn't worth my brain power to commit him to memory," Sutton replied and several around the table laughed.

Very proud of Sutton, Jackson looked up from the report and over at Paterson. "So, there still isn't any civil unrest?" he asked as

Sutton continued eating, tapping on his laptop and reading the papers.

"Very little, and most are families of those we've told their patient has been flown elsewhere," Paterson said.

The president stared at Sutton eating, reading his laptop and papers all at the same time. He watched how fast Sutton scanned the papers and then his laptop, knowing he was reading very fast. "When can we expect the stock market to crash?" the President asked, never looking away from Sutton.

"The day we announce the virus is deadly," Temple answered. "Wall Street is helping support the losses, but they want to know what's going on."

"Jackson, what's your thoughts on that?" the President asked.

Looking up from the report and setting it down on the table, Jackson turned to the President. "Sir, if you tell them, you tell the world," Jackson answered. "Our primary goal has been to buy time, but we are losing that fast because this virus is beyond anything we've ever dreamed of in our worst nightmares."

Still watching Sutton scanning pages and the laptop, the president nodded. "I agree, and that would only cause chaos," he said as Sutton put the last page down and picked up the report Sarah had put beside him. Before the president could ask, Sutton started reading.

Several others noticed the president staring and followed his gaze to Sutton. Sutton's eyes scanned each page from top to bottom quickly, then he flipped the page to start on the next. "Sorry, Dr. Sutton, but I have to ask, are you actually reading or scanning that report?" the President asked.

"Reading it," Sutton responded, not looking away from the report as his hand grabbed the soda and brought it to his mouth. When he set the can down, his hand moved over to the empty plate. Glancing at his empty plate, Sutton sighed and then turned his eyes back to the report.

Sarah moved up behind the President, whispering in his ear and the president nodded. With the President still watching Sutton, Sarah left the room.

Laying the report flat on the table, Sutton picked up the folder and thumbed through the papers. "Jackson, compare that to page one hundred and four," Sutton said, handing several pages to Jackson. "I'll be with you in just a second, Mr. President," Sutton called out, tapping his computer. "I hate giving half information and I'm sorry, but I didn't prep before coming."

"Quite all right," the President smiled as Sutton looked from his laptop to the report and flipped the page.

"The Atlanta team is right," Jackson said, handing the papers back.

Not taking the papers, Sutton handed the folder to Jackson. "There's a graph on age dispersion infection rates in there, compare it to what's in the report," Sutton said, flipping another page in the report and then typed on his computer. "Am I reading right that youth has the highest survival rate?"

Everyone started flipping through their reports as Paterson spoke up, "Page ninety-six."

The President flipped his report to the page and saw columns of numbers as Sarah came back in, carrying a plate loaded with sandwiches. She took the empty plate and set the full plate down, then opened the other soda before taking the empty can. "Sarah, my colleagues would love to have you around," Sutton said, not looking away. "You can read people like we can read viruses."

"Thank you, Dr. Sutton," Sarah smiled and carried the empty can and plate out.

"Holy shit," Jackson gasped, leaning back in his chair. "That's why the numbers are so skewed."

"Um, can you explain?" Paterson mumbled, looking at the rows of numbers.

"Prepubescent youth has a higher survival and recovery rate than any of the demographics," Jackson mumbled in shock. "What if we tried autoimmune drug classes?" Jackson asked, turning to Sutton.

"That's what I was thinking, but wanted confirmation," Sutton said. "When I ask Dr. Skannish, he will know for sure."

"Why aren't we seeing this in the elderly?" Jackson asked.

"I'm not sure, but elderly immune response may be diminished, but it would also have histologic response based in the adaptive immune system. Then you throw in the somatic hypermutation in the receptor gene segments, they would overload to bring on full shutdown," Sutton offered and everyone around the table sat opened mouth and stunned. When Sutton continued speaking, many were thinking it was another language.

Finally, Jackson leaned back in his chair, "Okay, you lost me at the MHC junction."

"Gentlemen," the President called out and Jackson turned to the president, but Sutton kept typing and raised his eyebrows to indicate that he was listening. "Care to explain in words that others can pronounce?" the President asked.

"Sorry, Mr. President," Jackson said and then leaned over, looking at Sutton's laptop screen. "Is that Dr. Skannish you're talking to?"

Scoffing, "No," Sutton chuckled. "He's back in the lab and I'll have to pry his ass out to talk this over with him. I'm typing the highlights of this report for the teams in Atlanta. Who put this together?"

"Um, I did. Last night," Paterson mumbled.

"Paterson, I need you to show some of my associates how to put together a report because they suck," Sutton said, typing away. "I'm sorry I didn't get to finish it yet, but can I ask you some questions while I type?"

"Sure," Paterson said, feeling very proud.

"Have you gotten numbers yet from the UK?" Sutton asked.

Nodding as he flipped over several pages, "Yes, and they are very similar to ours, percentage wise, with the exception of more dead," Paterson told him.

"Dr. Sutton," the President called out. "Would you like your team in Atlanta to have a copy of that report?"

Sutton's hands froze over the keyboard and he turned to the president. "We can do that? It says, 'Top Secret' on the cover," he asked.

"I am the President," he laughed and Sarah stepped up behind him. "You do have a secure fax there, don't you?"

"Yes sir. Let me pull up the number," Sutton said, grabbing the mouse and clicking it while Sarah walked down and stood behind him.

She leaned over his shoulder and pointed at the screen, "That's a secured fax number," she said.

"Perfect, that's right outside the main lab," Sutton sighed as Sarah wrote the number down on a scrap of paper.

As she walked past the president, she grabbed a report off a stack and then walked out another set of doors behind the president. "I thought I was going to have to type all that up," Sutton grinned, then stood up as he took a cable out of his laptop bag and plugged it into the back of his laptop.

Across from him, Paterson leaned over the table and grabbed the other end of the video cable and plugged it into a slot at the center of the table. "Okay, Mr. President," Sutton said, sitting back down. "As you've read in Paterson's report, he hypothesized that the virus has mutated. He's correct, it has into at least two different mutations. Atlanta sent me the information, that's some of what I was reading," Sutton said, tapping his keyboard.

"The thing nobody can figure out is how we found them dispersed over such a large area," Sutton told him as the screens around the room showed his laptop screen and they saw Sutton open up an e-mail. "Turns out, Mr. James Taylor flew out of London the day after he'd landed. First to Mexico City for a day, then he flew into New York and stayed for a few hours, then headed to Chicago, and then LA. Remember, my second report stated Taylor visited all three US cities over forty-eight hours but it turns out, Mr. Taylor also has a hobby," Sutton said, clicking an attachment.

A picture opened, showing a middle-aged man sitting in a park and feeding pigeons. Next to him was an older man, looking at the camera. "The man feeding the pigeons is Mr. James Taylor. The man sitting beside him is over Tong Shipping's New York office. It turns out that Mr. Taylor did this in every city he visited that had a park with pigeons. From Greece to L.A.," Sutton sighed and everyone gasped. "Yeah, now we know how it got around the globe into the bird population so fast."

Clicking open another picture, it showed the same scene but caught Taylor mid sneeze. "Holy mother," Jackson gasped.

"Was thinking the same thing," Sutton said, closing the pictures. "Birds spread the mutated viruses. Before we lost contact with the CDC team in Mexico City, they had reported large flocks of dead birds."

"What do you mean, 'lost contact'?" the President asked.

Looking up the table, "They lost contact with them twenty-four hours ago," Sutton answered, looking at the president. "Last contact, the team was reporting millions dead and the city had lost power."

Sitting up, the president flipped through the report. "I know I saw projections for Mexico," he mumbled.

"Yes sir," Paterson said, looking down and flipping over a few pages. "Page one hundred and fifty-two."

"The embassy has been sealed?" the President asked.

"Yes sir, but over a dozen inside are sick with four deaths, so we told the ambassador to stay in place until we could send assets to pull him out," Paterson answered.

"Mr. President," Sutton said and he looked down the table at him. "Mexico City is a packed city like New York. The fact that New York has better sanitation is the only reason it took a while to snowball."

Panting with wide eyes, "What did you mean by skewing the numbers?" the President asked.

"Kids skewed the numbers, showing we had a higher survival rate," Sutton said. "From birth to fifteen, the mortality drops to seventy-five percent or so. I would have to run the numbers, but I'm sure I'm close."

"Well, that's good," the President sighed as Sarah walked back in.

"Ah, Mr. President," Sutton said slowly. "No, it's not. Not with this death rate. Who will take care of the kids? The average kid thinks food comes from a box, can, or McDonald's."

Slumping his shoulders, the president leaned back in his chair. "Can you give me numbers that I can think about?"

Flipping a few pages back, Sutton looked at the page and then clicked his mouse, looking at the computer screen. "For every adult that survives, there will be six kids," Sutton offered and Jackson tapped his arm, showing him a page from the folder.

"Oh, sorry," Sutton said. "The same age group is also showing the largest non-infection rate."

Looking up at the ceiling as his mouth moved while whispering numbers, Sutton turned to the president. "Something like eleven kids for every adult that survives or is naturally immune, so the team's prediction of a mean of twelve million in a year won't be correct if we don't get a vaccine. Adults are over ninety percent mortality with no medical care."

"Sutton, if God came down and gave you the vaccine right now, how many could we save?" the President asked.

"Well, first I would ask God to give it to everyone," Sutton mumbled, grabbing a pen and started writing on a sheet of paper. "With a hundred chickens that don't die, in two weeks after we get the vaccine, we would have a thousand shots a day coming out."

"FUCK!" the President shouted, jumping up and agents burst in the room. "We are the most powerful nation in the world and are getting our asses kicked by a tiny virus!"

"Dr. Sutton," Paterson said in a low voice. "If you look toward the back, you will read about a dozen chicken farms losing half of their flocks over two days."

Sutton sprang to his feet with wide eyes, "Get me some of those damn chickens that survived! Our entire medical flocks were wiped out!" he bellowed and Paterson scooted back from the table in shock. "Paterson, what do we make our vaccines from? All the pharmaceutical chickens died because the virus is very lethal to them. In Atlanta, they have fourteen that survived out of our flock of three thousand. You get us some chickens that don't die, we have a shot!"

Paterson turned to the president, "Send someone to get the fucking chickens!" the President screamed.

"Paterson!" Sutton shouted as Paterson jumped up. "You might have just saved us, but keep the chickens outside. Have someone care for them in a hazmat suit."

"A hundred?" Paterson asked, grabbing the phone.

"You have troops around here, send some for chicken feed and bring as many as you can get," Sutton said.

Kenner, the Secretary of Defense, stood up, "How much does a chicken eat a day?" he asked, grabbing a phone.

"Just get all the damn chicken food you can!" the President bellowed and Kenner stabbed the phone with his fingers punching buttons. "I don't know where you get it, but I don't care if you shoot someone to get it!"

Everyone turned to Paterson as he bellowed into the phone. "You tell that cocksucker if he orders those chickens killed, I'll kill his fucking kids with his wife's teeth!"

Paterson stopped, listening to the phone. "I'm the damn Secretary of Homeland and you tell the Secretary of Agriculture that I outrank his ass! I will kill that motherfucker!"

The president stormed down the table and ripped the phone from Paterson. "This is the President. If he orders those chickens killed, I'll have a chopper fly him fifty miles out over the Atlantic and throw his ass in! Unless everyone there wants to die, shut the fuck up and listen!" the President bellowed so loud that his face turned purple.

Lowering the phone, the President turned to Paterson. "Where the fuck are they located?" he growled.

"Bunker in northwest Tennessee," Paterson answered and the President pulled the phone back to his ear.

"Is John nearby because I don't know why I'm talking to you?" the President snapped as Sutton grabbed a sandwich, taking a bite and watching the show. "Hello, John," the President said and tapped a button on the phone and the monitors around the room blinked before showing an older man with salt and pepper hair.

The President looked at the camera in the phone and everyone saw John sweating on the screen. "Are you disobeying a direct order from the President?"

"Sir, protocol clearly states we have to kill all livestock that are infected," John answered in a quivering voice.

"You're fired," the President snapped. "You, with the black hair behind John," the President shouted at a young intern who pointed at his own chest. "Yes, you. You're now the acting Secretary of Agriculture, get the word out now *not* to kill any chickens that survived on those chicken farms."

"Yes sir," the young man said. "What do you want done with them?" he asked, pulling out his cellphone and tapping the screen.

"The Secretary of Homeland will tell you," the President said, standing back up and Paterson reached over, picking up the phone and the screen went blank.

"Kenner, find someone to shoot John with a slow, dull bullet," the President said, walking past. "That bastard loves playing games."

Reaching for his soda, Sutton froze. Then he slowly started chewing again and grabbed his soda. "Um, Mr. President?" Sutton said and Jackson kicked him under the table.

"Yes, Dr. Sutton," the President said with a smile.

"Were you kidding?" Sutton asked. "Because if you weren't, can we, like, keep him in a cell? I don't have genetic mice here to test my vaccine on."

"Delay that order, Kenner. Throw John in a cell until Dr. Sutton finishes with him," the President said, sitting down. "Very good, Doctor."

"GENERAL!" Kenner screamed into the phone. "I don't know where you get chicken feed but if you find a chicken farm, I'm sure they will have chicken feed. Now get the hell out there and find some!"

Kenner slammed down the phone and reached in his pocket, pulling out a medicine bottle. "That's a good idea," the President said. "Sarah, can you get me some Motrin?"

"Yes sir," she said and left the room.

"Sutton," the President called out as he rubbed his temples. "How long would it take you to finish that report from Homeland?"

"Ten to fifteen minutes," Sutton answered, pushing the empty plate away and finally feeling full.

"Finish it, then I want to ask you some questions and you can tell me about this virus in words I can understand."

"Yes sir," Sutton said, grabbing the report.

"Paterson, how are your agents holding up outside?" the President asked as Sarah walked back in and handed the president some pills and poured a glass of water.

"Over a hundred have gotten infected and sixty-four have died," Paterson answered, hanging up the phone and sitting back down.

"Kenner, how are the troops doing?" the President asked before swallowing the pills.

"We have all troops locked down on bases, but have reports of outbreaks at multiple bases," Kenner answered, sitting down with a sigh.

The president went around the table as Sutton finished reading the report. When he set the report down, the president turned to him. "Finished?" the President asked and Sutton nodded, looking a little pale. "When will the deaths be so bad that we can't hide them?"

"Sir, I'm surprised your group has done as well as they have," Sutton told him. "But as Jackson pointed out, the deaths are growing exponentially. You only have two days because by then, the death rates will be over a million a day and by the end of next week, three million a day."

"What's the best way to spin this from a science point-of-view?"

"Just what we said, Mr. President," Sutton said and felt Jackson stepping on his foot. "We just talked about it; the virus mutated. We were holding our own and in the past twenty-four hours, we noticed mutations and notified the public."

The president's hands fell off the table and onto his lap as he looked at Sutton in shock. "You are a genius," the President gasped.

"Hardly," Sutton chuckled. "But tell people to avoid large crowds and only stay near family members. Tell the public we were close to the vaccine, but the virus mutated. But sir, to be honest, I would let Ernie do it. He can give straight information very well but anything he explains, nobody can follow it."

"Where's he at?" the President asked, looking around the table.

"He's in Atlanta," Sutton answered. "We don't let him in the labs, so he stays upstairs."

"Paterson, tell him what we want so he can start preparing. Tell him, we go public in two days," the President said.

"Mr. President, how many people are in this complex?" Sutton asked. "I need to know how many vaccines we need to produce here, so we will be able to go outside."

The President looked over at Kenner. "Five thousand, four hundred, and twenty-six," Kenner answered.

"That's doable," Sutton mumbled. "And I've asked Dr. Jackson to get me the samples of the two mutations," Sutton said and saw the President had raised his eyebrows. "Mr. President, the vaccine won't do any good if it doesn't work on the mutations."

"Jackson, have you taken care of that?" the President asked.

"Um, no sir, General Stonkly said he was busy," Jackson said, clearing his throat. "I was going to ask Paterson if he could send a chopper down."

"Paterson, throw this Stonkly in a cell for a lab rat," the President commanded with a wave of his hand.

"Yes sir," Paterson said, making a note.

"Dr. Sutton, will you and Jackson join me for dinner tonight?" the President asked. "The reason I ask, is I want to make sure you eat."

"Yes sir," Sutton sighed, closing his laptop.

"Sarah, you don't mind that I assigned you to Dr. Sutton?" the President asked, glancing back. "It seems he and his team needs someone to watch over them and make sure they take care of themselves."

"Happy to, Mr. President," Sarah smiled. "Who should I call, if someone doesn't give what I need to take care of Dr. Sutton and his team?"

"Me, of course," the President laughed. "Do you know who I made Secretary of Agriculture?"

"No sir, but Buddy knows him. I've seen them drinking together," Sarah answered.

Standing up, Sutton tilted his head to the president as he grabbed his laptop bag. "See you tonight, Mr. President. I'll shower, but I don't have a suit pressed and would really like to spend what time I can in the lab."

"You can wear underwear or boxers if you want, I don't care," the President chuckled and everyone joined in.

"I'll make sure you get any reports before the next meeting," Paterson called out.

"Thanks," Sutton said as Sarah walked over and opened the door. "Thank you," Sutton said with a frown.

"Oh, don't start the guy thing," Sarah groaned, pushing him out the door and then turned to Jackson.

"Hey, I have my own staff to tell me what to do," he laughed, walking out.

When they were in the golf cart with Sarah sitting in the back, "Dr. Jackson, will you let us off at Dr. Sutton's quarters across from the lab?" she asked.

"You bet," Jackson said, backing up and then leaned over to Sutton. "I'm just warning you, just do what she says, it's not worth the fight and tell your team the same."

Glancing back at Sarah and studying her appearance, Sutton would've been shocked if she was even twenty-five. The youngest member on his team was forty-one and he was fifty. "Just listen to Dr. Jackson," Sarah smiled.

Turning around, Sutton started having a bad feeling about this. Knowing he was old enough to be Sarah's father really didn't help.

Chapter Eleven
Answer a lie with a lie

May 4

Coming back from the morning chores, Arthur walked in the back door and stopped, tapping the completed chores off the list. He gave a long sigh, not feeling like doing anything at the moment and walked into his office. The e-mail Wendy had sent early yesterday morning was on the screen, telling him that a lot of passengers had come down with the flu.

She and the others weren't sick yet, according to her letter, but the captain had turned the ship around and was heading back early. That alone made Arthur feel better and he had already marked out a route to go and get her.

He glanced over in the corner and saw his AR standing against the wall, after listening to the local radio station. They had reported a rash of break-ins and riots starting in Little Rock. It had been just this morning that Arthur had heard of deaths from the flu, and it had been over a hundred and thirty in Clarksville alone.

In the living room, he heard the TV give off a blare of the Emergency Broadcast Network and then his computer blinked and started blaring as a scroll bar rolled across the bottom. 'This is not a test, stay tuned for emergency information'.

"Oh shit!" Arthur shouted, jumping up and running to the living room. He read the same ticker at the bottom of the screen, then the screen blinked and showed the national news anchor for the local station.

"Mark Bryant here, and we've just received word that all stations are now under the authority of the government," Mark said with a serious face. "We are awaiting a live report from the director of the CDC on the drastic turn of the flu outbreak that is spreading across the globe."

Mark stopped as if someone off screen was talking. "We are taking you live to Atlanta," Mark said and the screen cut to a podium with CDC across the front.

When Ernie stepped up to the podium introducing himself, Arthur groaned. "Oh, come on, can't you get someone there that at least understands medicine?! Get the guy who mops the floors!"

"I'm here today to tell you the virus that has broken out across the globe and here in our great country has mutated," Ernie said, looking out across the room. "We were dispensing the antiviral meds and holding the virus in check, but we have discovered that it has mutated into at least two different strains."

"What the fuck?" Arthur mumbled, dropping down on the couch.

"This virus is an H5N1 type and since the mutations, the mortality has climbed to over ninety percent," Ernie said and Arthur felt his heart flutter as the room exploded with reporters shouting.

Falling back on the couch and staring at Ernie holding up his hands for quiet, Arthur knew H5N1 was the virus that scared the medical community. Highly lethal and slow onset, but had never been recorded with human to human transmission.

"People, please. I can't give out the information the public needs with you yelling!" Ernie shouted. "You are killing people with your shouting!" The crowd fell silent at that accusation.

"Thank you," Ernie said. "People need to avoid crowds and public places. Stay indoors and only let immediate family in your house. Avoid all contact with all people as much as you can. People can look healthy but be infected. We have documented cases of people that once infected, can go for two weeks without showing any signs of illness. Then they will develop an itchy nose and sneezing. When coughing starts, death follows in twenty-four to forty-eight hours," Ernie paused, looking around the room at the stunned faces.

"That is why we have a sheet of glass between you and me," Ernie told the reporters and more than one ran out of the room. "We offered each of you masks and told you they were needed, but more than one of you told us it would mess up your makeup and distort your voice."

"Now," Ernie said, glancing at his notes and then back to the cameras. "Again, avoid people and closed in places where people have gathered recently; like schools and shopping areas. All schools are hereby closed and all students will be returned home and at home they should stay. If you need food, call your local Red

Cross, or hang a white sheet outside of your house. Police will inform the Red Cross and the military who are mobilizing to start food dispersion. I'm telling you now, if you go out to a store, you *will* get infected. Stay indoors unless you have a medical emergency, then call 911. A travel ban is in effect in all states."

Pausing, Ernie glanced at the teleprompter. "Anyone found off their property will be detained and that's the last place you want to be. The Attorney General has issued a draft that all prisoners will be on lockdown until further notice. All meals will be served in cells. Any confrontation with prison staff will be viewed as a deadly action."

"In public, any person not following a police officer's orders, deadly force has been authorized. You must understand, the police and soldiers don't want to get near people and they will instruct you to get in transport from a distance," Ernie said with a depressed expression. "This transport will be enclosed trailers."

"This virus is airborne, so you can catch it if a person gets within ten feet of you or you walk in a room they have been in. If you have someone sick or who passes in your house, hang something red outside. Separate them from everyone else and wash your hands repeatedly."

Taking a deep breath, Ernie looked around the room. "People, I'm not going to lie. The next few weeks will be very hard. We were very close to a vaccine before the virus mutated. That mutation killed most of the chickens we used to develop our vaccines. We have gotten more from secured sites, but our scientists have had to start over."

"How long?" someone shouted.

"I'm getting to that," Ernie snapped, looking hard away from the camera. "Our current projections based on the past work, we will have test batches in sixteen days," he said, turning back to the camera. "If those test batches work, then we can start mass producing the vaccines. Our scientists are working nonstop and many are sleeping right outside their labs. I assure you, we are working as hard as we can."

"Now, I will take questions but in an orderly fashion. But first, I must remind everyone that the President will be making a national address in two hours," Ernie said as everyone raised their hands.

He pointed and a voice asked. "What about the reports we've heard from Mexico?"

"Yes, it's been confirmed that there are horrifying death rates down there. The mutations reached them before making it here," Ernie answered, pointing at another person.

"So, the mutations came from Mexico?"

Shaking his head, "Not that we know of because the mutations have been discovered in Europe, the Middle East, and all the way to China," Ernie answered and pointed at another person.

"Have any survived the mutated virus?"

"Yes, no virus is one hundred percent fatal. If you get sick, you need to drink fluids and control your fever. Hospitals are pushed past their breaking point, so I caution you to use your own judgement about going to hospitals. I can guarantee you, the virus is at every hospital in the nation now," Ernie told the reporter as he pointed.

"Is this the Rudolph flu we've heard of on the internet?"

Nodding, "From what we've gathered, we have to say it is," Ernie said, pointing at another.

"What if people run out of food?"

"I suggest you ration what you have. It takes a long time to starve, but this virus will kill you in two weeks. Ration what you have until you are supplied by the Red Cross or the military," Ernie answered, pointing.

"People have to work?"

"No, they don't," Ernie said, frowning. "The President has signed a presidential order eliminating all bills and interest for sixty days. There can be no repossessions, evictions, shutting off of utilities or any repercussions for financial reasons. Any business that does can be sued with unlimited damages for claims."

"Whoa," Arthur gasped and heard several people in the room gasp in shock as well, as Ernie pointed again.

"How many deaths have occurred here?"

"We are still getting numbers because over the last twenty-four hours, the death rate has skyrocketed but I can tell you, it's over a million and climbing fast," Ernie said and all the hands dropped down in shock. "Are we done?" he asked, looking around. "You can e-mail me questions and I suggest you pick up the mask on your way out, but don't think that mask is a tank. Avoid people at all cost and thank you."

Before Ernie turned to leave, everyone in the room bolted for the doors and the screen cut back to Mark who was staring off screen with a wide-open mouth. "Mark, we are on the air," a voice said off camera.

Shaking his head, "Sorry, as you've just heard from Ernie Ostimer, Director of the CDC, the virus has mutated," Mark said, visibly sweating. "The Rudolph virus is highly contagious and people need to avoid all contact with others."

As Mark shuffled his papers, a ticker rolled across the bottom of the screen, repeating the answers to each question and all warnings. "Holy bitch balls, Batman," Arthur mumbled, struggling to stand up. All he could think of was Wendy. He was certain Joseph would be okay in the middle of the Indian Ocean.

Getting up, he headed to his computer. Dropping into his chair, he opened the folder for the servers in the basement, going through the library until he found a book on the avian flu virus and the different types.

He sat reading, just to keep his mind occupied for several hours. When his computer beeped, Arthur jumped in his chair and saw he had another e-mail from Wendy. He glanced at the clock on the computer and saw it was almost six p.m.

Moving the cursor over the e-mail, Arthur noticed it had been sent four hours ago as he clicked it open.

Hey Hun,

The captain just told us we can't put into port until we are quarantined and he is going to look for another port on the eastern seaboard. The flu is here and people are dying. I've tried to call over a dozen times, but can't get through. Got an e-mail from Joseph that he made it and is okay. He said he tried to get several to you, but they kept getting returned. He says he will find a way to get home before the end of summer.

I'm helping the doctor and nurse on the ship because I know I have it and can help others as long as I can. The sneezing started this morning and the fever will be starting soon. In the last three hours, we've had four hundred die and there was nothing we could do.

I promise you I will fight this, but you have to promise to stay safe for Joseph. Don't get around anyone, you have to help our baby boy. I love you and you were the best thing to ever happen to me. Please stay safe for Joseph, I know he's grown up, but he will need you after this.

I have to go, there is another code. I love you and if I make it through this, I will come home. If I don't, I'll wait for you.

Love you more than the world.

Arthur felt his chest get tight and had trouble breathing when he'd finished the message. Tears flowed from his face as he reread the letter. Through teary eyes, he clicked 'respond' and typed, 'I love you, Wendy'.

It was all he could write before he started wailing. Finally, he clicked 'send' and fell out of his chair, crashing to the floor. As he wailed, the dogs ran over and curled next to him, whining. He didn't hear the computer beep, telling him it was unable to send the message as he covered his face with his hands and cried.

The stuffy nose and slight fever Arthur would get in the next few hours from his lottery present were his antibodies killing the visitor and he would never notice. It would be buried in his grief as he cried on the floor until he fell asleep. Arthur wouldn't hear the computer give an alarm as the power from the grid was lost at seven a.m. on the dot. The computer turned off the feed from the grid, so it wouldn't drain the power that the land was producing.

Chapter Twelve
Symptoms show a killer inside

May 6

Coming out of the airlock, Sutton stopped, seeing Sarah looking at him as she tapped her foot. "I came out," he cried out in the bubble suit.

"I told you to come out an hour ago to eat," Sarah snapped.

Thinking about running back into the airlock, Sutton cringed as Sarah stepped over to unzip the suit and pull it off of him. "You will eat, then take a nap," she told him and then cringed her nose. "You will shower before taking a nap," she added.

Sutton looked at the dressing area where Sarah had a table and chairs brought in and the rest of the team was sitting down eating. None of them even turned around to watch Sutton get chewed out.

An elderly man pushed his chair back and started to stand. "Dr. Skannish!" Sarah shouted and the old man dropped back down in his chair like someone had shot at him. "I told you that you had to eat two plates and drink two bottles of fluids before you could leave!"

Sutton turned to the table as Dr. Skannish pulled his plate back over and continued eating. Dr. Skannish was almost seventy but seemed rather frightened of Sarah, as did everyone else.

Feeling a tap on his leg, Sutton looked down and saw Sarah waiting on him to lift his foot up so she could pull the suit off. "You know, I've been doing this longer than you've been alive," Sutton told her as Sarah pulled the suit off his foot.

"Sutton!" Sarah snapped and he lifted his other leg. "You and your team don't take care of yourselves for shit! I took on this job, so shove it! I'm surprised you get anything done with the way all of you document your progress."

Sutton stared at her with his mouth agape as Sarah carried his suit over and hung it up on the wall. "Sit. Eat," she commanded as she turned back around.

Almost running, Sutton moved to the table and dropped down into a chair. Grabbing his plate, he was about to take a huge bite when Sarah darted over and grabbed his hand. "Smaller bites," she said in a much gentler voice.

"I've finished two plates and have taken a shower. Can I go back to the lab now?" Dr. Skannish asked, but didn't move to get up.

"You will take a nap on the cots or go to sleep in your quarters. If you want, I will wake you in a few hours," Sarah offered, sitting down at the head of the table. "I put all of your findings in the computer and correlated them."

"Thank you," Dr. Skannish said with a gentle smile. "I have to say, with your help we will get to the vaccine much faster, but can't I go back to the lab?"

"No," Sarah said, but in a soft voice. "Your next batch won't be done for two hours and seventeen minutes, so you can rest. I know you want to do that different… whatever," she said, waving her hand off in the air. "But it can wait a few hours. You were stumbling around in the lab. I know, I was watching through the window."

Dr. Skannish turned to Sutton as he continued eating in small bites. "Sutton, a little help?" Skannish pleaded.

Shaking his head, "Nope, she knows how to use the intercom and it sounds really bad when she yells over it," Sutton replied and the others around the table nodded in agreement.

"Hey, I was about to get in a suit and drag your ass out," Sarah popped off at Sutton. Seeing Sutton emptying his mouth to protest, Sarah threw a hand up to stop him. "I don't try to understand what you're doing, but I can interpret the results you send out for me to put in the computer. Since I've been here, this group has progressed very quickly. I've been monitoring Atlanta and can tell they are just working away. If I was there, that would stop because I can see they are dead tired on their feet."

"Um, I didn't tell you to put them in the computer," Sutton mumbled and then took another bite, holding the fork up for a second to show that it was a small bite.

"I know," Sarah laughed and everyone loved the sound of her laugh. "But I'm sorry, that is not any of your strong points. You and your team continue to dictate your notes, and I will put them in the computer."

"You do know I have a great-granddaughter older than you, right?" Skannish asked from the end of the table and Sarah slowly turned and gave him a hard look. "I'm going to take a nap. Will you wake me in three hours?" Skannish mumbled, getting up.

"I would be very happy to, Dr. Skannish," Sarah smiled and then Skannish walked out, heading to his quarters.

The other four around the table turned to Sarah, holding up their plates to show that they were empty. "Very good. Anyone else want me to wake them in three hours?" Sarah smiled and the four nodded and broke for the door.

Sutton looked at their young general and couldn't help but grin. Sarah was barely five-foot-five and very slender, with long black hair that she always wore pulled back. Small black-rimmed glasses sat perched on her pert nose, giving her a bookworm appearance. After the first day with Sutton, she had stopped wearing the business suit and had donned jeans and a pullover shirt with tennis shoes.

"I set up your desktop in your quarters," Sarah said, grabbing a napkin and then reached over to wipe Sutton's mouth. "We have a meeting tomorrow at nine a.m."

Sutton gave a long sigh, slumping down in his chair. "Those meetings interrupt my work," he mumbled.

"I know. That's why I cancelled your appearance at the last two, but you have results the President can understand," she said, pushing a bottle of water closer to his plate and hoping Sutton would take a hint.

The vision of Sarah holding him down and pouring the water down his throat filled Sutton's mind and he snatched it up. "You can interpret the results that well?" he asked, then drank half the bottle.

Shaking her head, "No, but I understand your dictation. Give me a little while and I will understand the nuts and bolts better," she told him.

"I believe that," Sutton chuckled, setting the bottle down.

"May I ask you a question?" Sarah asked in a low voice.

"Sarah, you are part of this team now, so you can ask whatever you want," Sutton laughed. "I've never seen Skannish listen to anyone, including me."

Leaning back, the smile fell off her face, "How accurate do you think Dr. Skannish's death rates are?" she asked.

All cheer left Sutton's body and he looked down at his plate. "Accurate, but on the low side," Sutton said in a low voice.

"So, we will be losing six million people a day by the end of the week, and by next week it will be up to twenty million a day?"

Putting his fork down, "Yes, that will be the peak here," Sutton admitted. "In sixteen days, the numbers will start falling because those left will be isolated or immune."

"So, by May twentieth, the population of the United States will be less than thirty million? And a large portion of that will be kids?"

Nodding, "Yeah," Sutton mumbled. "This modern world we have was the perfect vector for this virus. Airplanes moved people around and one man got it into the bird population literally, around the globe. Then, a person can jump in a car and be on the opposite coast in two days."

"What are the numbers you feel that are isolated?"

"Ten to twelve million," Sutton answered. "Those are the ones we can help with a vaccine."

She leaned over and patted his cheek. "Go get in the bed, but shower first. I laid out new clothes and leave those in the bathroom, so they can be washed," she instructed. "Atlanta will be sending the next batch of results in an hour. I'll put them in the computer."

Getting up, Sutton looked down at Sarah, forcing a smile. "Thank you for all of your help," he said, really liking her but terrified of her. Sarah's language could make anyone blush when she got mad which it seemed, he and his team could do very easily.

***

Stumbling down her hallway, Wendy moved around a body that was lying on the floor. Wheezing hard, Wendy bent over coughing hard and spewing froth from her mouth. Ignoring the dead body, she clutched the handrail on the wall to keep from falling down. She had tried to continue the checkups on people in their cabins, but had finally had to stop. The cough had started gradually over an hour ago and then intensified fast. In two hours' time, the coughing had started doubling her over.

As the coughing fit subsided, Wendy lifted her head and saw a refreshment cart in the hallway ahead and stumbled up to it. Hitting the cart with her waist, Wendy leaned over it and used it like a walker to continue down the hall.

She stopped at her door and pulled the keycard attached to a bungie on her waist. The crew had given her that to check on people because it opened all the doors on the ship. Slipping the card in, she opened her door and pushed the cart in. She saw Gloria lying down on the bed, hacking hard as she coughed.

"Gloria, you have to sit up," Wendy croaked out. Letting the cart go, Wendy moved beside Gloria and touched her skin to feel that it was on fire. Seeing a bottle of Tylenol on the bedside table between the beds, Wendy grabbed it and took two out.

She pulled Gloria up and propped her against the headboard. "Take these," Wendy said, putting the pills in Gloria's mouth. When she lifted a bottle of water to Gloria's lips, Gloria grabbed it and turned it up. "Slow down some," Wendy said, taking the bottle away.

Gloria cracked her weary eyes open. "Nobody answered when the phone rang at home," Gloria told her in a raspy voice.

"I told you to wait for me and I would go with you," Wendy said, handing the bottle back. "The captain told me we will be able to quarantine in Miami. They are going to have us park in the bay."

Draining the bottle, Gloria dropped it as she gasped for air, wheezing so loud Wendy could feel the vibrations through the air. "How many died today?" Gloria asked.

"Don't know, I had to stop rounds," Wendy admitted, struggling to keep her eyes open. She saw Gloria tilt to the side to lay down. Reaching out, Wendy stopped her. "You have to keep your chest upright. Your lungs are filling with fluid. Upright, you have a chance to cough it out and use the top part of your lungs."

Giving a long moan as Wendy sat her upright, "I just want to lie down, I'm so tired," Gloria panted and then erupted into a violent coughing fit, spewing frothy sputum over the room until she covered her mouth.

Stepping back, Wendy tried to think of a way to keep Gloria upright. Wendy knew she had to get some rest as she looked around the room and an odd idea popped in her mind. She stumbled back into the cart as she thought about it. "Yeah, that could work," she croaked and then started coughing as Gloria stopped.

When Wendy finished coughing, she leaned hard against the cart, panting for air. When the stars left her vision, she pushed her body up and grabbed the extra sheets off the couch. Moving over to her suitcase, she pulled out the pocketknife she usually always carried, but she'd kept it in the suitcase since she had been on the ship.

Flipping it open, she cut the sheet in half and twirled the cut sheet until she had two long strands. Tying the two together, she moved over to the balcony door and tied one end to a light fixture. Then she threw the strand over Gloria's bed and saw it was too short to reach the far wall.

Grabbing another sheet, she cut it to repeat the process and tied the other end to the clothes rack bolted to the wall. Turning around she saw the sheet hanging over both of their beds. "Gloria, sit up," Wendy said, picking up the last sheet and cutting it in half.

After she twirled it into a strand, Wendy looped it under Gloria's arms as she sat her up. Wrapping it around Gloria's back, Wendy tied it to the overhead line. When she was done, Gloria was sitting up, or more appropriately, being held upright.

Moving to the couch, Wendy grabbed the cushions and put them behind Gloria and pulled Gloria's legs out in a more natural position. "I want to lay down," Gloria croaked, then started coughing.

Feeling lightheaded, Wendy toppled back into the cart. Catching herself before she fell, "You can't lay down. Upright you have a chance to keep your lungs clear by coughing," Wendy wheezed, feeling the fluid in her lungs trying to suffocate her.

She reached down and tossed half a dozen bottles of water around Gloria. Then she tossed some on her own bed. With the last of her strength, Wendy wrapped the other half of the sheet under her arms and tied it to the line, then sat down and found the loop held her upright.

Slumping forward, Wendy coughed as she flapped a hand out to the nightstand, grabbing the bottle of Tylenol. When she stopped coughing, she took two and set the bottle back on the nightstand. "Gloria, wake me if you need me," Wendy said as Gloria started another foaming mouth coughing fit and ended it by hacking out a mouthful of phlegm.

"Don't lay down, Gloria," Wendy panted, struggling to keep her eyes open. "When you cough it up, you can't drown."

As Gloria continued coughing, Wendy's head dropped down as her body gave out from all the exertion she had done trying to help others. Hanging from the line, Wendy started coughing hard but didn't wake up as the visitor tormented her body.

Chapter Thirteen
Finding an angel

May 7
Finished feeding the animals, Arthur dropped back down on the couch. Still wearing the same clothes since he'd read Wendy's message, Arthur had a look of defeat on his face as the dogs came over and surrounded him, putting their heads in his lap. "I'm sorry, guys," Arthur said with no emotion, getting up and walking to the kitchen.

He filled the dogs' bowls, then headed back to the couch and the dogs followed him. When he sat down, they again put their heads in his lap. Having no more tears left, Arthur reached down and rubbed the dogs. "Yeah, need to get it together," Arthur mumbled. "Joseph will be here after this subsides."

The dogs moved closer, since this was the first sign of affection Arthur had shown in days. When Don stood up on the couch, putting his maw in Arthur's face, Arthur couldn't help but give a small smile. "Yeah, boy, I'm going to get through this," Arthur said, rubbing his head.

That set off all the dogs to stand up on the couch in his face. "Okay, I get the point," Arthur said and the small smile turned into a grin he didn't feel. Hearing his phone vibrate, Arthur gave a startle since the power had been off, along with the phones, but then heard the ring of the front gate tone.

He got up and headed to his office and saw his phone moving across the desk as it vibrated. Picking it up, he tapped the screen to see Rudy at the gate. Before he tapped the phone to turn on the speaker, Rudy got out of his truck and moved to the control box and punched the keypad.

"What the fuck?" Arthur mumbled as the gate opened.

Rudy turned back and jumped in his truck as the grief Arthur felt turned to rage. He pulled his pistol out and press-checked it, seeing brass in the chamber. Keeping it in his hand, he moved into the living room and looked out the front window to see if Rudy would pull to the front or back.

Less than a minute later, Arthur saw Rudy's truck pull to the back and he headed to the back door. "Kit, Kat, sit," he snapped and the labs sat down as Don and Daisy followed him to the back door. Peeking out the small window, Arthur saw Rudy stop the truck and ease the door open, looking toward the shop.

Yanking the back door open, Arthur raised his arm and aimed the pistol at Rudy's chest. "I'm inside!" Arthur shouted and Rudy jumped, dropping his hand to his waist. Seeing Arthur aiming at him, Rudy raised his arms up.

"Hey, Arthur, it's just me," Rudy said sniffling and Arthur noticed Rudy's nose was a very bright red, almost glowing.

"I know. I'm only going to ask once, how did you know the code because we never gave it to you?" Arthur demanded, seeing a revolver shoved in the front of Rudy's pants.

"I, um, asked Jack last year when you and Wendy were in Dallas," Rudy said slowly, lowering his arms.

"Move your arms more and you will die," Arthur warned and Don and Daisy moved in front of him, growling at Rudy. Rudy's arms jumped up fully extended over his head. "Jack wouldn't just give you the code."

"I told him I had to bring your lawn mower back and forgot the code," Rudy admitted and then sneezed, but somehow kept his arms up.

"You come to ask for forgiveness for stealing from us?"

"No, I know you have power and food. I came to stay with you," Rudy told him. Then Rudy noticed Arthur's unkempt appearance. "I can help out, you know it."

"No, get out of here because if I see you again, I'll kill you," Arthur barked.

"No, you won't," Rudy grinned. "Arthur, either I stay or you leave, your choice," Rudy said, lowering his hands slowly. "I don't want to kill you, so I'll stay with you, or you can leave, or I will kill you. Those are your choices."

BOOM, sounded as Arthur squeezed the trigger and saw Rudy jump as the bullet hit him in the center of his chest. Arthur squeezed the trigger three more times, hitting Rudy almost in the same spot. As Rudy wavered back with the hits, Arthur saw the window in Rudy's truck shatter as the bullets passed through him.

Hitting the truck with his back, Rudy looked down at the blood flowing out of his chest. He looked up and noticed his vision was getting fuzzy. "I should've just killed you," Rudy gasped as blood dripped out of his mouth.

Lowering his pistol, "Yep, you should've," Arthur said and then saw Rudy grabbing for the revolver in his pants. Leveling the pistol again, Arthur squeezed the trigger one more time and Rudy's head snapped back as a hole was punched in his forehead.

Arthur kept his aim on the body for several minutes until there was no movement from Rudy. Finally lowering his pistol, Arthur ejected the magazine and pulled a fresh one from his mag holster. Putting the partial magazine in the holster, he shoved the full one into the pistol.

Holstering his pistol, Arthur shook his head counting up the days in his head. "Fucking asshole, you exposed me when you were here to get the auger."

He stepped up to the body and looked at the revolver in Rudy's pants. "You motherfucker, that's Jack's," Arthur snapped and then spun around and jogged to the house. Don and Daisy followed as Arthur ran to his office and pulled a box of shells from the gun safe. Topping his magazine off, he walked over and grabbed his AR.

"Dogs," he said, running for the back door. All the dogs ran after him as he ran outside and jumped on the electric buggy. Spinning tires as he backed up, Arthur shifted into drive and took off down the driveway.

As he sped down the driveway and saw the gate still open, "Shit-wad couldn't even close the gate," Arthur mumbled and breathed in through his nose and realized he could breathe better. "Yeah, you haven't cried," he mumbled, reaching the end of the driveway and turned onto the road. "I should be experiencing something."

Looking beside him, he saw the dogs running full speed and he slowed down some until they were at a trot. "Maybe I'm immune," he concluded.

Reaching Jack's house, Arthur pulled into the driveway and noticed the front door was open. Climbing out of the buggy, he grabbed the AR and moved to the front door. Jack's truck and Starlie's car were both in the driveway so he knew they should be home, but that had been Jack's prized 1873 Colt Peacemaker that Rudy had.

Moving to the door, Arthur jerked his head back after catching a whiff of rankness. Easing up to the door, Arthur peeked inside and saw Jack on the floor and Starlie on the couch. Even standing in the door, he could tell they had been dead for a few days.

"Sorry, Jack and Starlie," Arthur mumbled, closing the door and started thinking of just leaving and heading nowhere, just away from the land he and Wendy had turned into a home. As the idea started picking up steam in his mind, he looked up the valley and saw the next house as a tiny speck. "Lord, please let Ted, Tammy, and Nicole be all right."

Remembering them on the porch when he had taken Wendy to the airport, he jogged back to the buggy and just drove through the yard to reach the road. Fighting a growing apprehension, Arthur kept a steady pace for the dogs to trot along beside him. Ted and Tammy had moved into the old house two years ago and Arthur really liked them. They were a very young couple. Ted had gotten to legal drinking age last year and Tammy still had a year to go.

Two months ago, Tammy had given birth to their first baby, Nicole, a precious little girl. He and Wendy had visited them in the hospital but when Ted brought them home from the hospital, Wendy and Arthur came down to the house and gave them two hundred dollars for a baby gift and a prepared meal. Arthur had been trying to figure out a way they could talk Joseph into having a kid as he'd held the tiny baby. For the next two days, they had brought prepared meals down for supper and this had been Arthur's idea. Wendy picked up that he'd only wanted to play with the baby, which was true, but Wendy had held Nicole as much as he had.

Pulling into the yard, he saw their vehicles under the carport and remembered coming down and helping Ted put a new roof on, the month after they had moved in. "Please be all right, guys," Arthur mumbled, getting out and grabbing his AR.

Looping the single point sling over his head, Arthur walked across the yard to the front door. "Ted, Tammy, it's Arthur!" he shouted and heard a soft cry inside the house. "Shit," he sighed, feeling bad for waking the baby.

He stopped at the door and waited for it to open as the baby continued to cry. Then, Arthur noticed the cry sounded weak. Grabbing the door, he opened it and was hit with rankness once again. Looking inside, he saw Tammy slumped over on the couch but didn't see Ted.

"Tammy," Arthur called out and she didn't move. Knowing if he walked in and Tammy was sick or the baby, he was for sure exposed. "Sorry, Wendy. I could never live with myself for turning away from a baby," he said, walking inside.

He stopped at the couch and saw frothy phlegm on Tammy's mouth. Her breasts were exposed and a milk pump was in her hands. Reaching over, Arthur felt her neck but with his gloves on, couldn't tell anything. Pulling his hand back and pulling off the glove, he felt Tammy's neck again and felt she was cool but not ice cold and no pulse.

Moving over to the bassinet, Arthur looked down at the baby crying weakly. "Hey, Nicole," he said softly and immediately saw the diaper was full. Looking around, he found the diapers and wipes. Taking his other glove off, he opened the diaper up.

"Wow, you're awful little to be putting out a pile of shit like that," Arthur told the weakly crying baby. Tossing the full diaper on the floor, he wiped Nicole off and saw her skin was very red. "You've been laying in that awhile, huh?" he said, trying to be gentle. He was a nurse and knew it was a very bad diaper rash.

When he put on the diaper, he picked Nicole up and let his AR hang at his side. "I hope your mom took Wendy's advice," he said, looking around.

After they had visited them that third day, after bringing down an evening meal and had returned home, Tammy called Wendy crying because she wasn't making enough milk to fill Nicole up. Wendy left the house and picked up some formula and brought it to Tammy, telling her to supplement until she made the milk.

Looking around the house, Arthur sighed with relief when he saw a can of powdered formula on the kitchen counter. Grabbing a bottle from the dishrack, he saw bottled water in the corner and moved the still weak, crying Nicole to his left arm as he made a bottle. When he opened the formula, he saw it was almost empty.

"Shit," he snapped and Nicole stopped crying and he looked down at her to see her looking up at him. "Sorry," he said, dumping the measuring spoon of formula in the bottle and Nicole started crying again. Grabbing a bottle of water, he poured in four ounces.

"Almost," he said, putting the nipple on and shaking the bottle hard. When the nipple touched Nicole's lips, she started sucking hard and fast. Stepping back into the living room, he moved over and tried to move Tammy and felt that her body was stiff.

"That's at least eight hours and judging by that diaper, I'm betting you haven't eaten for ten," Arthur said, moving down the hall. He found Ted on the bed, sprawled out and gray. Grabbing Ted's leg, he found it wasn't stiff which told him that Ted had been dead for well over a day, but Arthur was thinking closer to two days.

"I should've been checking up on them," Arthur sighed, feeling guilty and then looked down and saw that Nicole was almost done eating. "We have to let that digest, princess."

Nicole's hair was so blonde it was white and her eyes were so blue they seemed fake. "You are still a tiny thing," Arthur smiled at Nicole.

Moving back to the kitchen, he looked in the formula can scooping up the formula around and making calculations. "Six, maybe seven bottles," he huffed, then looked at his watch. "We need to find you some formula."

Putting the top on the can of formula, he grabbed a plastic bag and set it inside. Then he moved over and put six bottles from the dishrack in. Grabbing the bag, he headed to the living room and saw there were only four diapers. "And diapers," he said, grabbing the diaper bag and putting the plastic bag inside.

Walking around, he gathered stuff up until the bottle was empty. He put Nicole on his shoulder and patted her back and she let out burp that Arthur felt in his chest. "All right, that's what I'm talking about," Arthur cheered, grabbing an infant carrier and the diaper bag.

Stepping outside, Kit and Kat jumped around him like: "What do you have? What do you have? Can we play with it?" Don and Daisy were sitting side by side in the yard just watching. "Kit, Kat, stop it," Arthur snapped in a whisper, hearing Nicole breathing steady.

Putting the stuff in the back of the buggy, he went back inside and brought more stuff out. On his last trip, he stopped and looked down at Tammy. Her blonde hair was matted as her vacant eyes stared at the ceiling. "I'll take care of her, Tammy," he said softly. "I'll come back and take care of you and Ted. I should've been checking on you kids."

Holding Nicole to his chest with his left arm and his right arm full of the last of the baby supplies, Arthur used his foot to close the door. Walking over to the buggy, he tossed the stuff in and climbed behind the steering wheel. Realizing Nicole was in a diaper only, he reached back to grab a baby blanket and draped it over her.

With his right hand, he steered the buggy back to the house and noticed the sky had gotten very dark. When he pulled up to the back patio, he looked over at the lifeless Rudy. "Hey, thanks for coming, I got to save Nicole, thanks to you," Arthur said, getting out of the buggy.

Opening the back door, he ferried the supplies inside and heard Nicole coo. He moved her off his shoulder and cradled her with two hands so she was looking at him, chewing on her fist. "Hey, sweetheart," he smiled and then leaned down to kiss her, but his beard stuck her and Nicole started crying.

"Oh, you don't like the beard?" Arthur asked, grabbing the diaper bag and pulling out the stuff for another bottle. Again, when the bottle hit her lips Nicole sucked hard, forgiving him about the beard.

It was two p.m. when Nicole finished the second bottle and Arthur grabbed the carrier and set her inside it. Sound asleep in the carrier, Arthur carried Nicole into the master bathroom and set her on the counter over Wendy's sink.

He pulled out his clippers and found his straight razor. In a few seconds, there was only stubble left of his beard as Arthur looked at his reflection in the mirror. Finding the shaving cream, he lathered up and opened the straight razor and cleaned the stubble off. Rinsing his face off when he was done, Arthur looked in the carrier to see Nicole staring at him.

"Stickers are gone," he smiled and Nicole squealed with a toothless grin. Picking the carrier up, Arthur headed back to the living room and dug out a little onesie and put it on Nicole.

"Let's go find you some food at the store and then you are getting a bath," Arthur said, getting up and heard thunder rumbling.

"Fuck!" he snapped and Nicole squealed with a grin. He looked down at her smiling. "Yeah, I can't get you out in the rain, your body has been stressed enough."

Nicole just cooed and then chewed on her fist as Arthur nuzzled into her neck, making her squeal again. Pulling his head back, he found a wide toothless grin of approval of the 'no beard'. "Let's see how much food you have, then make the call."

Putting Nicole back in the carrier, he set her on the kitchen island and grabbed a glass from the cabinet. It looked like Arthur was measuring cocaine as he carefully measured each scoop. When he was done, he looked down at Nicole. "Seven bottles. I think we should leave in the morning."

Nicole just chewed on her fist so Arthur took that as her agreement. Picking the carrier up, he talked to her as he moved through the house, gathering towels and rags. Thinking the rags were too tough for Nicole's skin, Arthur opened his dresser and pulled out a t-shirt. Everywhere he moved a line of dogs followed, wondering when they could play with what he was carrying around.

Grabbing the baby shampoo and soap he'd taken from Nicole's house, Arthur moved back to the kitchen and spread a towel out on the island beside the baby carrier. "You stinkie," Arthur said, making a face and turning on the sink, getting the water lukewarm.

As he talked to Nicole, he grabbed some scissors and cut his shirt into small squares for baby washcloths. When he was done, he laid Nicole on the towel and stripped her down. Putting her in the sink, Nicole looked around not really sure of this.

Arthur talked to her as he washed her and the skies opened up outside. Looking out the window over the sink, he could barely see Rudy's body out back with the rain coming down so hard. Nicole kicked her feet and splashed the water, really loving this sensation.

"Yeah, if Wendy was here, we would be closing all the shutters," Arthur smiled down at Nicole. "She really hates storms."

Giving a squeal when Arthur wet her head, Nicole looked up at him smiling, feeling the warm water on her body. When he was done, Arthur lifted her up and laid her on the towel, then wrapped her up. "You smell brand new," Arthur laughed as Nicole chewed on her fist as her head lay on his shoulder while he dried her off. Putting her down, Arthur pulled the baby lotion out of the water, hoping it was warmer. After lathering Nicole down, he swaddled her back up in the towel.

With his free hand, he dumped powder in three bottles and then poured water into one. When he started shaking the bottle up, Nicole tried to lift her head up. She knew that sound and liked it. Carrying her to the living room, Arthur sat down in his recliner.

"I know you don't have a diaper on, but we need to let your bottom breathe," he told Nicole, moving her to the crook of his arm. As the bottle headed for her, Nicole's mouth gaped open. When she'd latched on, Arthur started rocking the recliner.

Not able to help it, Arthur chuckled, seeing Nicole's eyes getting very heavy. He looked in front of him and saw all four dogs sitting, staring at the small form in his arms. "Yes, we have a new member," Arthur smiled.

Even asleep, Nicole never stopped sucking hard. When the bottle was finished, Arthur burped her and just let her sleep on his chest as he rocked. As he sat there, Arthur started making a mental list of what he was going to need, and calculated how much he would need as rain pounded the house.

At seven, Arthur made another bottle and tossed the towel away because Nicole had peed in it. Putting a diaper on her, Arthur carried her into his bedroom and laid her on the bed. As he got ready for bed, Mickey and Minnie jumped up on the bed and moved over to Nicole.

Hearing a growl, Arthur turned and saw Don growling at the cats. "Mickey, Minnie, get down!" Arthur snapped, moving over and picking up Nicole. "I should let Don use you for a chew toy."

The cats sat down and looked up at Arthur cradling Nicole to his chest as she cooed. "Back off, cats or I'll let Kong inside," Arthur warned and the cats just laid down.

Moving pillows around, Arthur climbed in bed. After Nicole had eaten, Arthur did something he hadn't done in over twenty years. Fell asleep with a baby on his chest.

Chapter Fourteen
Lives are saved

May 8

Not moving all night and still on his back, Arthur looked down on his chest watching Nicole sleeping peacefully. He'd woken every four hours and had fed her a bottle. The only time Nicole woke up was when she'd taken a dump and her butt had started burning from the rash. Arthur had cleaned her up with the speed of a NASCAR pit crew and Nicole had drifted back to sleep.

"Hey stinker, you hungry?" Arthur asked, kissing her head. Reaching to the nightstand, he grabbed the bottle as he sat up. Nicole gave a startle, then saw the bottle coming and opened her mouth. She looked up at Arthur as she latched on the bottle and he just grinned at her.

He walked into the kitchen and started a pot of coffee. Walking into the living room, Arthur almost started bellowing but took a deep breath, seeing the cats in the baby carrier, sleeping. Moving over, he kicked the carrier on its side and the cats jumped out and looked at him like he was insane.

"Oh, you're so lucky Wendy loved you two," Arthur announced in a quivering voice. Hearing whining, he turned to see the dogs at the back door. "All right," he sighed and moved over to let them out. Nicole gave a jump from the cool air and Arthur started to close the door until he saw the dogs heading for Rudy.

"No!" he snapped and the dogs changed directions. Leaving the door cracked, he went back for the baby carrier and set it on the island. Spotting cat hair, he placed a towel in first and then put Nicole in the carrier. Arthur made some breakfast and turned when the dogs pushed the door open.

"You guys are going to have to learn to shut the door," Arthur said, shaking his head and walking over to close the door. When his breakfast was done, Arthur moved the carrier over to the table.

Grabbing a cup of coffee and a notepad, he made a list of what he thought he would need.

Glancing over at the baby carrier, he saw Nicole asleep. Getting up, he carried her to the bathroom and sat her on the floor, then stripped and jumped in the shower. He got out grinning to see that Nicole was still asleep. Moving her into the bedroom, he dressed and then carried her into the office.

Setting her on the desk, Arthur moved over to the ham radios and turned one on. He gave a sigh, hearing voices talking. "Well, we aren't alone, blue eyes," Arthur said, listening. The more he listened, the more he wished they *were* alone.

Reaching up, he changed the frequency and listened again. Like before, they were talking about masses dying but also violence everywhere directed at anyone. "Yep, need to make some changes," he mumbled.

Rubbing his smooth face, he turned and saw Nicole looking at him. "What are you doing up?" he grinned and she squealed with a grin. Picking her up, Arthur moved to the linen closet and pulled out a silk sheet.

Putting Nicole back down in the carrier, he shook the sheet out, spreading it out over the bed and folded it lengthwise. Grabbing some string, he tied it around the rolled-up sheet while leaving a two-foot area unfolded. After he was done, he tied the two ends together and slung them over his head and right shoulder and the unfolded area was at his chest, forming a hammock or a baby sling.

"We have some work to do" Arthur said, taking Nicole out of the baby carrier. He dressed her and poured her a bottle, leaving two more to go. Wrapping Nicole up in a blanket, he tucked her into the sling across his chest and then moved the blanket away until it framed her face. She looked up at him with a toothless grin.

"We have to find you some boots," Arthur chuckled, grabbing his pistol off the dresser and clipping it to his hip. After grabbing the magazine carrier, he picked up his AR and the bottle. "Dogs," he said, heading to the back door.

As he drove the buggy to the barn, Arthur covered Nicole's face up so the cool air wouldn't hit it. It was a challenge to do the chores with Nicole on his chest. But Arthur even managed to feed Nicole a bottle as he hooked the milking machines up to the cows.

When the rooster crowed as the sun broke the horizon, Nicole gave a startle and started crying. If the gunshot wouldn't have scared her so bad, Arthur would've shot the rooster. As he fed the sheep, he looked at the thick wool on them and shook his head.

"Don't worry, we'll get you sheared in a few days," Arthur promised and then headed back to the buggy when he was done.

Reaching the back patio, Arthur headed over to the shop and climbed in the track steer, starting it up and Nicole looked around with wide eyes at hearing the diesel engine rumbling. When the track steer moved, she gave a startle and looked up at Arthur with an unsure expression. Seeing him smile down, Nicole moved her eyes to see the world move as Arthur drove.

Lowering the bucket, Arthur moved along Rudy's truck, scraping the side as he scooped up the stiff body. "I'll get the gun later, but I have to move you," Arthur told the body, raising the bucket up. He drove into the woods and dumped Rudy out, then drove back and parked the track steer.

"Dogs," he snapped and they ran out of the woods, falling in around him as he headed for the back door.

"You did so good doing chores," Arthur praised, taking Nicole out of her baby sling. She gave a squeal as he put her in the carrier. "We have to get you some food and more diapers, then figure how we are going to do some stuff around here to make it safe." Nicole just looked at him as she chewed on her fist.

He carried her with him to his office and set her on the desk as he went to the gun safe. Opening it up, he grabbed a suppressor off the top shelf. Arthur had three suppressors the government knew about, but over a dozen that they didn't. The one in his hand was one of those. It was his own design and worked better than the ones he'd bought.

At one time, he'd considered patenting it and leasing the rights, but hadn't wanted the thugs in DC breathing down his neck. Next, he grabbed a dual mag pouch for the AR. Clipping it on his left hip in front of the 1911 magazines, he shoved two magazines in the Kydex holster.

Stepping into the living room, he grabbed his AR and took the suppressor that was mounted off; it was one the government knew about. Putting the better one on, Arthur put the other in the gun safe and then checked his AR over. When he was done, he turned and saw Nicole staring at him in wonder.

"Yep, anyone messes with you and I'll skin them alive," Arthur sang out and Nicole giggled. Seeing his digital camera sitting in its cradle on his desk, Arthur picked it up and snapped two pictures of Nicole. "Gotcha," he grinned at her.

Shoving the camera in his thigh cargo pocket, Arthur turned around and closed the safe. Reaching up, Arthur took a black felt fedora hat with a three inch brim off the top of the safe and put it on. "You like my hat?" Arthur asked Nicole and she just gave him a toothless grin which Arthur took as yes and picked her up.

As he carried Nicole back to the kitchen, he noticed the living room looked like chaos with all the stuff he had brought over for Nicole. "Uh oh, we will have to clean the house when we get back," Arthur said, walking into the kitchen.

Pulling bottles out of the dishwasher, he fixed the last two and then made sure the last diapers and wipes were in the diaper bag. Holding up the pink diaper bag and looking at it, he turned to Nicole. "We are so getting another diaper bag," he said in a serious voice that tickled Nicole.

Turning away from Nicole to the diaper bag, "I can't walk around with a pink bag, Nicole," Arthur told her with a fake scowl that amused her even more. Putting the baby sling on, Arthur slung the AR over his head to let it hang under his arm.

"Kit, Kat, stay," he said, grabbing his keys off the key rack. "Donald and Daisy, come," he commanded, heading to the front door. He armed the pad he had just put up and then walked out, locking the door. Walking to the garage, he patted the baby sling as he looked around. Where he lived he rarely heard signs of civilization, but knowing what was going on in the world made the sounds of nature more distinct. What he did notice was there were very few birds chirping.

Opening the back of his Blazer, "In," he commanded. Donald and Daisy jumped in the back with ease. Closing the door, he moved into the garage and climbed behind the driver's seat. He looked down as he started the engine to see Nicole looking up at him, completely content. Backing out he gave a sigh, looking at Wendy's BMW.

"I found us a baby," he said softly and then put the Blazer in drive. Pulling down the driveway, he saw he'd left the gate open yesterday.

"Nicole, why didn't you tell me to close the gate?" he asked, driving through the gate and then pushed the remote clipped to his visor.

When he passed Nicole's house, Arthur tilted his head to the house as his left arm cradled Nicole. "We are doing good, guys," he whispered.

Driving north on small dirt roads that only locals would know, it took over twenty minutes for Arthur to reach a cabin rental area south of the hamlet of Murray. The area was only ten miles in a straight line but twenty by road, and Arthur had not taken the straightest route.

Passing houses of people he knew, Arthur would slow and look at their houses for any signs of life but didn't stop. At one house, he thought he saw someone but didn't know who lived there, so he didn't slow. Never going over forty, Arthur was sure if anyone saw him it might make them nervous, since he was going so slow. But he was worried about rounding a blind curve and finding it blocked. Needless to say, Nicole was making him overcautious.

He stopped half a mile from the small store that served the cabins but stayed open all year. You just had to honk your horn if the owner wasn't inside; Old man Turner lived behind the store. After listening to the ham, he really didn't want to risk taking Nicole into a populated area. Opening the glove box, he pulled out some binoculars and scanned the store.

"What the hell?" he mumbled, seeing three kids playing with something in a mud puddle in front of the store. "Those cabins aren't open for another month."

Zooming in, he saw it was three boys and none of them could be over ten. The way they were grinning as they played in the mud puddle, Arthur knew they were having fun.

Watching the three for half an hour, Arthur heard Nicole getting fussy. Without lowering the binoculars, he reached his other hand over to grab a bottle off the seat and put it to her mouth. Taking his eyes from the binoculars for a second, Arthur glanced down to see Nicole happily drinking.

When he put his eyes back to the binoculars, he saw the smallest boy had run into the store. After a few minutes, the boy came out eating something. The other two looked up and ran into the store and soon came back out, eating whatever the smaller one had gotten. "Well, I know they have formula there. I made a comment to Wendy when we stopped here after duck hunting this February. Wendy laughed because she said the formula was ten dollars more there," Arthur told Nicole, but Nicole didn't stop eating to answer.

Hoping he wasn't heading for a trap, Arthur dropped the shifter into drive and put the binoculars down on the seat. He eased up the road and when he was a hundred yards from the store, the boys turned to see the jacked-up Blazer heading for them and ran to the side of the store. They ducked down watching as Arthur stopped by the single pump and put the shifter in park.

Turning the engine off, Arthur glanced around and saw a minivan parked at one of the cabins. Opening his door, he held his AR to his side so it wouldn't bang around and held the bottle with his left hand. Finding coordination that he didn't know he'd had, Arthur climbed out easily while keeping his right hand on the pistol grip of the AR and Nicole never stopped drinking.

Letting the AR go, Arthur stepped away from the Blazer door and left it open, but held the bottle with his left hand. He could shoot with his left but was much better with his right. "Hey, guys!" Arthur called out and waved toward the boys, then headed to the store. "Donald, Daisy, stay," he said, hearing them move over the backseat.

The boys peeked around the corner as Arthur walked in the open door. Trash was scattered across the floor and from the looks of it, all of it was candy wrappers and soda cans. Having a good idea where that had come from, Arthur moved down the aisle he remembered and stopped.

"Oh, come on, one can?!" he cried out, grabbing the can of formula. He looked down at Nicole, shaking his head. "You believe this? They only have one can of your milk!"

Nicole didn't seem to care as she continued drinking. Moving further down, Arthur saw several diapers but all of them were too big. "Two of your little ass could sleep in these," he told Nicole who only wiggled, changing position in the sling.

Grabbing the smallest size, Arthur moved to the front and found the three boys standing in the door. Three very muddy and soaking wet boys. "Hi," Arthur smiled, still holding the bottle with his left and the stuff he wanted in the sling with Nicole. His right arm hung at his side casually near the pistol grip of his AR.

He wasn't worried about the boys, but who they might be with.

The two younger boys moved behind the oldest as he lifted his hand up. "Hi," he said in shock.

"Old Man Turner around?" Arthur asked and the boys looked at each other and then back to Arthur. "The old man who runs the camp?" he clarified.

"No, sir," the oldest answered, staring at Arthur like he was a ghost. "Is that a real gun?" he asked, pointing at the AR.

"Yes, it is. If someone tries to hurt my baby, they will learn quickly that is a bad idea," Arthur told him and was shocked when the three boys stepped into the store.

"Are you sick?" the oldest asked and Arthur noticed his lips were starting to quiver.

Cocking his head to the side, "Not that I know of, are any of you?" he asked.

"Jim and I was, but we got better," the oldest told him.

"Where's your family?"

The oldest boy pointed out the door and up at the cabin with the minivan. "Dad brought us here when people started shooting around the house. We camped here last summer."

"It's a good spot," Arthur said, pulling his wallet out and putting some bills on the counter and the boys looked at him in shock. They all turned to the stuff on the floor.

"We have to pay?" the oldest asked in shock.

Laughing as he put his wallet back, "Well, your dad will," Arthur said and all three got a scared look on their faces. "Old Man Turner will make you clean up your mess."

He was shocked to see the three relax, then the oldest spoke. "No, he got sick."

"You saw him?"

The oldest nodded, "When daddy wouldn't wake up, we went in the house behind the store and found him on the floor. He had bubbles on his mouth like everyone else after they get the Rudolph nose," he said.

"Anyone else in your family have bubbles like that?"

"Momma, our sisters, Judy and Gwen, then daddy," the boy answered.

Turning to the boys, "Son, how long have you been here?" Arthur asked.

"Four days."

"How long have you three been out here alone?" Arthur asked as Nicole finished her bottle.

He set it on the counter and pulled her up to his shoulder, patting her back and the boys moved closer to look at the tiny baby. "Daddy wouldn't wake up after we got here," the oldest told him.

"Momma and our sisters wouldn't wake up on the ride here," the youngest said with tears welling up in his eyes.

"Boys, are you telling me that you've been alone out here for three days?" Arthur gasped as Nicole let out a loud burp, making the three grin.

"Yes sir," the oldest said.

"It's scary at night," the youngest whimpered with quivering lips from fear and the cold mud and water covering him. "Can you stay here with us?"

"Boys, I can't because Nicole," he said, shifting the baby on his shoulder, "would get sick."

The three dropped their faces in despondency. "Please? It's scary at dark," the oldest begged in a breaking voice.

Moving to the back wall, Arthur sat down on a bench and patted Nicole's back as she slept. "Boys, come over here," he said and the three slowly moved over, hanging their heads low. "What's your names?"

"I'm Kirk," the oldest said and then pointed at the middle one who hadn't spoken yet. "He's Pat and he's Jim," he said, pointing to the youngest.

"How old are you guys?'

"I'm ten," Kirk answered, looking up with hope since Arthur was asking questions about them. "Pat is eight and Jim is six."

"You have any family close?" Arthur asked and all three shook their heads. Looking at the filthy boys, Arthur took a deep breath and let it out in a long-dejected sigh. "Okay boys, I want you to listen and don't say anything until I finish and ask for your answer," Arthur told them and all three looked up with hopeful smiles.

"I will take you with me, but you will do what I say because you will have to learn to work on a farm, ride horses, and learn how to shoot guns, not to mention a million other things. If you don't want to work, I can take you to a hospital and they can find you a place to go," Arthur said and at the mention of 'hospital', the smiles fell off to be replaced by looks of terror.

"Please, no hospital!" Kirk shouted and Nicole gave a jump.

"Shh," Arthur whispered, patting Nicole's back and rocking back and forth. Kirk clamped a hand over his mouth.

"Sorry," he mumbled around his hand.

"Okay, if you don't want a hospital, I will find you someplace else," Arthur said and Pat raised his hand, looking at Arthur timidly. "Yes," Arthur said, feeling Nicole drift back to sleep.

"Can't we just stay with you?" Pat asked, but it sounded like begging. "We'll be good."

"Boys, if you stay with Nicole and I, you will have to listen and work. There is no way around that and I'm the boss. I will work harder than you, but each of you will work and learn. I will protect you, but you will show me respect and I will show you respect," Arthur told them.

"Will bad men find us at your house?" Jim asked.

Arthur turned to Jim. "Jim, a bad man has already shown up at my house and I shot his ass," Arthur told them and all three stepped up, almost touching Arthur's knees.

"We want to go," Kirk said and his brothers agreed with wide grins.

"Have you guys seen lots of bad guys?" Arthur asked.

"Yes sir," Kirk answered. "They shot at our house in Memphis and at our car when we left."

Slowly, Arthur stood up and moved Nicole until she hung across his chest in the sling. "My name is Arthur, and we are now family," Arthur said and the boys took off, running out the door. When they were outside, they started jumping up and down and cheering. "Well, they waited till they were outside," Arthur nodded.

Stepping behind the counter and grabbing a bag, Arthur moved down the aisle and grabbed a can of the soy formula, just in case he ran out. Walking around, he filled the bag as the boys came back inside. "Thank you for not waking up Nicole. She gets cranky if you wake her up after eating," Arthur told them and started filling another bag.

When he had six bags filled, he walked past the boys and put the bags in the Blazer. "You have clothes?" he asked and they nodded, pointing at the minivan. "Have you boys been up to the cabin since your dad hasn't woken up?"

They all shook their head and Kirk pointed at the store. "We been sleeping in a closet in there," he said.

"Where are your clothes?"

"In the van," Kirk answered.

"Okay, follow me. You don't have to go up there, but I need you to tell me if it's yours," Arthur sighed and started walking.

The three boys ran up beside him and Jim reached up to hold his left hand. "We aren't scared if you go with us, you're big," he said and Arthur looked down at the small kid and smiled.

"And I'm mean when someone wants to hurt my family," Arthur informed him.

With a look of excitement, Kirk looked at Arthur. "That means us now, right?" he asked.

"You said you wanted to be part of mine and Nicole's family, so that means you three," Arthur chuckled and the boys grinned so big their white teeth seemed to glow against their muddy faces.

Getting closer to the minivan, Arthur's pace slowed at seeing the bullet holes in the back door and side panels. He opened the back hatch and was almost knocked over by the smell of rotting flesh. Stepping back, he blinked his watering eyes and looked down at the boys who were looking up at the front seat.

Following their gaze, Arthur saw brown hair. "Are any of these suitcases yours?" he asked, pointing at the pile shoved in the back. The boys dove in and Arthur saw he would've been able to pick their cases out, seeing superhero emblems on each one.

When each had a suitcase, they reached back in and pulled out backpacks with the same emblems as each one's suitcase. "That it for in here?" Arthur asked and they nodded. "Anything in the cabin?"

"Our camping backpacks," Jim said in a low voice.

"I want you three to wait here while I look in the van to make sure," Arthur told them gently and they nodded. He moved around to the driver's side and saw a woman in the passenger seat that was starting to bloat. Taking a deep breath, he opened the door and saw a purse in the floorboard. Yanking it out, he stepped back letting out the breath that he'd been holding and dug around inside, pulling out a pocketbook.

Opening it up, he found pictures and put it back. Closing the door, he moved back and handed the purse to Kirk. "So you'll have pictures and I'll know where you came from," Arthur told him as Kirk took the purse. "Guys, when we get to the cabin, stay on the porch. I'll get your packs."

"Thank you," Pat said with a weak smile.

"That's what family does, Pat," Arthur said, walking toward the cabin. Seeing the cabin door was cracked open, Arthur gave a thankful sigh. The boys stopped outside as Arthur walked in, trying not to breathe. Feeling Nicole moving from the smell, he scanned around and saw three small hiking packs and moved over to grab them quickly.

Arthur stopped, seeing a man on a bed. In his arms were a young teen girl and another girl that couldn't have been older than five. Not being in a hot car, their skin was only gray. Turning away from the sight, he saw a wallet on a bedside table and grabbed it.

As he headed for the door, Nicole gave a grunt as she wiggled in the sling. Stepping out into the clean air, Arthur looked down and saw Nicole relaxing and settling back down, drifting back to sleep. "Put this in the purse," Arthur said, handing the wallet to Kirk.

He watched Jim trying to lug his Superman suitcase. Moving all three of the backpacks to his left hand, Arthur picked up Jim's suitcase. "Guys, let's go," he said and the boys took off running to the Blazer.

With only his small Superman backpack on, Jim quickly pulled out in the lead as his brothers struggled with their suitcases. When Jim touched the Blazer, he turned around and raised his arms high, "I finally won!" he cheered out and then started jumping up and down.

"You weren't carrying your suitcase," Pat popped off.

Opening the passenger side, "Boys, don't worry about the dogs," Arthur chuckled at them and the boys looked in and saw the huge Rottweilers in the backseat. "Donald, Daisy, get in the back, right now," Arthur commanded and the dogs let out groans as they climbed over the seat to get in the cargo area.

Tossing the boys' stuff into the backseat, Arthur was very glad he had seat covers. "Boys, all of you need to sit up front because you're muddy and the backseat doesn't have a cover," Arthur told them and they just smiled at him.

Helping the boys in, Arthur closed the door and walked around to the driver's side and climbed in. "Boys, am I the first person you've seen since you got here?" he asked, starting the engine.

"No, sir," Kirk answered as Arthur turned around. "We saw a sick man the day after we got here and another man yesterday."

"Did you talk to either of them?"

"No, sir. The man yesterday saw us playing in the creek and stopped," Kirk told him. "He tried chasing us, but we hid in the woods. He drove away but came walking back later, but we were still hiding."

"Why didn't you talk to him?" Arthur asked, glancing over at the three.

All three turned to look at him as Kirk spoke. "He was scary."

"Guys, don't you think I'm scary?" Arthur chuckled, glancing at the road and then back to the boys who were all shaking their heads.

"No, sir," Kirk answered. "You look nice and then we saw you had a baby."

"Would you have talked to me if Nicole hadn't been with me?"

"Yes sir," Kirk said and then turned to look out the window. "The other man gave us scary feelings. Even if he'd had Nicole, we wouldn't have talked to him."

"And never talk to sick people," Jim pipped in.

"Why?" Arthur asked.

"Dad told us they sometimes act crazy from the fever," Pat told him.

Very impressed, Arthur turned to the road. "Guys, you're very smart but from now on, you see someone, you come get me. You're right about trusting bad feelings, but I don't want a bad man hiding his bad feelings from you. I'll talk to them and if they're bad, you won't have to worry anymore."

Sitting next to Arthur on the bench seat, Jim leaned his head over to rest it on Arthur's side. "Thank you, Arthur," Jim said in a tired voice.

Glancing back at the boys, Arthur saw Kirk's head resting on the window, sound asleep. Pat was leaned over asleep, laying on Kirk. He looked down and saw Jim's eyes closed and his mouth hanging open.

Looking up at the road, Arthur gave a sigh, "Three little boys terrified out of their minds for three days. I'm willing to bet none ever slept more than an hour."

When he reached the gate, Arthur slowed and hit the remote. "Guys, we're home," Arthur said and the boys all sat up yawning as he pulled through the gate. When they saw the huge house, they all gasped as Arthur pulled into the garage.

"Boys, you're going to strip to underwear and get in the tub. I don't like mud all over the house," Arthur said, turning the engine off.

"Yes sir," the boys said in unison and climbed out.

They helped Arthur pull their stuff to the front door and all of them froze as Donald and Daisy walked up to them, sniffing. "They are getting to know you," Arthur explained, unlocking the front door.

Kit and Kat charged out and Donald and Daisy took off after them as Arthur ducked inside, turning the alarm off. Stepping back outside, he found the boys stripping down. Seeing the mud caked under their fingers, toenails, caked in their hair, and packed in every crease of skin, Arthur knew the mud wasn't going without a fight.

He led the boys into the house to his bedroom and they all gasped at the huge garden tub. "Don't get in till I get back," Arthur told them, turning on the water and leaving. When he came back carrying a sleeping Nicole in the baby carrier, Arthur grinned at the boys who were leaning over and looking into the tub.

Setting Nicole down, Arthur reached over and squirted some of Wendy's bubble bath in and the boys grinned wider at seeing the bubbles.

Taking off his weapons, Arthur pulled his shirt off. "Get in and let's get you three cleaned up," he sighed, grabbing a rag. When the boys climbed in, Arthur had to admit for their size the tub looked like a small swimming pool.

Arthur handed a rag to Kirk and to Pat as he got on his knees, leaning over the tub. Starting on Jim, Arthur never remembered having to work so hard to get a body clean. Working on a farm and being a nurse, that was a statement.

When the tub was full, Arthur turned off the water and then turned on the jets, making the boys laugh as he grabbed the baby shampoo and finishing Jim off by washing his hair. Seeing Pat hadn't made much progress knocking the mud off, Arthur took over. He was halfway done when Nicole announced it was feeding time.

Arthur stopped and fed her and then put her back in the carrier. Undoubtedly, Nicole thought the boys taking a bath was hilarious because she squealed and laughed as they splashed around. When he reached Kirk, Arthur was pleasantly surprised that Kirk done a fair job. But Arthur grabbed a nail brush, going after the fingers and toes.

When he was done, Arthur let the water out and the boys all let out a moan. "Boys, we have a swimming pool that you can swim in but not for a few days, we have work to do," Arthur told them while standing up and grabbing towels.

Jim jumped out and Arthur dried him off, then wrapped the towel around his waist. Kirk and Pat saw that and tried to copy it, so Arthur came over and showed them how. "Boys, you want to take a nap until I get some food ready?"

"I thought we had to work?" Kirk asked with heavy eyelids.

"No, first you need to rest," Arthur chuckled, leading them into the bedroom. "You can take a nap here. I'll get one of the beds upstairs made up for you tonight."

With no protest, the boys climbed in the bed and before Arthur was out of the room, they were all asleep. Leaving the door open, Arthur carried Nicole into the living room and started cleaning up. The boys didn't wake up until Arthur woke them the next morning.

Chapter Fifteen
Surviving a killer takes a toll

May 9

Feeling very painful needles stabbing her legs, Wendy struggled to open her eyes and then felt sharp, searing pain in her throat. Trying to swallow, she almost passed out from pain that filled her vision with bright lights. Grabbing a bottle of water beside her, Wendy sighed before tossing the empty bottle on the floor.

Blinking the crust and haze out of her eyes, she saw empty bottles around her and an empty bottle of Tylenol. Slowly moving her gaze, Wendy spotted an unopened bottle under her right leg and that thought brought the *pins in legs* to the forefront of her mind.

Rolling to her right, Wendy unfolded her left leg from under her butt and stretched it out. Extending her left leg, Wendy gave a wince and then grabbed the bottle of water. She could feel how dry and scaly her throat had become as she opened the bottle of water. Grimacing beforehand, Wendy took a drink as searing pain shot out from her throat with each swallow.

The only satisfaction was the wetter her throat got, the more the pain diminished. With half of the bottle gone, she smacked her lips while lowering the bottle and then realized, she tasted blood. Wendy looked down and saw she was naked from the waist down and blood covered the front of her shirt. Lifting her eyes up, Wendy saw from where she sat to the end of the bed was covered in dried blood.

Moving her feet to get blood flowing to them, Wendy winced at the pain of the circulation returning.

Rolling her eyes up, she gave a small thank you that the sheet rope she'd been hanging from had held up. She could remember from dream-like states that she had gone to the bathroom and had struggled to get back into the loop of sheet that was holding her up. So many times, she could recall just wanting to lie down, but a small voice in her mind would scream, '**NO**!'

Then, Wendy noticed a putrid smell and opened her eyes wider to look down. Seeing the mess under and on her, Wendy realized she hadn't made it to the bathroom every time because the bed was covered in dried urine and feces, as were her legs.

Turning the bottle up and draining the rest, it suddenly occurred to her that excrement didn't stink like that. Dropping the empty bottle, she turned to Gloria's bed and saw Gloria lying back on the bed. Her skin was gray and her eyes were staring at the ceiling.

A small cough erupted from her chest and Wendy felt slicing pain in her throat and tasted fresh blood.

Slowly, she moved and flexed her legs as she glanced around, but didn't see any more water bottles on the bed. Afraid to take a deep breath because it would make her cough, Wendy pulled her body out of the loop that had been holding her up. Holding the loop, she rotated her body slowly until her feet slid off the bed.

When her feet hit the floor, tingling pain shot up as blood flowed back into her legs. Seeing a bottle of water on Gloria's bed, Wendy leaned over to grab it and opened it up. Bracing her body and mind, she turned it up to drink and felt the searing pain again.

This time, she didn't stop drinking until the bottle was empty. Dropping it on the floor, Wendy reached over and grabbed another bottle of water from Gloria's bed. Opening it up, she just dumped it over her head. Dropping the bottle and holding onto her loop, Wendy struggled to stand up on her wobbly legs.

The sharp, stabbing tingles slowly abated from her legs and she was able to lessen the amount of weight she was having to support. Slowly letting the loop go, Wendy leaned over and felt Gloria's wrist. Gloria's skin was ice cold and her wrist moved freely with no rigor mortis.

Bringing her left wrist up, Wendy blinked her eyes trying to see the date and time. "Over eighty hours," she said, but only heard a coarse whisper. Then her throat informed her that it wasn't ready for that by unleashing a wave of sharp pain that made her waver on her feet.

Pushing off Gloria's bed, Wendy stumbled to the cart and snatched another bottle of water. This one she sipped, wanting the cake of funk in her mouth to wash away. Very slowly, she shuffled to the door to the balcony and opened it up.

She gave a sigh as she stepped outside and looked at Miami, or what she hoped was Miami. Studying the skyline for a second, Wendy was certain it was Miami. Turning toward the front of the ship, Wendy could see the anchor line out and then realized that they were parked about a mile off the coast. Looking back at Miami, Wendy saw columns of smoke dotting the horizon across the city.

Feeling the afternoon breeze as she sipped the water, Wendy realized there were gunshots coming from the shore. Shading her eyes with her hand, she glanced at the shore but couldn't see anything. Looking to her right and left, she didn't see anyone else on their balcony. Looking down, she saw the lifeboats and then she noticed at least two were missing. Very gently, Wendy turned around and headed back into the room, leaving the door open.

Stopping just inside the door, she looked at Gloria and felt very bad that she hadn't stayed awake and forced Gloria to remain upright. But Wendy slowly realized that if she had tried sitting at Gloria's bedside, she too would be dead. Sluggishly, Wendy shuffled into the bathroom and gave a shiver at seeing her pants lying in front of the commode, looking like a dirty diaper. Dried blood was sprayed across the wall in front of the commode and the floor was a mess.

Turning to the mirror, Wendy gave a startle when she saw her reflection. Her eyes were sunken in and her skin had a pasty cast, not to mention the blood over her face and chest. Opening her mouth, she could see thick crusty pieces of dried blood on her teeth and tongue.

Stepping closer, Wendy opened her mouth as wide as she could and felt the pain in her throat increase. Tilting her head back, she could see scabs at the back of her throat and spots where it was bleeding. Closing her mouth, Wendy reached down and turned on the faucet. Grabbing a washcloth, she dropped it in the sink and took her shirt off.

Throwing her shirt over her jeans, Wendy picked up the washcloth and wiped her face off. Then she noticed how boney her shoulders looked. Dropping her gaze in the mirror to her chest, Wendy gasped at seeing her ribs. 'I look like a stick figure model', she thought, not wanting to talk.

Turning the faucet off, Wendy opened the shower and turned it on, not caring if the water would be hot or cold. Stepping in, she just stood under the water before wanting hotter water. Adjusting the handles, she grabbed the soap and washed as well as she could while struggling to maintain her balance.

When she stepped out, Wendy felt better and moved to the sink and grabbed her toothbrush. Brushing her teeth, Wendy gave a sigh of contentment, imagining the toothbrush scraping the fur off her teeth. Almost dry by the time she'd finished brushing her teeth, Wendy brushed her hair out and then studied her reflection again.

She was still skinny and pale with sunken eyes, but she didn't look like a zombie.

Moving back into the room, she dug in her suitcase to pull out some jogging pants and t-shirt. After she was dressed in clean clothes, again she felt better. Avoiding looking at Gloria's body, Wendy moved to the cart and grabbed several Jell-O containers. She opened them up and grabbed a plastic spoon and carefully ate, grimacing with each swallow.

Forcing herself to finish the second one, Wendy dropped the cup and almost headed for the door but turned, heading back to the bathroom. Using her fingers, she dug out the card the crew had given her to check on passengers that were in their rooms. Unclipping the bungie line from her pants, Wendy moved over to the sink and washed the card and bungie off.

When the crew had started dropping, one of the ship's officers had taken her and two other nurses, like Wendy they were passengers but were willing to help, to a lifeboat and gave them instructions on how to operate it. They had no range and depended on rescue, but being this close to land if she needed to, Wendy would drop one in the water.

Stepping out of the bathroom, "Sorry, sis," Wendy sighed and it came out with a little voice this time, but still hurt.

Heading for the door, Wendy grabbed a bottle of water and her knife before walking out. In the hall, there were several bodies that she didn't remember from when she'd gone into her room.

With a goal in mind, Wendy headed to the bridge. Part of her duties had been to check the crew manning the bridge after the main doctor had gotten sick, so she knew the way.

After walking a hundred feet, Wendy felt her lungs wheezing and stopped, grabbing the handrail on the wall. She tried not to cough but lost in the end, giving a few coughs but nothing like she remembered from before. There were times when Wendy had expected to see her lungs fly out of her mouth.

Bracing her sore stomach muscles with her hands, Wendy stayed in place until she felt better. Turning her head, she spit and noticed it had a little blood in it. Taking a drink of water, she continued on but slower.

Reaching an elevator Wendy hesitated, knowing the ship was operating under its own power. Not sure how long that would be, she took the stairs having to step around a few bodies. When she reached the bridge, Wendy swiped her card and walked inside.

She saw the captain laying on the floor, but no other bodies. Walking over, Wendy picked up his hat and put it over his face. The captain was Italian and spoke English, but you had to listen hard to understand. "Thank you," she said, moving away.

On a chart table, she saw a map of lower Florida and a red dot beside Miami. Giving a sigh of relief, Wendy moved over to the windows to grab one pair of huge binoculars and scanned the coast.

Zooming in, Wendy's mouth fell open at seeing several bodies on the beach and along the shoreline. Scanning the buildings, she thought she caught sight of movement, but it ducked into one of the buildings, or she thought it did.

Putting the strap for the binoculars around her neck, Wendy left the bridge and headed to the infirmary. Moving slowly it took her awhile, but Wendy wasn't in a race and she was also looking for people: live people. There were bodies everywhere.

Passing the shops on the main deck, Wendy stopped suddenly, swearing that she'd heard a baby crying. Tilting her head and trying to trace the noise, it stopped abruptly. Moving over to a bench, Wendy sat down to take a break and listen.

She could hear the music from inside the stores and shops, but nothing else. Not hearing the cry again, Wendy struggled to stand as the smell was getting to her.

Continuing on, Wendy saw the daycare area and fought not to cry. She had watched so many kids die as she had tried to help, Wendy had thought she was going to go insane. Long ago, she had formed the shield against adults passing, but she didn't think anyone could do that for kids.

As she passed the daycare, Wendy stopped when hearing a muffled coo from inside. Very slowly, she moved up to the door and looked in through the glass. Parents got a card to access the daycare area when they dropped off a child. If you didn't have one, you had to use the phone on the wall to ask the workers inside to let you in.

Using her card, Wendy slid it in the handle and heard it click. She opened the door slowly, not seeing anyone in the main play area. "Hello?" she said hoarsely.

Walking in, she let the door close and moved to the nap room. Hearing a gasp, Wendy turned and saw double. Shaking her head,

Wendy stumbled back into the wall and waited until the spinning stopped. Turning back to the corner, Wendy saw twins looking at her in fear.

Wendy smiled and held up her hands, "I'm not going to hurt you," Wendy said, trying to force her voice to work. "I was one of the nurses helping out those that got sick."

The girls stared at Wendy with wide eyes. "We remember you. Are you sick?" one asked.

"Not anymore," Wendy said, dropping her tired arms. Taking the top off the bottle of water, she drained it and recapped it. "Have either of you been sick?"

They both shook their heads. Wendy waited for them to talk, but they just stared at her. She did notice they didn't appear as terrified after recognizing her. "Are your parents around here?" Wendy finally asked.

Again, they both shook their heads. "Do you know how long we've been stopped?"

"Two days," one answered.

"Is anyone else on this ship besides you two?"

They both nodded and Wendy saw the fear return to their faces. "Girls, has someone tried to hurt you?" Wendy asked and they nodded.

"Yes," they said together.

Feeling lightheaded, Wendy moved over and sat down in a kid-sized chair. "You know him?"

"He shouted out his name was Anthony when he got Timmy," one said.

"And there's nobody else on this ship besides you and this Anthony?" Wendy cried out and heard a coo. She turned to the wall and saw one of the baby cribs shaking. Grabbing her knees, Wendy struggled to stand up and then moved over and saw a baby looking up at her, kicking its legs. "Guys, there's a baby here."

"That's Ryan, his mom and dad got sick," one of the twins said. "Timmy told us to watch him until he got back."

Spinning around, "Got back?" Wendy gasped. "People have left this ship and left you here?"

The twins nodded as one spoke. "Daddy said he was going to shore and make sure it was okay because some army guy said we couldn't get off the ship for two weeks."

"Did any of the crew stay?"

Both nodded and the other twin spoke. "The captain, but we can't find him."

Glancing at the door, "Girls, we can't stay here," Wendy told them.

"Ryan ran out of the powder to make his milk," one twin said. "We were hiding in our room."

"What's your names?"

"Jo Ann," one said.

"Sally," the other answered.

"When's the last time you saw Anthony?" Wendy asked, moving to the office.

"Yesterday, when he got Timmy," Sally answered.

Turning on the office light, Wendy grabbed the file cabinet and opened the top drawer, grabbing a folder. Of the three thousand and seventeen passengers, Wendy had been told that eighty-four were children under the age of twelve. Wendy knew for a fact, thirty-three were dead because they died on her shift.

Opening the folder, she flipped through the ID pages that parents had to fill out for their kids, complete with a picture in the upper left corner. Finding the twins' info sheets, Wendy found out they were eight and lived in Nashville.

Continuing through the pages, she pulled out two Timmys. The two-year-old she remembered dying and put that one aside. The next was a picture of a ten-year-old boy with a big grin. Putting that sheet with the girls, Wendy continued through the stack until she found Ryan.

Ryan was seven months old.

Putting his with the others, Wendy folded them up and shoved them in her pocket. Looking around, she saw a backpack and dumped it out. Seeing the stuff on the desk, she knew the pack had belonged to a woman.

Walking back into the nap room, Wendy headed to the cabinets and opened them up. She glanced at the counter, seeing a can of opened formula. She took the other four of that kind and then grabbed diapers and wipes. "Girls, how did you know how to take care of a baby?" she asked, filling the pack up.

"We helped Aunt Lisa take care of her baby," one said and Wendy could almost hear the smile.

"Girls, is your mom in your cabin?" Wendy asked, zipping the pack closed and looking over at the girls.

Both had watery eyes as they nodded. "Girls, we can't go back there because if Anthony is still on the ship, he can find out where you are," Wendy told them and they both gasped. "You can come with me until someone comes back."

The twins looked at each other, then back to Wendy and nodded. "Okay," one said and Wendy looked around on the counter and saw barrettes. Grabbing a yellow and pink one, she handed them over.

"Sally put the yellow one in your hair and Jo Ann, put the pink one in yours," Wendy pleaded, then smiled. "Please? Until I learn to tell you apart."

The twins smiled, grabbing the barrettes.

"Do you two have any trouble carrying Ryan?"

"No," Jo Ann answered, moving over to the crib. She lowered the side rail all the way down and picked up Ryan who was just cooing away. "Ryan, you have to hush," Jo Ann whispered, grabbing a pacifier and putting it in his mouth.

Ryan stopped cooing as he sucked away on the pacifier and Jo Ann moved back beside Sally. Wendy saw Ryan was either big for his age or the girls were really small for their age. "Stay close because we are going to the crew passageways," Wendy told them, moving out to the playroom.

Looking out the windows, "Let's go," she said, heading for the door. Leading the girls out, Wendy forgot the infirmary and moved to a small door that was tucked back in a recess in the wall marked 'Crew Only'.

Swiping her card, Wendy ushered the girls in and closed the door behind them. "These are the crew passageways," she told them, walking down the hallway. When one of the crew showed them to her when she'd gotten her card, Wendy had been amazed that this many passages were tucked and hidden away on the ship.

Stopping several times to rest, Wendy saw the twins passing Ryan to each other as one got tired. "We are stopping at the kitchen and will load up a cart with some food. I know a room we can hide out in," Wendy told them and they smiled.

Reaching the kitchen, Wendy grabbed a serving cart and moved to one of the refrigerators. Loading up several prepared trays, Wendy tossed a case of bottled water on the bottom and then grabbed a case of sports drinks, shoving them beside the water.

Closing the fridge, Wendy leaned over the cart panting and felt the fluid rattling in her chest. "Hold on, girls. I need to catch my breath."

The girls nodded with smiles as Ryan laid his head on Sally's shoulder, closing his eyes. "We didn't know this was here," Jo Ann said, looking around.

"Passengers aren't allowed in these passageways. I was shown them, so I could help out," Wendy explained, reaching down and pulling a bottle of sports drink out. She drank several gulps, then put the top back on. "That elevator there moves between all levels and that's where we are headed."

As Wendy pushed the cart over, the girls followed still looking around. Swiping her card, Wendy pressed the button and heard the elevator moving. Seeing a table next to the elevator with utensils, plates, and napkins, Wendy put some on the cart.

When the elevator opened, they saw a body sprawled out on the floor and none of them jumped. "Jo Ann, hold the door," Wendy told her as she grabbed the dead woman by the legs and pulled her out so the cart would fit.

Pushing the cart in, Wendy waited for the girls and swiped the card and punched her level. "Girls, we are stopping at my level. I have to get something from my room and then we will go to the spot I was talking about," Wendy told them. "Let the door close and flip this switch," she pointed at the control panel. "It will make the elevator stay there. Only someone with a card can open the door and I won't be long."

As the elevator stopped, the twins nodded and Wendy stood at the door as they parted. Poking her head out, she looked up and down the hallway, seeing only the bodies that had been there before. Stepping out, she heard Jo Ann flip the switch as she moved down the hallway to her door.

Almost tripping on a body, Wendy grabbed the handrail as the elevator door closed. Holding the rail, she moved to her door and swiped the card to go back inside. Leaving the door open, she moved over to Gloria's suitcase and opened it up.

Digging through it, Wendy pulled out a spear gun and smiled, remembering Gloria tell her that she was going spearfishing. Gloria never went spear fishing, but Wendy needed it. Digging out a holster that held three metal arrows, Wendy doubled over coughing. When the fit passed, Wendy stood up panting and cradling the spear gun to her chest.

Moving back to the door, she closed it and hurried back down the hall as fast as she could to the elevator. Swiping the card, she gave a sigh to see the girls smiling as the door opened up. Stepping in, she flipped the switch to unlock the elevator, swiped her card, and punched two floors up.

When the doors opened, Wendy pushed the cart out and let the girls out. Leaning back inside, she swiped the card and pressed the bottom floor. Pulling back as the doors closed, Wendy grabbed the cart to steer around a body and headed down the passageway.

"Why did you send the elevator away?" Jo Ann whispered.

"You can hear it on the floors and if Anthony's here, I want him looking somewhere else," Wendy whispered back, stopping at a door marked 'Suite'. Swiping her card, she pushed the door open and stepped into the large room that was untouched.

The people who had paid for this suite hadn't made the boarding call; she had found out when she was checking passengers. When she'd first seen the room, she didn't even want to know how much it had cost.

When they were inside, Wendy closed the door as Jo Ann put Ryan down on the bed and they moved over to a sliding door. Opening it, they stepped out onto the balcony and looked at the coastline. "Our room only had a round window," Sally said.

Moving over to the bed, Wendy grabbed the pillows and surrounded Ryan with them as he slept. Picking up her bottle of sports drink, Wendy took the backpack off and then sat down on the couch. When the twins came back inside, they smiled at her as Wendy finished the bottle off.

"Can we see your binoculars?" Sally asked and Wendy took the massive binoculars off and handed them over.

"Be careful with them, they are heavy and we will need them to watch for someone coming to rescue us," Wendy told them.

Wendy watched them head back over to the balcony to use the binoculars. Turning to Ryan, Wendy gave a sigh looking at the baby sleeping peacefully. Then, she saw his diaper. "Girls, when was the last time you changed Ryan?"

"Yesterday, he ran out of diapers," Sally said, coming back inside.

Getting up, Wendy grabbed the pack and unloaded it. "How did you two get stuck taking care of Ryan?" she asked, carefully changing the baby's diaper.

"Timmy's mom told him to, but he heard a man yelling for help and gave us Ryan. Timmy ran down the hall and then later, he yelled out for us to run and hide," Sally explained with a sad face.

Coming back inside, Jo Ann put the binoculars on the table. "We heard Anthony calling out for us last night," Jo Ann said with a quivering lip.

Finished changing Ryan, Wendy smiled at herself for doing it without waking him up. "Girls, let his ass show up, I'll take care of it," Wendy said, grabbing the spear gun. Sitting down on the couch, she put her feet in the loops and pulled back one band, locking it in the housing. Pulling back the second band, Wendy found more difficult.

Pulling out one of the spears, the girls gave a shiver while looking at the wicked-looking tip. “You will shoot him?” Sally asked hopefully.

“He tries anything, you bet I will,” Wendy told her.

Chapter Sixteen
The destroyer comes inside

May 9

Sutton walked out of the airlock and smiled at Sarah waiting on him. "I came out as soon as you said."

Giving a laugh, "I know, and that means we'll be early," Sarah told him.

"How do they expect me to make progress if they keep pulling me into meetings?" Sutton asked, pulling the suit off and hanging it up.

"Dr. Sutton, I've gotten you out of three meetings," Sarah reminded him. "They are basing their decisions on what you tell them."

Sitting down on the bench, Sutton kicked his crocs off and put his shoes on. "Really?" he asked, not looking up.

"No," Sarah said in a low voice as she moved over and sat down beside him. "We lost another government facility to the virus."

Jerking his head up, "How? They are supposed to be locked down." Sutton asked.

Shaking her head, "Just like the last one, they don't know," Sarah told him. "What we do know is everyone inside is infected. The screening test proved it."

"They're scared," Sutton mumbled and Sarah nodded.

"Aren't you?" she asked.

"Sarah, I've worked with the most lethal viruses we've ever discovered. And before you ask, this isn't the most deadly. That title belongs to a virus from the Philippines. It just has a number. When you catch it, you are dead three days later. All our tests show it's one hundred percent fatal. But that virus moves too fast, so it would be very hard for it to become a pandemic," Sutton told her with a smile. "Because of you, I can say we are very close here. You have become indispensable to this team."

"Please," Sarah scoffed, getting up. "I'm just the mother hen and typist."

Getting up, Sutton shook his head, "Nope, even Skannish agrees. We are making more progress because you are making sure we aren't tired. That we eat. That all our research is in the system and all links with Atlanta are downloaded. For someone who doesn't know viruses, when one of the team asks for something, you know where to find the answer or who to ask."

Taking a deep breath, "Thank you," Sarah beamed.

Glancing at his watch, "Let's do the dog and pony show," Sutton said, heading for the door and stopped.

"I have your laptop, notes, and the latest report from Homeland," Sarah said, walking past him. "You can read on the way over."

"Like I said," Sutton chuckled, following her outside. "Indispensable."

When Sarah pulled up to the presidential area, Sutton was finished with the report. He followed Sarah through the doors. Walking into the room, he saw everyone was just taking their seats. "Damn, even early," he mumbled and Sarah stifled a laugh.

"Sutton, what do you have for us today?" the President asked, sitting down.

Pouring a cup of coffee, Sutton walked over to the table and put his coffee down but didn't sit. Turning to the president, Sutton pointed at him with his hand. "Mr. President, you are a genius," Sutton sang out, then dropped his hand as the President gave a startle.

"How so?" the President asked hesitantly.

"When you assigned Sarah to the team, I had to admit, I was against it. I'm not going to tell you what the others said, but I'm here now saying we were wrong," Sutton admitted and then looked around at those seated, then back up to the President. "She leads that team like a general. Never in my life would I have ever believed someone forcing people to nap and eat would make such a difference, but holy shit are we making progress."

The president sat up straighter with a big grin as Sutton continued. "Then, she types up all our dictation and when a question is asked, she knows which one of us can answer it. Even in Atlanta, Sarah has made a difference. I want to make her the director, but that would take her out of the trenches. But when the time comes, Mr. President, I'm begging you to make her Senior Executive Director of the CDC," Sutton said, sitting down.

"She made that big of a difference?" the President cried out.

Standing back up, "Last dictation, please," Sutton said, holding his hand out and Sarah passed him a stack of papers. Turning to the president, "If you have someone who understands viruses, let them read that," Sutton said, tossing the stack on the table and sliding it toward the president.

"Mr. President," Sutton said, jerking his thumb back at Sarah. "Because of her, we will be starting cultures of the first batches of vaccines in two days."

The room erupted in cheers as everyone jumped up, clasping their neighbors' hands and shaking them. When everyone stopped, the president yelled at the person sitting next to Sutton. "Get your ass up and let the Senior Executive Director sit down," the President bellowed.

Sarah was looking around in shock as the man got out of the chair and moved to the chairs along the wall. Moving over timidly, Sarah sat down. "We'll work on your credentials soon, Sarah," the President smiled. "You need any help?"

"No, sir," Sarah said quickly. "I hate to say it, but the scientists talk to themselves a lot as they work. Even asking questions out loud, and since I'm always near them or the lab radio, I know who to direct them to."

"You keep up the good work," the President said and everyone around the table smiled at her.

"Mr. President, I can tell you this. If you want the vaccine this fast, let's move these update meetings with us to once a week," Sarah said. "Dr. Sutton was talking to himself in the airlock about the culture slots…" she paused, looking around. "Sorry, he was trying to remind himself, so he could pick up the same train of thought when he gets back. I've learned their little telltale signs and know when not to talk to them or let anyone else talk to them."

"Sarah, you tell us what day the weekly meeting is to be," the President said with a nod. "Sutton, from half a year to days, that's incredible."

"Sir, she takes care of the team and it seems we needed it because everyone is performing at top level," Sutton laughed. "Like I said, the first batch will be out no later than three days, but that doesn't mean it will work. But we will put out batches every day with alterations, checking for results."

"Outstanding," the President sighed.

"I read about losing the bunker in Ohio. Do we have any idea how?" Sutton asked, turning to Paterson.

"None, but it didn't come in through the vents or water," Paterson told him.

"They either let someone or a bird inside," Sutton said.

"I have a team going over all the security footage," Paterson said.

"Dr. Sutton," Kenner, Secretary of Defense called out. "I had a company go through a small town of ten thousand and they didn't find anyone alive. I thought this virus only killed nine out of ten, not all of the ten."

"Kenner," Sutton said, picking up his coffee. "It's the roll of the genetic dice. The virus chooses the one in ten at random, not us. You could pick ten and all ten survive or none. I've got reports of spouses surviving, but none of their offspring. Some offspring survive and everyone else dies. It's a crap shoot depending on your DNA. Now, after we get this vaccine, I will devote some time to it and get some better answers."

"Did you read the findings of sick people moving to water?" Patterson asked.

Nodding, "Yeah, they are delirious with fever and water is a driving human need," Sutton explained. "That will be a problem later because those bodies are going to contaminate the water supply."

"Anyone else?" the President asked, looking around. He turned to Sutton and Sarah. "Sarah, keep me up to date and no one will bother you."

"Thank you, Mr. President," Sarah said, standing up. As Sutton stood up, she reached over and grabbed his stuff.

"You are over me now, so I should carry that," Sutton told her and tried to take it.

"I have it. Now get in the buggy, so we can get back to work," Sarah snapped and Sutton headed for the door.

"See what I mean?" Sutton laughed as he walked out.

When they were gone, the President looked around the table. "That's why I wasn't sad about letting her go. Sarah can be a bitch," he grinned. "A real bitch."

On the other side of the base, Greg Lunston walked up a narrow flight of metal stairs in a very poor mood. He was part of the crew that manned this facility. For the last three years, he had spent half of every month in this mammoth complex.

For the first few months it was cool, seeing where the president would go if something happened, but that faded very fast. Of course, he couldn't tell anyone what he did working for the

Park Service and the two-week tours made it very hard to have a relationship.

Even the Secret Service had a full-time detachment of four agents assigned here all the time. If his job was bad, then theirs sucked. The agents had to pull one month shifts. But even for a facility built to house five thousand people, it only took twenty-five to maintain it. There were only two teams of twenty-five, red and blue.

Greg was three days into his blue shift when the call went out to lock down the mountain. Thinking it was an exercise, Greg tried his hardest to impress anyone, so he could get out of this tomb. Then the choppers started landing with the scientists. A few days later, convoys of limos and heavily tinted SUVs started dumping off members of Congress.

Two days before the president arrived, two thousand troops had shown up and manned the top floor. It was then Greg knew, this was real. He'd wanted to call his family and tell them to run, but couldn't because all phone lines were turned off and routed through a switchboard now that you had to have approval to call out on.

All cellphones were of no use because the towers around them had been shut down.

It took three days after the president's arrival for him to even find out what was going on. By then, he knew his mom and dad who lived in New York City were screwed.

Reaching the top of the stairs, Greg looked at the ship-style hatchway door. Flipping the lock open, he started turning the steering wheel handle. When the door moved away from the frame, Greg swung it open. He stepped out into the sunshine and took a deep breath, then pulled a pack of cigarettes from his shirt pocket.

"I'm not a mole," he mumbled, shaking a cigarette out. He and several others had been warned not to smoke anymore in a storage area. "I know every inch of this place and you think you can stop me?" he snorted, pulling out his lighter.

Taking a long drag when his cigarette was lit, Greg gave a sigh filled with smoke. Putting his lighter back in his pocket, Greg looked down and saw a dead pigeon. He turned back to the small ledge over the hatchway where the pigeons roosted.

"Frankie better start getting rid of the birds he kills," Greg mumbled, turning around and kicking the pigeon's corpse out of the recessed doorway. Unless he stepped out on the grass where a camera could spot him, nobody would ever know about the new smoking area that was now used.

This maintenance tunnel had no alarm on the hatchway. The door that led to the maintenance tunnel did, but it was part of his job to patrol that area and check the hatchway.

When his cigarette was finished, Greg ducked back in the door and closed it. Spinning the handle like a wheel of fortune until it stopped, Greg flipped the lockdown. "Maintenance entrance seven secured," he grinned, then started down the long metal staircase.

Chapter Seventeen
Learning is hard for everyone

May 10

As Nicole finished her bottle, Arthur took the bottle away while grinning at her heavy eyelids. Moving her up to his shoulder, Arthur patted her back as he rocked in his recliner. A very loud burp sounded from her tiny body making him chuckle as her body shook with the burp. "I think you do that to make me laugh," he said softly, rubbing her back.

Glancing at the clock and seeing it was almost five, Arthur continued to rock Nicole and thought about the boys. After they had gone to sleep that first day, Arthur hadn't had the heart to wake them up so he'd just let them sleep in his bed.

It had been forever since Arthur had slept with a kid and memories came flooding back of Joseph beating him and Wendy to death in the bed. The three boys had flipped and flopped throughout the night. After getting a bruise on his thigh, Arthur had moved to his recliner when it was time for Nicole's four o'clock bottle.

He'd made up one of the guest rooms upstairs for the boys that had a queen-sized bed. When he had put the boys in the bed last night, Arthur had been ready for some good sleep in his bed alone with Nicole on his chest.

After he'd woken Nicole up for her first bottle of the night, Arthur could do it by memory. When she gave her burp, he just cradled her to his chest. Not long after that, he had felt something burrowing under him. Waking up to pop one of the dogs, Arthur had found that it was Jim burrowing under him.

Looking across the bed, he saw Pat and Kirk sound asleep. Not wanting more bruises or one of them to hit Nicole, Arthur had gotten up and headed to the recliner.

All day yesterday the boys followed him around, learning how to feed the animals and take care of them. It only took Arthur a few seconds to realize the boys had never been around any farm animals. When he saw young Jim running for his life from two small lambs chasing him, Arthur gave a sigh realizing this was going to take some time.

The boys were scared of the big dogs for a little while, but they had been around dogs. To Arthur's disgust, the boys loved Mickey and Minnie and lugged the cats around the house. He found out they'd had cats at their house and Arthur told them to stay away from all the cats outside because they were more or less wild.

Feeling Nicole snuggle into his neck, Arthur smiled as he closed his eyes in bliss. Getting up, Arthur put Nicole in the baby carrier softly and buckled her in. Grabbing her blanket, Arthur covered her up.

Picking up the carrier, Arthur headed to the bedroom and set Nicole on the dresser. "Time to get up, boys," Arthur said softly. Moving over to the bed, he shook each one until they opened their eyes. "We have to feed the animals before we leave."

Hearing 'leave', the boys sat up rubbing their eyes. "I'm up," Kirk yawned.

"Make sure your brothers get up," Arthur said, grabbing the baby carrier. "I'll start breakfast."

Hearing 'food', Kirk shook the others, "Breakfast, come on," he said, bouncing across the bed until he reached the edge. He stopped as he got off the bed and saw three neatly folded outfits. Seeing one was his, Kirk moved over and started dressing.

"It's dark outside," Pat yawned, looking at the window.

"We are big now and have to get up early," Kirk huffed, pulling his pants on. "Get Jim up."

Shaking Jim, "Quit being a baby, Jim," Pat said, then climbed out of the bed.

Hearing the boys, Arthur chuckled as he started breakfast. Jim and Pat looked up to their older brother. "I'm not a baby," Jim pouted out in his small voice.

"Come on, boys," Arthur called out, looking at Nicole to make sure he wasn't too loud. Only seeing Nicole twitch, Arthur continued gathering stuff on the kitchen island. Yesterday, the boys had watched in wonder as Arthur had made each meal.

When Jim had asked, "Where are the boxes?" Arthur had busted out laughing.

It'd taken some explaining, but the boys had finally got the concept down of cooking from scratch.

Kirk walked in, rubbing his eyes and Arthur smiled, "Wash your hands and let's start on the biscuits."

Taking off for the sink, Kirk stood up on his toes to turn the water on. Hooking a step stool with his foot that Wendy used to reach the top shelf in the cabinets, Arthur pulled it over to the sink. "Thank you," Kirk said, climbing on the stool.

Pat and Jim followed as Kirk stepped down and they ran to the sink to wash their hands. Even with the stool, Jim had to stretch hard to wash his hands. Arthur could've prepared breakfast much faster on his own and without them in the way, but he needed them to learn and learn fast, just in case he wasn't immune or something happened to him.

Holding up a strip of raw bacon, "Where does this come from on a pig?" Jim asked and then laid the strip in a pan very neatly.

"I'll show you soon," Arthur grinned. He didn't want to introduce them to the real world too fast.

When breakfast was done, the boys helped him clean up. Arthur fed Nicole her bottle, letting the boys wipe the island and table down because the next part required him. The boys didn't have toothbrushes but luckily, Wendy had boxes of them.

Yesterday, Arthur had watched the boys trying to brush their teeth and had shaken his head. Taking each one's toothbrush that he had given them, Arthur had brushed their teeth, one at a time, explaining how and what he was doing. Then Arthur promptly put electric toothbrushes on the list to pick up.

Today wasn't as bad, but Arthur still had to brush after each one.

Gathering up his weapons, Arthur put the baby sling on and moved Nicole over. When she was in the sling, Nicole looked up at Arthur and gave him a wide smile. "You are a happy baby," Arthur said, patting her butt.

"The dogs want outside," Kirk said and Arthur looked over and saw the dogs filed up at the door.

"Let them out and let's take care of the animals," Arthur told him, checking his AR.

Watching Arthur press check the AR, "We are really going to learn how to shoot guns?" Kirk asked with a wondrous grin.

"Yes, like learning the farm, that's not negotiable," Arthur answered, leading them out back.

"Big kitty," Jim sang out and Arthur turned to see Jim approaching Kong.

"Jim!" Arthur snapped and Jim jumped a foot in the air, spinning around and putting his hands behind his back. "That's an outside cat and what did I say?"

"Outside cats are feeuris," Jim mumbled.

"Feral, that means wild like I explained yesterday," Arthur corrected, turning to Kong. "But of all the outside cats, you leave that one alone. Even the dogs are terrified of him."

Jim cut his eyes at Kong to see Kong looking at him as Kong relaxed on the porch. Slowly, Jim eased away and then darted behind Arthur to hide. "It's that bad?" Kirk asked and noticed that as Kong was sitting, his head was well above Arthur's knees.

Walking over to the buggy, "Kirk," Arthur sighed, sitting down in the buggy. "That monster kills stuff a cat shouldn't be able to. I know he's killed raccoons, opossums, snakes, rats, rabbits, squirrels, and at least one fawn."

"What's an opossum and fawn?" Pat asked, climbing in the backseat with Jim who was looking at Kong with wide eyes.

"I'll have to show you pictures of opossums, but they can be mean as hell. A fawn is a baby deer," Arthur told him.

"That cat killed a deer?" Kirk cried out in shock, whipping his head over to stare at the massive Kong.

"A baby deer and yes, he did," Arthur said, cradling Nicole in the sling with his left arm as he backed up and headed down to the barn.

"Are you scared of him?" Kirk asked as they rode in the dawn's early light.

"I respect the son of a bitch, but he does a job on the farm. Kong kills wild animals that want to hurt the farm animals," Arthur explained and almost added. 'But if that fucker ever looks at me wrong, I'll shoot his ass.'

"What about the other cats?" Pat asked, pulling up to lean over the front seat.

"Oh, they kill the mice and other small things that hurt the farm," Arthur told him as he stepped inside the barn.

The boys looked around, seeing the horses and sheep running from the fields on the right. They turned to see the cows already waiting on the left for the doors to open. "Are you sure the little sheep don't bite?" Jim asked in a quivering voice.

"Jim, you need to worry about the sheep with the big horns and not the babies," Arthur told him, climbing out.

Jim looked at the big rams, "They don't chase me."

Pulling Nicole out of her sling, Arthur put her in the carrier and tucked a blanket around her. "That's the problem; you don't see them till they knock the shit out of you. When those turds hit, it really hurts."

The boys stayed close to Arthur and today, he made them actually help. They all laughed while washing the cows' udders and hooking up the milking machine. "You mean all the milk I poured on my cereal at home came from here?" Pat asked, pointing at the milking machine pumping the teats.

Reaching down, Arthur grabbed the teat of the next cow and milked it a few times by hand and the boys almost dropped on the ground laughing. "That's how they use to do it and all your milk came from a cow, but not these," Arthur explained as Kirk ran over.

"Can I do it?" he asked with a grin.

After Kirk, Pat, and Jim had to try, then Arthur let Kirk hook up the milking machine by himself. "Very good," Arthur grinned and then led them across the barn to feed the horses and sheep.

When one of the lambs knocked Jim down and the other lambs came over, Jim screamed bloody murder, "They're killing me!"

Casually, Arthur walked over and brushed the lambs away and picked Jim up. "Use your knees when they get close to push them away. Don't kick or the rams come over and they're mean," Arthur told him, brushing the dirt off. When Jim was brushed off, Arthur showed him how to use his knee to push the sheep away but being little, Jim had to use his hands.

Arthur wouldn't let them get in with the horses until the boys had calmed down a bit.

Finished in the barn, Arthur led them out to the pigs and chickens. Walking in the chicken coop, the boys all jumped back as Arthur punted a rooster that tried to get his leg. "Now a rooster tries that, kick his ass," Arthur instructed them, but the boys didn't want near the roosters. All they could see were the thorns sticking out from their legs.

Pat cried out when a hen pecked him as he tried to grab the eggs she was sitting on.

With Nicole in the sling, Arthur walked over as Pat looked at the hen with wide eyes. "Watch," Arthur said and reached up, brushing the hen out of the nesting box by using the back of his hand. "Don't act scared because animals can sense it."

"Okay," Pat said, moving to the next box and pushed the hen out and grabbed the two eggs.

Turning and holding up the eggs in triumph, "I did it," Pat cried out.

"Very good," Arthur laughed, holding up the egg basket.

With the chores done, Arthur led them to the buggy. "Kirk, sit behind the steering wheel," Arthur said, scooting to the middle so his foot could still reach the brake.

"I can't drive," Kirk said, not moving.

Looking down at Kirk, "Neither could I until I learned," Arthur told him.

Slowly, Kirk got out and walked around the buggy and climbed behind the steering wheel, acting like the steering wheel was going to reach out and kill him. Listening to Arthur, Kirk did what he was told. Arthur had Kirk drive around the fields to the office house and then onto the road.

Like all new drivers, Kirk didn't have the concept of easing the pedals down and they lurched with each press of the pedals. Holding Nicole tight, Arthur told Kirk to drive down to Jack's farm. He glanced back to see Pat and Jim staring at Kirk in awe.

Turning around, Arthur had Kirk pull through the yard to Jack's chicken coop. "What are those big barrels on the side?" Pat asked from the backseat.

"Automatic feeders. I filled them a few days back and need to check them," Arthur answered and held Nicole tight. "You can stop here," he told Kirk and he slammed the brake down and the buggy skidded to a stop.

Glancing back, Arthur smiled at seeing Jim and Pat holding on tight. The boys climbed out and Arthur showed them how to fill the auto feeders and get the eggs out without ever walking into the chicken coop.

"Your house makes power down here?" Kirk asked, bringing eggs over to the basket as Nicole started complaining.

"No, Jack has solar panels that run this and his water pump," Arthur explained, grabbing a bottle with powder already inside out of the buggy and pouring water in. Nicole gave a wide grin, hearing the bottle shaking. "Yes, I have your food, baby blue eyes," Arthur grinned, putting the bottle in her mouth.

"Why don't you have your chickens like this?" Pat asked. "You don't have to go inside here."

Shaking his head, "I want to make sure the animals are okay," Arthur shrugged. "This seems like cheating. Besides, half of these chickens have died and I'm wondering if they would've died had I went inside to check on them."

They all climbed back in the buggy with Kirk driving and headed back to the house. When they stopped at the gate, Arthur glanced back at Pat. "See that keypad, punch in one, seven, nine, three," Arthur told him and Pat jumped out. Running over, he punched in the numbers and the gate started swinging open.

"We can close it from the house," Arthur called out as Nicole finished her bottle.

After Pat climbed back in, Kirk almost stomped the accelerator. "Wait," Arthur said, moving Nicole to his shoulder and Kirk looked up at him. "Make sure your passengers are ready before you take off."

Glancing back at his brothers, "Are you guys ready?" Kirk asked with a huge grin.

"Yeah, just don't stomp so hard," Jim moaned, holding onto the seat.

"I'm trying," Kirk groaned and slowly pushed the accelerator and the buggy slowly took off.

"Now, that was a good takeoff," Arthur said as Nicole let out a loud echoing burp. "Shit, I wish I could do that," Arthur mumbled.

Pulling up to the patio, Kirk let off the accelerator to slow down and then pressed the brake. The buggy gave a jerk as Kirk did the latter too hard. "Sorry," Kirk said, looking up at Arthur.

"Hey, you did great," Arthur laughed, reaching over patting his leg then moved to get out and saw Kong walk from behind the grill. The laugh fell off Arthur's face. "Kong, I have guns and will use them."

Kong just looked at Arthur with indifference as the dogs trotted up from behind the buggy. Slowly, Kong turned to the dogs and yawned, showing his teeth. "Booger eater," Pat gasped. "You see how big his teeth are?"

"Yeah," Arthur said curtly as he eased out of the buggy, holding Nicole to his chest with his left hand. His right had the AR, just in case. "I've seen and trapped smaller full grown bobcats than Kong."

"Has Kong ever hurt the lambs?" Kirk asked, getting out of the buggy.

Shaking his head, "No, because Kong would've died," Arthur replied, leading the boys inside. He walked into his office and showed them how to close the gate from the computer.

"Okay, time to head out. Empty your backpacks and get back down here," Arthur told them and the boys just stood rooted to the floor. "What?" Arthur asked.

"Mean people are out there," Kirk reminded him.

"Guys, Nicole has to have diapers that fit. I'm tired of cleaning her poop off of me and everything near me, every time she goes,"

Arthur told them. "I asked if you wanted to stay here and all of you said no. Have you changed your minds?"

All three shook their head rapidly. "No, but it's scary," Pat said.

"Guys, if something can get past me, then it will get us here," Arthur told them. "Guys, if we don't leave soon, we will be out after dark. I really want to be back by then."

Like magic, the three boys vanished from where Arthur was talking to them. He turned and caught sight of all three running upstairs at a very impressive pace. Moving Nicole off his shoulder, Arthur smiled to see she was fast asleep.

Putting her in the baby carrier, he moved it into the kitchen and made some sandwiches. The boys came back down and found Arthur packing a cooler. "Need food," Arthur smiled and then headed back to his office.

Grabbing four radios, Arthur turned to carry them to the boys and found them right behind him. "You know how to use walkie talkies?" he asked and the boys' eyes widened in wonder. "You will always be close but if not, you can call me."

The boys grinned as Arthur clipped a radio to each one's belt. After showing them how to turn them on, Arthur headed back to the kitchen.

"Donald, Daisy," Arthur called out and the Rottweilers trotted over.

"You like Disney," Kirk stated as Arthur put Nicole in the baby sling.

"Why?" Arthur asked.

"Your cats are Mickey and Minnie and your dogs are Donald and Daisy," Kirk pointed out.

Shaking his head, "I named the dogs Donald and Daisy hoping they would beat Mickey and Minnie's butts," Arthur huffed.

The boys laughed, following Arthur outside and not letting Kit and Kat out. "Why don't Kit and Kat ever get to go?" Pat asked.

"Donald and Daisy have been trained to attack. Kit and Kat haven't," Arthur answered bluntly, leading the boys over to the Blazer. The twenty-foot trailer was already hooked up so Arthur opened the door and folded the seat up.

Pat and Jim climbed up, having to use the step mounted under the door. Arthur saw the passenger door open and Kirk climbed up into the passenger seat. As Arthur climbed in, he saw the boys buckling up.

Cranking the engine up, Arthur turned in the seat to look at all three boys. "Okay, you have to stay alert. I'm driving, so each of you needs to keep looking out the windows and behind us. If you see people, call it out but try not to shout. Just let me know. I'll be looking, but you three have to help," he told them very slowly.

"Will you shoot the mean people?" Pat asked.

"Yeah," Arthur replied nonchalantly. "But I'm not shooting everyone we see. Only if they pose a threat."

"Okay," Kirk said, looking out the window and appearing very at ease.

Pulling his 1911 out of the holster, Arthur shoved it under his leg while glancing down at Nicole sleeping soundly. "Let's go shopping," he said, putting the Blazer in gear.

Chapter Eighteen
Feeling overwhelmed isn't always bad

Driving down the valley with his fedora pulled down, Arthur took the south road where a creek forked into Piney. "Can we go fishing?" Kirk asked, looking at the stream running beside the road.

"We can go in the pond closest to the house and then I'll take you to fish in the stream," Arthur told him and glanced over to see a grin fill his face. "Don't forget to keep an eye out."

"I'm not," Kirk said, glancing around at the woods and then back to the water.

Fifteen miles later Arthur slowed, seeing a wrecked car in the ditch. Glancing at the driver leaned over the steering wheel, Arthur could tell the crash hadn't killed him. "That's why I'm driving slow," Arthur explained, speeding up to forty. "If I round a curve and see something in the road, I will have time to stop and not wreck."

Almost pale and panting hard, Kirk turned to Arthur. "I don't want to drive," he gasped.

Letting out a chuckle, Arthur reached over and patted Kirk's chest. "Don't worry, you can wait on cars for a little while," Arthur said and could feel the relief wash over Kirk.

Keeping his eyes on the road, Arthur pulled his hand back, gripping the steering wheel as his left dropped down to pat Nicole in the baby sling. Half an hour later, "I see someone," Pat shouted behind him.

Nicole jumped with a startle, opening her eyes with a grumpy expression. "Shh," Arthur calmed her as he looked around and saw a figure sitting on a porch. "Are they alive?" Arthur asked, driving past the house.

"He waved," Pat answered.

"Very good," Arthur said, looking ahead. "Now we will learn positions. To our front is twelve, our right is three, to our back is six and to the left is nine," he said, then explained how to call out using the clock face.

"So that guy was at our nine o'clock," Pat said proudly.

"Yes, he was," Arthur grinned and saw the retail store ahead. He slowed and coasted off the road, pulling beside the store then easing around the corner and stopping at a large rolling door in the back.

"It's closed," Kirk said, looking at the trees behind the store. There was a loading dock with another rolling door in front of them.

"I have a key," Arthur said, pulling the sling off and putting Nicole in the baby carrier between him and Kirk.

"They have alarms," Kirk whispered.

"Powers been off for too long," Arthur said, looking around. "Batteries for alarms are only good for a few days at most."

"Oh," Kirk said, not looking away from the trees.

"I'm going to open the door and check the store. Have your radio in your hand. I'm taking Daisy and if you see someone, call me. If they come toward the truck, open the door and let Donald out," Arthur said, opening his door.

Kirk turned to Arthur and gave a slow nod. "I won't be more than ten feet away and trust me, Donald will kill anyone that messes with you. He and Daisy love you guys," Arthur grinned.

All three gave a sigh of relief as Arthur closed the door and walked to the back of the Blazer. Opening the door, "Daisy, out," Arthur said, grabbing something from the back and then closed the door.

"I'm scared, Kirk," Jim whispered, watching Arthur walk up to a pedestrian door and holding a box that had a metal bar sticking out from it with a wedge at the end.

"He won't be far Jim, stop being a baby," Kirk said looking around.

"He's breaking in," Jim gasped in shock, watching Arthur shove the small end of the arm between the door and the frame. "You remember how much trouble we got in when we stole Ms. Sponder's apples and those just fell on the ground."

"Arthur is taking care of us. Now, do what he asked," Kirk commanded.

Jim just nodded as Arthur flipped a switch on the box and they heard a whine. "Whoa," Jim said, watching the metal arm split into two arms, spreading the door away from the frame. The door gave a 'tang' and flew open. When Arthur put the box down, Jim leaned over and saw the two arms spread out with the wedge split in half. "That is cool."

"Jim, keep watch," Pat snapped, looking out the back and patting Donald on the head.

Turning around, Jim looked at the trees at the back of the store. To him, they were a long way off but in reality, only fifty yards. In a few minutes, Arthur came back out and picked up the machine and flipped a switch. The two arms closed until they looked like one arm again and then the others noticed the sharp wedge at the tip.

Opening the back, "Donald, out," Arthur said, putting the machine in the back.

"That is so cool," Pat said, pointing at the machine.

Shrugging, "I wasn't always a good boy," Arthur admitted as Donald jumped out. "I grew up in foster homes and didn't always hang around the right people."

Closing the back door, Arthur moved to the driver's door and opened it up. Gently, he picked up Nicole and slung the sling over his head. Reaching under his seat, Arthur held out flashlights. "Use these because it's dark inside, but stay with me," Arthur said as Kirk opened his door and jumped out. "Kirk, close your door easy," Arthur whispered loudly.

Barely closing his door, Kirk walked around the Blazer as Pat and Jim climbed out. They followed Arthur in and he turned around, pointing at the door. "Donald, guard," Arthur commanded and Donald turned around, looking out the door.

Arthur led them into the store. "Try not to shine your lights toward the front. We don't want people to know we are in here," Arthur told them, walking to the front.

He stopped and read the aisle headers and almost took off running for the baby aisle. Grabbing a small shopping cart as he ran past them, Arthur glanced back to see the boys running after him. Arthur stopped, seeing the small diapers and gave a contented sigh.

"Won't they fly off the trailer?" Kirk asked.

Reaching over and patting Kirk's back, "Very good," Arthur told him, glad the boys were thinking. "Yes, they would, but there are boxes in the back we will put them in."

They watched Arthur rake the shelf clean of the small diapers, filling the buggy all the way up. "Get us another buggy," he said, pushing that one to the back of the aisle. The boys ran to the front and came back with three buggies. Arthur filled them up with the bigger sizes and then pushed them down the aisle.

Before he asked, the boys came back pushing three more carts. "Boys, you are getting good," Arthur said as he started grabbing the baby formula. "Grab all those bottles," he said and the boys started putting the bottles in one of the carts. Seeing bouncer chairs, Arthur grabbed all four boxes thinking he could leave one in the barn and the others around the house. When the carts were full, they pushed them to the back storeroom.

Then Arthur headed back to the store, walking along the aisles. He stopped and grabbed rolls of tape and then headed back to the storeroom. Finding a stack of broken down cardboard boxes, Arthur showed the boys how to fold them up and tape them.

Setting the first one on the floor, "Start filling it, Kirk," Arthur said, grabbing another box. Soon, the three boys were filling the boxes with the baby stuff. After he'd made a dozen boxes, Arthur moved over to the rolling door and unlocked it. When he rolled it up slowly, the boys all jumped.

"Need more light," Arthur told them as he stopped the door, only leaving a seven-foot opening. Grabbing a handcart, Arthur pushed the sling to his side and put the boxes the boys had filled up on the trailer.

When they were done, Arthur had them grab the carts and head back to the baby aisle. Not seeing anything else he really needed, Arthur turned to the boys. "Next aisle is toys, you can take what will fit in your packs."

The boys took off, not caring at that moment if Arthur came or not.

He grinned and then stepped over as the boys were stuffing toys in their packs. "Boys, I'm heading to the front to see if anyone is about," Arthur said.

"We have our radios," Kirk said, shoving a small car in his pack.

Grinning at the excitement of the boys, Arthur spun around and headed to the front of the store where he'd be able to see the gas station across the road. Before he had reached the front, he dropped down as a car drove past heading toward town. "I swear that was the car in front of that house that man was sitting at," he mumbled, feeling his pulse quicken.

Glancing at his watch, Arthur relaxed to see they had been in the store for well over an hour. "They weren't after us," he concluded, moving to the side of the large window. He glanced to the south where Clarksville was and saw a few columns of smoke rising in the air.

He was guessing they were on the far side of town near the electric company. In the distance, he heard a pop and knew that was gunfire. "Had to come," he mumbled, patting Nicole and glanced down and saw her sucking her pacifier and looking up at him.

"Got you some diapers, but we will make you some better clothes; these are cheap," he smiled at her and Nicole smiled under her pacifier. Lifting his head up, Arthur cocked his ear toward the glass when he heard a hum. Moving to the sliding doors, Arthur reached up to flip the lock and release of the electric motor.

He pushed the doors open about an inch, and then stepped back to the side. He cocked his head, hearing the hum was a steady buzz. "We're ready," Kirk said, coming up behind him and Arthur held up his hand and Kirk stopped talking.

"You hear that?" Arthur whispered.

"Yeah, sounds like a lawnmower," Kirk answered and his brothers nodded.

The boys moved behind Arthur as he stared outside and the buzz continued getting louder. Then they saw a small go-kart coming down the road rather fast. Arthur watched as the kart pulled off the road and up to the pumps at the small gas station across the street.

The driver was an older kid who took something from his lap and passed it to his passenger who was much smaller. When the driver got out of the go-kart, he reached back and pulled out a rifle that had been sitting beside him. "Smart kid," Arthur mumbled as the kid looked at the pumps and then at the store.

Arthur could see the kid's shoulders slump as he walked to the doors and looked inside the dark store of the gas station. When the kid turned around, Arthur saw him cradle his rifle up to his shoulder but not lift it. Following the boy's gaze, Arthur saw a little girl running across the road to the gas station.

"That's a girl," Kirk said and looked at the boy. "He will get in trouble, riding that go-kart on the road."

"Yeah, it's too loud," Arthur said, watching the boy lower the rifle as the girl reached the parking lot.

"Don't move!" a man's voice bellowed and Arthur turned to see a man step out from behind the gas station. "Got 'em, Ash!" he called out and another man stepped out from the other side of the store.

"Mean guys," Kirk whispered as the men aimed at the kids.

"Put the gun down, boy, or I'll just shoot ya," the first one shouted, aiming at the boy.

"Boys, step back and lay on the floor," Arthur said, pulling his AR up.

The boys dropped down as the boy across the road put his gun down. "Very good," the first man called out. "You girl, get over here before I shoot you in the leg!" he shouted and the girl moved up closer to the go-kart.

When the men lowered their rifles, Arthur stepped up to the door and eased it open. Lifting his rifle, he sighted in on the speaker and flipped the safety off. He squeezed the trigger twice and the AR coughed. The man let out a grunt as the bullets hit him and Arthur was on number two when he looked over to see his friend fall to the ground.

Just as the man realized what was happening, two rounds slammed into his chest and blew out the back. Dropping his rifle, the man grabbed his chest as he dropped to his knees. Frothy blood poured out his mouth as he fell face first onto the pavement.

"Boys, on me," Arthur said over his shoulder as he walked to the road, glancing around with Daisy beside him. The little girl that had run across the road gave a squeal as a man and a large dog walked toward her, and took off when the boys came out. When she'd reached the shoulder of the road, the little girl slowed seeing three little boys follow the man and big dog across the road.

Scanning around, Arthur watched the boy pick up his rifle. "Don't aim it at me," Arthur warned, walking into the parking lot keeping his rifle toward the two he shot and saw the passenger was a little girl around four or five. "A word of advice, get something that's quieter," Arthur said, walking past the boy who looked like a young teenager.

"It's all I had," the boy said, looking at the three small boys following Arthur. "Thank you, mister."

"Welcome," Arthur replied, walking up to the body of the first one he'd shot. The man let out a moan and Arthur moved his AR and pulled the trigger, shooting the man in the face. "Boys, if you ever shoot someone, you make sure they are dead," Arthur said, turning back to look at the boys.

All three were pale after watching Arthur casually shoot the man in the face. "Boys, people like that will hurt you for no other reason than they can," Arthur told them, walking over to the other body. Kicking it over, Arthur saw the man was dead and Daisy sniffed the man.

Looking at the man's bright red nose, "Rudolph is a real good name," Arthur mumbled, turning to see the boys behind him. "Boys, I told you I would protect you. This is what it will take. We couldn't have left and they needed help."

"Yes, sir," Kirk gulped, swallowing hard.

"Boys, don't feel bad defending family. We fought evil today and won. Just be happy we are alive," Arthur told them as Nicole started crying. "My gun was quiet," Arthur groaned, pulling a made bottle from his left thigh cargo pocket.

He glanced around and saw the teen boy was standing next to the go-kart and the young girl was coming back across the road. "Name's Arthur," Arthur said, putting the bottle to Nicole's lips with his left hand. The teen boy noticed Arthur's right hand never let his AR go.

"I'm Shawn, and thanks again," Shawn said as the girl came over.

"Like I said, get something that's quieter to ride around on, Shawn. We heard you from a long way off," Arthur said, heading back to the retail store.

"Hey, is there any place safe around here?" Shawn asked.

Stopping at the pumps, Arthur looked at the small girl in the go-kart, cradling a blanket. "Only what you make. I'm hearing on my radio that this is going on everywhere," Arthur said, feeling the boys stay behind him. He glanced down and saw Daisy looking around and panting.

"Arthur, can we come with you and your sons?" Shawn asked with a pleading expression. "We've had four people shoot at us just today. Someone shot my mom yesterday when she went to the diner to try to get some food. She was sick, but wouldn't let me go. When I saw people coming into the trailer park, we took off."

Giving a long sigh, Arthur looked around and saw a car fly through an intersection, heading east toward the interstate. "Shawn, you come with us, I'm the boss and you learn how to work," Arthur finally said.

"Yes sir," Shawn cried out and turned to the go-kart. "Beth, give me Lucas," Shawn said, slinging his rifle over his shoulder.

"That's a baby?" Arthur cried out, letting the AR go.

"Yes sir. His mom lived next door, but died four days ago," Shawn said, taking the bundle.

Moving over, Arthur pulled the blanket back to expose a small face, but the skin was cool. "Shit, the baby's cold," Arthur said, letting Nicole's bottle go. Grabbing his shirt, Arthur ripped the snap buttons open and took the baby out of the blanket as Nicole started crying.

"Nicole, I only have two hands, baby," Arthur panted, seeing the baby boy wasn't much older than Nicole but wasn't moving much. He thrust Lucas into his shirt and buttoned up the bottom of his shirt, then grabbed the blanket from Beth and draped it over his chest, tucking it under the sling.

Lucas felt the warmth from Arthur's chest and tried to burrow in. "I had him wrapped up," Shawn gasped with wide eyes.

Arthur turned and saw Shawn was on the verge of tears. "Son, you didn't know and were doing your best," Arthur told him, holding Lucas to his chest with his right hand and grabbed Nicole's bottle with his left and put it back in her mouth.

When Nicole started drinking, "Get your stuff and bring it to the truck," Arthur said, walking off. "We are in the open and that's bad."

"What about my go-kart?" Shawn asked, grabbing a backpack and picking up Beth.

"Leave it, we'll find you something that doesn't make so much noise," Arthur replied over his shoulder.

The other little girl ran across the parking lot and around the go-kart to stop in front of Arthur. "Can we come?" she asked, clasping her hands.

"Um, I thought you were?" Arthur said, turning to Shawn.

"I don't know her," Shawn confessed, looking around.

"Car, nine o'clock," Kirk said and Arthur turned to his left and saw another car go through the same intersection. It was going much slower, but heading toward the interstate.

"Come," Arthur said, moving into a jog back to the store. When everyone was inside, Arthur closed the door as Lucas started moving around, getting warm against his chest.

"Shawn, you know how old Lucas is?" Arthur asked.

"Four months," Shawn answered, putting Beth down. "I had to babysit him a few times so his mom could work."

"How old are you and Beth?" Arthur asked as Nicole finished her bottle.

"I'm fourteen and she's five," Shawn answered as Arthur turned to Kirk.

"Kirk, get Nicole and burp her just like I taught you," Arthur said. He didn't want to let him, but Lucas was still latched to his chest hair. Very gently, Kirk pulled Nicole out and put her on his chest, patting her back.

Turning to the little girl, "And you are?" Arthur asked.

"I'm Vicki," she said very anxiously. "Please let us come. People are shooting and chasing me when I go out to look for food."

"Why are they chasing you?" Pat asked.

Clearly confused, Vicki shrugged her shoulders, "One man thinks I have a little cat," Vicki told him and Pat just cocked his head. "He keeps yelling he wants my little pussy," Vicki explained. "The other two just chased me and shouted for me to stop."

Arthur felt his face flush as anger flooded his system and so did Lucas, burrowing into Arthur's chest at the added warmth. "How many are with you, Vicki?" Arthur asked.

"Three more," Vicki told him, clasping her hands in front of her. "Please," she moaned, bouncing on her toes. "I'm scared."

"Okay, how old are you and the others?" Arthur asked and Vicki flew at him, throwing her arms around his waist.

"Thank you," she wailed out.

Dropping his hand down and stroking Vicki's nasty and nappy brown hair, "Shh, it's okay," Arthur said softly as Nicole let out a loud long burp. Kirk and the boys laughed and then everyone joined in.

Vicki looked up with a dirty tear-streaked face. "I'm ten, Jodi is seven, Robin is two and Pam is a six-month-old baby."

Hearing baby, Arthur wanted to just go home as he looked out the windows. "Where are they?"

"At the daycare. We are out of food, but we have formula for Pam," Vicki answered, still holding on to Arthur.

"Shawn, can you drive a car?" Arthur asked, hearing Lucas cooing under his shirt.

"Yes, sir. I drove the work truck at the salvage yard I worked at," Shawn told him.

Pulling Vicki off his waist, "Can you show us where the others are if you ride with us?" Arthur asked.

"Yes, sir," Vicki nodded.

"Let's go," Arthur said, grabbing Vicki's hand and leading them through the store. When they reached the storeroom, Vicki gave a gasp seeing Donald at the door.

Never breaking his pace, "He's with us," Arthur told Vicki. "Kirk, Pat, Jim, put your packs in the back with the dogs," Arthur said, opening the back up.

"Shawn," Arthur said and Shawn turned. "Passenger seat and get a bottle ready for Lucas."

"Have one," Shawn said, heading around the Blazer with Beth.

Taking Nicole from Kirk, Arthur just held her as the boys threw their packs in and just climbed in the cargo area. Arthur chuckled as he watched the boys just climb over the backseat. "Donald, Daisy, in," Arthur commanded and they jumped in.

"Where do you want me to sit?" Vicki asked, standing beside the driver's door.

"You will sit beside me," Arthur said, managing to get his door open with two babies in his hands. "Beth, I need you to sit back with the boys. Boys, introduce yourselves," Arthur said and Beth climbed over the seat to join them in the back.

Arthur laid Nicole in his seat and then took Lucas out of his shirt and Lucas let out a small cry to let everyone know, he wanted back where it was warm. "Wrap him in this," Arthur told Shawn, handing the blanket and then Lucas over.

When Lucas was wrapped up, Shawn fed him the bottle and that made Lucas content.

Putting Nicole back into the baby sling, Arthur picked up Vicki and put her in the middle on the car seat. "How far?" Arthur asked, climbing in.

"Not far," Vicki said. "I can't go far and stay gone long because Robin starts crying and people hear it."

Nodding as he started the engine, Arthur put the shifter in drive and pulled around the store. "Turn right here," Vicki told him at the next road.

Pulling into a subdivision, Arthur noticed a few bodies lying around in yards and the road but then, he noticed there were dead birds also. "See that white sign? That's the daycare," Vicki said with a smile.

When Arthur stopped, Vicki looked at him with a serious face. "You won't leave, will you?" she asked with a trembling lip.

Arthur turned off the Blazer and pulled the keys out. "I gave my word, little lady," he smiled, reaching over and clipping the keys to her belt loop. He opened his door and let her out. "I don't want to scare them, so we'll wait here," Arthur said, putting Vicki down.

When her feet touched the ground, Vicki took off running and Arthur held his AR across his body, looking around. The smell was harsh, but if he breathed through his mouth he could taste the smell of death and that was worse. Turning as Vicki reached the door, Arthur watched her knock in a code on the door.

When the door cracked open, Vicki pushed it open and ran inside. She soon came back out with a baby on her hip and holding the hand of a toddler, with seven-year-old Jodi following. Vicki ran around the front of the truck and stopped.

Taking the keys off her belt, "Guys, it's going to be crowded, but just hang on," Arthur said, reaching for the baby. The baby pulled away so Arthur just picked up Vicki and turned, lifting his seat up to help Vicki into the back.

He turned to see Robin, the toddler holding out her arms to him. Smiling as he picked her up, Arthur put her in the back and then watched Jodi climb in. "Won't let me pick 'em up, but will get in my ride," Arthur chuckled.

Climbing in, Arthur cranked up, put the shifter in drive, and pulled off. Hearing a small burp, he looked over to see Shawn patting Lucas on the back. "That sounded wimpy," Arthur chuckled, hearing Jodi whispering to Vicki.

Avoiding a body in the road, Arthur saw a nude woman standing in a yard. The woman's face was emotionless as she watched him drive past, but did nothing else.

Taking the next turn that would take him out of the subdivision, Arthur kept his head on a swivel. "You are looking, right, boys?" he asked, seeing several people walking on a side street.

"Yes sir, people at nine o'clock," Kirk said.

"A man at six o'clock riding a bike," Pat called out and Arthur glanced in his mirror and saw a man peddling fast behind them to catch up.

"Hey, that's the man who wanted my cat," Vicki cried out and Arthur slammed on the brakes.

In one motion, Arthur shifted into park, grabbed the AR pistol grip and jumped out as the man started to stop as he yelled, "Give me those kids! They're mine!"

Flipping the safety off, Arthur was already raising his AR up as the man reached for his waist. Arthur squeezed the trigger three times, watching the rounds impact across the man's chest.

A pistol fell from the man's hand as he fell over with the bike crashing hard on the road. Giving a glance around, Arthur saw a young woman looking at him and a few others further away. Calmly, Arthur strolled over and aimed the AR like a pistol with his right arm and shot the man in the face.

It wasn't for dramatic Hollywood effect. The reason he'd aimed with one hand was Nicole was crying and his left was putting the pacifier in her mouth.

Spinning on his heel, Arthur pulled a magazine from the pouch on his belt. Ejecting the partial, he slapped the full one in as he continued looking around. He climbed in, letting the AR hang from the sling propped on the seat. "Worthless cocksucker wasn't sick," Arthur growled, putting the Blazer in gear.

"My mom would never let me have a cat," Vicki said.

"Um, that's not what the man-," Shawn stopped as Arthur spoke.

"Shawn," he snapped, patting Nicole with his left hand. "Not now, I'll explain to her later. I'm mad enough as it is."

"Sorry, sir," Shawn mumbled.

"Shawn, you did nothing wrong. You did everything you could and people tried to hurt you. And that's what has me pissed off like a madman," Arthur growled. "Now people will know, screw with my kids and I'll kill you, three of your best friends and your pet hamster."

"Car, three o'clock," Kirk announced and Arthur spotted a car speeding out of a parking lot to the main road. They heard the squeal of tires as Arthur slowed to turn onto the main road and the car headed away from them.

"Sir, I don't want to sound like a sissy, but can we, like, leave town?" Shawn asked, feeling his mouth was bone dry.

"We are, but we have to make one stop," Arthur told him, pressing the accelerator and getting up to fifty.

"That man was never that close to us," Vicki said from the back.

"He had tracked you down and was waiting on you to go back inside," Arthur mumbled, but everyone heard him.

"There are a lot of dead birds," Kirk noted, but didn't mention the dead bodies everywhere that dotted parking lots and the road.

"Flu is killing a lot of them as well," Arthur said, turning onto a bigger road and picking up speed while dodging a stalled car.

"I thought you said to go slow," Kirk called out, but didn't look away from his window.

"Can't here. Too many people. You shoot at something, you better hit it or it might hit you. Kids, I want you to get a little lower in the seat," Arthur advised, seeing his destination ahead.

When he started to slow down, Shawn looked around to see a car dealership on one side of the road and a building on the other. Glancing around, he didn't see any people as Arthur turned into the dealership.

Pulling up behind a row of brand new trucks, Arthur put the Blazer in park. "Can you drive that?" Arthur asked and Shawn followed his finger to a gray Suburban.

"Holy shit, that's big," Shawn gasped. "Um, I've never driven anything but a truck. Can I just drive this?"

"It's pulling a trailer," Arthur said and Shawn shrugged.

"I've never driven a truck without one," he admitted.

"Boys, have your radios ready, I'll be right back," Arthur said, getting out.

Walking around to the back of the Blazer, Arthur opened the cargo gate and grabbed the box with the protruding arm. "Donald," he said and Donald jumped out.

"Why's he getting another car?" Jim asked.

"Because there's so many, goofy," Kirk laughed, watching Arthur walk up to a door and shove the arm in it. The others watched as the arms popped the door open and Arthur walked inside with Donald.

"That box is so cool," Pat said in awe, looking around.

"Are we going to get in trouble?" Jodi asked Vicki.

"No, Arthur knows what he's doing," Vicki said, bouncing Pam in her lap.

Only gone a few minutes, Arthur came back out the door and raised his hand at the massive Suburban and they heard it crank up. "Wow," Kirk said.

Walking over to the idling Suburban, Arthur pressed the fob and the back hatch opened up. He put the box inside and motioned for Donald to jump in. After Donald was in, he hit the button to close the hatch and walked around the Suburban.

It was completely loaded with off road tires and lights, side bars, four-inch lift and a nice cattle guard and winch. When Arthur stopped at the passenger window, he gasped. "Six figures for a Suburban, are they insane? I better be able to push a button and get a blow job for that kind of money!"

Continuing his walk around, he opened the driver's door and saw a quarter of a tank. Knowing that was enough to get home, Arthur headed back to the Blazer. He opened Shawn's door, "Give me Lucas and everyone but Kirk, get in the new truck," Arthur told them.

The kids piled out as Shawn scooted over and Kirk got in the front passenger seat. Reaching over, Arthur grabbed Kirk's arm. "You are his eyes, so keep them open. Use your radio if you see anything, okay?"

Nodding with a gulp, "I will," Kirk promised.

Arthur climbed in the Suburban and pulled out with Shawn following. Shawn and Kirk both jumped when the radio in Kirk's hand went off. "We are taking a different route home Kirk, so don't get worried," Arthur called over the radio.

"Okay," Kirk answered.

"Man, Arthur is cool," Shawn said with a grin.

"Oh, you haven't seen anything yet. He has a huge house and all kinds of farm animals that he just hits with his knee and they run off," Kirk cried out in wonder.

Chapter Nineteen
I may be weak but you're dead

May 11

Feeling someone shaking her, Wendy cracked her eyes open. "Wendy, the power went off," Jo Ann whispered. "We think Anthony did it."

Smiling as she sat up in the bed, "No, baby, the ship makes its own power and probably ran out of fuel," Wendy said, seeing it was late in the afternoon. Waking up this morning, she had picked back up on doing simple exercises and knew she had pushed too hard. After lunch, she had only intended to let Ryan take a nap, but had passed out with him.

Not leaving the room at all yesterday, Wendy would pace and do lunges while trying to clear her lungs. During the day between her limited exercises, they ate and played cards and then Wendy had the twins shower, then took one herself with Ryan. With all of them clean, they'd piled up in the bed together going to sleep. During the night, Wendy thought she heard something in the stairwell and got up to put another chair in front of the door.

With the spear gun clutched in her hands and sitting on the edge of the bed, Wendy had waited up for over an hour but the sound never came back, so she'd gone back to bed.

Still feeling weak but much better both mentally and physically, Wendy leaned over to check on Ryan on the floor, lying on a blanket. Ryan was kicking his legs as Sally sat beside him, shaking a stuffed doll over his face.

"Are you sure?" Jo Ann asked, stepping back as Wendy stood up.

Turning to the little girl, Wendy reached over and cupped Jo Ann's face in her hand. "Yes, baby. He wouldn't know how, for one. Only a member of the ship's crew could do that and then, only a few of them would know how," Wendy told her in a reassuring voice.

Jo Ann gave a relaxing sigh and Wendy heard another come from Sally on the floor. "Sorry we woke you then," Jo Ann said sheepishly.

Giving a shrug as she let Jo Ann's chin go, Wendy turned and saw they only had a few bottles of water left. "Is the water on?" Wendy asked.

Nodding, "Yeah, but we didn't drink any like you told us," Jo Ann answered.

Walking over to the small table, Wendy sat down and looked at the spear gun. "Guys, we need more bottled water," Wendy told them. In normal times, she knew the ship's water plant would and could put out drinkable water, but didn't want to trust it. Wendy was sure it would be okay to wash in, but didn't want to risk drinking any.

Putting a pacifier in Ryan's mouth, "They have some in the store beside the daycare," Sally said, getting up.

"That's only a few levels down," Wendy nodded, looking at the wall with an unfixed gaze as she thought. When she turned, Wendy saw the girls standing side by side, holding hands in front of her. Both had small trusting smiles on their faces.

Reaching out, Wendy put a hand on each of their shoulders. "Jo Ann, Sally, I'm going out to get us some water," Wendy said and the smiles fell off as both gasped, taking a breath to argue. "Hold on," Wendy said and both girls closed their mouths.

"Ryan can't come and we can't leave him alone. It takes both of you to look after him. This room is more or less soundproof unless you bang around. When I come back, I'll give this knock," Wendy said tapping the table three times, then two, followed by three more. "One of you will put your ear to the door and I'll whisper 'it's me'. Then and only then, will you open the door."

"What if Anthony comes?" Sally blurted out with tears welling up in her eyes.

"Sally, I won't be that far away and if you keep the door locked, I'll hear him trying to get in," Wendy explained, taking her hands off their shoulders. Gently, she caressed each one's cheek. "I'll be back long before he could get in," Wendy assured them.

"What if you don't come back?" Jo Ann asked with a few tears running down her cheeks.

"Girls," Wendy snorted with a chuckle. "If that virus didn't kill me, Anthony doesn't stand a chance."

Hearing certainty in Wendy's voice, both girls visibly relaxed and the tears in their eyes dissipated. Jo Ann and Sally leaned over, hugging Wendy. "Please be back before dark," Sally begged.

"Girls, I'll try, but I have to find us some flashlights," Wendy told them, hugging them tight.

Both girls leaned back and looked at each other. Unspoken thoughts passed between the twins, and then they turned to Wendy. "Okay, just bring us some," Sally said with a serious face and Jo Ann nodded.

"I will," Wendy chuckled.

Wearing only shorts and t-shirt, Wendy put on her shoes and then emptied out the backpack that had held all of Ryan's supplies. "Need some more diaper wipes," Wendy mumbled, putting the pack on.

Grabbing the hard-plastic spear holster, Wendy strapped it to her left leg. She looked at the two shiny metal spears. The shaft of the spear that the gun fired, or what Wendy called the arrow, was twenty-eight inches long, with a large metal tip that was over an inch wide. Under the spear gun was the line connected to the arrow so you could pull fish that you'd shot back to you.

Knowing the thing wouldn't be very accurate, Wendy had taken the reel line off the spear shaft. She didn't know how much power the two rubber bands had, but it'd taken her a lot of effort to pull them back. One was relatively easy, but the second one was very hard to pull back. "Gloria would've never been able to pull back that second rubber band," Wendy mumbled.

No sooner than her sister's name escaped her lips, memories flooded Wendy's mind, making her take a deep breath and push them away. "Keep your mind on the here and now," Wendy reminded herself as she moved over and helped the twins remove the chairs from around the door.

"When I'm gone, put the chairs back and the door stop," she said, pointing to the wedge under the door. They had found it in the bathroom but since the bathroom door could be locked open, Wendy hadn't known why it'd been there.

"What if you need in fast?" Sally asked, kicking the door stop out from under the door.

Glancing at the yellow hair barrette in Sally's hair, "Sally," Wendy said, resting her hand on the door. "I won't need in fast, but you have to make sure nobody but me comes in."

"Okay," Sally mumbled unconvinced.

Undoing the privacy latch and unlocking the door, Wendy eased the door open and stuck her head out. The smell in the hall was much stronger today and Wendy was sure it was going to get much worse. With the emergency lights on in the hallway, Wendy poked her head out and didn't see anything.

Turning back to the twins, "I'm waiting here until you have the door locked, so give one light tap when you are ready for me to leave," Wendy whispered. As one, Jo Ann and Sally nodded.

Closing the door, Wendy checked the keycard attached to the bungee cord on her waist. Hearing the door lock Wendy turned, looking up and down the hall as the twins pushed the chairs back. Wendy glanced at the door, hearing one of the twins putting the door stop back.

When a soft knock sounded, Wendy moved down the hall and stepped over a body. Keeping her finger off the trigger of the spear gun, Wendy held it up like she would any gun; aiming where she looked.

Reaching the stairwell, Wendy opened the door and almost coughed as the stench of death washed over her. Suppressing the cough, Wendy eased the door open and slipped inside to close the door softly behind her. Thankful for the emergency lights, Wendy stepped over and around the bodies in the stairwell as she headed down.

When she reached the level she wanted, Wendy froze when she heard a muffled thump below her. Waiting for several seconds and not hearing it again, Wendy gripped the door handle to open the door when she heard the thump again below her.

Letting the door handle go, Wendy rounded the stairwell landing and headed down, hearing the thump several more times. Each time she heard it, the thump sounded further away into the ship as she went down the stairs.

Stopping two levels lower, Wendy froze at hearing a voice. "Come on, girls. I need to play with you." The voice was male and was definitely on this level. "I played with Timmy and now it's your turn."

"Fuck," Wendy breathed out. More than once she had doubted the twins about Anthony but now, she knew they had been telling the truth and not talking about some hallucination.

Gripping the door handle, Wendy gently eased it open. "Girls, you're making me mad. Uncle Anthony needs to break you in," Anthony grunted and Wendy heard the thump again. Now that she knew Anthony was further down the hall, Wendy peeked out the door and saw the doors along each side of the hallway were open.

Glancing further down the hall, Wendy saw a rather round figure stepping out of a room with a long pole. Pulling her head back, Wendy felt her pulse speed up. "I'm going to find you," Anthony sang out and Wendy heard the unmistakable sound of a card being slid into a card slot and a door opening.

Easing up to the door jam, Wendy eased one eye out and saw Anthony walking into a room. When he walked out, Wendy studied him for the first time. The twins had described a hound of hell, but Anthony couldn't have been more than five-foot-five. Wendy knew he was shorter than her five-foot-six.

But Anthony was fat, a very round fat, and balding. Only a thin strip of black hair rounded his head and Wendy dropped her eye back to Anthony's body. She was almost certain that Anthony's girth would surpass his height. Seeing Anthony dressed only in shorts and sandals, Wendy knew that any other time, she would have had to suppress a laugh. His arms and legs while big, were out of proportion with his girth. In her mind's eye, Wendy saw him working behind a desk.

"Timmy loved the games," Anthony said, moving to another door to shove a card in and tried to open it. The door only opened an inch as the privacy latch engaged. Pulling the pole up, Anthony put one end in the opening.

"Oh, are you girls being bad?" Anthony cooed and then gave a grunt, leaning against the pole. The door flew open, thumping against the wall and answering Wendy's question of where the thumps had been coming from.

Wiping his forehead, Anthony stepped in the room. When he was gone, Wendy looked down the hall and saw Anthony was only halfway through searching the row of rooms. Pulling her head back when Anthony stepped out into the hall, Wendy took a few breaths to calm herself.

If she hadn't gotten sick, Wendy knew she could've kicked Anthony's ass with her bare hands. He may have the weight and might be a little stronger, but she and Arthur had both trained in hand to hand. But she was still weak and couldn't just go down there and kick his ass.

Hearing another door open, Wendy peeked out the door and watched Anthony walk into another room. Looking down the hall, Wendy saw a few dead bodies under the emergency lights. "I want to see little twin pussy," Anthony called out as he stepped back into the hall.

A coldness spread over Wendy that she wasn't prepared for when she heard Anthony. Watching Anthony check two more rooms, Wendy glanced across from the stairwell to an open cabin door. When Anthony stepped in the next room, Wendy eased out the door and closed it softly, then stepped into the room.

"It will only hurt for a little while," Anthony chuckled, stepping back into the hall.

When Anthony opened the next cabin's door and walked in, Wendy eased two more cabins down and stepped in the room before Anthony came back into the hall. "You can't hide forever," Anthony said, opening another door and it stopped as the privacy latch held. "It's only us now," Anthony sang out, putting one end of the pole into the door. "I took care of the others, so they can't interrupt."

When Anthony let out a grunt, Wendy peeked around the door jamb and saw Anthony was facing away from her as he pried against the door. 'Blam' sounded as the door flew open and Anthony waddled inside quickly.

Stepping out into the hall, Wendy dodged four bodies and she crept down the hall as fast as she could. Darting into an open door of a room Anthony had already searched, Wendy leaned back against the wall, hearing Anthony step back into the hall.

Moving down the hallway, Anthony started whistling softly and then opened up another door. When he stepped in, Wendy moved into the hall. Before Anthony came back out, Wendy was only two doors away when she ducked back inside.

Not risking a look, Wendy heard Anthony open several more doors, getting further away. When she heard a door being held by a security latch, Wendy peeked out and quickly eased back. Anthony was facing her as he put one end of the pole into the door to pry it open.

When the door gave, Wendy glanced out and saw Anthony was nearing the end of the hall. There were only five doors left on each side of the hall. Moving out into the hall, Wendy again closed the distance, darting into the room next to the one Anthony was searching.

Holding the spear gun in both hands, Wendy stayed back from the door but kept her aim in the center of the doorway. Afraid Anthony could hear her heart beating, Wendy tried to calm down but heard the heavy breathing of Anthony as he stepped back into the hallway, still whistling softly.

In the hall, Wendy heard Anthony put the card into the next door slot. When Anthony tried to open the door, it stopped as the privacy latch held. Lowering the spear gun, Wendy was certain this door didn't open toward her so Anthony would have to face away to pry it open.

Leaning around until she could see out, Wendy saw Anthony's back to her as he put one end of the metal pole in the gap. Stepping out into the hall, Wendy raised the spear gun and aimed at Anthony's back ten feet away as she took two steps closer.

When Anthony leaned against the pole, Wendy squeezed the trigger. The sound of the release and impact were almost simultaneous. Letting the pole go, Anthony gave a cry as Wendy watched the spear sink under his left shoulder blade and disappear.

Stepping back, Wendy pulled the light rubber band back until it locked as Anthony stumbled into the wall and looked behind him. "You fucking cunt!" Anthony yelled out and then gave a cough that spewed blood out onto the wall and over his chest.

Still stepping back, Wendy pulled another spear from the holder on her leg. Putting it on the rail of the spear gun, Wendy finally looked up to see Anthony looking down at his chest. The head of the spear was sticking out from under one of his flabby pecks.

"Damn, you have bigger tits than I do," Wendy said, finally stopping and aiming at Anthony. Judging where the arrow had come out, Wendy was certain she had hit Anthony's heart. She had been bow hunting enough to know Anthony was on borrowed time and she could outrun him with the injury she had given him.

Trying to stand upright, Anthony pushed off the wall only to stumble over and crash into the opposite wall. Very little blood was coming out of Anthony's chest but as his lung filled with blood, Anthony started coughing and spewing blood out.

Anthony took a step toward Wendy and crashed down on his face. Like a seesaw, Anthony's legs flipped up as his belly provided the pivot point. Using his arms, Anthony pushed against the floor until he was on his side and blood rolled out of his mouth.

Stepping closer, Wendy aimed the spear gun at Anthony's face. "I'm a nurse and will stop the bleeding if you tell me where Timmy is at," Wendy told him with her voice quivering in anger.

Spewing pink blood across the floor, "Deck four, room one oh seven," Anthony coughed out.

Lowering the spear gun, Wendy turned around and headed for the stairs. "Help, I told," Anthony coughed out, reaching a flabby hand out.

Glancing over her shoulder at Anthony, "I have to make sure you weren't lying," Wendy told him, walking down the hall. "How many adults did you take care of?"

"Three, but they were already dying. I just ended their misery," Anthony coughed, spewing out blood as Wendy continued walking away.

Reaching the stairs, she headed down until she reached deck four. Walking out, she wasn't surprised to find all the doors open. Rounding the hallway, she stopped at the only closed door she had walked past to see 107 on the door.

Taking out her card, Wendy opened the door and stepped inside. The spear gun fell from her hands at seeing a small body tied spread eagle on the bed. Stumbling back, Wendy started dry heaving. Glancing up and seeing the large wounds on Timmy's young body and the gray cast of his skin, Wendy straightened up, fighting the revulsion.

Knowing Timmy was dead, Wendy eased over to confirm it because she knew that it would haunt her if she didn't. When her fingertips touched the cold skin, Wendy gave a sob while holding them on Timmy's neck. Satisfied Timmy was dead, Wendy pulled out her knife and cut the restraints.

Covering Timmy up with the bloody blankets, Wendy was certain this scene would be in her nightmares for the rest of her life and if there was reincarnation, her next one.

Picking up the spear gun, Wendy stepped out into the hall and closed the door. Narrowing her eyes, Wendy jogged back to the stairs begging God or any power that was listening, that Anthony would still be alive when she reached him.

Reaching the floor she'd left Anthony on, Wendy doubled over as she wheezed from the physical exertion. Bending over, Wendy coughed up mouthfuls of phlegm and spat them on the floor. It took almost ten minutes, but Wendy finally stopped coughing.

Looking at what she had coughed up, Wendy was happy to see it wasn't bloody.

Walking out into the hall, Wendy saw Anthony had moved by rolling on his other side. "Motherfucker," Wendy snarled, heading down the hall toward Anthony.

She came to a stop as a small voice of reason sounded in her mind. 'Don't waste your shots. You might not be able to retrieve them and there could be more like him aboard'.

Freezing in her steps, Wendy stared at Anthony. "Fine," she told the voice of reason and set the spear gun on the floor.

Grabbing her knife, Wendy flicked her wrist and the blade popped out with a satisfying 'Thwack'.

Raising her arm, Wendy dropped down onto her knees, driving the blade into Anthony's neck. Even when Anthony didn't move, Wendy yanked her knife out and buried it again. Crying out, Wendy kept plunging the knife into the corpse.

When she stopped, Wendy saw a divot in the side of Anthony's neck. Pulling her knife out, Wendy stood up and folded her knife. As she clipped it back in her pocket, Wendy noticed she was covered in blood. Not caring, Wendy looked at the corpse with disgust and then saw the tip of the spear sticking out of Anthony's chest.

Stepping into a room and over a dead body, Wendy dug in a suitcase. Grabbing a shirt, she stepped back in the hall and wound the shirt around the tip. Putting her left foot on Anthony's chest, Wendy pulled the shaft out with a grunt, falling back into the wall.

Taking the shirt off, Wendy shoved the bloody arrow into the holster on her leg. Walking over and picking up the spear gun, Wendy pulled the second strap back until it locked. Lifting her left arm up, Wendy wiped the blood off her watch and saw she only had a few hours until dark.

She headed to the stairs and back up to the main concourse. Using a cart, Wendy loaded up water and then grabbed a small display of flashlights and batteries. Pushing the cart out of the store, Wendy stopped at a closet marked 'Emergency Staff Only'. Swiping her badge, Wendy opened the door and grabbed large flashlights, knocking over a stack of life jackets.

After leaving the closet, Wendy stopped in another store and grabbed some clothes for her and the kids. Glancing at the price tag of the shirts she'd grabbed for the twins, Wendy gave a scoff. "Thirty dollars for a t-shirt, are you kidding?"

Filling the cart with other supplies, Wendy pushed it back to the stairwell. Then she headed down to the kitchen. Loading another cart up from the refrigerator, Wendy pushed it to the stairs and then ferried it up to her floor, one armload at a time.

Then, she carried up the first cart she had loaded up one armload at a time. When she was done, Wendy glanced at the end of the hall at a window to the outside and saw it was almost dark.

Walking down to the room she'd left the girls in, Wendy gave the knock and put her mouth near the crack of the door. "It's Wendy," she said in a low voice.

Hearing movement behind the door, Wendy gave a sigh of relief as she stepped back from the door. When the door opened, Jo

Ann and Sally gave a small cry to see the blood covering Wendy's upper body. "It's not mine," Wendy assured them. "I found Anthony and he won't ever bother us again."

"What about Timmy?" Sally asked and saw Wendy's lips tremble.

Shaking her head slowly, "He's…," Wendy whimpered. "He's dead and please don't ask," Wendy finally forced out. Jo Ann and Sally stepped out and hugged Wendy tight, ignoring the blood.

"Girls, I need your help getting the stuff," Wendy said and they noticed she was breathing hard and could hear a wheeze rattling in her chest. They let Wendy go and Wendy waved a hand inside the room. "Get that cart we have inside. I need to lie down."

The girls grabbed the cart and Wendy saw Ryan asleep on the bed surrounded by pillows.

It took three trips to bring the stuff into their room and they still had to use the flashlights to guide the cart around a few bodies in the hallway that the emergency lights weren't near. Ryan woke up as they were relocking the door.

As the twins moved to get Ryan, Wendy stepped in the bathroom and gave a startle at seeing her reflection in the mirror. Setting her flashlight on the counter, Wendy turned on the shower and was happy to hear and feel the water coming out. When the water never warmed up, Wendy stripped and gritted her teeth as she stepped under the cold water and washed off.

Wrapping a towel around her body and another around her head, Wendy stepped out to see the twins playing with Ryan. Glancing around, Wendy smiled when seeing the twins had stacked the stuff around the room in neat piles. "Girls," Wendy said, walking over and closing the curtains over the balcony door. Then turning around, Wendy stepped over to the bed and sat on the corner. "We don't know if Anthony was alone, so you have to help me make sure the door stays locked."

"Okay," Jo Ann replied with a sad expression. "Why hasn't daddy or the others come back?"

"I don't know baby, but we have to wait until I'm stronger before we can risk leaving. Until then, we will wait," Wendy said, reaching over and taking Ryan from Sally. "Was your daddy sick?"

"Yes," Jo Ann answered.

"You're leaving?" Sally cried out.

Hugging Ryan to her chest, Wendy nodded. "Yes, and *we* will leave a note for your dad telling him where we are going because you can't stay here."

The twins looked at each other and then back to Wendy. "Okay," they said together.

"Girls, at night if we have a light on in here, I want those curtains closed," Wendy told them, motioning to the balcony with her chin.

"So people can't see us?" Jo Ann asked.

"Kind of," Wendy answered as Ryan curled up in her arms. "The emergency lights are on batteries and will go out soon. Any light on the ship will let others know we are here. They might be good or they could be like Anthony."

Both girls gave a shiver and nodded. "How long until we leave?" Sally asked, glancing at the barricaded door. "It's really starting to stink."

Looking at the twins with a gentle smile, "I'm hoping I'll be strong enough in a week," Wendy told them and both nodded.

Sally glanced at Jo Ann and then turned back to Wendy. "Are you sure Anthony won't get us?" Sally asked hesitantly.

The smile left Wendy's face as she nodded. "I shot him in the heart and almost chopped his head off with my knife," Wendy answered, making the twins gasp. "If anyone tries to hurt you kids, they will have to step over my dead body to do it."

Jumping up, Jo Ann and Sally wrapped their arms around Wendy as she held a sleeping Ryan. Leaning over, Wendy kissed each one on the top of the head and then stood up. Putting Ryan on the bed, Wendy helped the twins into pajamas and helped them brush their teeth.

When they were all in bed, Wendy turned out the flashlight and crawled in bed. Putting Ryan on her chest, Wendy felt a twin curl up on each side of her. Soon, they all drifted off to sleep as a new world continued to evolve.

Chapter Twenty
Babies and kids everywhere

May 14

Asleep on a pile of pillows, almost sitting up and hearing a soft coo, Arthur opened his eyes. Blinking his eyes, Arthur looked down at Nicole asleep on his chest with Lucas beside her, chewing on his fist. Glancing over, he saw Pam beside him on the bed and kicking her feet in the air.

Looking at Nicole's two-month-old frame beside Lucas's four-month-old body, Arthur turned to six-month-old Pam. "I know you're little, but you look half growed next to these two," Arthur grinned.

Seeing movement past Pam on the other side of the bed, Arthur looked up expecting the dogs and did a double take seeing two-year-old Robin and six-year-old Jim. Both were sound asleep, sprawled out over the bed.

"Wonder when they came in?" Arthur mumbled, slowly getting out of bed with Nicole and Lucas in his arms. Very gently, he placed both back in the bed and grabbed a bottle off his nightstand with a 'P' written on it with marker. Two more were on the stand with 'L' and 'N' already made up.

Giving a big yawn, Arthur picked up Pam and put the bottle in her mouth. Pam latched onto the bottle like she was starving, trying to hold it herself. "Oh, come on, I fed you four hours ago when I fed Nicole and Lucas," Arthur moaned through the yawn.

After chores the last two days, Arthur had taken the kids out visiting several houses around them and then the church he and Wendy went to. He grabbed every bottle, diaper, and can of formula they came across. The nursery at the church was now bare.

Even though Arthur knew he needed the stuff, he was very reluctant on leaving the house. It seemed every time he left, he added kids. No sooner had that thought crossed his mind, Arthur felt like shit and had told the kids to load up. He'd let Shawn drive his Blazer with Kirk and they'd followed Arthur around as he drove the kids in the Suburban.

Bringing back the trailers filled up with the stuff they had gathered, Arthur would tell the others where to unload as he fed the babies one at a time. They had only made two trips out before running out of daylight and Arthur was worn out.

They never found or saw another living person the last two days, but they had seen a bunch of dogs and dead bodies that had been eaten on. Most bodies looked like they had been eaten on by dogs, but there were other bites as well. One body, Arthur was certain had been eaten on by a bear.

Hearing air being sucked on, Arthur glanced down to see Pam had finished with her bottle and was fighting to keep her eyes open. Putting Pam on his shoulder, Arthur patted her back as he leaned his head over onto Pam's. "Give up the burp," Arthur hummed softly with a smile.

When Pam burped, Arthur gently laid her down on the bed as Lucas started fidgeting and getting louder, with his coos turning to angry grunts. Picking up Lucas, Arthur grabbed the 'L' bottle and cradled Lucas in his arms. "Pam cries louder than you do, so she gets fed first," Arthur laughed as Lucas attacked the bottle.

Looking around the room, Arthur saw the three baby beds that needed to be put together with a sigh. "They will be put together tonight," he vowed.

When Lucas was finished, Arthur laid him down and saw Nicole looking at him with wide eyes contently. "Hey, blue eyes," Arthur cooed and scooped her up, making her smile. Feeding Nicole the bottle, Arthur walked around the bed to see the dogs asleep on the floor with the cats curled up next to the Rottweilers.

"Weird," Arthur mumbled. Glancing at the clock, Arthur gave a sigh seeing it was time to get up.

After Nicole finished her bottle, Arthur put her up on his chest, patting her back and Nicole let out her now customary earth-shattering burp. Putting her on the bed, Arthur changed her and then grabbed the baby sling and slipped Nicole inside.

Moving down the line, he changed Pam and Lucas and then put them in bouncy chairs and carried them to the kitchen. Putting them on the kitchen island, Arthur headed upstairs. Tapping on the first door where Shawn was sleeping, Arthur walked in and found Shawn asleep with his sister beside him. Also in the bed was Kirk and Pat. "Shawn," Arthur whispered, shaking him.

Shawn opened his eyes and sat up. "Get the others up while I start breakfast," Arthur said and then left.

Looking down at the bed, Shawn grinned at his little sister. "Beth, time to feed the animals," Shawn said in a soft voice and Beth's eyes shot open.

Yesterday, one of the hauls they'd made had been bringing in over two dozen goats and Beth loved chasing the four baby goats around. "I'm awake," Beth said, rubbing her eyes.

"I thought you were sleeping with the girls," Shawn said, shaking Kirk and Pat awake.

With her hair going everywhere, Beth yawned out. "I wanted my bubba."

Leaning down as Kirk sat up, Shawn kissed his sister on the head. "Let's get ready," Shawn said and then grabbed his pants.

Walking to the next room, Shawn tapped the door and walked in to see Vicki and Jodi curled up to each other. "Time to get up, guys," Shawn told them as he shook both.

When both opened their eyes, he stopped and stepped back. "Arthur is working on breakfast, so come on."

"I'm awake," Vicki mumbled, sitting up and slowly moving to the side of the bed.

"Vicki, we need to hurry so we can help Arthur with the babies," Shawn told her as he walked toward the door.

Glancing back at the bed as she got out, "Where's Robin?" Vicki asked lifting the covers up. Not finding Robin, Vicki rolled Jodi over to check under her.

"I don't know, but Jim left my room around midnight to sleep with Arthur," Shawn told her, walking out.

Heading back to his room, Shawn saw the others up and getting dressed. As Shawn moved to help Beth, Beth took off out the door, carrying her clothes in her hands. "Man, for a five-year-old, she can move," Shawn mumbled.

Walking over to a gun rack on the wall, Shawn pulled down the AR Arthur had given him on the first day. Arthur had taught Shawn how to use it and then made Shawn drill after each meal. Shoving his feet in his boots, Shawn looked over at Kirk.

Kirk was looking at the AR in Shawn's arms in awe. "When will Arthur teach me?" Kirk asked.

"He said soon, so you'd better be paying attention when I drill," Shawn told him. "You've never been around guns and he has to teach you and Pat, so you'll need to pay attention."

"I will," Kirk said with a grin and then pulled on his shirt.

Following Kirk and Pat out of the room, Shawn made a mental note to not look as tired as he felt. The last two nights they had sat around as Arthur had listened to the CB and HAM radios for several hours. Most were people calling out in sick voices for help, but not all.

From Little Rock, they'd heard a man talking about people running around and shooting anyone they came across. Men, women, and children were shot for no other reason than being alive. Other people talked about the raw violence.

One man from Clarksville was on the CB, talking about all the dead in the city and how he couldn't find anyone alive in his subdivision.

Reaching the bottom of the stairs, Shawn headed for the kitchen as Vicki ran down the stairs and flew past him. Vicki skidded to a halt, seeing Robin on the floor playing with a doll.

Walking around Vicki, Shawn hung his AR up and turned to see Kirk and Pat already helping Arthur with breakfast. "I need to feed Lucas?" Shawn asked.

"Nah, fed him just before I woke you up," Arthur answered, watching Kirk cracking eggs.

Shawn turned to see Jodi walking over while carrying a stack of plates and started setting them around the table. "What are we doing today?" Shawn asked, moving over to the counter and grabbing a coffee mug. He had never drunk coffee, but learned it really helped in the waking up process.

"Going into Clarksville to get more stuff," Arthur answered, reaching into the bowl Kirk was cracking the eggs into. Pulling out a small piece of eggshell, Arthur wiped it off on a kitchen towel. "We have a lot to do around here and need supplies."

Spooning sugar into his coffee, "Um, shouldn't we wait?" Shawn asked.

"No," Arthur answered, moving over and helping Pat with the dough for the biscuits. "People aren't really moving around now and I think after the shock wears off they will. We need to be done by then."

"How long do you think that will be?" Shawn asked, then took a test sip. Shaking his head, Shawn headed to the refrigerator, grabbing the milk.

Moving over to the stove, Arthur made sure Jim and Jodi were doing all right with the bacon. "Don't know, but we will hear about it on the radios," Arthur told him.

After adding milk, Shawn gave a smile after his next sip. "I'm tired of getting shot at," Shawn admitted, putting his coffee mug down.

As Shawn started taking glasses down, Arthur looked over at him. "As you should be," Arthur said. "But humans aren't the only thing we have to worry about."

Almost dropping a glass, Shawn spun around and gasped. "What else?"

Moving around the island, "Dogs, for one," Arthur answered, bending over and helping Beth get dressed. "We have to get better fences up for the livestock and one around the house. Dogs have enough food now that they aren't a problem but in a few months, we are going to be inundated with wild dogs."

Giving a long sigh, Shawn carried the glasses over to the table. "Come on, Arthur. They're just dogs," Shawn chuckled.

When Shawn turned around, he saw Arthur stand up and look at him. "Shawn, you realize there were almost a hundred million dogs in the US? Let's say only half were big breeds and the others die off to leave only fifty million. Most dogs give birth to large litters. By winter, there could be over two hundred million. I'm talking about huge packs roaming around. How many could you shoot before a pack of a hundred were on you?"

As his mind went into overdrive, Shawn felt goosebumps spring up as a vision of a hundred dogs charging him filled his mind's eye. "What do we do?" Shawn mumbled in terror.

"They will die out till they reach equilibrium with the environment but I hate to say it, they will see us as food," Arthur told him as Pam started crying. Before Arthur could get her out of the bouncy chair, Vicki walked over. "If a pack wipes out our animals, we will be hard-pressed to make it."

Picking up his coffee mug, "Let's go to town and get three times what we need," Shawn said with a shudder.

Watching Vicki take Pam out of the bouncy chair, Arthur nodded. "That's my thinking," Arthur said and then moved over to check on the kids cooking.

"So, you don't think people are going to be a problem?" Shawn asked, moving over and watching the others work on breakfast.

"Hardly," Arthur scoffed. "But we are way back off the beaten path and they will have to look for us hard, and it's a big world. Dogs and other animals can sniff us out."

"Other animals?" Shawn mumbled, looking up at Arthur.

"Yeah, the day before I found you, someone called over the radio saying that someone had let all the animals from the zoo in Little Rock go free," Arthur said in a low voice. "I hope they won't be able to sustain breeding populations, but I'm not holding my breath."

Nodding, "That makes sense," Shawn said. "They didn't have that many animals in the zoo."

"I'm worried about all the zoos doing that," Arthur told him, moving over to help Kirk. "There is a big cat sanctuary south of Little Rock…"

Shawn interrupted while watching Arthur help Kirk. "Yeah, mom took us there."

Looking off, Arthur gave a long sigh. "Yeah," he mumbled and then spoke in a normal voice. "I took Joseph and Wendy there when we first moved here. Went back a few years ago and it had nearly doubled in size. There were over fifty large cats there and, I know because I asked, most weren't sterilized. I know animals, and those cats can get out of those cages if someone doesn't let them out."

"Whoa," Shawn said, leaning over and grabbing the kitchen island when he felt his legs get weak. "That's not cool," he said, realizing the implications.

Bouncing Pam on her hip, Vicki stepped over to them looking a lot older than her ten years. "But we are people and animals are afraid of us," she said.

Reaching down, Arthur caressed her cheek as he smiled at her. "True, but there aren't that many people to be afraid of now," Arthur pointed out and Vicki stopped bouncing Pam. "Cats in the wild breed at certain times of the year. In time, I think those will as well but until then, they will breed as each litter grows up. The big cats are hunters so they will secure food and when they have litters, they'll have large litters."

"So, we have to worry about tigers?" Vicki asked and the older kids stopped and turned to Arthur.

"In time we will, but there will be other things as well," Arthur said, looking around at the scared faces. "But by then, each of you will know how to shoot, work the farm, and our farm animals will be protected."

They all relaxed at hearing the confidence in Arthur's voice.

Hearing a squeal, Arthur turned to see Robin chasing the cats. "Robin," Arthur moaned. "I just put your clothes on you."

Stark naked, Robin chased the fluffy cats into the living room. All four dogs looked up at Arthur as kids moved around the kitchen and dining room. "Don't start, bitches," Arthur told the dogs and then bent over, grabbing Robin's clothes off the floor. Shawn snickered when Arthur swore at the dogs.

"Robin doesn't like clothes," Vicki told Arthur, putting Pam back in the bouncy chair as Lucas started crying. Before Vicki could grab Lucas, Shawn came over to take Lucas out of the bouncy chair.

"Figured that out in the first hour on the day we met," Arthur sighed, walking into the living room with Robin's clothes.

After breakfast, the older kids helped the younger ones get ready and Arthur put Lucas in a baby carrier. Making sure Vicki had Pam strapped into her car seat, Arthur let his AR hang under his right arm as he picked up both car seat carriers and Kirk opened the back door. Looking down in the baby sling, Arthur found Nicole looking up at him with a smile. "I know, blue eyes," Arthur said.

Vicki got in the backseat of Arthur's side by side with Jodi. Arthur put the baby carriers on the backseat and used bungee cords to hold the baby carriers in. He glanced to the driver's seat and saw Kirk climbing behind the steering wheel.

Looking over at the new side by side they'd hauled back, Arthur saw Shawn in the driver's seat as the other kids piled in. "Make sure they are holding on and don't go fast," Arthur called out and Shawn nodded.

Counting heads, Arthur felt his pulse quicken only counting ten. Counting again as he named off kids and touching Nicole in her sling to make sure he counted her, Arthur again reached ten. Turning around and realizing he was missing Robin, Arthur let out a groan to find Robin standing behind him with her clothes on the ground. "Oh, come on," Arthur cried out, throwing his hands up.

Picking up a naked Robin, Arthur grabbed her clothes. "You keep on and I'm taping them on," Arthur grumbled as Robin giggled and then kissed his cheek. "Let's go, Kirk, but drive slow because we have little ones."

As Kirk followed Shawn down the small road cut in the steep slope to the barn, Arthur redressed Robin who was actively fighting him. By the time they reached the barn, Arthur had only managed to get Robin's panties on. "Fine," Arthur finally snapped and grabbed Robin's sandals, putting them back on her feet.

Arthur let Robin run off as he moved around and watched the kids tending to the animals. Everyone could tell Kirk, Pat, and Jim had done it the most, even though Jim still freaked out when the lambs came near him.

After finishing up with the chickens, Arthur turned around to see a naked Robin chasing the baby goats. "Robin, stop chasing the kids," Arthur called out, looking around for Robin's panties but thankful she still had on her sandals.

"Kids? She's chasing the baby goats, not us," Vicki said, closing the chicken coop.

"That's what baby goats are called," Arthur answered, not seeing Robin's panties anywhere. Giving up, Arthur reached down and pulled a bottle from his cargo pocket when Nicole announced that she was hungry.

"Shawn, grab the nudist," Arthur said, putting the bottle in Nicole's mouth and her cry stopped.

"Um, she's naked," Shawn said, turning and watching Robin chase the goats. "I'm a boy," he offered, but moved toward Robin.

As Lucas and Pam started crying in their baby carriers, Arthur turned to the buggy and let out a sigh. "Vicki, start feeding Lucas and Jodi, feed Pam. Just leave her in the baby carrier and hold her bottle," Arthur said, feeling a headache coming on and the sun was barely up for the long day ahead.

Turning around, Arthur saw Shawn scoop up Robin holding her at arm's length like she was contaminated, he carried her back to the buggies. Really wanting to go back to bed, Arthur piled in the buggies with the others as Kirk and Shawn drove them back to the house.

"Shawn, Kirk, make sure the trucks are full of gas," Arthur told them, climbing out. "Everyone else, get in and stay with your buddy."

Seeing Vicki carrying Pam to the Suburban, "Pat, get Pam's baby carrier," Arthur said, walking over to the Suburban. When he opened the back door, Arthur looked down to see a naked Robin climbing in using the running board as a ladder.

Arthur didn't move until Nicole had given him a burp, then he strapped her in the car seat carrier in the backseat. The car seat carriers just snapped into the car seat mounts and Arthur was certain the person who'd invented it had more than one kid to deal with.

When all the kids were loaded, Arthur started having thoughts of leaving Shawn here to babysit and going to get the stuff on his own. "Can't do it," Arthur finally sighed and let Donald and Daisy in the back of the Suburban. He had already left the kids alone the night before last. Only taking Nicole, Arthur had driven into Clarksville and then east to Russellville to scout. Russellville was three times larger than Clarksville with a population of over thirty thousand, but Arthur had spotted more lights from houses in Clarksville. Since the power was out, lights meant people.

Only gone for four hours, the kids had waited up for him, even after working their asses off all day moving stuff.

Holding his AR to his side, Arthur climbed in the driver's seat and glanced back counting. After counting heads in his Blazer, Arthur grabbed his radio. "You ready, Shawn?" he called out.

"Yeah, I have Kirk, Pat and Beth," Shawn answered. "I put Kit and Kat back in the house."

"Okay, and stay behind me. If we have problems, we are coming home," Arthur called out and then released the transmit key.

"Understand, take back road home and get everyone inside," Shawn called back.

Nodding, Arthur pressed the transmit key. "Tell your guys to keep an eye out," Arthur reminded him, then turned the truck on.

Pulling down the driveway, Arthur reached up and pressed the gate button. He slowed to let the gate swing open, then pulled through. Glancing back, Arthur saw the gate closing after Shawn had pulled through. "Very good," Arthur mumbled.

Driving past Jack and Starlie's farm, Arthur looked at all the stuff parked around the yard; everything from two more skid steers to a mini excavator. Glancing over at Jim in the passenger seat, Arthur grinned to see Jim scan around them with a serious expression.

Looking in the rearview mirror, Arthur saw Vicki and Jodi had their hands full with Robin, getting her dressed. Risking a quick glance back, Arthur saw all three babies asleep even though Robin was yelling 'NO' as Vicki and Jodi struggled to dress her.

Halfway to town, Robin finally gave up and let them dress her.

Passing the retail store, Arthur glanced at the gas station across the street and saw crows picking at the two bodies he'd shot. Next to the pumps was Shawn's go-kart.

Keeping his speed around forty, Arthur kept swiveling his head around but didn't see anyone. "Where is everyone?" Vicki asked from the back.

Knowing each of the kids had seen their families die, Arthur cleared his throat. "Either dying or inside," he told her.

Reaching their first stop, Arthur pulled around the large home improvement center to stop at a large roll up door at the back of the store. Putting the Suburban in park, Arthur looked around before he got out.

Walking to the back-cargo door, Arthur opened it up and let the dogs out as he got his mini jaws of life and moved over to a small pedestrian door. Checking the knob and finding it locked, Arthur put the wedge in between the door and the frame and flipped the switch.

A few seconds later, the door popped open. Putting the mini jaws down, "Donald, Daisy," Arthur whispered and the dogs trotted inside.

The kids all looked around with wide eyes as Arthur followed the dogs inside. When the large overhead door started rolling up, all the kids jumped. Even the babies jumped in their sleep but thankfully, didn't wake up.

Walking back out, Arthur climbed in the truck and pulled it inside almost to the front of the store, stopping at another rollup door that led out the front. Turning off the truck, Arthur looked over at Jim and then turned to Jodi. "You two have to keep an eye out, plus watch the little ones," Arthur said in a serious tone. "It's a hard job, but you can't let anyone sneak up on us."

Grabbing his radio, Jim climbed between the seats and stopped in the middle row with Jodi. "We will," he said with a nod but his six-year-old voice was trembling.

Turning to Jodi, Arthur saw the seven-year-old force a smile as Vicki opened her door and climbed out. Giving the sleeping babies a last glance, Arthur stepped out as Shawn put Beth in the Suburban with them. Arthur grabbed Kirk and climbed on a forklift. Having already shown Kirk how to drive one, Arthur hung on the side to make sure Kirk was doing all right.

Directing Kirk to scoop up a stack of empty wooden pallets, Arthur guided him around the store to drop one off and then move on. The first ones Kirk dropped off, Arthur pointed at what they needed and Shawn, Pat, and Vicki started stacking the items on the pallets. "You have your list for the other areas," Arthur told them and they just nodded.

Then Arthur guided Kirk over to the cement aisle. "Just like you practiced yesterday, put them on the trailer," Arthur said, climbing off.

After watching Kirk load up two pallets, Arthur left to get on another forklift. Driving to where he'd left the kids loading, Arthur found a pallet filled with buckets and boxes of screws. Moving on, he found the kids when he saw the dogs sitting in the main aisle.

"Pat, come with me," Arthur said and Pat stood up, wiping the sweat off his face. Pat ran over and climbed up. He gave a startle when Arthur put him behind the steering wheel. "You drove one yesterday," Arthur told him and then turned to the dogs. "Daisy, guard. Donald, come."

"But you stand up and drive on this one!" Pat gasped with wide eyes as Daisy moved closer to Shawn and Vicki.

"It's the same," Arthur smiled, putting Pat's hands on the steering wheel and moving to the side.

Barely able to see over the top, Pat lightly pressed the pedal and the forklift moved. Letting out a cry, Pat took his foot off the pedal and looked up at Arthur. "That's what you want to happen when you press that pedal," Arthur told him with a grin.

Nodding, Pat turned back and pressed the pedal again and the forklift crept along and Donald walked along beside them. Stopping at the doors that led outside to the outdoor area, Pat was drenched in sweat as Arthur climbed off and tried to push the doors open. When they didn't budge, Arthur stepped over to grab a long pry bar and helped the doors to see things his way.

Leading Pat outside, Arthur climbed up behind Pat and directed him to an aisle of fencing. Helping Pat the first time, Arthur pressed the lever to lift up a pallet of chain-link fencing. "We need this entire row," Arthur said, waving his hand around at the pallets.

"Some of those are barbed wire," Pat said almost panting.

"Yes, and in the next aisle, you will see the metal poles for each type of fence," Arthur chuckled as Pat gave a groan.

When they backed up, Arthur lowered the load until it was almost on the ground. "Lower your load so you can see," Arthur told Pat and Pat just nodded, turning the forklift around and driving back toward the trucks.

After dropping the load off, Arthur rode back as Pat drove slow enough to be passed by a turtle. Donald would take a few steps and wait, then take a few more. "Very good driving because if we break this, we would have to load this stuff by hand," Arthur said and Pat tried to swallow, but his mouth was too dry.

After the second load, Arthur stepped off and told Pat to continue loading. Watching Arthur walk away, Pat felt sick to his stomach as he drove off.

"Holy shit!" Arthur gasped, coming to a stop and seeing ten pallets of cement on the trailer he was pulling. He turned to see Kirk driving from the back of the store with another pallet and stacked it on top of another pallet of cement.

Jogging over as Kirk was backing up, Arthur stopped him. "Where are you finding the cement?" Arthur asked. He'd used this store a lot and had never seen more than six pallets of cement.

"In the back," Kirk said, jerking his thumb over his shoulder.

"How many more?" Arthur asked, turning to the twenty-foot-long trailer. Even with three axles, he could tell it was strained under the weight.

"Fourteen," Kirk answered and Arthur gave a jump.

Giving a nod, "Go ahead and load what you can fit," Arthur said as he walked off. Speaking under his breath, "If the Suburban breaks, we'll just get another one."

Moving to the electrical wire aisle, Arthur started loading up spools of wire and turned to see Pat driving slowly past the aisle he was in. The concentration on Pat's face, one would think he was on the Indy Five Hundred. When the pallets were full, Arthur moved to the front of the store and found Vicki and Shawn loading tools up on pallets.

"Why the little tools?" Vicki asked, holding up a child's hammer.

"For you guys," Arthur replied. "You have to have tools to help me turn our place into a fort that we will be safe in."

"Oh," Vicki said, tossing the hammer in a plastic bin.

Hearing a forklift coming, Arthur turned around and held his hand up, blocking the driving lights from shining in his eyes until the forklift pulled up beside him. "I filled the trailer," Kirk said, but wasn't smiling.

"What's wrong?" Arthur asked.

"I don't think that trailer can carry that much," Kirk admitted.

Nodding at the intelligence Kirk showed, "Very good," Arthur said. "It can't, but we can't afford to make a hundred trips because the trailer is acting like a pussy."

"The trailer is acting like a cat?" Vicki asked, looking up clearly confused.

Shawn snorted, then turned and walked off. "Vicki, load your pallet," Arthur said, lifting his radio. "How are you doing in the truck, Jim?"

"Okay, haven't seen anything. Just finished feeding the babies and they are back asleep. Robin took off her clothes again and we are just letting her play naked in the back," Jim called back.

Shaking his head and dropping the hand holding the radio to his side, "That girl was raised by a nudist," Arthur decided. Lifting the radio back to his mouth, "Very good, we will be leaving soon."

Hearing that, Shawn spun around. "There's no way we can get just the stuff we loaded on pallets on my trailer," he cried out.

"You're right, your trailer will be filled with fencing," Arthur told him. "We will be coming back for another load, just not today."

Thinking it over, Shawn gave an impressed nod at the thinking as Arthur turned to Kirk. "Go help your brother load up the fencing stuff," Arthur told him and Kirk took off. Arthur couldn't help but grin at watching Kirk stretch out his leg and use his tippy toe to push the accelerator.

Moving to another aisle, Arthur saw large plastic bins already on a pallet. Moving his AR so it would hang off his back, Arthur started loading the plastic bins that were on the pallet. Hearing the forklifts, Arthur looked up to see Kirk move past his aisle on the forklift at a walking pace.

A few minutes later, Pat crawled past on his forklift at a drunken moonwalk pace that an old woman with a broken hip using a walker could outrun. "Don't push him," Arthur told himself and went back to loading the pallet.

As the two continued on the forklifts, Arthur found out that for every load Pat did, Kirk did two. Moving to another pallet, Arthur stood up to stretch his back and saw Kirk pull to a stop at the end of his aisle. Walking down to Kirk, Arthur saw Pat creep past with Donald walking and stopping beside him.

"I don't think we can get much more on," Kirk said with a grimace. "I'm scared it's going to fall off."

Giving a nod, Arthur headed toward the trucks. Getting closer, his eyes widened in surprise. The twenty-foot double axel trailer Shawn would be pulling was stacked two pallets high all the way back as Pat dropped off the last load.

Very impressed the boys could even load rolls of fencing like that, "Very good, boys. Turn your forklifts off and let's secure the load and drop it off," Arthur told them and then called Shawn and Vicki on the radio.

Grabbing several packages of straps, Arthur pulled his knife out and cut them out of the packages. Hearing a small cry, Arthur looked up to see Jodi climbing out of the Suburban with a small bundle. Dropping the straps, Arthur folded his knife up as he ran to meet her. "What's wrong with Nicole?" he gasped, locking his legs and skidding to a stop in front of Jodi.

"She won't stop crying no matter how much I rock her, and I just fed her," Jodi winced as Arthur took Nicole into his arms.

"What's wrong, baby blue eyes?" Arthur sang out and Nicole stopped crying. She opened her eyes and saw Arthur and smiled. "You didn't have to throw a fit to get me to hold you," Arthur said and then pulled a glove off with his mouth. Stroking Nicole's face with his fingertips, Arthur felt very giddish to see Nicole smile wider.

"Knew that would work," Jodi said with a nod and headed back to the Suburban.

Grabbing the baby sling from his seat, Arthur put Nicole in it after he'd draped it on. Seeing Nicole give a small yawn, Arthur pulled his glove back on. Being very careful, Arthur showed the kids how to strap the load down. When he was done, Arthur had to admit, never in his life had he seen so many ratchet straps holding loads down.

Walking to the front, Arthur unlocked a pedestrian door beside the overhead door at the front. "Donald, Daisy," he called out softly and the dogs ran over. When the dogs stopped beside him, Arthur eased the door open and looked around.

Stepping outside with the dogs, Arthur very slowly scanned around. Off to his left, he saw five dogs running up the road away from him. The way they were bouncing he could tell they were playing. Off to the west, he heard the faint report of a gunshot and figured it was outside of town and they weren't heading that way.

Stepping back in with the dogs, Arthur closed the door and moved to the roll up door and unlocked it. Grabbing the chain, he pulled it hand over hand and heard Nicole give out a cry from the noise the door was making. "Sorry, puddin'," Arthur told her, but didn't stop until the door was open enough for them to drive out.

"Everyone is accounted for," Shawn told him, standing beside the Blazer.

"Heard a gunshot, so tell your lookouts to keep their eyes peeled," Arthur called out, opening his door. Climbing in with Nicole still crying, Arthur started the truck and put it in drive. When he hit the accelerator, the massive Suburban's engine revved up but didn't move. "Fuck me," Arthur gasped, pushing the pedal down more.

Slowly, the Suburban moved forward while pulling the heavy trailer. Pulling outside, Arthur turned toward the road and stopped, leaving enough room for Shawn to pull out.

Climbing out, Arthur let the dogs jump in the back and then ran past Shawn into the open bay door and grabbed the chains. Pulling the door closed, Arthur pulled Nicole up to his neck as he walked out the small pedestrian door. “It’s okay now,” he said softly over and over.

By the time he climbed back in the Suburban, Nicole had stopped crying and was looking up at him. “Let me have her, so I can put her back in the seat,” Vicki said.

“Nah,” Arthur replied, putting the transmission into drive. Pulling out slowly, Arthur took a different route home. Glancing back, he saw Vicki’s hair was plastered to her head. “You guys are doing an excellent job,” Arthur said, looking around the truck.

“I want our house safe,” Vicki said, holding a bottle for Lucas. “Can I hold Lucas? He doesn’t like drinking in his seat.”

“Sure, we aren’t going fast and we don’t really have to worry about cops,” Arthur said, cradling Nicole to his chest. “I know it’s for their safety, but we need quiet.”

Glancing in the rearview mirror, Arthur saw a naked Robin standing in the cargo area with the dogs. Not in the mood, Arthur just headed home.

Stopping at Jack’s, Arthur pulled near the barn and turned the Suburban off. Looking down and seeing Nicole sound asleep, Arthur climbed out to see Pat and Kirk moving to the track steer and rough ground forklift. Letting Pat take the forklift, Kirk climbed up on the track steer that had forklift bars over the bucket.

The others moved over as Arthur let the dogs out. When he turned back around, Arthur chuckled to see Shawn carry over the cooler. “Guess it’s time for some sandwiches,” Arthur laughed.

“Nah, I know how to make sandwiches,” Shawn grinned as the track steer and forklift fired up.

After unstrapping the loads, everyone gathered around as Shawn made sandwiches. Standing in the shade of the barn, Arthur watched Kirk unload the pallets of cement and drive them into the barn. It seemed Kirk was much surer of his abilities with the track steer and its ability to pivot on the spot.

Both trailers were unloaded before anyone ate a second sandwich. When Pat and Kirk walked up, they both smiled as sandwiches were held out for them. “Why aren’t we heading back today to load up the pallets we left?” Shawn asked as he made another sandwich.

“You think we made noise others could hear?” Arthur asked and then shoved the last of his sandwich in his mouth.

The older kids nodded as Shawn spoke. “Hell yeah, those roll up doors alone were loud.”

“Think of it like this,” Arthur explained, pulling off his gloves and grabbing a bottle for Nicole as she started to squirm in the baby sling. Arthur would feed himself with gloves on, but never Nicole. "If someone comes, they will see stuff loaded. If they are bad they will wait around, but we won't show back up. They can't stay there long because there isn't much food there and they will know others may have heard, so they will leave."

The older kids thought about that as Shawn looked at Arthur in awe. "How long would you stay there?" he asked.

"Oh, I wouldn't," Arthur replied, looking down at Nicole as she drank the bottle. "I would find supplies somewhere else."

"No, if you were bad," Shawn blurted out and then looked at Arthur in shock. "Not that you are," he said quickly.

Laughing, Arthur looked over at Shawn. "I know what you meant," Arthur winked and Shawn relaxed. "I wouldn't wait around more than a day. That building is too big to secure with only a few people. To hole up, you need someplace that's easy to defend and that building isn't it. Anyone with a brain knows there are bad people out there. Hell, even other bad people know there are others meaner than them and will move off."

"What if someone is there?" Kirk asked, finishing off his sandwich and then gulping down a bottle of water.

"We kill them," Arthur said with a shrug. "If they are there, then that means they are waiting. Now, if we see someone loading up, we move on. There's more stuff we can gather elsewhere."

None of the kids showed any surprise when Arthur said 'kill'. They were adapting to this new world very fast.

Chapter Twenty One

Survival is easy compared to taking care of kids

After eating, everyone loaded up and Arthur led them to another store. This one was a smaller hardware store and they had to park along the back. Since there was only one forklift, Kirk started loading as the others pulled stuff over to empty pallets.

With those in the Suburban keeping watch, Arthur left it running since it was rather warm.

The hardware store only had half as much cement and fencing, so Kirk was done loading that rather fast. Then he started on the pallets the others were loading. No sooner than one was loaded than Kirk would scoop it up and run it to the trailers.

Feeling cocky and thinking he had the hang of this driving down, it was then that Kirk knocked over a small shelf. Thankfully, it was small and only blocked off one aisle. After that, Kirk slowed back down and had no other mishaps.

After an hour of loading, the trailers were full. Never taking the sling holding Nicole off, Arthur helped strap the loads down. When they were finished, Arthur turned to Shawn. "This time, you lead us home," Arthur said and the color drained from Shawn's face. "Shawn, you have to know how to get home without me leading."

Slowly, Shawn started to nod. "Okay, but if you see me making a wrong turn, please call out because I can't back up that long trailer."

Reaching over and squeezing Shawn's shoulder, "We will practice that later, now let's get home," Arthur said with a grin.

After loading the dogs up, Arthur saw Robin lying in the cargo area sound asleep, naked. "Don't wake her up," Arthur told the dogs, then closed the cargo door.

It took Shawn longer to lead them home because he drove slower, but he never made a wrong turn. Stopping at Jack's barn,

Pat and Kirk jumped out and ran for the forklift and track steer. Taking the straps off his trailer, Arthur stepped back as the boys headed over and started unloading the trailers.

Helping the others undo the straps on Shawn's trailer, Arthur turned back and saw Pat taking the last load off his trailer. Stepping back as Kirk drove over, Arthur patted Nicole and watched Kirk lift the first pallet off Shawn's trailer.

When both trailers were empty, they gathered up the straps and loaded back up. Pulling over to the fuel tanks beside the barn, they filled the trucks up. It was just after one when Arthur led them out of the valley, heading to Russellville.

It was after 2 p.m. when Arthur led them into Russellville and stopped at another large box chain home improvement store. After pulling the trucks inside, Arthur didn't have to tell anyone what to do. Pat and Kirk took off with the dogs and found the forklifts and were soon dropping off empty pallets around the store.

As Arthur, Shawn, and Vicki loaded the pallets, Pat and Kirk started loading the trailers. Unlike last time, Arthur stopped them before the trailers were completely loaded. Loading up several pallets of plastic storage bins, Arthur let the boys load them up on the trailers and then strapped the loads down.

Pulling out of the store and closing it up, Arthur headed back to the Suburban and stopped. Off to the east he heard gunfire and then turned to hear more shots off to the west. "Don't shoot at me and I won't shoot at you," Arthur mumbled, patting Nicole in her sling.

Climbing back into the Suburban, Arthur pulled out on the road weaving around a few stopped cars. Having shopped in Russellville since he'd moved into the area, Arthur turned off the main roadway he was on and took side streets as he headed east.

Driving through the neighborhoods, Arthur had to weave around a wreck. He slowed and looked at the small car that had plowed into a parked truck and saw bullet holes along the car. The door was open and there wasn't a body inside, but Arthur glanced around as he drove off.

Rounding a curve, Arthur took his foot off the gas at seeing a figure ahead in the middle of his lane, pushing a grocery cart. As the Suburban slowed, Jim called out. "Man at twelve o'clock."

"Good eye, keep an eye out in case he has friends," Arthur said as the man stopped and looked back at the vehicles coming toward him. Grabbing his grocery cart, the man pushed it into the opposite lane. Getting closer, Arthur saw a pistol at the man's hip and what looked like a AK resting on the seat of the cart.

Pulling his pistol out and holding it low, "Kids, get down," Arthur said, reaching over to roll down his window and slowed. The man took a step back, almost touching the opposite curb and raised his hands up, watching the Suburban slow to a stop in front of him.

"Afternoon," Arthur called out, tilting his head but not taking his eyes off the man. At one time, the man had been younger than Arthur, but had aged decades over the last weeks.

Tilting his head to Arthur, "Afternoon," the man said and stifled a cough. Looking at the man, Arthur saw the man's nose was very red; almost shining.

"Not my business, but you should stay off the roads," Arthur told the man.

"Can't drive," the man said, then turned and coughed violently for several seconds. Spitting out a bloody mouthful, the man rasped, "Tried that a few days ago and wrecked when a coughing fit hit me."

"Just saying, we've seen several moving around and shooting," Arthur said, gripping the pistol tight and aiming through the door at the man. Then it dawned on Arthur, the man had been coughing for days and concluded he was fighting off Rudolph.

"You had Rudolph?" the man asked, taking a step back and raising his hands back up.

Shaking his head, "Not all of us yet," Arthur lied.

"Then stay back," the man wheezed. "You're right about groups moving around, though. Saw a group pull a woman out of her house yesterday, but they took off before I could help. Seen you with kids at that store, so knew you weren't a threat if I wasn't."

Glancing at the cart quickly, Arthur moved his eyes back to the man. "You take care of you and yours and drink lots of fluids," Arthur said, impressed with the man's reasoning.

"Thank ya," the man smiled with bloody teeth. "Stay away from the interstate. That's where a group of kids hang out, chasing any that they see. You have kids and they won't care."

"You do the same," Arthur replied with a slight nod. "Please don't grab for a weapon until we are out of sight because the kids behind me shoot first and ask questions later."

The man doubled over in a coughing fit and to the west, Arthur heard the sound of engines. As the man stopped coughing, Arthur barely heard the squeal of tires. "That would be them," the man panted and then spit a glob of blood on the blacktop. "You need to get those kids under cover."

"Will do and you do the same," Arthur said and the man shrugged.

"I'll be dead in a day," he answered. "I've watched too many die after they started coughing up blood."

"You're still alive now, and I haven't heard of many making it a day or two and you have to drink fluids," Arthur told him and the man just nodded. Pulling away, Arthur watched the man in the mirror as Shawn drove past. When Shawn was passed, the man grabbed the shopping cart and steered it back to the proper lane and continued on.

Only when he'd rounded a curve did Arthur take his eyes off the mirror. "He's got Rudolph," Vicki said in a small voice from the backseat.

"Yes, he does," Arthur said, knowing they had all been exposed long before now. "I want both of you to notice how neither Donald nor Daisy growled at the man. They knew he posed no danger."

"They were both looking out the window at him," Vicki noted, looking around at the houses.

"Yes, just in case he became a threat. That's what you do. Keep ready and if someone poses a threat, pull the trigger until they go down," Arthur instructed, driving across a major road and back into a subdivision.

"I saw a car to our three o'clock when we drove over that road," Jim said, glancing over at Arthur.

Looking over at Jim, "Which way were they heading?" Arthur asked and Jim pointed north, the same way they were going. Thinking for a second, Arthur turned right at the next street and stayed in the subdivision. Rolling down his window, Arthur heard the high-pitched whine of engines off to the east getting fainter.

"I heard engines," Shawn said over the radio.

Letting the pistol rest in his lap, Arthur lifted the radio up and pressed the transmit key. "I heard 'em," Arthur called out. "That's why we are taking back roads."

A few minutes passed, then Shawn came back over the radio. "Think we should head home?"

"Not unless we are attacked. Guys, it is going to take us weeks to pull in all the stuff we need to fortify our place. The longer we wait, those that aren't sick will start to group together," Arthur said over the radio and to those in the Suburban with him.

"Like the man who said I had a kitty cat," Vicki said and Arthur felt his blood pressure rise, just thinking about the man.

"Yes, he wasn't sick but wanted to hurt you," Arthur replied in a tense voice and then lifted the radio. "Shawn, just keep your eyes peeled and let's get this done."

"Copy," Shawn answered and Arthur set the radio on the center divider, seeing a large road ahead they were going to cross. Barely slowing, Arthur looked each way as he crossed over the road and back into another subdivision.

Driving slow with the window down so he could hear, Arthur kept looking around as the houses slowly gave away to an industrial park. Pulling onto a main road, Arthur rolled up his window as he sped up.

Turning off onto another big road, Arthur looked over at a large bookstore. "Might need to visit you," he mumbled, driving past. Passing vacant lots, Arthur looked ahead and saw the red and white sign of their destination; a large agriculture supply store.

Pulling into the parking lot, Arthur pulled to the gate of a fenced-off area on the side of the store where equipment was stored outside. Putting the Suburban in park, Arthur climbed out. Leaving his door open, Arthur trotted to the back and opened the cargo door. Grabbing massive bolt cutters, "Donald, Daisy," Arthur said and the dogs jumped out.

Pulling on the cargo door, Arthur trotted off as the door slowly closed automatically. Reaching the gate, Arthur cut the lock and pulled the chain out before dropping it on the ground. Grabbing the gate, he glanced at the bicycle chain at the bottom that electronically rolled the gate open, but Arthur just forced it open.

When the gate was open, Arthur moved around and cut the bicycle chain, then ran back to the Suburban. Nicole opened her eyes up as Arthur climbed in and drove inside the fence while leaving his door open. Glancing in the rearview mirror, Arthur stopped when he saw Shawn's trailer was inside the fence.

Putting the truck in park, Arthur jumped out and jogged back to the gate. With the bicycle chain cut off, Arthur didn't have to fight the dead motor this time and the gate easily rolled shut. Picking the chain up off the ground, Arthur fed it through the gate and fence so it looked like it was still locked.

With all the banners on the gate, nobody could see through it and with all the stuff stacked along the fence, no one could see them from the side. Glancing around, Arthur thought the tops of the vehicles could be seen in a few places over the fence but that was it.

Patting Nicole in the sling, Arthur walked back as Shawn stepped out, holding his AR. Putting the loop of the sling over his head, Shawn let the AR hang down as he helped Beth out. "We are checking the building before letting the little ones in, right?" Shawn asked, turning to the west and hearing engines in the distance that seemed to be racing.

"Yeah, you stay here. My rug rats are still in the Suburban," Arthur said, patting Beth on the head.

Walking back to the Suburban, Arthur grabbed the back-hatch handle and stepped back as the door opened up. Putting the bolt cutters back, Arthur grabbed the mini jaws and headed for a side door. Holding Beth's hand with his left, Shawn gripped the AR and then heard the whine of the mini jaws and grinned, looking over just as the pedestrian door popped open.

"That thing has to be illegal in every state," Shawn chuckled as Arthur let Donald and Daisy inside. Putting down the mini jaws, Arthur followed them inside. A few minutes later, a rolling door beside the pedestrian door rattled as Arthur opened it, making Shawn glance around in alarm.

Realizing he couldn't see out of the fence, Shawn concentrated on his hearing as Arthur walked over. "Let it air out for a second," Arthur said, walking over. "A few died inside and have been shut inside for a few days. Don't think my place of work would be my primary spot to go and die."

"Does it have skylights?" Shawn asked, following Arthur to the Suburban.

"Not really," Arthur said, pulling a stroller out of the back. "We'll have to use the lights."

Shawn watched as Arthur unfolded the dual seat stroller. Smiling, Arthur pushed the stroller up to the back door as Jodi opened it up. Taking Pam, Arthur put her in the front seat and buckled her in. Reaching back, Arthur took Lucas as everyone climbed out of the Suburban holding their flashlights. "Who has front door duty first?" Arthur asked, looking around.

Holding up his hand, "I'm taking it first," Kirk answered.

"Follow me," Arthur said, leading them inside and they found the dogs waiting. Everyone jerked and covered their noses as they walked inside, getting hit with the pungent odor of rotting flesh.

"There are the bins. Everyone grab one and older ones assist the younger group before starting on your own," Arthur said, pointing.

Kirk followed as Arthur led him to the front of the store pushing the stroller. Letting the stroller go, Arthur moved to the door and unlocked it. Pushing the doors apart, Arthur stopped when he had a foot-wide gap. Feeling the air rush in, Arthur turned to Kirk.

"Remember to listen as well as watch, and stand back from the window," Arthur told him, walking back to the stroller. "Anything at all, you call me," Arthur said, grabbing the stroller and moved back into the store.

Pushing a shopping cart, Shawn moved along with Beth and picked out clothes for her. Coming to shoes, Shawn stopped and sat Beth down. Taking off her shoes, Shawn moved over and grabbed some boots as Vicki forced a naked Robin to stay in the shopping cart.

When Vicki had stopped, Robin had tried to climb out but Vicki grabbed her and pulled her out of the cart. When Robin saw racks of clothes, she let out distressed cry and tried to climb back into the shopping cart. Hearing the battle with Robin as he tried boots on Beth, Shawn shook his head. "Glad I got my sister," he mumbled.

Finding a pair of small cowboy boots that fit Beth, Shawn looked over to see Vicki sitting on Robin's back, holding Robin's legs up while Jodi brought over shoes. "That girl really doesn't like clothes," he chuckled and Beth grinned as Shawn put the boots in the bin.

Reluctantly, Arthur came over and helped dress Robin in jeans and a shirt, even putting pink cowboy boots on Robin as she tried to kick her feet.

"Arthur, I hear a car coming," Kirk called over the radio in a panic.

Standing up and gripping his AR, Shawn saw Arthur pushing the stroller back to the front of the store. "Vicki, hold the others here and let me check out where Arthur wants us," Shawn said and Jodi came over to grab Beth as Vicki let Robin up.

Feeling tension from the group, Robin stopped fighting and clutched Vicki as Jim and Pat came to them, pushing shopping carts. Trotting to the front of the store, Shawn slowed to see Arthur open the doors wider. Even as he ran toward the front, Shawn heard the whine of an engine getting closer.

Skidding to a stop behind Arthur, Shawn watched Arthur take the sling holding Nicole off. "Shawn, take her and move to the side of the windows," Arthur said. "The dogs are guarding the side doors so if we have to leave fast, you call them to load up in your ride."

Taking the sling, Shawn put it over his head and looked down to see Nicole sleeping peacefully. Wanting to leave, Shawn did what he was told, moving to the side and Kirk joined him. Watching Arthur step through the small opening, Shawn gripped his AR as Arthur checked his pistol and AR and then moved behind one of the columns that supported the overhanging roof at the front.

Putting his back against the concrete column, Arthur turned to the west where the noise of the engine was coming from. Hearing the high-pitched whine, Arthur knew the engine was redlining. Glancing around the column to the parking lot, Arthur saw four cars, three pickup trucks with trailers, and a minivan.

Pulling back behind the column, Arthur moved to the other side and glanced out, hearing the car getting closer. All of a sudden, a gray car screamed along the main road in front of the store and then the brakes locked up as the car turned and drove over the curb. The driver stomped the gas, throwing dirt up as the car sped over the grass before jumping off the curb and into the parking lot.

Steam was pouring out from under the car as the engine whined, but the car barely rolled toward the store. Finally, it seemed the car had just given up as the engine whined louder, but the car didn't move. Arthur recognized the car as a Mitsubishi Lancer as all four doors opened.

"That's not the trucks we saw," a teen-aged girl cried out, looking at the pickup trucks with trailers.

"They have to be close," the driver shouted, looking toward the road from the way they had just come. "They were carrying fencing stuff and their trailers weren't full, so they have to be close because this store sells stuff like that."

Very impressed with the reasoning power, Arthur looked toward the driver and saw she was a young woman and noticed a boy not much older than Kirk get out of the back with a girl about the same age. "They can't be far behind, we have to hide," the boy said, closing his door and looking around.

As the steam from the car turned thicker, Arthur realized it was smoke and then he saw the car was riddled with bullet holes. At first, he thought the kids were lucky and then noticed the bullet holes were all over the front of the car like someone had aimed only at the engine.

When the oldest girl pulled a pistol from the back of her pants, Arthur gripped his AR tight and stepped around the column, giving Shawn and Kirk a heart attack inside the store. "Play nice," Arthur said, stepping out and the four turned in shock.

"Little lady, don't raise your gun and I won't raise mine because if I do, you're dead because I'll win," Arthur said casually. The girl kept her pistol aimed at the ground as she turned, glancing west down the road she'd just driven off of.

"You have to help us," she cried out, turning back to Arthur. "These guys have been chasing us for the last few hours. Every time we think we've gotten away, they show up shooting at us and now my car won't work."

Glancing at the car, Arthur moved his eyes back to the one holding the gun. "I suggest you move away from your car because that's smoke coming out now," Arthur informed her and the four moved to the front, getting behind the oldest girl that held the gun.

The boy looked at Arthur and his eyes got wide. "He's the one that was driving that big gray SUV with the kids," the boy told the others.

Turning to the boy, "Just how the hell do you know that?" Arthur snapped.

The young woman let the pistol hang at her right side and took a step closer and watched Arthur move the AR in response. "We saw you driving out of a hardware store on the other side of town. We tried to follow, but you kept changing directions. Running through the neighborhoods, we would catch glimpses of you and even found a man pushing a shopping cart. He told us to hide, but said you had passed him," the young woman said very fast, glancing back to the street.

A 'whoosh' sounded and they all jumped and turned to the car as flames erupted from underneath. "I take it, you don't know the ones chasing you?" Arthur asked, lowering his AR.

"They are trying to kill us!" the young woman shouted with tears streaming down her face.

Watching the other three holding each other as they hid behind the young woman, Arthur took his left hand off the foregrip and motioned the young woman forward. When she was at arm's length, Arthur held out his hand. "Give me your gun and get inside," he said, staring at the young woman. She let out a gasp as Arthur continued.

"My kids are inside and they have weapons and two big ass dogs so if you try anything, you won't live to see if it works. If you have other weapons, don't pull them out. If your friends show up, I'll have a chat with them and ask them to leave you alone."

The four stared at Arthur with gaping mouths as he spoke calmly. "Mister, they are trying to kill us," the young woman said slowly.

"Then I suggest you hand over that Glock and move inside. If your friends are rowdy, I'll have to be firm with them," Arthur told her, still holding out his hand.

Glancing back at the kids with her, the young woman reached down and grabbed the barrel with her left hand, then held the gun out to Arthur. "If you hurt us, I swear you'll pay," she said in a trembling voice.

Taking the gun, Arthur ejected the magazine and then racked the slide, catching the bullet in the air. "Little lady, I could've done that before you even got out of the car," Arthur replied, putting the bullet back in the magazine. He slapped the magazine back in the gun and held it out to the young woman.

"Don't you dare chamber a round in that store or you'll be shot," Arthur told her. Not believing Arthur was returning her pistol, the young woman reached out to take the pistol back and visibly relaxed. "Don't wake the babies, now get inside," Arthur instructed, hearing tires squealing from the west.

Shoving the Glock in the small of her back, the young woman led the others into the store and Arthur moved back behind the column. Leaning to the side so his left eye could see the road, Arthur tried to relax while hoping he hadn't made a mistake.

After waiting for what seemed like a year, Arthur glanced at his watch and saw only ten minutes had passed since he'd heard the squealing tires. Dropping his left hand back to the AR, Arthur watched the road in front of the store.

A few minutes later, he heard the thumping of loud music and a small sports car drove along the road and stopped where the young woman had pulled over the curb. There was no entrance to the store off the main road. One had to turn onto the road on the west side to come into the parking lot.

The small sports car stayed stopped in the road and then backed up and pulled down the side road, then into the parking lot. It stopped twenty yards from the smoking car and both doors opened up. Two young men climbed out, both holding AKs. The driver was white and the passenger was black as another young white male climbed out from behind the driver.

"You can't run and we need some pussy!" the driver shouted, looking around.

As the driver reached up and pulled his forearm across his nose, the black man glanced around. "They couldn't have gone far," he said.

"Fuck this, let's find some more bitches," the young male that had climbed out last said and then started coughing.

"We are going to fuck every bitch we see until we die!" the driver bellowed and Arthur stepped out from behind the column, aiming his AR.

"Too late, you're dead," he said, pulling the trigger twice and watching the driver twitch as the rounds punched through his chest. Swinging over, Arthur shot the black male twice in the chest and then moved his AR to the last one who was watching the driver clutch his chest.

Squeezing the trigger, Arthur watched the young man drop, letting out a wail that ended in a coughing fit. As the three rolled on the asphalt, Arthur calmly walked over to aim his AR like a pistol and shoot each one in the head. When he was done, Arthur aimed his AR inside the car and squeezed the trigger and the music shut off.

Kicking the guns away from the bodies, Arthur gave a sigh while looking at the red noses and knew none of the kids were over twenty-five. "Should've played nice, cocksuckers," Arthur said and then headed to the door. "Motherfuckers better realize I'm a dangerous son of a bitch."

Chapter Twenty Two
No place like home

Before walking inside, Arthur glanced back feeling very satisfied as he looked at the bodies of the three he'd shot. Then he turned and saw the young woman's car still smoking as the flames continued to grow. Giving a sigh, Arthur stepped into the store as the young woman and kids stared at him in shock and awe. Not paying them any attention, Arthur walked over to the wall and grabbed a fire extinguisher and headed back outside.

Keeping his rifle low but covering the new group, Shawn stayed behind the group as they watched Arthur spray under the car and up into the engine. When he was done, the flames were gone and very little smoke was coming from the car. Tossing the fire extinguisher away, Arthur headed back to the door as it landed with a loud 'clank' and rolled over toward the three bodies.

The group parted as Arthur walked toward them and watched him step over to Shawn. Taking the baby sling, Arthur looked down and saw Nicole was awake. Speaking in a baby tone, Arthur winked at Nicole. "Did you see me teach those mean boys a lesson?"

Putting the sling over his head, Arthur adjusted Nicole across his abdomen and spoke without looking up. "I talked to your asshole friends and they promised to leave you alone."

Turning away, Arthur grabbed the stroller as the young woman ran up and stopped beside the stroller. "Thank you, sir," she said with sincerity.

"You're welcome, ma'am," Arthur said and strolled past her, pushing the stroller. "Kirk, back on guard and Shawn get Beth outfitted. Start the war with Robin again."

"Sir," the young woman called out and ran up to the stroller and walked backwards as Arthur moved down the aisle. "Do you have room for a few more?" she asked, coming to a stop and Arthur walked past her and stopped.

Giving a long mournful sigh, Arthur's head dropped with his chin touching his chest. "I'm kind of busy with the kids I got," Arthur mumbled. It made Arthur feel bad but he had taken pictures of each kid and printed their names on each picture just so he could learn all the names. A part of him wanted everyone to wear name tags for a few weeks but thought that might hurt the kids' feelings so he never brought it up.

Darting over, the young woman looked up at Arthur with pleading eyes. "Please?" she begged as her eyes teared up and then pointed at the other three. "If nothing else, take them."

Biting her bottom lip, the young woman watched Arthur pull a pacifier from his pocket as the baby gave a complaining grunt. "You would willingly do that?" Arthur asked after Nicole took the pacifier and the young woman nodded. "If you stay with us, you all stay. I'm the boss and what I say goes. Everyone here has to learn to work."

Like the weight of the world had been taken off her shoulders, the young woman staggered back to sit down on a small table. "Thank you," she panted as relief that she had help filled her being.

"Names, ages," Arthur stated, looking at the young woman. "We'll get to the rest later."

Nodding as she stood up, "I'm Andrea and I'm eighteen," the young woman told him and then pointed at the redheaded teenaged girl. "That is Shelia and she's thirteen and the next young lady is Betty, she's ten. The last is Tony, he's eleven."

"Very good, Andrea," Arthur said, grabbing the stroller. "Find Shawn and he has a list of what you need and since you're now the oldest, you get to double check that the younger ones have their list filled," Arthur told her, and then walked away. "You know how to use any other weapon besides that Glock?"

"No, sir," Andrea answered. "It's the only gun I've ever shot."

Hearing that, Arthur stopped and gave another long sigh. "My son learned guns at the age of five. What is the problem?" he grumbled. Hearing the clatter of running feet, Arthur turned to see Robin stopping beside him, wearing only the pink cowboy boots they'd put on her.

"How in the fuck did you get your pants off over cowboy boots?" Arthur whined. Robin let out a squeal and took off.

Holding his right hand flat, Arthur pointed up at the ceiling with his hand. "You can ease up on the challenges anytime! You give someone an easy one like make bricks without straw; any idiot could do that!" Arthur shouted. "I'll take parting the fucking sea compared to a nudist toddler that's not potty trained!"

Grabbing the stroller, Arthur walked off grumbling. Feeling a tap, Andrea turned. "I'm Shawn," Shawn introduced himself and then held out a sheet of paper. "I suggest moving," Shawn advised Andrea. "When Arthur starts cursing at God, he's really cranky."

"Shawn, could you point out and name everyone?" Andrea asked and Shawn nodded and pointed around the store, naming their group. He stopped as Robin, still only wearing her cowboy boots, ran from Vicki.

Hearing an electric motor, Andrea and her group turned to see Arthur driving a standup forklift. As Arthur passed them, they noticed a pallet full of welders was on the forks and Arthur was holding onto the stroller with his left hand. The stroller was following along like a trailer and from the squeals of Pam and Lucas still in the stroller, it seemed fun.

Andrea felt Shawn grab her arm and she turned to look at him. "I'm serious, you need to move. Arthur moves all the time and expects us to do the same," Shawn told her in a low voice.

Hearing the forklift returning, everyone turned to see the stroller up in the air on the forks and heard the babies now laughing as Arthur headed to the front of the store. As he drove past, Andrea saw Arthur was feeding a bottle to Nicole in the sling. "That can't be safe," Andrea said, looking at the stroller.

Shaking the shock off, Andrea moved over to her group and pulled them to the work clothes. When Andrea picked up a pair of women's Carhartt pants, she gasped doing a double take at the price tag. "These cost as much as my designer jeans!"

"Yeah, but they will last twice as long until you can make your own," Arthur said, driving past her very slowly on the forklift. Lowering the pants, Andrea saw Arthur had loaded up a stack of green John Deere bunkbeds. In awe, Andrea's eyes widened at seeing Arthur still feeding Nicole and driving along. Arthur had his left foot out and hooked under the handle of the stroller, pulling it behind him.

"Make my own?" Andrea asked, but Arthur was already past her. "Now that's multitasking," Andrea mumbled as Vicki walked past.

Carrying Robin under one arm, "All the clothes Arthur has on, he and his wife made," Vicki told her and then put Robin down.

"Robin!" Vicki snapped and Robin stopped fighting and looked up at Vicki. "You stay beside me and I won't put your clothes on but leave, and I'll glue them on."

Robin just looked at Vicki with an innocent smile.

Looking at her list, "Am I supposed to try them on?" Andrea asked.

"If you do, do it fast," Shawn answered and Andrea turned to see him pulling up a pair of pants on Beth.

Turning to her group, Andrea looked at the list Shawn had given her. "Everyone, get one pair of cowboy boots, but make sure they have grips on the bottom. Next, get lace up work boots, one tall lace ups and the other short. If you can, get some tennis shoes. When you find your size, get another pair that's one size larger."

Looking up, Andrea saw her group was gone. Turning around, she saw them digging through the boxes. Folding her jeans up, Andrea moved over to the boots, finding her size and kicking off her shoes. Hearing the forklift stop, Andrea looked up to see Arthur getting off and the forklift was loaded with large storage bins.

"Each of you, load your stuff in these and use the markers to put your name on it," Arthur said, pulling off the bins and setting two at each new person. "If you have room get extra boots, pants and shirts until the bins are full."

As Arthur climbed back on the forklift, Andrea saw the others had put their bins in shopping carts. Running to the front of the store, Andrea came back pushing four carts.

Driving to the front of the store, Arthur stopped the forklift and climbed off. "Kirk, I'll take watch, go load up," Arthur told him. As Kirk moved to leave, "Will you take the stroller? I'll come and get the babies in a minute," Arthur asked. "I'm going to glance around outside."

With a big smile, Kirk nodded as he grabbed the stroller. "Pam and Lucas are easy compared to Robin," Kirk declared, pushing the stroller to the back of the store.

Glancing outside, Arthur saw Andrea's car was barely smoking and he didn't see anything else noteworthy. He turned to the pickup trucks in the parking lot. "Daisy," Arthur called out, lifting Nicole to his shoulder and putting the empty bottle in his cargo pocket.

When Daisy sat down beside Arthur, Nicole let out a loud burp that the others heard back in the store. Lowering Nicole down, Arthur let her hang in the sling and lifted his AR up. Ejecting the magazine, Arthur pulled another one out and slapped it home. Putting the partial magazine in the magazine pouch, Arthur stepped through the door. "Daisy, heel up," Arthur said and Daisy followed him out.

Glancing in the minivan, Arthur didn't see the keys so he stopped and again stared at the pickup trucks. Two were three quarter ton with hitch trailers; a Chevy and a Ford. The last was a black Dodge quad cab dually, with a thirty-foot heavy duty triple-axle goose-neck trailer.

Getting closer, Arthur saw it was a brand new Dodge 3500. "Damn, even four-wheel drive," Arthur mumbled and then a grin spread across his face, seeing it was gas powered. He loved diesel but they made too much noise, that's why he wasn't in his truck. Stepping up to the door and glancing in, Arthur saw it was locked and a small flashing light was blinking. Knowing that car alarms were good for a long time, Arthur moved over to the Chevy and Ford trucks and found them locked as well.

Looking around and then down at Daisy to see she was relaxed, Arthur had an idea and went back inside. Pulling out his flashlight as he moved to the office and taking a deep breath, Arthur looked at the two male bodies lying on the floor. Feeling Nicole squirm as the smell filled her tiny nose, Arthur shined the light around the room and saw Ford and Chevy keys on the wall.

Shining his light on the bodies, Arthur saw keys clipped to the belt of one of the bodies and quickly darted in, seeing they belonged to a Dodge. Stepping out of the office, Arthur patted Nicole back to sleep as he moved away from the door and noticed Daisy had stayed back.

"Oh, some guard dog you are," Arthur snorted, trying to clear his nose. Seeing Arthur heading for the door, Daisy followed. When he reached the door, Arthur raised the massive key fob and pressed unlock and saw the lights flash on the massive truck.

With a huge grin, Arthur pressed the start button and heard the Dodge crank up. "I like the automatic start," he mumbled, walking over to the truck. When he opened the door, Arthur stepped back as a blast of heat hit him in the face.

Reaching in, Arthur turned the A/C on full blast and glanced at the instrument panel and saw the truck only had three thousand miles on it. "If that Suburban cost six figures, I don't even want to know what this one would set you back," Arthur said, looking around.

Far to the west, he saw a column of smoke in the air. "That is near the river," Arthur noted, looking down at Daisy. Seeing Daisy just looking around panting, "I know they call it Lake Dardanelle, but they just put a dam on the Arkansas River and the backed-up water they called a lake," Arthur huffed at Daisy.

Daisy just looked around, apparently not wanting to get into the argument Arthur was having with himself.

When the inside of the truck had cooled off, Arthur pulled it over to the front of the store. Putting the shifter in park, Arthur groaned to see the gas gauge at a quarter of a tank. Then he noticed that the meter read 'Auxiliary'. Looking around, Arthur found the switch on the dash and flipped it to primary.

"Suck my ass!" he said, hitting the steering wheel as the gas gauge dipped to 'Empty.' Feeling Nicole squirm in the sling, Arthur cringed realizing he had shouted. "Sorry, puddin'," Arthur whispered, patting Nicole and turning the truck off.

Climbing out, Arthur headed back in and found the kids still packing storage bins. Jogging to the office, Arthur grabbed the truck keys and patted the other body down to find the keys to the minivan. "Wondered who the minivan belonged to," he mumbled after running back out of the office.

Checking the trucks, Arthur found both had half a tank and the minivan had a full tank. Moving back into the store, Arthur grabbed some supplies and a fifteen-gallon rolling fuel can that pumped fuel. Pulling the stuff outside, Arthur hooked up a small pump and fed a hose into the first tank.

Turning on the pump, Arthur grinned as the gas flowed out into the rolling can. He turned to see Daisy sitting down and looking up at him. "Yeah, the other way is faster, but I really don't want to destroy the trucks unless we have to. We might need them," he told Daisy and then waved at the trailers. "If nothing else, we can get the trailers."

After all the fuel had been put in the new truck, Arthur sighed to see he now had a tank and a half. He almost put the stuff he'd used back in the store but instead, loaded it in the bed of the truck. Walking to the back of the trailer, Arthur pressed a switch and watched the ramp lower. "Yeah, I love that," he said and then headed to the store.

Pushing the door all the way open, Arthur went in and climbed on the forklift. Driving outside, Arthur loaded up two hybrid buggies on display that had front and back bench seats with a small bed. Driving back inside, Arthur saw Kirk on another forklift picking up a pallet that held stacked storage bins.

"What are you getting?" Shawn asked, walking over.

Pointing to the back, "Feed. I don't like it, but we will have to bring in more animals and until we can make enough feed, we'll have to use this. They put too much shit in this stuff," Arthur told him.

Looking out the front of the store, "I hope you're driving that big ass truck," Shawn gasped, seeing the Dodge with the gooseneck trailer hooked up.

"I am, Andrea will drive the Suburban," Arthur said as Pat ran over.

"I have my list done, want me to load?" Pat asked with a huge grin.

Climbing off, Arthur pointed at the stacks they needed and then turned to Shawn. "Can you keep watch with Beth beside you?" Arthur asked.

Chuckling as he nodded, "Yeah, I take her fishing with me. Beth listens," Shawn told him.

"Your lists done?" Arthur asked.

The chuckle died on Shawn's lips at the question, but he nodded. "Yes sir, but, um, I hope you don't mind, but I loaded up another two bins for Beth and I. We ain't never had nice clothes, boots, and shoes like this before. I was goin' to ask, but forgot. I'll put them back if we don't have room. I marked the bins," Shawn said nervously.

Stepping over as Pat took off at a crawl on the forklift, Arthur grabbed Shawn's shoulder and squeezed it as he smiled. "Son, you take whatever clothes and stuff you want. In time, we will have room but I promise you, you'll like the clothes we will make much better," Arthur told him and felt Shawn relax before he took his hand off Shawn's shoulder. "I can't make boots or shoes yet, so load up on those."

Relieved he hadn't let Arthur down, "Thank you," Shawn sighed, then grabbed Arthur and moved him to the side as Pat came creeping back up, carrying a pallet of chicken feed.

"Keep an eye out, but stay under the cover of the awning," Arthur said.

"I will," Shawn assured him. "I'll stay beside that column like you did."

When Arthur nodded, Shawn walked over and grabbed Beth's hand and led her outside. Turning around, Arthur saw Andrea going through bins and then closing them up and writing a name on the lid with a permanent marker. Looking over, he saw Vicki feeding Pam, "Has Lucas…," Arthur stopped when he saw Shelia feeding Lucas.

"I tried feeding Pam, but she didn't want me," Shelia said with a smile.

When Andrea moved to another bin, Tony came over and picked up the one she had finished. Stacking it on a pallet, Tony moved back while carrying another empty bin and set it down near a stack of boxes with boots and shoes.

"Jim, Betty, with me," Arthur said and felt Daisy rub against his leg and looked down. Pointing to the front door, "Guard," Arthur commanded and Daisy trotted off to the front of the store. When he looked up, he saw Jim and Betty beside him.

Knocking the electric lantern over, Andrea gave a groan as she picked it back up. Setting it on a bin, Andrea turned and watched Arthur move off into the store. "You know what he's getting?" she asked, glancing back at Vicki.

Holding Pam's bottle under her chin, Vicki leaned back and pulled out a stack of folded papers. Unfolding them with one hand, Vicki glanced where Arthur had headed and then down at the papers. "Stuff for the horses," Vicki answered. "We were only supposed to load it in bins to pick up later, but Shawn thinks we can load it up since we now have another truck."

Standing up and looking out the front door, "Um, I hope he doesn't expect me to drive that," Andrea mumbled.

"Arthur always says, 'just drive slow, so mistakes are made slow'," Vicki quoted as Pam emptied the bottle. "If he tells you, just do your best," Vicki offered.

When the babies were fed, they were laid down in the stroller to nap. Vicki laid a blanket out on the floor for Robin and Robin just dropped down and went to sleep, still only wearing the pink cowboy boots. Leaving Tony with Andrea, Vicki led Shelia out in the store to fill up storage bins.

An hour later, Pat called out that the trailers were full and Arthur gathered everyone up. "I'm leading in the new truck. Andrea, you will be driving the Suburban with most of the kids, so be careful. You will follow me with Shawn at the back," Arthur explained and everyone nodded. "Vicki, you will explain to Shelia how we keep watch in the Suburban. Tony, you're riding with me and Jim, so he can explain it to you."

Tony raised his hand slowly and Arthur nodded at him. "Where are we going, sir?" Tony asked in a low voice.

"Home," Arthur sighed with a grin and then felt Nicole move and pulled another bottle from his cargo pocket. "We are only making one more stop. The only ones getting out are me, Tony, and Shawn. We won't be stopped long and everyone needs to keep a lookout."

Everyone nodded and Arthur told Jim and Tony to head for the truck as he led the group out the side. "I'll open the gate so just drive and turn around but remember, you have a long trailer so swing wide. Shawn, when you clear the gate, jump out and just roll it closed, then we'll take off," Arthur told them as they loaded up in the vehicles parked inside the storage yard. Putting the dogs in the back of the Suburban, Arthur folded up the stroller after Lucas and Pam were put in their car seats.

Closing up the side doors, Arthur headed to the front and closed the front doors. Looking at the trailer, Arthur gave a wry grin at all the stuff piled on. "Just might make this," he said to himself.

Climbing in, Arthur saw Jim and Tony were both in the front seat looking around. Pulling the truck up, Arthur climbed out and opened the yard gate. Holding Nicole so she wouldn't bounce, Arthur trotted back over to the truck and climbed in. Unlike the Suburban or Blazer, the massive Dodge barely acknowledged the heavy ass trailer it was pulling.

Avoiding what big roads he could, Arthur headed north leaving town. As the businesses and houses spread out, Arthur saw the interstate ahead. The exits formed a cloverleaf and an Army detachment was set up in the eastbound exit ramp. Having stopped there already when he had scouted the towns, Arthur had only found four troops there. All four had been in the tents, lying on cots and coughing up chunks of blood.

Pulling to a stop on the road the ramps fed from and ran under the interstate, Arthur glanced around as he put the truck in park. "Jim, keep an eye out and if you see anything, start calling on the radio," Arthur instructed and Jim gave a nervous nod while holding up his radio.

Climbing out, Arthur looked back and saw Andrea had pulled up beside his trailer and Shawn was right behind her getting out of the Blazer. "Let's go," Arthur said, gripping his AR but didn't jog, so he wouldn't jar Nicole.

Following Arthur, Shawn held his AR to his shoulder and scanned the area, seeing several military vehicles near some tan tents. They smelled the stench long before they reached the area. Slowing, Arthur eased up to the first tent and glanced inside.

Cots lined both sides of the tent with bodies and Arthur only spotted movement from one at the other end. Slipping inside, Arthur moved down the tent and stopped at the cot with movement. A young man not even old enough to buy beer was sprawled out on the cot. Breathing shallow, fluid rattled in the young soldier's lungs as the young man coughed weakly, never opening his eyes.

Moving over, Arthur propped him up using pillows from other cots and then placed water bottles on the soldier's lap. "Gather the weapons and backpacks," Arthur told Shawn and Tony as he tried to get the soldier to drink some water.

When the soldier coughed after drinking a few sips, Arthur put the bottle of water in his hand. "You have to drink, but sit up," Arthur said, standing up. "Sorry, but that's all I can do for you."

The soldier never opened his eyes as he continued to wheeze when Arthur walked off. Stopping at three cots, Arthur grabbed the combat vests off the floor and headed for the door.

He saw Shawn and Tony coming back for another load. Moving back to the truck, Arthur tossed the vests in the back and then moved to the driver's door. Taking the sling off, he placed Nicole in the seat and then gently closed the door.

Breaking into a run, he passed Shawn and Tony carrying a load back to the truck. Emptying the first tent of equipment, Arthur pulled the boys over to a five-ton truck and started tossing out ammo cans and other boxes. The boys would grab them off the ground and carry the thirty-pound ammo boxes back and toss them into the bed of the truck.

Jumping out of the supply truck, Arthur helped the boys carry over what he had tossed out.

Twenty minutes later, they loaded up and Arthur led them north. Before they drove off, the soldier in the tent weakly opened his eyes, wondering why he was sitting up. Wanting to lay down, the soldier pushed the pile of pillows from his cot and lay back down.

Just as Arthur drove through the gate at the house, the soldier gave a grunt as his last breath escaped. Nobody knew that the soldier had joined the billions that were already dead and still had billions more to go. The virus was now at its peak, with over fifty million dying an hour around the globe.

Chapter Twenty Three

Preparing for a journey through hell, tickets please

May 16

Standing out on the balcony, Wendy scanned the shore for any signs of life. Lowering the binoculars, Wendy glanced up at the dark clouds of the storm that had rolled in last night. Her fear of tornadoes had kicked into overdrive as the ship had rocked back and forth during the night.

Looking around at the ocean, Wendy gave a shudder at all the floating bodies. The beach was lined with them and several days ago, they'd watched sharks feeding on the dead bodies. Even as she looked on now, Wendy saw a body two hundred yards away get jerked under the water. When the body bobbed back up, a large splash appeared at the body and it went back under.

Turning away from the feeding, Wendy saw Jo Ann and Sally looking at the shore with binoculars they had scavenged up. "Ready for some breakfast?" Wendy asked.

Lowering her binoculars, Sally looked up at Wendy. "I think we're closer to shore," Sally blurted out.

Taking a deep breath, Wendy nodded. "Yeah, I know we are," she said, just thankful that the sea had calmed down and the ship wasn't rocking that badly today. "I'm just guessing, but I think we moved in a few hundred yards."

Still looking at the buildings of Miami and Fort Lauderdale, "I'm just glad we didn't move further out," Jo Ann admitted.

Suppressing a shiver, "Me too," Wendy agreed, watching Jo Ann lower her binoculars.

"Daddy isn't coming back," Jo Ann said in a low voice.

Reaching over, Wendy pulled the twins into a hug. "Girls, we don't know that. I put a note in your cabin so he can find us, but we can't stay here," Wendy told them. "The computer in the bridge shows a bigger storm coming and I don't want to have to travel miles to get back to shore."

Squeezing Wendy tight, Jo Ann and Sally nodded.

After the night Wendy had taken care of Anthony, she and the girls had carried Ryan to the kitchen and found the emergency lights were still on. Reaching the kitchen, they'd found that the freezers and refrigerators still had power.

On a hunch, Wendy had tried the service elevator she had used at the stern and found it still worked. It may have worked, but they didn't use it. Instead, they would load it with supplies and then walk up to their level and call the elevator up.

None of the passenger elevators worked, so Wendy led the girls up to the bridge and found it still had full power. It took some time on one of the computers, but Wendy found out that the ship was only running emergency systems. The computer had given a readout that said those would shut down in fourteen days when the last of the fuel ran out.

That was the only day Wendy had tried the radio. When she'd called out for help, a stern voice had answered and told her if anyone left the ship, they would be shot.

After the warning, each day Wendy exercised more and scouted the ship with the girls, and the spear gun in hand. They even searched the crews' quarters and engine rooms, but found no one else. Searching the rooms of all her friends, Wendy found them all dead, with the exception of Alicia. What gave Wendy some hope was Alicia's purse and small suitcase were gone. All the twins knew was that a bunch of people had left, but not who. Saying a prayer that Alicia had made it to shore, Wendy continued scouting the ship. It was on those scouting missions that Wendy finally knew how they were getting off.

At St. Lucia, Wendy and the others had rented jet skis from the onboard marina and had ridden around, even up to the beach. She hadn't forgotten about it but when thinking of getting off a ship, a lifeboat was always the first thought. Wendy did wonder why the crew hadn't used them, but was thankful because they were there.

Another change they made was clearing the large suite beside them and opening the door between the two rooms. Their room sat at the corner of the starboard stern and the balcony looked over the stern. The balcony for the other room looked starboard or to the right of the ship, if you were facing the bow or front.

Hearing Ryan babbling, Wendy moved inside and saw Ryan kicking his legs in the air from the pallet they'd put him on before going to the balcony. The day before yesterday, Ryan had showed them that he knew how to roll over, even rolling over the pillows they'd surrounded him with. As they had scanned the shore, they'd all heard the thump and turned as Ryan had let out a scream.

Only scared by the fall, Ryan had been okay. Now, if they weren't in the bed with Ryan, he slept on the floor.

Picking Ryan up, Wendy watched the twins pull over the highchair they had moved into the room. "Don't feed him the green beans," Sally grumbled.

Laughing as she put Ryan in the highchair, "Sally, he has to eat and Ryan really likes the green beans," Wendy told her as she buckled Ryan in.

The girls grabbed bowls and cereal and then pulled a jug of milk from an ice chest. Wendy sat down, opening up the baby food jar. "What do you want me to cook today?" Wendy asked, dipping the baby spoon in the jar. Ryan slapped his hands on the highchair and opened his mouth before the spoon was even out of the jar.

"Grilled cheese," the twins cried out and Wendy gave a sigh, putting the food in Ryan's mouth.

"Girls, I've cooked that every day. How about soup to go with the grilled cheese?" Wendy offered as she refilled the spoon. When Wendy had found out the kitchen stoves still worked off stored propane, she'd cooked them one meal at least every day.

After looking at each other, the twins nodded while picking up their spoons. "Okay," they said in unison.

Glancing over at the girls, Wendy no longer needed the barrettes to tell them apart. Even when they spoke and Wendy wasn't looking at them, she could tell which one it was, most of the time. "Sally, you need to brush your hair again," Wendy said and then spooned more food into Ryan's gaping mouth.

Sally gave a groan and then scooped up a spoonful of cereal. "I can do it," Wendy offered.

"You brush hard," Sally mumbled.

"Not as hard as she brushes teeth," Jo Ann said under her breath.

"Girls," Wendy said, guiding the spoon to Ryan's mouth. "You have to brush your teeth, so you don't get cavities. I can assure you, neither of you want me to fix a cavity."

"What about the dentist?" Jo Ann asked.

Refilling the spoon, the tiny bit of joy Wendy had felt left. "Girls, I'm sure some are alive, but the world is changed now," Wendy told them with her voice breaking.

Dipping her spoon into her bowl, Sally just pushed the cereal around. "You think those people on the radio were telling the truth about all the sick people, don't you?" Sally asked in a small voice.

Wendy and the girls had listened to the radio, but never called out again. In truth, Wendy had been hoping to hear from the other dozen cruise ships parked around them. Before the storm, there had been sixteen cruise ships around them. The other ships were about half a mile apart but this morning, they'd found one just a thousand yards away. Also, there were only fifteen around them now. Wendy was hoping when they headed to the bridge they would see the missing ship further out to the northeast, since they couldn't see in that direction from the balcony.

"Girls, what I think is a terrible virus has hit us, killing many and those of us left have to rebuild," Wendy said solemnly.

Slowly, the girls ate because if they didn't, Wendy would feed them and to them, that was worse than the teeth brushings.

"What if the sharks eat the jet ski?" Jo Ann asked, taking a bite.

Looking over as she refilled Ryan's spoon, "Then I won't slow down," Wendy smiled, but even she was worried about that.

With the balcony door open to let a breeze in, they all turned when they heard the soft report of a gunshot. They all stared at the open balcony door. "Wendy, do you think Anthony has friends on the land, waiting?" Sally asked.

Turning away from the door and feeding a spoonful to Ryan, "If he does, then I'll do the same to them," Wendy said with iron in her voice. "I'll kill anyone that threatens any of you."

Hearing Wendy tell them again, Jo Ann and Sally perked up again and continued eating.

After breakfast, the group grabbed flashlights and backpacks. "How many diapers does Ryan have?" Wendy asked, putting Ryan in a baby body carrier on her chest so he faced her.

Leaning over, Sally counted. "Thirty-four," Sally reported. "Do we have to find more in the cabins?" Sally asked with wide eyes. Wendy never let them go inside the cabins, but standing outside in the hallways with dead bodies was just as terrifying to the eight-year-olds. On one scouting trip, Wendy had found the body of a man that had been bludgeoned to death and knew it'd been Anthony's work. So far, she hadn't found the others Anthony had claimed.

"No, we won't be able to take that many with us," Wendy said, picking up the spear gun.

The twins gave a sigh of relief and then moved up behind Wendy, putting on their backpacks. Even though they had been all over the ship, they all were apprehensive as Wendy opened the door each morning.

All of them shook their heads as Wendy opened the door and the powerful stench of rotting flesh flooded their noses. No matter how much they shook their heads, they couldn't stop the smell.

Moving out into the hall, Wendy watched Sally close the door and make sure it was locked. Giving a nod, Wendy moved down the hall toward the concourse. In areas they used frequently, they had moved the bodies to the side, so they could get carts up and down the hallways. Not having to dodge bodies as they walked was also an added bonus.

Wendy stopped, letting the girls go into a shop they visited each morning. The girls giggled, running into the store and pulling off their backpacks. Each one grabbed a coloring book and put it in their backpack. That's what they did after playing a board game each night, they colored.

When they came back out putting their backpacks on, Wendy led them through the ship until they reached a large staircase and headed up. Even though she was much better, Wendy knew she was nowhere near her previous health. She got winded much easier and it took her much longer to recover.

Not to mention, she was still fifteen pounds lighter than when she'd boarded the ship. Wendy's body had always been athletically toned. Now she was thin, but Wendy was just glad to not have the gaunt appearance and most of all, to be alive.

Reaching the upper deck, they all stopped, digging out binoculars and scanning to the northeast. "I don't see it," Sally said, standing on Wendy's right.

"How could a boat that big just disappear?" Jo Ann asked, standing on Wendy's left.

Lowering her binoculars, Wendy turned to Jo Ann. "Jo Ann, there are several ways," Wendy said. "One, it could've been pulled out to sea and be drifting. What's another way a ship can disappear?"

"Oh," Jo Ann mumbled, lowering her binoculars. "It can sink."

Reaching over and patting Jo Ann, "That's why we have to go," Wendy sighed. "We should've left days ago, but I'm sorry I didn't feel strong enough yet."

"It wasn't your fault you got sick," Sally declared, lowering her binoculars.

Laughing, Wendy put her arms around each one's shoulders. "Girls, I'm going to be honest. The reason I've waited so long is to make sure I can fight if we have to."

"I'm glad we waited then," Sally said, putting her binoculars up.

Heading back to the stairs, they continued up until they reached the bridge. Walking in, they found a seagull inside. They had moved the bodies out and had left the doors open to air it out. Sally ran over and the seagull hopped across the room and flew out the door.

Moving over to the chart table, Wendy pulled out a small notepad, reciting the trip she would take on the jet ski in her mind. When she was done, Wendy opened the notepad and smiled, seeing she hadn't missed anything. Then she compared her notes to the map on the chart table.

"Wendy, there is a lifeboat going down to the water," Sally said behind her and Wendy spun around.

Sally was standing on a chair and looking out to sea with the massive binoculars they'd left on the bridge. Moving up beside Sally, Wendy saw one of the cruise ships a mile away lowering a lifeboat. Pulling her binoculars out, Wendy watched as the boat touched the water.

"There's still people on the ship," Jo Ann said beside her and Wendy glanced over to see Jo Ann standing in another chair so she could see out the windows.

Turning back to her binoculars, Wendy zoomed in and could see people waving at the lifeboat as a man climbed out on the roof of the lifeboat. After unhooking the cables that had lowered the lifeboat, the man climbed back inside. Watching the lifeboat pull away from the ship, Wendy gasped while watching someone jump off the ship.

The body missed the lifeboat and hit the water hard. Moving feebly, Wendy watched the body sink and realized whoever it was hadn't been wearing a life jacket. "Why did they jump?" Sally asked, watching the lifeboat steer for shore.

"I don't know," Wendy admitted. "There are other lifeboats."

"Another one jumped," Jo Ann mumbled and Wendy lowered her binoculars.

"Sally, can I use those?" Wendy asked, holding hers out.

Sally passed the large ones over while taking Wendy's. Raising the massive binoculars, Wendy could almost make out faces. "I count seven still on that ship," Wendy said, moving her gaze to the lifeboat. Through the small windows, she could see a few shadows of heads but not much else. "I only count ten on the lifeboat but can't see inside. There may be more."

The lifeboat passed between their ship and the one that had moved closer during the storm. "Should we wave?" Jo Ann asked.

"No, we don't know what's going on," Wendy told her. "They may have left just sick ones on board, but we aren't taking the chance."

Following the lifeboat with the binoculars, Wendy saw a small boy's face pop up in a side window, looking back at the ship the lifeboat had left. The boy was clearly crying as he reached at the window and back toward the ship. A man came up behind the boy, pulling him away from the window and the boy kicked and fought the man until Wendy lost sight of them.

Moving her binoculars to the ship that had drifted closer, Wendy gave a startle to see two men standing outside of the bridge, looking at the lifeboat with binoculars. "People on the ship that got closer," Wendy announced. "Look up at the bridge."

When the radio squawked behind them, they all jumped. "Lifeboat that just passed between the two ships, don't head for the city," a female voice called out in panic. "We had a group put to shore two days ago and three were shot."

"We have two that we sent ashore last night waiting," a male voice answered. "There is a storm coming that could develop into a hurricane."

Looking over at the monitor that showed a satellite image, Wendy saw the glob was closer but wasn't kidding herself, she wasn't a meteorologist. Watching the two men on the bridge of the ship, a woman soon joined them as they all watched the lifeboat slowly make its way to shore.

"Lifeboat, you had two people jump, why didn't you help?" the female voice asked.

"All left on board are sick and anyone that's sick is shot on sight," the male voice responded.

"When do you think the storm will hit?" the female asked.

A few minutes passed before the male voice answered. "Two days but even if it doesn't, it will send high seas here. That's what pulled the Emerald out to sea last night."

The female called out several more questions, but the man never answered. Jo Ann jumped off the chair and was heading for the door when Wendy ran over and grabbed her arm. "Let's go out the other door, so they can't see us," Wendy suggested, motioning to the other ship that now had six people watching the lifeboat.

Grabbing the girls by the hand, Wendy led them out the starboard side to keep the bridge between them and the other ship. They raised their binoculars and followed the lifeboat. Wendy had expected the lifeboat to head for a marina to dock, but the boat just headed straight for a grassy beach.

From a mile away, they watched thirteen people get off the lifeboat and even though they were a mile away, Wendy could tell over half were kids. "That ship is bigger than ours and I didn't count more than twenty people," Wendy said, talking to herself. Lowering the binoculars, Wendy chewed on her bottom lip. "We had almost forty-five hundred on board. Let's say they had five thousand," Wendy mumbled doing the math.

"Shit!" Wendy gasped softly as the numbers filled her mind.

"What?" Jo Ann asked, finally lowering her binoculars.

"This flu has killed most of mankind, if it's this bad onshore," Wendy said and then looked down at Ryan as he woke up. "I need a bottle," Wendy said, walking back into the bridge.

The twins followed and Jo Ann turned around and Sally dug inside Jo Ann's backpack to pull out a bottle. "Here," Sally sang out with a smile.

Pulling Ryan out of the pack carrier, Wendy sat down and fed Ryan his bottle as the twins moved back to the windows to look at the other ships. "I see people on the other ships," Sally said.

"All the people from the ship beside us have gone inside," Jo Ann announced.

Before anyone could ask anything, a loud thumping and clanking sounded over the water. Knowing that sound, Wendy jumped up in panic and looked at the consoles around the bridge. "What is that? I've heard it before," Jo Ann asked, still looking at the ship beside them.

"They are pulling their anchors in," Wendy panted, setting Ryan's bottle down and touched one of the screens. When she found a touchscreen for the anchors, Wendy heard a deep rumble over the anchors being pulled in.

She turned to the ship beside them, praying it wouldn't get any closer. "Do they know how to drive that?" Sally asked in a very worried voice.

"Girls, we head to the first lifeboat at the bottom of the stairs if that boat heads this way," Wendy said, grabbing Ryan's bottle as he cried. He stopped when Wendy put the bottle in his mouth.

They were all watching as two anchors were slowly pulled out of the water. The boat beside them was pointed to land, but black smoke belched out of the stacks as the ship pivoted, turning north away from them.

"Can we do that?" Sally asked in wonder.

"No," Wendy said flatly. "If they hit something with their bottom, they'll sink. If they run aground, the boat could tip over. Let's stick to our plan."

They watched the ship pull two miles further out to sea and head north. Before the ship was gone, they watched lifeboats from two other ships drop down and head to shore. When Ryan was asleep, Wendy put him back in the pack carrier.

"Girls, let's get our stuff ready and then eat," Wendy told them and the girls jumped off the chairs, putting their binoculars up.

After stopping in the kitchen for a snack, Wendy led them down into the hold to the onboard marina. The only light now came from the emergency lights, so they all carried flashlights just in case. When Wendy walked into the large bay, she sighed while looking at the rows of jet skis.

Jo Ann pulled a blanket out of Sally's pack and spread it out and Wendy put Ryan down, then put her spear gun on the counter before moving over to the first jet ski in the rack. It was the same one she had driven already. It had carried her, Gloria, and Alicia with no problems so she was certain with the twins, she wouldn't have a problem.

Pulling the lift over, Wendy hooked it up and pressed the controller and gave a groan when the motor didn't turn on to lift the craft up off the rack. Grabbing the chain, Wendy started pulling and just as she'd feared, the grinding of the chain woke Ryan up.

Pausing, Wendy glanced over to see Sally run over to Ryan and lay down with him on the blanket. With Ryan tended to, Wendy continued until the craft was up. Moving over to the craft, Wendy pushed and guided the lift over to the closed bay door.

A ramp was in front of the door with several V grooves formed along the ramp to guide the jet skis out to the water. When the door was opened the ramp was hand-cranked, extending it to the water. Wendy was just happy she had watched the workers because they'd all spoken Filipino, so she couldn't ask them.

Seeing Wendy struggling to move the jet ski, Jo Ann ran over and tried to help. It took some serious effort, but they managed to get the craft over the ramp. "See that groove?" Wendy asked, panting hard.

Jo Ann looked at the ramp and then at the bottom of the craft and realized the bottom of the jet ski would fit in the groove. "It needs to come more to the right," Jo Ann told her.

"When I lower the jet ski, you pull and guide it and it will set down into it," Wendy panted, wiping sweat off her face.

As Wendy started to lower the craft, Ryan cried out as the chain woke him up again. "Sorry, Ryan," Wendy called out but didn't stop. When the jet ski slipped into the groove, Wendy wanted to cheer but she was exhausted. "Should've started this sooner," she mumbled, trying to catch her breath.

Walking over to the counter, Wendy saw the key box on the wall was closed and locked. "This is starting to piss me off," Wendy moaned, looking through the desk and finding several keys, but none fit. Giving up, Wendy walked over to a toolbox and dug around until she came up with a crowbar.

"Here's a key," she grinned and then grabbed a hammer. Luckily for Ryan, Wendy didn't need the hammer as she popped the box open. Glancing at the jet ski and making sure she had the right number, Wendy grabbed the key with the number eight. Feeling exhausted, Wendy stuck the key in and turned it on. Seeing the gas tank was full, Wendy gave the key another turn, and the engine fired right up.

Quickly turning the motor off, Wendy left the key in the ignition and headed back to the desk. Grabbing the keys she'd found, Wendy moved back to a walk-in cage that held wetsuits and scuba gear. Finding a key that unlocked the cage, Wendy gave a silent thank you as she opened the door.

Already knowing her size but knowing she was smaller now, Wendy grabbed the size below it and moved around to a rack that held kid sizes. Grabbing one, Wendy turned to call for Jo Ann but found Jo Ann behind her. "Let's see if this fits," Wendy said, holding it up to Jo Ann.

"I thought we were riding. Why are we getting diving suits?" Jo Ann asked as Wendy pulled another one out and held it against Jo Ann's body.

"We will be riding over ten miles and this will keep us from getting cold," Wendy said satisfied. "Try this one on."

Kicking her shoes off, Jo Ann stripped down as Wendy moved over and grabbed diving shoes in the girls' size. Moving back over, Wendy helped Jo Ann pull on the neoprene suit and zipped up the back. "Very nice," Wendy nodded and then bent down, putting the shoes on Jo Ann and zipped them up.

"How do the shoes feel?" Wendy asked.

"Flat," Jo Ann answered.

Laughing, Wendy moved over and grabbed a suit in the same size for Sally. "They weren't meant to run in, so that's okay," Wendy said.

Jo Ann looked down at the black and blue suit and then at her bare arms. The suit was armless.

Coming over with diving gloves, Wendy tried several pairs until she found a size for Jo Ann. When Wendy went to get a second pair, it hit her how easy it was fitting the girls. She only needed one of them.

Grabbing a duffel bag, Wendy loaded it with their stuff and walked over to find Sally keeping Ryan entertained. "Let's eat," Wendy said, still breathing hard but not gasping.

Jo Ann picked up her clothes off the floor and picked the spear gun up off the counter. Wendy had taught them how to use it and had even let them shoot it at pillows, but the weapon sent shivers down Jo Ann's spine just looking at it. After Wendy had Ryan in the baby pack, Jo Ann held up the spear gun like it was about to jump out of her hands and kill them all.

Giving Jo Ann a wry smile, Wendy took the spear gun. "Don't be afraid," Wendy said.

"I'm trying," Jo Ann said, putting her backpack on. Jo Ann stepped over and helped Sally lift the duffel bag with Sally's and Wendy's boots, suits, and gloves.

When they reached the kitchen, Wendy wasn't in the mood to cook much more than soup. Finding cans of tomato soup, Wendy carried them over to the stove and grinned, seeing Sally and Jo Ann already starting on the grilled cheese. "If I would've known how easy it was to make grilled cheese, I would've made them at home," Sally said, spreading butter on slices of bread.

"We got in trouble boiling eggs for Easter," Jo Ann smirked. The first time Wendy had cooked, the twins had looked at her like Wendy held some magical power.

"How about tomato soup with the grilled cheese?" Wendy asked and the twins made not so pleasant faces. "Tell you what, if you try it and don't like it, you'll never have to eat it again," Wendy offered and the twins nodded.

With their food prepared, they put it on a cart to move to their rooms and ate. To the surprise of the twins, tomato soup went very well with grilled cheese.

Chapter Twenty Four

The team decides who is a member

May 16

Carefully working under the microscope, Sutton gave a startle as Sarah's voice came over the intercom. "Dr. Sutton, I need to see you in the ready area now," Sarah called out. "Please, it's an emergency," she added and Sutton lifted his head up from the microscope.

He looked around the lab and noticed everyone else was looking up at the window that overlooked the labs. Even looking through the face plates on the suits, Sutton could tell the faces were worried. Like him, they'd heard Sarah's voice trembling.

Dr. Skannish came over, pushing Sutton out of the way. "Where are you at?" Skannish asked.

"Prepping a second batch of eggs," Sutton answered, stepping back as Skannish picked up the pipettes Sutton had been using.

"I'll finish this, go see what's bothering her," Skannish said, bending over the microscope. "Sarah showing emotions of worry upsets the natural order of the universe."

Disconnecting his suit from the air hose, Sutton headed for the decontamination chamber. Closing the door, Sutton held up his arms as the shower started. When he walked out, he found Sarah waiting on him, clearly worried.

"The flu is inside the complex," Sarah blurted out and Sutton stumbled back, hitting the outer chamber door.

"How?" he gasped, pulling the suit off. "I've looked at the filtration system and the decontamination procedures of stuff that's brought inside. Nobody is allowed inside for twenty days and are held in quarantine."

Nodding, Sarah came over and helped Sutton take off the suit. "I know, but the first ones to come down with the flu were part of the base crew that mans the installation. Homeland and the FBI retraced their guard routes and found that some were going outside to smoke. At one entrance, they found dead pigeons right outside the door."

Feeling lightheaded, Sutton moved over and sat down in a chair. "How many infected inside?" he asked.

"So far over four hundred, but the testing has only started and there are over five thousand in the main bunker and fifteen hundred troops in the outside bunker. So far, they haven't found any infected among them," Sarah said, sitting down. "I know the team has had minimal contact, but we have to test them."

Looking up at Sarah, "You've had more contact with others than we have," Sutton said fearfully. "I need to test you," he added, quickly moving to get up.

Reaching out, Sarah stopped him. "I showed negative," she said and Sutton gave a sigh of relief. "I have to admit, getting attached to the team probably saved my life. Since you and the team don't like leaving to eat and I never know when I can get any of you out of the lab, that's why I've prepared your food in the office."

"I'm glad you got the president to let us do the conferences via video," Sutton mumbled and then looked up. "The president?"

"Not infected, but several others on his cabinet were, so everyone is in isolation. He wants to talk to you," Sarah said, grabbing a test kit off the table beside her.

Watching Sarah open the kit up, Sutton gave a nervous chuckle. "Turns out smoking is dangerous for everyone."

Uncapping a swab, Sarah inserted it in Sutton's nose and then pulled it out and put it in a test tube, breaking it off and closing the top. "You do that rather well," Sutton said, clearly impressed.

"Well, you go and get me promoted to the upper ranks of the CDC, I'd better know how to do some of this stuff," Sarah grinned, putting the tube in the rack. "The only contact the others have had with the outside are the guards at the entrance to the lab and private quarters. I thought I was going to have to beat Skannish yesterday just to get him out of the lab to eat."

Sutton grinned, "Tapping on the observation window with a baseball bat did have some effect."

"It was all I could think of," Sarah shrugged.

Dropping the grin, Sutton asked. "Sarah, may I ask you a question?" When Sarah nodded, "Why aren't you wearing a mask? You know you're not infected, but we could be."

"I know you're not, but if this team is sick, my team, I go with them," she said with a straight face.

Jerking his head to the table, "Well, I'm not," Sutton told her and Sarah glanced over to see the liquid was still clear.

Getting up, "We need to brief the president and then test the rest of the team," Sarah told him, holding out a hand. Sutton grabbed her hand and she pulled him up. Letting her hand go, Sutton followed Sarah to her office. Walking in, he grinned at the large fridge, hot plate, and microwave that Sarah had put in the day she'd been promoted just so she could cook for the group.

"Not many bosses cook for their team," Sutton chuckled, walking around the desk and sitting in one of the chairs.

"All of you better be happy I took classes," Sarah told him, dropping in her chair. Tapping the keyboard, the two monitors came to life. On one screen was the President, looking at them and the other was subdivided into multiple sections, showing the rest of the cabinet. Even though he didn't know all of them, Sutton could tell there were missing faces.

"Dr. Sutton, please tell me you have some good news," the President cried out.

"Yes sir. The first batch for testing is nearly ready. We'll start testing in twenty-four hours," Sutton answered and the President gave a very relieved sigh before dropping back into his chair. "All the preliminary information looks good and it's a viable vaccine."

"You and that team are owed a debt that can never be repaid," the President told him.

"Mr. President, you have to understand, this vaccine works like any other. It will take those given the shots up to fourteen days to develop antibodies. If they get the virus before then, they will still get hit with the full lethality," Sutton explained.

Holding his hands up, "I understand," the President said. "Dr. Sutton, we are getting reports from outside of unprecedented violence. Is there any way the virus could be the cause?"

"Not by altering the brain, if that's what you mean," Sutton answered. "But sir, you have to understand, people have watched masses die; including family. That is enough to push many past the breaking point. If you have the time, I have a report from a psychiatrist and two psychologists that have done follow-up work after an outbreak. They show a clear correlation between deaths from the outbreak and the increase in violence afterwards."

"I've read that one," Paterson said and Sutton looked over at the subdivided screen and saw Paterson's tiny image in the upper right corner. "We had them do another study after Katrina and Sandy to draw up strategies in other disasters."

"Paterson, send both to me," the President said and then looked at the camera. "Dr. Sutton, the reason I mention it is because our troops have been attacked in the field. We've had to pull out of all major cities. Across the globe, it's much worse."

Sarah cleared her throat, interrupting, "Yes, Mr. President. I've just compiled a report that third world countries will have a one in fifty survival rate. Even though they have the knowledge to live off the land, they have become dependent on foreign aid. The secondary diseases from unclean drinking water will hit them hard over the next year."

"I see you are taking your position by the horns, so to speak. Sarah, I'm very pleased," the President smiled. "Are the new numbers Dr. Sutton gave us holding up?"

"Yes sir. In North America by next year, there will only be four to six million people. From our current projections, in two years the population will continue to fall for another year by half. Before the epidemic, there were almost eighty people for every square mile of the US. In two years, it will be less than one. By then, people will learn to sustain themselves. In two years, the global population will be under half a billion, but we don't think it will fall much lower. As the current predictions are, the way of life we once knew won't be attained for over a century."

"Sarah, we had over a hundred troops attacked and wiped out near Boston. What I need to know is, will this change with the vaccine?" the President asked.

Looking at the screen in shock, Sarah slowly looked down and shuffled the stack of papers she was holding. "Mr. President, they've watched their world destroyed in front of their eyes. The numbers we have right now suggest only one in five of survivors is an adult over the age of eighteen. We just passed the peak death rate here in the states with a projected twenty million dying an hour. That number will continue to fall drastically, since there won't be anyone left to infect," Sarah summarized from the papers.

"Sarah," the President snapped. "Will the vaccine stop the violence we are facing?"

Looking back up at the screen, "No, sir," Sarah answered. "Just the opposite. Once they know we have it, reports suggest others will attack to make sure they get a dose."

"Thank you," the President smiled. "What are your projections of those not infected right now?"

"Less than twenty million," Sarah answered.

"Paterson, that sound near your numbers?" the President asked.

"Yes, Mr. President, but there won't be anyone on the North American continent that hasn't been exposed by winter. Current projections have over sixty million mobile-infected in the US. I've ordered what troops we have to pull back to isolated areas. As of right now, only this facility, along with Groom Lake are running. We lost our bunker in Virginia to a group of civilians trying to get inside," Paterson read and then looked up at the camera. "We have confirmed Diego Garcia has been lost, along with two of our carriers. The sub fleet has remained intact, but our forces as of now are under twenty percent. And will drop to ten percent before the flu runs its course."

"Dr. Sutton, how long to put this vaccine into large scale production?" the President asked.

Sutton glanced at Sarah and then back to the screen. "Mr. President, we would have to seize a manufacturing plant to do that. We are setting up here in the labs to do what we can. If this vaccine works, we will be able to produce a hundred a day. But that's only if we can keep getting eggs from those chickens that the troops are protecting topside," Sutton explained. "We lose those chickens, and we are done."

"Mr. President," Paterson interrupted. "I've sent you a report outlining this. After key cabinet personal are vaccinated, we'll need those troops topside vaccinated and then let it filter down."

"Agreed," the President said. "What's the news inside?"

"Not good," Paterson sighed. "We are still testing but so far, almost a thousand have tested positive. If the numbers continue to hold, over two thousand inside the main bunker will be positive. We are trying to come up with a way to feed the rest, who are isolated in their rooms until we can vaccinate them."

"That won't work," Sutton said, leaning toward the camera. "When I got here, I looked at the air system. That large main complex with all the stores and apartments doesn't filter the air inside as it's circulated around. Only the air systems at the presidential complex and this lab complex do that. Everyone in that main complex will be exposed and eventually infected unless they are naturally immune."

The President nodded, "Thank you, Dr. Sutton. Sarah, I expect daily reports, by video of course."

"Yes sir," Sarah said with a nod and the screens blinked as the feed was cut.

Pushing up from his chair, "Come on, we have to tell the others," Sutton sighed.

As she got up, Sarah turned to Sutton. "The president was asking very troublesome questions," Sarah admitted, as Sutton headed for the door.

"Yes, he was," Sutton said, opening the door. "My guess is he's going to use the vaccine to force compliance on those who receive it."

Following Sutton out, "It makes sense, but it's wrong," Sarah mumbled as Sutton stopped at the intercom, telling everyone they needed to come out for a meeting. After listening to Skannish yell for five minutes, Sarah stepped over to the wall to open a fire station and pull a fireman's axe out. Walking over to the window, she tapped the blade lightly against the thick glass.

Skannish gave a yelp and took off running for the decontamination chamber. Putting the axe back, "I feel so bad when I threaten Skannish," Sarah admitted with a sigh.

Laughing, "I don't, that old fart has yelled at me for decades," Sutton told her.

They met the team in the dressing area and told them what was going on. As Sarah spoke, she watched each member of the group test themselves and all were negative. "Best case is twenty days before we can start handing out vaccines," Skannish blurted out.

Rolling her eyes, Sarah walked over to a small fridge and pulled out a tray of sandwiches. "Dr. Skannish, you will eat two of these because when your blood sugar gets low, I want to strangle you with a yo-yo," Sarah growled, putting the tray in front of him. Looking up at Sarah behind his thick glasses, Skannish tried to scoot back, running his eyes over Sarah for a yo-yo.

Hooking her foot around one of the legs of the chair Skannish was sitting in, "I ran track and always placed. I also had three older brothers. I promise, I can catch you," Sarah said, narrowing her eyes. "Don't think I won't force feed you."

Reaching out, Skannish grabbed a sandwich and took a bite. As he chewed, Sarah reached over the table grabbing a napkin and putting it in his hand. Walking over to the coffee pot, Sarah poured a cup as the others on the team dove over the table to grab sandwiches before she started on them.

Walking back over to the table, Sarah smiled at everyone to see they were eating. Putting the cup of coffee she'd just fixed in front of Skannish, "Just like you like it," Sarah smiled as Skannish shoved the last of his sandwich in his mouth. "Don't choke," Sarah told him as she patted his cheek.

"How are we for supplies before we have to go out?" Sutton asked.

"For regular people about two weeks but for this group, we can go three with ease," Sarah answered. "But the troops can resupply us from storage."

Feeling much better after his second sandwich, Skannish drained his coffee. "I have shoes older than you," he mumbled with a grin as he got up and headed over to the coffee pot. "Well, seems like as good a time as any," he called over his shoulder, refilling his cup. "I have seventeen vaccines ready for trial."

"The eggs were just put in for incubation!" Sutton shouted. "How in the hell did you manage that?"

"Used the human DNA based bacteria cell cultures," Skannish shrugged. "That's why I only have seventeen. Had to use some on mice twelve days ago and exposed them on day eight. Antibody response was immediate."

"That's not in your reports!" Sarah mumbled with shock.

"Sorry, but working under Scott has taught me to hide some of my work," Skannish said, glancing over at Sutton. "He doesn't like me going off on my own, wasting resources."

"What's the production rate?" Sarah asked, moving to a table and sitting down.

"The culture set puts out enough for one shot every four days," Skannish answered, walking back to the table. "That's all we have and I got that from Atlanta before we left. Even with what they have, we could make one shot every two hours. Sorry, but I was working on this because the virus was so lethal to chickens. Since I was almost done when we got some chickens that were immune, I just continued on the side."

"How certain are you that it works?" Sarah asked.

Setting his coffee cup down, "I took my shot six days ago," Skannish answered. "I tested for antibodies this morning and have them. By day ten, I should have full antibody response."

"You tested negative!" Sarah gasped.

"Sarah, as our boss you should know, getting the shot doesn't give you the flu. We only inject pieces of the flu that we've killed. You don't spread the flu with the shot. The only downside is if the shot doesn't work on what's going around," Skannish grinned.

Rolling her eyes, "I know how it works. I've read so much on virology, I want a damn degree," Sarah huffed, throwing up her arms. She looked around at Sutton and Skannish, then to the five other researchers.

"If everyone agrees, let's get the team vaccinated," Sarah said, looking each person in the eyes. "All it would take is for someone that was infected to burst in here and without this group, there isn't a hope. That means the president will have ten vaccines to give out."

Sutton looked around the room and then back to Sarah. "I know you can count, you prove it each day. There are eight of us," he told her.

"I'm not a researcher, nor in the continuity of government," Sarah said and Skannish jumped up, trying to yank his belt off but was having serious trouble.

"I haven't spanked someone in forty years, but I'm damn sure about to fix that!" he bellowed, still trying to get his belt off.

"Sarah, you are part of this team and without you, we wouldn't have made the progress we have. Either you do this with us or we hold you down," Sutton grinned. "One on one, we are intimidated by you but as a group, we aren't."

As Skannish pulled and tugged at his belt, Sarah looked around at the others and saw them nodding. Reaching up, she wiped a tear from her eye, "Okay, I'll take the shot willingly," she smiled.

"Hold her down!" Skannish yelled out as he finally got his belt undone and was pulling it off.

"Skannish, she said she would take the shot!" Sutton shouted, moving over and stopping Skannish from moving toward Sarah.

Looking at his belt in his hands, "You have any idea how hard it is for me to get this damn thing on?!" he shouted. "I should spank you just for making me pull it off!"

Walking over, Sarah took the belt from Skannish's elderly hands. "I'm almost sorry I sat you down and force fed you," Sarah smiled and started putting Skannish's belt back on him.

Sutton and everyone turned to Skannish and saw he wouldn't look at them. "It was a few days ago and Sarah told me I had been in the lab too long, but I was checking viral culture reactions. She suited up, came into the lab, and pulled me to the decontamination chamber. When she got me out, Sarah put me in a chair and forced two bowls of soup down my throat," Skannish mumbled.

Pulling Skannish's belt tight, Sarah buckled it and straightened his shirt up. Skannish was the only researcher that didn't wear scrubs. "I looked up those words you called me, that's why I'm not sorry," Sarah grinned.

Looking at Sarah, Skannish saw his great-granddaughters but in Sarah's eyes, he saw a determination that they didn't have. "I shouldn't have called you Coccydynia Bescumber," Skannish mumbled.

"Haven't heard that one," Sutton chuckled, thinking the meaning out.

"Pain in the butt shit sprayer," Sarah grinned.

Everyone laughed as Skannish moved over to his locker. "Let's take our shots and let the president decide who gets the other nine," Skannish said. "Sarah goes first."

Rolling up her sleeve, "Fine," Sarah moaned and dropped into a chair.

Chapter Twenty Five
Don't go swimming

May 17

Crossing her fingers, Wendy flipped the lever for the door on the hull. When she heard the whine of the motor, Wendy sighed with relief. There was a crank that said, 'Manual Operation' but Wendy knew that would wipe her out.

As the ten-foot-tall door pulled in, the smell of the sea filled their noses. They watched the door slide down the wall on tracks, exposing a twenty-foot opening. The sun was just peeking above the horizon as Wendy flipped the switch that lowered the ramp into the water over ten feet below the door.

Making sure the winch line was hooked into the front of the jet ski and what few things they could bring already loaded, Wendy leaned and pushed against the jet ski. Slowly, the craft rolled back until it reached the slope of the ramp. Feeling the jet ski getting lighter, Wendy stopped pushing as the craft slid down the ramp and into the water with a splash.

Walking back, Wendy locked the winch line to stop the jet ski at the bottom of the ramp. Looking at the girls, Wendy could see how nervous they were. "It's just like riding a four-wheeler or a bike. Jo Ann, you hold onto Sally, and Sally, you hold onto me," Wendy told them and they both just nodded.

Glancing down at Ryan in the baby pack on her chest, Wendy patted his back as he chewed on his fist. Since Jo Ann was riding in the back, she was the only one with a backpack on. Since each had on a life jacket, Wendy had had to adjust the backpack so it would fit.

Putting on her sunglasses, Wendy tightened up her diving gloves. "Follow me," Wendy said, walking down the ramp and pulling the winch line. The jet ski moved to the ramp and Wendy guided it so it sat sideways to the ramp and climbed on. Checking the spear gun strapped to the handlebar, Wendy was glad she had decided to unload it.

Reaching out, Wendy helped Sally climb on and throw one leg over the seat. When Jo Ann was on, Wendy grabbed the Velcro strap on the bungee cord line that connected to the key and wrapped the strap around Jo Ann's wrist. It was a safety feature so if the driver fell off, the motor would shut off.

Since Jo Ann was in the back, nobody could fall off without knocking her off, but Jo Ann could fall off and not take the rest.

Wendy gave a last glance at the ship and then started the motor. "I'll never leave the sight of land again," Wendy vowed, gripping the handlebar. Turning the handlebar, Wendy gave the engine gas and the jet ski pulled away from the ship heading north.

Moving closer to shore, Wendy glanced to her left at Miami Beach. Turning to her front, Wendy turned the handlebar to dodge a floating body. Seeing the body was missing its legs, Wendy suppressed a shiver.

Guiding the jet ski so she was only a few hundred yards from shore, Wendy continued north but kept the speed at a nice cruise. She had jet skis at home and she and Arthur had ridden them every summer, but she didn't want to worry the twins. Plus, she had never ridden with an infant strapped to her chest.

Glancing down, Wendy grinned to see that Ryan had buried his face so the wind wouldn't hit him. Tilting her head to see around Ryan to the instrument panel, Wendy saw she was holding around twenty miles an hour.

Feeling Sally's arms relax around her, Wendy glanced toward shore and saw the high-rise hotels. Several had caught fire and they had watched a few, but none had collapsed. Quickly, Wendy glanced back and saw their ship anchored and getting smaller. Hoping she wasn't making a mistake, Wendy turned her head back around and drove on.

Another reason Wendy wanted to go slow was she knew from experience that the faster these jet skis went, the louder they were. She wanted to go fast enough so if someone shot they would have problems, but not so fast that they could be heard from a long way off.

So, fighting the urge to gun the engine, Wendy just kept up a cruising speed. As she continued to monitor the shore, Wendy was amazed at all the tall buildings right on the beach.

The sun was well up when Wendy saw the channel that cut through the beach. Barely slowing, Wendy turned to guide the jet ski into the channel and saw Sandspur Island ahead. Driving under the bridge that spanned the channel, Wendy turned and saw bodies piled up under the north embankment.

Not even entertaining the idea to investigate, Wendy turned north to follow the sheltered bay behind the beach. Ahead, she saw a few boats in the channel but it was over three hundred yards wide, so she didn't have to get close to any of them.

None of the boats looked manned and they didn't see anyone aboard.

Reaching the drawbridges at Bella Vista, Wendy sighed with relief that she was on the right course. A nautical person, Wendy wasn't and she knew it. Going under the bridges, Wendy looked ahead to see buildings on each side of the narrow bay. She'd known they would be there but from the charts, three hundred yards had looked wider.

Ahead, the channel narrowed to just over a hundred yards. To her left on a balcony of a six-story building, she saw a figure watching them. Staying in the center of the canal, Wendy couldn't tell if it was a man or woman. She was shocked when the figure casually waved at them. Not knowing what else to do, Wendy waved back.

The person just watched as they passed. Feeling Sally tapping her right leg, Wendy turned to her right. A woman and man were walking along a walkway. Before she turned away, Wendy saw the woman double over coughing. "I see them," Wendy shouted over her shoulder.

Looking ahead to Dumfoundling Bay, Wendy's grip on the throttle lessened. Thousands of bodies bobbed in the water with dozens of drifting boats. "God help us," Wendy gasped, pressing the throttle but staying at a cruise as she started weaving around the floating corpses.

Halfway through the body-filled bay, a body to their right was jerked underwater. The girls screamed as a shark's tail splashed the water and Wendy felt Sally's grip almost squeeze her in half. Reaching down, Wendy patted her arm and then reached back to pat Jo Ann's leg.

"That was a shark! I watch Shark Week, I know!" Sally yelled. Wendy just nodded as she reached forward, gripping the handlebars. She didn't have the nerve to tell the twins that she had seen dozens of sharks swimming below them.

Ahead, she saw the bay shrink back down to the narrow channel just over a hundred yards wide. On their left, huge, towering buildings reached for the sky and on the right, were very nice houses. Continuing her weaving around the floating bodies and boats, Wendy looked ahead at the bridge and saw people looking down at them.

Wendy knew there were over a dozen people looking down at her and all of them were waving frantically toward the shore. As she got closer to the bridge, several started pointing at the water and then over toward the shore. It didn't take a genius to figure out that they were telling her to get off the water, but Wendy continued on. Like the people on the bridge, she could see the sleek forms around her under the water, but not as many.

On the bridge, the group could see hundreds of shadows of sharks swimming around with the bodies.

Coming out from under the bridge, Wendy saw a boat coming toward her and 'boat' was a light term. The yacht was over a hundred feet long and Wendy moved to the side, giving the craft the right of way. The yacht paid no mind to the bodies, but wasn't going fast enough to produce a wake.

As they passed, Wendy saw a woman with six kids standing on the bridge with another woman at the controls. They all waved and Wendy returned the wave and then moved back to the center of the channel. Wendy smiled because the twins hadn't unlatched their grasps since they'd started off.

Thankful for the yacht, Wendy used the path it had created through the floating bodies, but still had to dodge a large, drifting speedboat. Seeing splashes to her left, Wendy turned to see another body get pulled under and several shark fins splitting the water. "Well, they said sharks were endangered. They won't be for long," Wendy mumbled.

Seeing the houses getting larger, Wendy could only imagine what they would cost, but was sure she wasn't even close.

By the time she reached the next bridge, the bodies had floated back out. Weaving around a body, Wendy glanced at the Hallandale Bridge and knew she only had one more to go, hopefully. On the east side under the bridge, she saw a group of people. Only a few turned to watch them and when Wendy gave a casual wave, none returned it.

"Okay, so not everyone is friendly," she mumbled, fighting the urge to just haul ass.

Keeping in the center of the channel, Wendy started tallying up how many people they had spotted. "Not even fifty," she finally said, knowing before the flu they would've seen thousands.

Glancing down at Ryan, Wendy saw him asleep with his head flopped back. Moving his head until it looked more comfortable,

Wendy second-guessed her plan. She was putting in at a large residential area. The ship had had satellite links, but she couldn't connect to the internet because she'd really wanted Google Earth.

To put in at an area with a low population density, Wendy had mapped it out that they would have to ride the jet ski over a hundred and sixty miles along the coast. Like the girls, Wendy wanted off the damn ship and on land. There were canals that fed into the cities, but they had all heard people calling for help on the radio from deep in the cities. Before they ventured into urban areas, Wendy wanted a vehicle and a gun, not necessarily in that order.

Ahead, she saw a bridge over the channel and reached down to pat Sally's arm. Turning, Wendy yelled over her shoulder. "That's the last bridge. If we don't see a lot of people, we are getting off the water. If not, the next area that looked good is thirty miles further."

"Can we get a boat?" Sally yelled back, having seen too many shark fins slicing through the water.

"Damn, that *is* a thought," Wendy mumbled and then yelled out. "Let's check this area first and decide later."

Going under the bridge into North Lake; just another bay, Wendy slowed to ten miles an hour and glanced around. Tall buildings still dominated the left, but the right side had houses lining the area around the lake. Seeing a sandy beach ahead, Wendy sped back up.

Having no intention of stepping into the water and pulling the jet ski ashore, Wendy only slowed when she neared the beach and braced her body. The bow hit the sand and skidded up, leaving only the very back in the water. Turning the engine off, Wendy climbed off and saw a massive mansion on the corner where the lake flowed back into the channel that continued north.

Taking the spear gun off the handlebar, Wendy cocked the two rubber bands back and pulled a bolt from the holster strapped to her leg. With a spear loaded, Wendy turned to see the twins already off and looking around. "I don't like the ocean anymore," Jo Ann admitted.

"Me neither," Wendy smiled and then opened the cargo area, pulling out hers and Sally's backpacks. "Let's find a car," Wendy said, pulling off her life jacket. With the baby carrier on her chest, that was a chore because she didn't want to wake up Ryan.

Ryan didn't get the memo about staying asleep and woke up as Wendy fought to get the life jacket off. Giving a groan, Wendy unbuckled the baby carrier and handed Ryan to Jo Ann, then pulled her life jacket off.

Taking Ryan back, Wendy tightened up the straps and put the pacifier in Ryan's mouth. "Have either of you heard or seen anyone since we landed?" Wendy asked in a low voice.

"Sharks," Jo Ann said, pointing out to the water as a fin split the surface twenty yards away.

"Baby, if they come on shore, we are screwed," Wendy chuckled. "You two stay behind me."

As Wendy moved off and crossed the street that ran along the water, they saw she was moving through the yards of houses. Sally grabbed Wendy and stopped her. "We'll get in trouble for going through people's yards," Sally whispered.

"Sally, it's easier to see us near the street," Wendy told her, moving up to the first house. She glanced at the cars in the driveway and sighed, seeing both were tiny sports cars. The next house had a van and a BMW. Tempted with the beamer, Wendy continued on.

Two houses down they spotted a Toyota 4Runner, but it had crashed into a palm tree. It didn't look damaged that badly, but Wendy continued on. The next house they crept past Wendy saw a large SUV, but heard coughing inside and quickly hurried off with the girls.

In two more houses, they heard coughing and Wendy started having bad thoughts because at each house was a large SUV. Seeing the garage closed at the next house, Wendy moved up to a window and peeked inside. A black Tahoe was on the other side of the window. "Yes," Wendy hissed and moved around to the back door.

She pressed her ear to the door and listened. After a few minutes, Wendy pressed her nose against the doorframe. She breathed in deep and jerked back, swatting at her nose. "Did something sting you?" Sally asked in alarm.

"No, it stinks real bad inside," Wendy said, wiping her nose. Wendy tried the back door and groaned, not feeling the knob turn. Stepping back and looking at the back of the house, Wendy saw a sliding door that led out to a patio. Walking over, she grabbed the handle and pushed.

When the door slid open, Wendy stopped as a wave of putrefaction washed over her. Fighting not to gag, Wendy stepped to the side and saw the twins holding their noses. "It didn't stink this bad on the ship," Jo Ann said in a low voice.

"These bodies have been locked up in a house under a blazing Florida sun," Wendy said. "I want you two to move inside, but stay beside the door. I'm going to check the house."

"Can't we come?" Sally asked, glancing around with her eyes but her head never moved.

"Okay, but if I say run, you run to this door," Wendy told them and braced her body for the odor to come.

Walking inside, Wendy's eyes started to water, swearing she could *see* the smell. Moving into the kitchen and seeing the back door she had tried, Wendy unlocked it and opened it up. Then she moved over to the sink and opened the two windows.

Feeling a breeze, Wendy still didn't take a deep breath as she led them into the house. In the living room, she stopped at seeing the bloated form of a man holding a woman that was equally bloated lying on the couch. Continuing through the living room, Wendy opened the door she thought would lead her into the garage.

Opening the door, Wendy sighed to see the Tahoe. Then she saw very dark tint on the windows. "How the hell can they have tint that dark?" Wendy mumbled and then saw the post-mounted lights on each side of the windshield. Turning, she looked at the other vehicle for the first time and saw it was a sedan, also with the post-mounted lights by the windshield. But on the sedan, she saw forward mounted flashing lights beside the rearview mirror.

"How in the hell could cops afford to live in this neighborhood?" she asked, walking over to the Tahoe and opened the door. Not seeing the keys, Wendy closed the door and headed back inside. Stopping in the living room, Wendy saw the man and woman were only wearing shorts.

"At least you died together," she mumbled and then moved over to the front windows and opened them up a few inches. The breeze blew in, pulled through the house, and out the back open doors and windows.

"That's better," Jo Ann said, looking around. "Are those the keys on the bar?"

Turning to the kitchen, Jo Ann saw the bar that separated the kitchen and living room. On the bar were two sets of keys. Walking over, she saw the keys for the Tahoe. Snatching them up, "Very good. Now, since they were cops, let's find the guns," Wendy said, moving around the first floor and very happy she hadn't had to entertain those earlier bad thoughts about the occupied houses with SUVs.

She found an office and a gun safe in the corner. "Come on," she groaned, stomping her foot.

"Try the keys," Sally said, moving over to the safe.

"Baby, it needs a combination to open," Wendy told her, looking at the safe and wondering how to break into it.

"No, look," Sally said, pointing at the combination dial and a key slot.

Holding up the keys, Wendy moved over and started trying them out. On the third try, the key slid into the lock and to Wendy's surprise, it turned. Grabbing the handle, Wendy turned it and heard the bars in the door unlock. "Why didn't Arthur make us gun safes like this?" Wendy wondered, opening the door.

"Wow," Sally said, looking at the rows of guns.

Jo Ann moved over to look inside. "Can you shoot them?" she asked hopefully.

"Girls, not only can I shoot them, I can take them apart and put them back together," Wendy said, putting the spear gun on the desk. "For once, I won't complain about a Glock," Wendy said, pulling out a pistol.

Ejecting the magazine, Wendy smiled at the full mag. Press checking the pistol, Wendy saw brass and let the slide lock back and then slapped the magazine back in. "Glock 17, I'm betting this was hers," Wendy said, looking back in the safe and pulling another pistol out. "Glock 37, I'm sure this was his."

"They have boy and girl guns?" Jo Ann asked as Wendy put the Glock 37 on the desk.

"No, but boys tend to go with bigger bullets," Wendy said. "Can I get you two to sit and feed Ryan? Then can you play with him, but stay in this room. I'm going to check the rest of the house."

They looked at the ease with which Wendy held the pistol in her hand and felt much safer. "Okay," they said in unison.

Taking Ryan off, Wendy left him with the girls and grabbed the keys from the lock on the safe. Walking back into the living room, Wendy stopped and looked at the second set of keys and saw the same key on it that had unlocked the gun safe. Grabbing the keys, she moved back into the garage and climbed into the Tahoe.

Turning the key on, Wendy saw the gas tank was half full. "I'll take that," she said and moved over to the sedan and turned the key on, finding it only had a quarter of a tank. Moving to the trunk, Wendy almost used the key but then saw a trunk button on the fob. Pressing it, she stepped back as the trunk popped open.

Seeing an equipment bag, Wendy pulled it out and set it on the floor. In a gun rack was an M4 and Wendy went through the keys until she found the one that unlocked it. Taking the M4 out, Wendy set it on the duffle bag and dug through the trunk and found a garment bag with a pair of tactical boots. It only took a glance to tell Wendy they were female boots. Looking at the size, "Six and a half is almost a seven, I'll try them," Wendy mumbled.

Unzipping the garment bag, Wendy found a spare uniform. "Girl stays prepared," Wendy nodded, setting the boots next to the bag.

Walking back inside, Wendy headed upstairs and walked in the first room and found it was the master bedroom. Seeing a picture on the dresser, Wendy walked over and picked it up. It showed a nice-looking man and woman in sheriff uniforms. They both looked around Joseph's age. "So, there are young people that get married and haven't had kids," Wendy said, caressing the picture and outlining the couple with her fingertips.

Setting the picture down, Wendy saw walk-in closets. Walking into the first Wendy stepped out, since it clearly belonged to the guy. Looking at the back of the door, Wendy saw his duty rig hanging up. Stepping over quickly, Wendy opened the other closet and saw a duty rig hanging from the door. Pulling the rig off, Wendy saw a gun in the holster.

Pressing the release, Wendy pulled it out and put the one she'd been carrying on the bed. "Glock 23," Wendy said, ejecting the magazine and saw it was full. Giving the gun a press check, Wendy saw brass in the barrel. "My kind of people," Wendy said, slapping the magazine back in.

Wendy put the rig and the suspenders on and found it was a little large. From the photos and clothes, Wendy knew the woman was near her size but after the flu, Wendy still had some weight to regain. Even going down one size with her wetsuit, the suit had still been loose. Putting the rig on the bed, Wendy adjusted the belt and suspenders and then put it back on.

With the rig on, she adjusted the suspenders because the woman clearly had been much better endowed than Wendy ever would be. Moving into the closet, Wendy grabbed some pants and shirts and tossed them on the bed. On the floor, she saw another pair of tactical boots, but these were well-worn but in good shape. Picking them up, Wendy was shocked to see they were a size seven.

Grabbing the boots and clothes, Wendy picked up the pistol from the bed and headed back downstairs. Tossing the stuff on the desk, Wendy saw the girls playing with Ryan. "You found a holster," Sally grinned.

"Yep," Wendy smiled, looking at the girls in their wetsuits. None of them had brought clothes because they'd needed room for diapers and formula, baby food and juice, water and then finally, a little food for them. Wendy had reasoned it would be easier to find the girls stuff than Ryan. "Are you two okay? I'm going to check the truck out."

"Can I take this off? It's hot," Jo Ann groaned, grasping at the wetsuit.

"Not yet, baby. We will look around for some clothes," Wendy said and then jerked as a gunshot sounded off in the distance.

"Was that close?" Jo Ann panted.

Shaking her head as she glanced toward the windows, "No, that was a mile or so away, but keep an ear out," Wendy said and they nodded.

Moving back to the garage, Wendy opened up the back of the Tahoe with the fob and saw it was empty. "Oh, I can fix that," Wendy tittered, grabbing the duffel from the sedan and setting it in the cargo area. Opening it up, Wendy saw a tactical vest and magazines for the M4.

Laying the stuff out, Wendy had to admit that the woman could pack. Reaching the bottom, Wendy found a hard case and opened it up. "Holy shit! Cops around here get night vision goggles?" Wendy gasped, pulling out the PVS 14 monocular. "I bet they didn't pay what my husband did," Wendy snickered.

Putting the monocular up, Wendy repacked the duffel bag. Looking further into the vehicle, Wendy saw another duffel bag and climbed in before pulling it to the back. Inside she found another vest, but there was also a satellite phone, crime scene tape, notepads, a tape recorder, cameras, and a video camera.

Taking out the vest and ammo, Wendy set the bag on the sedan. Walking around and looking in the back, Wendy didn't see another M4. "Where's his?" she thought out loud. Shrugging her shoulders, Wendy moved to the front of the garage and a workbench.

Seeing a small chainsaw, Wendy grabbed it. "Need this just in case of road blockage, but I'll have to get rid of this before I get home. Arthur would freak out, seeing me with something other than a Husqvarna."

Putting the chainsaw in the back, Wendy froze. "I wonder how long I'm a carrier?"

Thinking for several minutes, "We'll stay at the office house for a month," she finally said and moved back to the workbench. Grabbing a small gas can, Wendy opened it to see it was mixed fuel. Setting it to the side, Wendy grabbed a large Phillips screwdriver and a hammer.

Setting them to the side, Wendy laid a small crowbar in the stack and dug through a toolbox, pulling out a few other tools. "Thanks to my husband, I know what every tool I've come across is used for," Wendy mumbled. "I wonder if that is alarming to some people?"

Bending down, Wendy saw a plastic oil pan reservoir. Pulling it out, Wendy felt it was empty and after looking at it, she wondered if it had ever been used. The reservoir looked like it would hold well over a gallon with a long spout off the side that was capped off.

"Almost have my fueler," Wendy said, grabbing a water hose. Picking up the utility knife she'd laid out, Wendy cut off two sections, one four-foot-long and the other, eight-foot-long. Finding a hose clamp in the toolbox, Wendy put one end over the oil spout after taking the cap off. With a lot of shoving, she got the one end of the shorter hose over the spout. Then she put the hose clamp on and was sure it wasn't needed, but this was how Arthur had taught her so she would do it.

Putting the tools in a small plastic toolbox, Wendy moved the stuff to the back of the Tahoe. Glancing over at the sedan, "Where the hell are their private vehicles?" Wendy asked out loud.

She knew there weren't cars in the circular drive at the front of the house, so Wendy moved to the windows on the garage door. The driveway led to a communal cement drive that ran behind the houses like an open alley. Looking down the driveway and with the gate open, Wendy could see the house opposite of the one she was in. The only difference was it was much bigger and didn't have a six-foot fence around it.

Moving to a door on the side of the garage, Wendy unlocked it and peeked outside. "Oh," Wendy said, seeing two Harley Davison motorcycles and a Jeep. The Jeep was jacked way up and Wendy knew Arthur would've liked it, but there wasn't a top. Turning to the motorcycles, they just looked expensive to Wendy.

Closing the door, Wendy went and checked on the girls. "I'm going to the backyard, do you want to come?" she asked and the girls grabbed Ryan, flying out of the office.

When they were outside, Wendy looked at the swimming pool. "No, you can't swim," she told them.

"I'm kind of tired of water," Sally admitted and Jo Ann agreed with a nod.

"Have to say, I am too," Wendy said, walking over to a small shed in the corner. Finding a lawn mower and weed eater, Wendy also found an axe, a machete, and a hatchet and tossed them out the door for road debris removal, but hoped she wouldn't need them. Seeing two five-gallon fuel cans and a long flexible funnel, Wendy tossed them out after feeling that the fuel cans were empty and grabbed a spool of rope.

Walking out, she saw the twins playing with Ryan in the grass. The twins were being very quiet and like he knew, Ryan was being quiet with his coos. Gathering the stuff on the ground, Wendy carried it to the garage and finished gathering tools, then grabbed a five-gallon fuel can from under the workbench.

Looking at the sedan, "Nope, I'll just siphon the gas. Punching a hole in the fuel tank will be loud and we aren't ready to leave yet," Wendy reasoned and grabbed the long hose.

Shoving the end in the gas tank, Wendy blew into the hose and then briefly sucked and took the hose from her mouth, putting it in a fuel can. Letting that one fill up, Wendy pulled over another one that was empty. When the fuel stopped, Wendy figured she had only gotten seven gallons from the sedan.

Using the funnel, Wendy poured the gas into the Tahoe and then moved up to turn the key on. "That's bullshit! You didn't even move up to three quarters of a tank," she moaned at the gas gauge. Turning the key off and yanking it out, Wendy clipped it on her suspenders.

She emptied the Jeep and found a full metal gas can in the back. Saving that, Wendy emptied the motorcycles and was happy that the Tahoe was now full. Putting the metal gas can in the back, Wendy started arranging the area.

Climbing out, Wendy went inside to the kitchen and started opening cabinets. "What the hell did you eat?" she asked toward the couch. Besides a few boxes of cereal and crackers, the cabinets held dishes and glasses.

Not about to open the fridge, Wendy closed the cabinets and headed back to the office. Collecting all the magazines for the pistols she had, Wendy grabbed AR magazines and set them on the desk. Inspecting the rifles as she turned back, Wendy saw four ARs and then looked closer and realized one was an M4. She grabbed it, and one of the ARs that had everything one could put on an AR.

"You must be kin to my husband," Wendy mumbled, setting the rifles on the desk. Seeing a closet door, Wendy moved over and stopped at the wall that was covered with pictures. One was of the same young man and woman with a date of last February.

On the young man's collar were shiny sergeant pins. "You got promoted. That's why your stuff is set up different," Wendy mumbled as she opened the closet. Seeing metal and plastic ammo cans, Wendy started pulling them out.

"There's no way I'll need this much ammo," Wendy said, looking at the ten cans she had pulled out. "Screw it, I'm taking it."

Checking the safe before she closed it, Wendy saw a .38 revolver and two compact 9mm Glocks. Tossing them onto the desk, Wendy closed the safe and then started carrying the stuff to the Tahoe. Instead of moving through the house, Wendy walked out the back to check on the kids and used the side door on the garage. Placing one Glock in the door bin on the driver's door, Wendy put the .38 in an overhead storage rack after removing stacks of forms. The last Glock, she set on the center console. Grabbing the PVS-14, Wendy put it in one of the overhead storage bins so she could grab it fast.

Leaving the AR with all the attachments out, Wendy opened the storage drawer that covered the cargo floor. Removing more stacks of forms, Wendy put the other weapons she was taking inside and then filled the drawer with the other supplies that would fit.

When she was done, Wendy looked at her watch and saw it was just after noon. "It took me three hours to load all that?" Wendy mumbled in shock.

Shaking her head, she walked over and saw the twins eating peanut butter and crackers. That was the staple Wendy had packed for them. Between the twins, Ryan was on a blanket fast asleep.

"We ready?" Sally asked, handing over a cracker loaded with peanut butter.

"We could leave, but I want to check the house next door and the one after it," Wendy answered and then shoved the cracker in her mouth. As she chewed, Jo Ann held up a bottle of water.

As Wendy took the bottle, Jo Ann asked. "Why do you want to go to the next houses?"

Smacking her lips, Wendy drained half the bottle of water. "They have kids play equipment in the backyards, I saw it upstairs. They may have clothes for you and formula and diapers for Ryan," Wendy told her and then drained the bottle.

Jo Ann looked over at Sally and then back to Wendy. "We can come, can't we?" Jo Ann asked.

"I'm not going without you," Wendy smiled.

Chapter Twenty Six

Miracles can happen anywhere

After filling up on crackers and peanut butter, Wendy put the baby carrier back on and put Ryan in it. As Wendy situated Ryan, the twins packed up the supplies. "Okay, we are going to the houses to see if there is anything we can use. If I say run, you run and climb into the black truck in the garage," Wendy explained, turning to the twins. "Don't get out because you don't see me, because I'm coming and then we will leave."

"Okay," the twins said in unison and smiled.

"Why aren't we going to search other houses like that one?" Jo Ann asked, pointing at the massive house behind them.

"The next two houses have fences like this one and we can move around the backyards without being seen easily," Wendy explained.

When no more questions came, Wendy headed across the yard and opened a gate that gave access to the next yard. Looking at the swing set and other toys, Wendy could tell they were new. She looked down the driveway and saw the gate was open.

Turning back to the house, there wasn't a garage but a Mercedes was parked beside the house. The space between the house and Mercedes told Wendy another vehicle had been parked there. "Hope they don't come back," Wendy mumbled, moving up to the back door.

Listening for several minutes, Wendy didn't hear anything then reluctantly, she put her nose next to the door and sniffed. When Wendy didn't jerk back, the twins sighed. Trying the doorknob, Wendy raised her eyebrows when the door opened.

When the door opened, a cat ran past them and out into the yard. Ignoring the cat, Wendy slipped inside and put her finger on her lips as she looked back at the twins. Walking through the kitchen, Wendy smelled the odor of a very full litter box.

Searching the house, Wendy found a family picture of a man and woman with two boys. One looked around ten and the other about six. Looking at the pictures on the walls, Wendy found one taken in the backyard with the dead couple next door.

Going upstairs, they found the boys' rooms. "Girls, see if these clothes will fit until we can find more," Wendy told them. The first was the older boy's room and he was bigger than the twins. From the pictures, Wendy would've called him chunky. Finding a school backpack, Wendy emptied it and handed it to Jo Ann who was going through a drawer full of shirts.

Only grabbing a few shirts, the twins followed Wendy to the next room and started searching. They both pulled out tennis shoes from the closet and shoved them into the backpack. Watching the girls pull out some light jackets, Wendy figured the smaller boy had been very close to their size.

Moving to the closet, Wendy pulled out several pairs of jeans and held them up next to Sally. Going through seven pairs, Wendy found two that looked close and shoved them in the pack. Then she moved over to the dresser and grabbed socks. Finding a few more items, Wendy led the girls to the kitchen.

Seeing a few cans of soup, Wendy put them in the pack.

Not finding anything else in the house or the keys to the Mercedes, Wendy led them back outside. Walking over to a shed, Wendy saw a small utility trailer with two plastic gas cans strapped on the front. Shaking them, she found one was full and the other almost half full.

Opening the shed, she found a lawn mower and other stuff, but nothing they needed. "Let's go to the next house," Wendy told them in a low voice.

"What about the cat?" Jo Ann asked.

"If we wouldn't have let him out, the cat would've died," Wendy answered, heading for the side gate. Opening it, she led the girls in and moved to the garage. On impulse, she looked back and saw the driveway gate closed.

Stopping at the garage door, Wendy stood up on her tiptoes and saw a massive SUV and a minivan parked inside. "Oh, now I find another SUV," Wendy mumbled, but liked the Tahoe much better.

Leading the girls across the patio, Wendy grabbed her nose and looked at a window that was open. Gritting her teeth, Wendy moved to the window. Not only could she smell it, Wendy could feel the stench rolling out of the house. Glancing in, she looked at a kitchen that had cereal everywhere.

Stepping back from the window, Wendy turned and looked at the yard and saw a very small swing set and other small toys. Almost talking herself out of facing another house of stench, Wendy shook her head. "We'll just look fast," she mumbled.

Reaching for the back door, Wendy tried the knob and found it was locked. "I can get in through the window," Sally offered, taking her backpack off.

Before Wendy could tell Sally that it wasn't worth it, Sally was gripping the window ledge and pulled her body in. Watching Sally climb in Wendy sighed, knowing she would search the house since Sally had put in the effort to get them inside.

Hearing the deadbolt unlock, Wendy turned to the door as Sally opened it and the stench rolled out. Walking past Sally, Wendy looked at the kitchen again. In with the cereal poured on the floor were animal crackers. "Ryan would've liked those," Wendy sighed.

A thump sounded from inside the house and Wendy yanked the pistol out, shoving the girls behind her. "We won't hurt you," Wendy called out. "I'm with kids and looking for food. We thought everyone inside was dead because of the smell."

The thump turned into a patter that was closing in. Gripping the pistol tight, Wendy held it low while staring at the corner of the kitchen. All of a sudden, a naked boy toddler popped out from the hallway grinning. He was filthy, with feces down both legs and dried food over his face.

"Hey," Wendy said, letting the pistol hang at her side. "Is your mom and daddy here?"

"Da," the little boy said and took off.

"Girls, stay close," Wendy said, following the boy around the corner. Going down a short hallway, Wendy stopped in the living room and saw the little boy standing beside the couch, smiling.

"Da," he said, pointing at a corpse on the couch.

"Oh my God," Wendy gulped. Holstering the pistol, she moved over to the boy and looked down at the dead man. "Where's your mama?"

"Ma," the boy said and took off for the stairs, running up them on all fours.

Wendy took off after him with the girls right behind her. Reaching the top of the stairs, Wendy saw the boy climb up on a bed and she ran into the room. She stopped as the boy curled up next to a dead woman. "Momma," the boy said, smiling.

Stumbling back into the wall, Wendy could tell the mother had been dead longer than the father. "They've been dead over a week, how?" Wendy asked, panting and watching the toddler curl up next to the corpse.

Pushing off the wall, Wendy clapped her hands, "Come here," Wendy said with a smile and the boy jumped and ran across the bed. Reaching the end, he leapt into the air and Wendy caught him while turning her body and pulling him to her side so he wouldn't hit Ryan.

"Oh," she said, jerking her face back at smelling the stench from the boy. As Ryan woke up, Wendy saw an open doorway and a bathroom inside. She took off to find anything to wipe the boy down and then remembered the swimming pool at the first house. Walking in the bathroom, Wendy stopped.

A huge garden tub sat in the floor and it was half full of water. "Wawa," the boy pointed at the tub.

"He drank that?" Jo Ann asked in a tearful voice.

"Yes, that's all he had," Wendy said, putting the boy down. "Thankfully, his parents filled up the tub. It has steps so if he fell in, he could get out."

Taking the baby pack holding Ryan off, Wendy passed Ryan to Sally. When Wendy turned around, the little boy was holding onto the metal handrail beside the steps. He bent over and used his hand to scoop up water to his mouth. Walking over, Wendy grabbed a rag and bent down to get it wet.

"Wawa," the boy said, shaking his head and pointing at the rag.

"Jo Ann, pull out a bottle of water," Wendy told her, moving to the boy. "Water," Wendy said as Jo Ann held up the bottle and the boy smiled. Wendy started wiping him off as the twins moved over.

"I'm sorry," Jo Ann cried out.

"What for?" Wendy asked, but didn't stop wiping the boy off.

"I didn't want to come inside," Jo Ann whimpered.

Turning around, "Jo Ann, I didn't either. If Sally hadn't crawled in, we would've been getting the gas from the vehicles outside and then leaving," Wendy admitted and then went back to washing the boy off.

With most of the dried feces off, Wendy picked him up. "Let's get his stuff and see if we can find out his name."

"It's Noah," Jo Ann said, wiping her eyes. "There were birthday invitations on the refrigerator."

"Can you go get one and meet us in Noah's room?" Wendy asked and Jo Ann took off running.

If Jo Ann hadn't known the name, they would've found out since there was a sign on Noah's bedroom door with his name. Toys covered the floor and Wendy saw several places where Noah had taken a dump.

Walking over to a dresser, Wendy grabbed a backpack diaper bag. Inside, she found some pull-ups. Opening the dresser, Wendy started grabbing clothes as Jo Ann ran back and held out a card.

Wendy took it reading, 'Join us for Noah's Second birthday. Cake and ice cream will be served'. The date was May fourteenth. "Can we have a birthday party for him?" Jo Ann asked with dried tear streaks still on her face.

"Yes, when we get home, Noah will have his party," Wendy promised with a nod, shoving the card in the bag. Grabbing some shoes for Noah, Wendy led them out of the room. Seeing a picture of Noah as a baby with his mom and dad, Wendy took the picture off the wall and shoved it into the backpack.

Walking downstairs, Wendy saw a small table by the front door with a purse on it. She walked over and took the wallet out and opened it up and saw the mom's license. Closing it, Wendy tossed it in the bag and then saw a wallet on the table. Not looking inside, Wendy tossed the wallet inside the diaper bag as well. Before she turned, Wendy noticed a key rack and grabbed the keys.

As Wendy walked out the back door with Noah in her arms, Noah looked at his house. "Momma, bye," he said and kissed his palm and slung his hand out, throwing the kiss. Then Noah kissed his palm again throwing it out. "Bye Da," he called out.

Tears were pouring out from Wendy's eyes as she walked through the gate and Noah hugged her neck and kissed her cheek. Noah leaned back to look at Wendy, "Luv ou," he said with a smile.

Wendy stopped and hugged Noah tight, "I love you too, Noah," Wendy cried as she dropped to her knees. Jo Ann and Sally, with Ryan in her arms, came over and hugged Wendy and Noah. "We all love you, Noah," Wendy whimpered.

If a gunshot in the distance hadn't have broken the moment, there was no way of telling how long the group would've stayed there. Jo Ann let go and looked west where the sound had come from. "That sounded further," she said, wiping her face.

"It was," Wendy said, getting to her feet. "Let's get Noah cleaned up and dressed. I still have to get the gas from the vehicles."

"If you take Ryan, we can do it," Sally offered and Wendy looked down at her. "We can swim, but we will wash Noah on the steps that go into the swimming pool."

Nodding as she looked from the girls to Noah, "Okay, but please, be quiet. I will never be far, but I don't want anyone to know we are here," Wendy said and the girls nodded.

Putting Noah down, Wendy took Ryan and put the carrier back on. "I fed him already," Sally said as she and Jo Ann took Noah by the hands and headed to the swimming pool.

Wendy followed them over and set down the diaper bag. "I have the baby shampoo, washcloths, and towels in the diaper bag," Wendy told them.

As the girls got ready, Noah seemed to be thrilled as he watched them. Since they were in wetsuits, the girls just sat down on the first step and started washing. When Noah didn't fight them, Wendy moved off while grabbing the empty fuel cans.

She stopped at the house with the small utility trailer and set the gas cans down. Walking over, she picked up the tongue and pulled the trailer back through the fence to see the twins washing a very happy Noah. Putting the trailer down, Wendy went into the garage. Saying a soft prayer as she reached for the roll up door of the garage, Wendy saw the electric motor over the cars. 'Battery Backup' was in huge white letters on the box.

Debating on whether to try it, finally Wendy moved to the side and pressed the open button. The door rolled up as the motor hummed and Wendy was surprised at how quiet it was. When the door was open, she climbed in the Tahoe and backed it out into the yard. Climbing out, Wendy looked at the open gate and walked over, closing it but not locking it.

Patting Ryan as she walked back to the trailer, Wendy wondered how many more Noahs were out there. Finally, she reasoned not many because not many would have had access to water like Noah had. "I'll take care of any I find," Wendy pledged, picking up the trailer's tongue and moving it over to the Tahoe.

Putting the trailer on the ball hitch, Wendy was thankful for that as she locked the trailer down. She stopped as she was about to hook up the lights. "Be damned if I drive with lights," she mumbled.

It was four p.m. when Wendy stopped. She looked at the small trailer with six full red five-gallon gas cans strapped on. The minivan still had a full tank of gas, but Wendy hadn't found any more gas cans and several more gunshots had sounded out to the west.

She walked over to where a very clean and dressed Noah played with Jo Ann and Sally. Before Wendy spoke, everyone stopped at hearing engines to the west. They all listened as the noise faded away. "That was more engines that time," Sally said, looking up.

"Yeah, and they were heading the same way that the last ones were," Wendy said, looking back down at the kids. "Guys, I want to leave at dark. I'm not driving with lights because I don't want people to see us."

"How will you see?" Sally asked, clearly not liking that idea.

"We will have a full moon tonight and the skies are clear," Wendy answered, kneeling down and patting Sally's leg. "But I have a night vision scope if I need it."

"Oh," Sally said, feeling a little better about it.

"Guys, can I ask a big favor?" Wendy grunted as she sat down on the grass.

"You don't have to ask," Jo Ann giggled.

"I need to get some sleep before we leave. Do you want me to sleep out here and you keep watch or inside?"

The twins didn't even look at each other as they spoke simultaneously. "Outside."

"Okay," Wendy said, laying her head down on Ryan's blanket. "You have your watches, so wake me at eight p.m. or if you hear anything close."

"We will," Jo Ann promised as Wendy closed her eyes. Before the twins went back to playing with Noah, Wendy was already asleep.

Chapter Twenty Seven

When in doubt, just aim and pull the trigger

Wendy felt a hand grab her shoulder and jerked back as she sat up. "It's me," she heard Sally say. Turning around, Wendy saw Sally kneeling in the grass beside her. "It's almost eight."

Blinking her eyes, Wendy looked around and realized the sun was already setting. "Did either of you hear anything?" Wendy asked, getting up and seeing Noah asleep beside Ryan on the blanket.

"A few gunshots and engines. One was from where we left the jet ski and it sounded like that big boat that passed us," Jo Ann told her. "Um, we only have one pack of crackers, half a jar of peanut butter and one can of soup. Sorry, but Noah was really hungry."

Reaching out and caressing Jo Ann's face, "Baby, don't apologize for taking care of the little ones," Wendy smiled.

"But we have to find more food," Jo Ann moaned.

"And we will, but not around here," Wendy said, stretching out. Finishing the stretch, Wendy moved over to the Tahoe. "Follow me."

The twins followed as Wendy opened the back passenger door and they saw something taped to the inside of the door. "This is a bulletproof vest. There is one on the other side and one behind the seat. If someone shoots at us, lay down on the seat."

"What about you?" Jo Ann asked.

Opening the passenger door, Wendy pulled out the tactical vest. "I'll be wearing this and I have a smaller one for when one of you sits up front," Wendy answered.

"Are you going to shoot back?" Sally asked.

"My first job is to get you out but if they chase, I'll shoot the assholes," Wendy said, holding up the concealable vest.

"How far are we going?" Jo Ann asked.

Letting out a long sigh, "Fifteen hundred miles," Wendy said, already feeling tired.

"When can we leave?" Sally asked, looking back at Noah and Ryan.

"Don't know about you guys, but I'm ready to leave now," Wendy said with a grin.

"I'll ride up front first," Jo Ann said, tossing her backpack in.

They went back over and Wendy picked up Noah as Sally picked up Ryan and carried them to the Tahoe. Jo Ann packed up the stuff left as Wendy and Sally put the sleeping boys on the back seat. With a comforter spread over the backseat and pillows stuffed in each floorboard, Sally looked over at Wendy as she put Noah on the driver's side back seat.

"They can't wear seatbelts," Sally whispered.

"I'm not wearing mine," Wendy answered as she covered Noah up with a sheet. "If we wreck, we all get hurt. If we find car seats for them, then I will."

Covering up Ryan with the sheet, Sally nodded. "I'm not wearing mine until we do either," she said with a nod.

Smiling over at Sally, "Get in the middle and remember, you have to help keep an eye out until we get out of town," Wendy said as Jo Ann ran over with the blanket and diaper bag.

As she tossed them in, Wendy came over and draped a bulletproof vest over her. Even though it was the female officer's vest, it still swallowed Jo Ann's body. Looking down at the vest, "I know you said we were driving without lights, but what about when we stop? The red lights at the back come on," Jo Ann stated.

Shaking her head, "Not anymore, I pulled the fuse," Wendy said, reaching up and scuffing Jo Ann's hair.

Staring at Wendy in awe, "You think of everything," Jo Ann mumbled.

"No, I learned from my husband. In his youth, Arthur was a bad boy, a very bad boy," Wendy grinned, guiding Jo Ann to the passenger seat. "He stopped for the most part when we met, but he never lost his rebel heart of independence."

Reaching out and grabbing Wendy's arm as she was about to close the door, "Did he go to jail?" Jo Ann whispered in shock.

"He was arrested once when he was thirteen, but was found not guilty. After that, he became much 'more sneaky' I say; 'careful' he says," Wendy chuckled and then closed the door.

Walking around the Tahoe, Wendy opened the driver's door and pulled the M4 she liked the best off the dashboard. Checking it over and press checking it, Wendy put the M4 back. Grabbing her vest from the seat and throwing it on, Wendy looked down at the four magazines for the M4 on her chest as she tightened the straps down. Pulling the pistol from her holster and checking it, Wendy put it back. Looking down at the bin in the door and the Glock resting there, Wendy turned to the Glock 17 resting on the console.

"Don't have to reach far for a gun now," Wendy sighed with relief, walking over and opening the gate. When she climbed in, she glanced around and saw the twins almost vibrating with excitement and anxiety. Closing the door, Wendy started the Tahoe up.

"Wendy," Jo Ann said, looking down in her floorboard. "Why did you bring the spear gun? You have real guns now."

Shrugging as she put the shifter in drive, "It protected us, so call it good luck," Wendy answered. "It's not loaded, as you can see."

"Okay, but why did you take the tires from the truck at Noah's house?" Sally asked from the backseat.

"They are the same size as the ones on this truck and I only took the back tires," Wendy said, tapping the GPS mounted on the dash. Out of everything she had done to get ready, the GPS system had proved the hardest. Using an atlas, Wendy had known the way she wanted to go, but the GPS hadn't liked her route. Just as Wendy had been about to break the unit, she'd figured out how to program the route she wanted.

Pulling out the gate, Wendy turned on the back communal drive and drove along behind the houses. Reaching the road, Wendy turned and started driving west. Even with the GPS unit on night, the screen was too bright. Reaching over, Wendy tapped the screen until the contrast came up and turned it all the way down. Realizing that was too low, Wendy increased it until she was satisfied.

"There's someone ahead," Jo Ann said and Wendy's hand dropped from the screen to the Glock resting on the center console as she looked ahead.

Pulling the pistol to her lap, Wendy saw a man standing in the yard of a very nice house. The man just stared in front of him at the road. Keeping her eyes on him as they drove through his line of sight, Wendy never saw any recognition on his face as she drove past him.

"What was wrong with him?" Jo Ann asked, scanning the road ahead.

"He's in shock," Wendy said, letting the pistol rest on her lap and turned the dash lights down to a very low dim.

"His nose didn't look red," Jo Ann noted.

"Think of shock as an injury to the mind," Wendy explained, gripping the steering wheel with her left hand and dropping her right to the pistol. "He didn't look sick, but he's seen the world he knew die. He may look awake, but his mind is asleep, kind of."

Leaning forward between the front seats, Sally looked at the speedometer staying at thirty. "Can't we go faster?" she asked in a soft voice.

"The faster we go, the more noise the car makes; just moving the air and noise from the tires on the road," Wendy explained. "When we get to our bigger roads I'll speed up some, but a car going sixty can be heard from a long way off."

"Where did you learn this stuff from?" Sally gasped in wonder.

"Arthur," Wendy grinned. "He found out when he was younger that he could hear cops or security driving toward him if they drove fast, even if they turned off their lights and sirens. But if they drove slow at forty, he couldn't hear them until they were right on top of him."

"Did he steal from people?" Jo Ann asked as the GPS told them to turn right ahead.

"Not the way you're thinking. Arthur broke into corporate warehouses and even government buildings," Wendy answered. "Even when he was little, Arthur didn't like the way the little guys were treated."

"He was like Robin Hood," Jo Ann said cheerfully.

Making the turn, Wendy laughed. "No, he didn't give to the poor, baby. Most of the times, he broke in just to break in."

"Didn't his parents get mad at him?" Sally asked and then let out a gasp as a man ran out of a house, waving his arms in the air.

Wendy just gripped the Glock and pressed the accelerator, passing the man's yard long before he'd made the road. "Sorry," Jo Ann mumbled. "He just ran out."

"Baby, I saw him at the same time," Wendy said, slowing back down and glancing back in the mirror to see the man was stopped in the middle of the road, still waving his arms over his head.

"Sally, Arthur never knew his parents," Wendy said, looking ahead.

"He was adopted?" Jo Ann asked with her eyes scanning to their front.

"No, Arthur lived in foster homes his entire life. Nobody ever adopted him," Wendy sighed. "When our son was born, I finally tracked down his birth record. His mom died two years after he was born from a drug overdose. The father wasn't listed on the birth certificate."

"That's sad," Sally mumbled as she glanced behind them.

"Yes, it is, but it taught Arthur independence," Wendy said.

With the full moon and clear sky, the twins looked around in amazement. "Could you always do this?" Jo Ann asked. "Move around without lights?"

Laughing, "Yes, baby, even on cloudy nights you can see, just not as far," Wendy said. "I wouldn't be driving this fast if it was cloudy."

Wendy slowed at seeing a wreck in the intersection ahead and steered to the side. Even at twenty miles an hour, the twins held on as Wendy weaved around the wreck and heard the tires squeal a little. After they rounded the wreck, "Person at the house," Jo Ann called out. Everyone turned and saw a woman walk out of a house and look at them, clearly shocked to see a car rolling down the road without lights.

With Wendy accelerating back up to thirty, Sally turned around to keep watch on the woman. "She's just staying there and holding a bunch of stuff in her hands," Sally reported.

"People to the left," Jo Ann called out and Wendy jerked her eyes over and saw several people next to a neighborhood grocery store. "I think one has a gun."

"Get down," Wendy said, hitting the window button and her window rolled down as she aimed the pistol across her body and out the window. Knowing it would be near impossible for her to hit the group, Wendy just wanted to be able to shoot back.

The group turned and saw the Tahoe just as they were even with the store. Only fifty yards away for a split second, Wendy could tell all were armed. None raised their weapons as Wendy drove past, never speeding up. Lowering the pistol, Wendy set it in her lap and rolled the window up. "You can get back up," she told the twins.

"At least they didn't shoot," Jo Ann said in a quivering voice.

Feeling the adrenaline leaving her system, Wendy held up her right hand and saw a slight tremble. "Yes, that is good news," Wendy admitted. "Jo Ann, open the center console and give me one of those small bottles."

The young cop couple hadn't had food, but they'd had flats of small energy drinks. "Can I have one?" Jo Ann asked, taking the top off the small bottle.

Taking the bottle, "One," Wendy said and then drained the bottle. Cringing at the aftertaste, "Sally, you can have one if you want," Wendy coughed and tossed the empty bottle in Jo Ann's floorboard.

"It's not that bad," Jo Ann noted after draining her bottle.

When the GPS announced left turn ahead, Wendy noticed the houses along the road had been replaced with businesses. Guiding the Tahoe into the opposing lane, Wendy passed a bus that had hit a delivery truck. "Shit," Wendy mumbled, seeing abandoned cars in the road ahead.

Taking her foot off the accelerator, Wendy left the pistol in her lap as she gripped the steering wheel with both hands. Slowing to fifteen, Wendy weaved through the stalled cars and then tapped the brakes, seeing the packed intersection ahead where they had to turn.

With a quick glance at the intersection, Wendy was sure she could get through but would have to slow to a crawl. "Screw it," she growled and tapped the accelerator, jerking the steering wheel to the left. Bouncing over the curb, Wendy drove across the sidewalk and bounced down over the curb into a large parking lot.

As the GPS told her she needed to turn around and get back on the road, Wendy drove across the parking lot, weaving around the few parked cars. "Turn left, Sheridan Street," the GPS called out as Wendy reached the entrance of the parking lot.

"I was," Wendy snapped at the GPS, speeding up and pulling out onto the four-lane road.

"People in those trees," Jo Ann called out.

As she turned onto Sheridan, Wendy glanced over and saw a dozen figures at a park. All were standing around several cars. One of the group, pointed at the blacked-out Tahoe and before Wendy turned her eyes back to the road, she saw the group running for vehicles.

"Fuck!" Wendy snapped as she pounded the steering wheel and pressed the accelerator.

"I see lights coming on," Sally announced from the backseat.

"Girls, if something happens to me, get Ryan and Noah and run," Wendy said as she picked up speed and weaved around a car. Speeding over an overpass, Wendy glanced in the mirror and saw the two cars pulling out.

"Go faster," Sally cried out, seeing the cars following.

"Baby, one person shooting out of a car only works in the movies," Wendy said, seeing an intersection ahead. "Pick your own battlefield," she mumbled, stomping on the brakes. Sally reached down to stop Noah and Ryan from sliding into the pillows on the floorboard.

When the Tahoe came to a stop, Wendy grabbed the AR off the dash and jumped out. Pulling the stock to her shoulder, Wendy aimed behind her as the cars topped the overpass. Flipping the selector to auto, Wendy took a breath and let half out, centering the red crosshairs between the lights of the first car.

Brushing her finger against the trigger, the M4 roared as Wendy squeezed off a six-round burst. She saw the car jerk to the right as she squeezed another burst off and saw several sparks as the bullets impacted the front of the car.

This time, the car jerked to the side of the road and hit the curb as Wendy turned to the other car and saw it was slowing. Wendy brushed the trigger two more times to send out short bursts and felt the bolt lock back. Ejecting and replacing the magazine, Wendy sent two more bursts into the second car and then moved back to the first and shot short bursts until she felt her bolt lock back again.

Jumping in the Tahoe, Wendy slammed the shifter into drive while tossing the M4 on the dash. Her door slammed shut as the Tahoe took off down the road. Glancing in the mirror, Wendy saw the lights of both cars not moving, but saw several gun flashes.

Jerking the steering wheel back and forth and making for a harder target to hit, Wendy weaved around an abandoned truck. When she glanced back to the mirror, Wendy couldn't see the car lights anymore.

Like a switch had been thrown in her mind, all of a sudden, Wendy heard Ryan screaming at the top of his lungs. Glancing to the backseat, Wendy saw Sally lying flat, holding Ryan and trying to calm him. Next to Sally, Noah was curled up in a ball, clutching Sally's leg and crying. He just wasn't crying as loud as Ryan.

"I'm sorry Ryan," Wendy said, turning back and saw Jo Ann climbing out of the floorboard. "Is everyone okay?"

"My ears hurt," Jo Ann shouted, opening and closing her mouth.

"Sally, do we have enough water to make Ryan a bottle?" Wendy asked and then noticed she was doing eighty. She slowed down as Sally sat up, digging in her backpack.

"Jo Ann, see if you have a bottle of water," Sally said, not finding one.

"I got two," Jo Ann said, holding one up. Sally passed a bottle and the can of formula up. As Jo Ann made up a bottle, Wendy slowed back to forty. Wendy never called out the few people she saw coming out of houses, looking in the direction they had come.

"I miss my suppressor," Wendy mumbled and then opened and closed her mouth, trying to pop her ears and reduce the ringing.

Holding Ryan to her chest, Sally put an arm around Noah and rocked back and forth, trying to calm both. "Are the bad guys still coming?" Sally asked and Noah's cry turned into a whimper as he looked up at Sally.

"No, I stopped them," Wendy reported with her voice quivering.

"You never said you had a machine gun," Sally snapped.

"Baby, a gun is a gun. The reason I used full-auto was to scare the bad guys. I could've hit the cars more if I had shot single-shot," Wendy explained, weaving around cars. Seeing a congested spot ahead on her side of the road, Wendy jerked the wheel into the opposing lanes.

"Don't make me spill the milk!" Jo Ann panted, looking at the powder in the scoop like it was gold.

"Sorry, but our side was clogged and I saw two people in a yard," Wendy said.

Carefully, Jo Ann dumped the scoop into the bottle. "I just didn't want to spill it," Jo Ann said, refilling the scoop. "You think you shot any of the bad guys?"

"Oh, I know I hit two," Wendy admitted.

Closing the can of formula, Jo Ann poured in the water. "What if they weren't bad?" Jo Ann asked timidly.

"Then why chase us?" Wendy asked back. "Baby, we are doing the best we can, but you don't chase people for any reason. They had cars, so they didn't need ours. I don't care if they wanted to sell us flowers. If I think someone is a threat to us, I'm shooting."

Passing the bottle back, Jo Ann looked up at Wendy. "I just don't want to hurt nice people," Jo Ann mumbled as Sally put the bottle in Ryan's mouth.

Taking a deep breath, Wendy exhaled to calm her nerves as Ryan stopped crying. "Jo Ann, have we chased anyone?" Wendy asked. "We didn't stop when we saw them so they should've known, we didn't want to be around people. But that didn't matter to them, they chased us."

Getting comfortable in her seat, Jo Ann thought about what Wendy had said. "Person in the other road," Jo Ann said, still keeping watch.

When they were half a mile away, the figure turned and ran over into their lane. Jo Ann tensed up to see the figure running right at them, waving its arms. "Do you think we should stop?" Wendy asked, not slowing down.

"No," Jo Ann answered as Wendy guided the Tahoe into the other lane. They could see the figure was a woman now as she moved with them. A hundred yards from the woman, Wendy jerked the steering wheel and crossed through an intersection to the westbound lanes.

The woman continued running and just barely missed running into the trailer. "There are cars everywhere. If she needed one, she could get one," Jo Ann said with a sigh.

Reaching over, Wendy patted Jo Ann's leg. "Baby, I know it's hard, but you and Sally have to know these rules for this new world. Just because that was a woman doesn't mean she wasn't bad. You have to be careful, even around other kids unless I say they are all right. When you get older, you and Sally will be making that call for Ryan and Noah."

"I understand," Jo Ann said.

"Right turn, US Highway 27," the GPS announced.

After Wendy turned, everyone relaxed as the houses fell away and fields surrounded them. "Where did you learn to shoot a machine gun?" Jo Ann asked.

"My husband," Wendy smiled. "He made several because he thinks we shouldn't let the government decide who has what."

With a big grin, Jo Ann turned to Wendy. "He sounds cool."

"Oh, he is," Wendy said.

Still rocking Ryan with Noah's head in her lap, Sally asked. "Will Arthur like us?"

"Girls, Arthur is going to spoil you," Wendy chuckled.

"What if he got sick?" Sally asked.

The burst of happiness left Wendy as she slumped in the seat. "We live way out in the country and he didn't have to go into town, so I'm betting he never came into contact with anyone that was sick. But if he did, Arthur is a nurse like I am, he knows how to take care of himself," Wendy said.

For several minutes, the Tahoe was quiet and then Wendy spoke again. "Even if he is gone, we have to wait for Joseph at our home. We can live there," Wendy told them in a low voice.

Nobody spoke for over an hour until Jo Ann spoke up, seeing a sign ahead. "Lake Placid, is that where that big alligator is from in the movie?" she asked.

"I hope not," Wendy said as the houses started getting closer together. Seeing a dark billboard ahead, Wendy slowed down so she could read it. "If we can, we are stopping there," Wendy said, pointing at the sign telling them a truck stop was ahead.

"What if people are there?" Jo Ann asked.

Speeding back up, "Then we don't stop," Wendy told her.

Ten minutes later, they saw a group of buildings near an intersection ahead and Wendy slowed to a stop. They all looked at the dark truck stop ahead. "Anyone see anything?" Wendy asked in a low voice.

"A cow," Sally said and Wendy glanced back and saw Sally pointing out the driver's side. Turning around, Wendy saw a cow standing in the ditch.

"I missed him," Wendy admitted, turning back to the truck stop. "I'm pulling up. Everyone, keep your eyes open."

On pins and needles, the twins scanned around as Wendy pulled up to the truck stop, only going five miles an hour. When she reached the building, Wendy stopped to see the glass door was busted open. "It's been robbed," Jo Ann said.

Not wanting to inform Jo Ann that what they had done would be seen as robbing, Wendy stared into the dark store and then around the area. Pulling up sideways to the store, Wendy stopped when the back of the Tahoe was in front of the door.

"Okay, Jo Ann, roll down your window and if either of you see anything, call out and let me know."

Jo Ann shook her head, "How about I stand at the door, so I can yell in the store and you can hear."

Looking around again, "Okay, but I want in and out," Wendy said, getting out.

"What about your machine gun?" Jo Ann asked.

"I have my pistol. I need arms to carry stuff," Wendy answered, pulling her pistol out.

Walking around the Tahoe as it idled, Wendy met up with Jo Ann as they headed for the door. They both jumped when they heard Sally roll down the back window.

Peeking in the store, Wendy didn't see anything moving and opened one of the glassless doors. Walking in with the glass crunching under her diving boots, Wendy made a mental note to see if those boots she'd found fit.

Holstering her pistol, Wendy pulled the flashlight off the duty belt and walked over to a clothes rack selling t-shirts. Grabbing a white one, Wendy wrapped the shirt over the flashlight and turned it on. Even that dimmed light made her blink. Walking around and making a mental inventory, Wendy saw all the beer, cigarettes, chips, and most of the candy was gone.

Seeing cases of bottled water stacked by the register, Wendy gave a sigh of relief. Setting the flashlight down, Wendy grabbed one case and carried it out. Seeing Wendy coming, Jo Ann opened the door to let Wendy out and then ran over and grabbed the cargo door and stepped back as the cargo door lifted up.

Putting the water inside, Wendy headed back to the store and saw cases of bottled sports drinks and grabbed one. Going back in, Wendy grabbed the boxes of trail bars someone tossed on the floor as they'd grabbed the candy. Putting the bars in bags, Wendy passed the bags to Jo Ann and then grabbed cans of soup and crackers.

Handing them off, Wendy stopped at seeing loaves of bread. Waving her flashlight around, Wendy saw peanut butter and jelly. Grabbing them, Wendy passed them off and started filling more bags, even grabbing a portable coffee maker.

Coming back inside, Wendy headed over to a display of audio books and grabbed several that they could all listen to. Walking by a busted display, she saw a portable DVD player. Grabbing the player, Wendy headed over and grabbed several movies and then filled bags with all the batteries she could.

Wendy froze when she saw canned formula behind the counter. Breaking into a run, Wendy rounded the counter and took all three cans of Ryan's brand of formula. Struggling to hold all the bags, Wendy came back out and looked around for diapers and saw two packages of pull-ups and one pack of diapers that would fit Ryan.

Putting them under her arms, Wendy headed for the door.

"We're running out of room," Jo Ann whispered from the door.

Walking out with her hands full, "We are done," Wendy said, grunting to get the last load in. As Wendy yanked the cargo door to make it close, she heard Jo Ann climb back in the Tahoe. Running around and jumping in, Wendy dropped the Tahoe into drive and rounded the store, pulling back on the highway.

As they were driving away, Jo Ann let out a gasp. "We just robbed that place!"

Chapter Twenty Eight
Growing up fast isn't always a choice

May 18

Hearing an alarm, Shawn sat up rubbing his eyes. Reaching over, he swatted at the alarm until it shut up, then turned to the bassinette and didn't see Lucas. "Shit," he grumbled, throwing his legs out of the bed. Getting up, he walked around the room to wake up the other boys. Kirk, Pat, and Tony all sat up and Shawn looked at Jim's empty bunk bed.

"Jim went to sleep with Arthur," Pat yawned out.

Jumping off the top bunk, "Yeah, he followed Arthur when Arthur got Lucas because he was crying," Kirk told him.

"Why didn't you wake me up?" Shawn moaned.

"Because Arthur had already got Lucas," Kirk snapped. "I was getting out of bed to feed him, but Arthur walked in."

"Oh," Shawn said, pulling on his pants. "We have to help more with the babies. They are wearing Arthur out."

"I told Arthur I was getting up to feed Lucas, but he told me to go back to sleep," Kirk said, pulling on his clothes.

"Are we working out today?" Tony asked, struggling to stand as he dressed.

Heading for the door while putting on his shirt, "We'll find out at breakfast," Shawn said, grabbing his AR. Stepping out into the hallway, he saw Andrea pulling on her shirt. "Where's Pam?" Shawn asked.

"Arthur got her last night," Andrea groaned and then looked at Shawn.

"Yeah, he got Lucas," Shawn said as they headed for the stairs. "I swear, I never heard Lucas wake up."

As both trotted down the stairs, Andrea looked over at Shawn. "Lucas doesn't cry loud, so you have an excuse. Pam screams bloody murder and I can't believe I slept through that," Andrea huffed.

Feeling somewhat better after hearing that, Shawn headed for the kitchen and stopped, not seeing Arthur already up. Andrea bumped into him and looked around not seeing Arthur. "I feel like shit now," Andrea moaned. "How can he function going that hard and that long?"

Waving a hand at the kitchen, "Undoubtedly, he can't," Shawn pointed out. "There has to be a way to wake up when a baby cries."

Pushing Shawn out of the way, Andrea walked through the kitchen and stopped at the master bedroom door. Arthur was sitting up in bed with pillows behind him. Sound asleep, Arthur's head was tilted back and his mouth was hanging open. Nicole and Lucas were cradled in his arms and Arthur's legs were bent forming a box, with Pam sleeping in the box formed by his legs.

Curled up next to Arthur were Robin, Beth, and Jim. "How the hell does he get Robin to wear pull-ups?" Andrea asked as Shawn eased past her.

"He puts them on her after she goes to sleep," Shawn answered in a low voice, moving to the bed. Carefully, he picked up Lucas and Arthur's eyes cracked open. "I'm changing him," Shawn whispered and Arthur's eyes closed back.

Andrea moved in and tried to get Pam and Nicole, but Shawn stopped her from picking up Nicole. When Andrea picked up Pam, they left the room. "I found out that if you take Nicole, he always wakes up," Shawn told her, walking through the kitchen.

They put the sleeping babies in bouncy chairs as the rest came downstairs. Shelia came in, putting her long red hair up in a ponytail and looked over at Andrea. "I swear, I never heard Pam wake up," Shelia said, holding up her hands.

Andrea just nodded and looked around the kitchen. Fourteen kids were here, plus her, and they couldn't even wake up when the babies cried. Being the oldest of the group, Andrea felt she should be the most responsible, but she didn't know how to take care of babies. She was the baby of the family and the youngest kid she had ever babysat had been eight.

Turning to the kitchen island, she saw Kirk and Pat already at work and starting breakfast with Vicki and Jodi. Taking a deep breath, Andrea moved in and started the coffee and then moved over, helping and learning.

After Betty pushed him back from doing the bacon, Shawn moved to the cabinets and grabbed the plates. Carrying the stack to the table, Shawn started setting the table.

Smelling coffee, Arthur's eyes struggled to open up. When his eyes finally opened, Arthur looked down at Nicole sleeping peacefully. Feeling bodies next to him, Arthur looked at the little kids beside him and groaned. "Robin, you don't sleep in your cowboy boots." Robin, nor Jim and Beth moved when Arthur groaned.

Looking at Robin's pink cowboy boots, Arthur wondered if he found her pink clothes, maybe Robin would keep them on. As that thought bounced around in his head, Arthur stood up and felt Nicole squirm in his arm. As a yawn erupted from Arthur, he glanced down to see Nicole giving a small yawn.

With her yawn finished, Nicole opened her eyes and saw Arthur looking down at her. "Hey, blue eyes," Arthur smiled and Nicole let out a coo. Setting Nicole on the bed, Arthur took off his shorts and pulled on his pants. Shoving his feet in his crocs, Arthur changed Nicole and then walked out of the bedroom and stopped.

The kitchen was a buzz of activity. Kids were moving everywhere. He would follow one with his eyes for a few minutes just to make sure progress was being made and to his surprise, each one was doing a task. Tony was feeding the dogs and cats. Shawn was setting the table. Shelia was putting the dishes up from the dishwasher and the others were cooking.

"Your mug is fixed," Arthur heard Andrea call out and turned to see her closing the waffle maker.

"Thanks," Arthur said, grabbing his mug and heading for the back door.

The eastern sky wasn't bright yet as he stood out on the patio. 'Meow', Arthur heard and glanced over and saw Kong approaching him. Stepping back, "You just go on," Arthur snapped, thinking about throwing his mug at the monster cat.

When Kong sat down, Arthur noticed a mound of fur beside the patio and made a wide circle around Kong. "How in the hell can you kill a raccoon that big?" he asked, looking at the huge dead raccoon. "The dogs can't even kill one that big, I'm sure."

Turning back to Kong, Arthur saw him cleaning his paws. "Okay, thank you," Arthur said, but still didn't get close to Kong. Hearing the back door open, he turned to see Shawn and Andrea walking out.

"Arthur, I'm sorry," Shawn started as he walked toward Arthur and then jumped back, seeing Kong. "Nice kitty," Shawn said, glaring at the cat and side-stepping around it. If the cat scared Arthur, Shawn would run from Kong and would feel no shame whatsoever.

"It's just a cat," Andrea huffed, throwing up her hands and saw Arthur pointing at the side of the patio.

As Andrea looked over and saw a mound of fur, Arthur spoke. "That is a thirty-pound raccoon that Kong killed and carried to the house. Coons that size, kill dogs."

Jerking her head back and staring at the cat in shock, Andrea side-stepped around Kong with Shawn. "Are you sure it's a cat? I've seen bobcats at zoos that weren't that big," Andrea said when she was standing beside Shawn and Arthur.

"Not sure, but he kills shit that tries to hurt the animals on the farm so he can stay," Arthur said, taking a sip and then smacked his lips. "To be honest, I'm scared to shoot him. It might just piss him off."

Shawn's body jerked as a shiver ran down his spine and then he turned to Arthur. "Arthur, I'm sorry. I should've heard Lucas and I don't know why I didn't. I'm…," Shawn stopped as Arthur raised his coffee mug up.

"Shawn, you're fourteen and have been busting ass since you joined this family. You have nothing to be sorry for," Arthur told him. "You wanted to try and did feed Lucas once. I'm head of this family and I heard Lucas crying after I fed Nicole. So, I went and got him."

"I'm eighteen!" Andrea snapped. "And Pam doesn't cry, she screams. I should've woken up."

Turning to Andrea with a huge grin, "Andrea, anyone can tell, you've never been around babies until now. You tried to get Pam to use the toilet two days ago. Granted, if you had gotten a six-month-old to use the toilet, I would've been impressed," Arthur chuckled and Shawn snorted, turning away. "Vicki did get up when Pam cried because she's been around babies, but I knew she was tired so I took Pam and fed her."

Cocking her head to the side, "Vicki got up?" Andrea asked, clearly confused.

"Andrea, Vicki alone took care of her group until she found us. She went out looking for food for Jodi and Robin, then fed and changed Pam," Arthur told her with a serious face and then turned to Shawn. "If you think back, Shawn, Beth is the one that woke you up when Lucas cried. I know because the first few days here whenever Lucas cried, Beth ran and grabbed you."

"I'll get Beth to sleep in my room again," Shawn nodded.

"If she wants to," Arthur said and then took a sip of coffee. "Don't get me wrong, I've never had to sleep with more than one little kid at once. One beats you half to death; a group beats you into submission."

Watching the way Arthur cuddled Nicole, Andrea gave a soft smile as she sighed. "Arthur, can I ask you something?"

"Sure," Arthur said, jerking his head to see movement and watched Kong walk over to the corpse of the raccoon. Grabbing it by the neck, Kong carried his trophy off.

"Eeww," Andrea shivered, seeing Kong carry something off that looked bigger than him. "Sorry," Andrea mumbled turning to Arthur and then asked. "I know you love and care for all of us, but Nicole is special. Can I ask why?"

Looking down at Nicole chewing her fist, Arthur smiled at her. "Nicole saved my life," Arthur answered bluntly. "I had given up and was looking for a fight. Rudy came along and any other time would've gotten the drop on me, but not that day. I went down in the valley and in my heart, knew I wasn't coming back to this house. Even though my wife's dying wish was for me to stay alive and keep the farm ready for our son to come home."

Hearing the sorrow in Arthur's voice, Andrea wiped tears off her face and then saw Shawn do the same.

Still looking down at Nicole, "Then I reached Tammy and Ted's and felt even more guilt because I'd never checked on them," Arthur said, smiling as Nicole closed her eyes slowly. "That's when I heard her crying out weakly. She had held on long enough for me to find her. Picking Nicole up that day, I knew I had a purpose. I had met Nicole on the day she was born and even then, knew she would always be special to me."

"Wow," Shawn sniffled. "Nicole saved all of us."

Arthur looked up from Nicole and over at Shawn. "Nicole saved you, so you could save all of us," Shawn explained, dragging his forearm across his nose.

"Never thought about it that way," Arthur nodded. "But Andrea is right; I care for all of you the same," Arthur said with a wide grin.

Hearing the back door open, they all turned and the grin fell off Arthur's face. "Robin, will you please wear some clothes?" Arthur whined just like a kid, even stomping his foot.

"No," Robin said, stomping her pink cowboy boot on the patio.

"Can you say anything besides 'NO'?" Andrea chuckled, walking over.

"No," Robin said, stomping her foot again.

When Arthur had brought Vicki and them to the house that first night, he'd checked all the kids over. Being a nurse, Arthur had plotted all of them on growth charts and had made sheets up for each one. Vicki's group had been easy because he had gone back to the daycare and gotten the files on them. Kirk and his brothers were harder, but he had the birthdays and found a medical emergency card in the mother's purse that gave basic health information. Shawn, he had asked and Andrea's group was old enough to answer.

Giving Robin her physical, Arthur had found out she was thirty-two inches tall which was perfect for her age, but only weighed twenty-four pounds. That gave her a lanky appearance which made her look smaller and younger than she was. The one thing that put him at ease was in the daycare file, it had clearly said that Robin didn't like clothes.

Andrea picked Robin up and brushed Robin's light brown hair out of her face. "Are we working out today?" Shawn asked as Andrea walked back over.

"No, everyone's too sore from the work and working out would do more harm than good," Arthur answered.

"Are we going out to get more loads?" Shawn asked with a grin, ready to drive the huge truck and trailer again.

"Not today," Arthur said and then drained his cup. "Today, we are working on the southern road that leads into the valley."

"Okay," Shawn said, remembering Arthur talking about that. "How in the hell do you hide a road?"

Grinning, Arthur glanced at Shawn, "Easy, if you're a sneaky motherfucker."

"Arthur, keep on with the language and I'm sure Robin, Pam, Lucas and Nicole will pick it up," Andrea sighed.

"Joseph's first word was 'Fucker'," Arthur chuckled and then stopped. "Holy shit, I didn't know Wendy could punch that hard."

Bending over and slapping his thighs as he laughed, "What happened?" Shawn asked.

"Someone cut me off in traffic and I rolled down the window and called him a Fucker. Sitting in the backseat in his car seat, I heard one-year-old Joseph say, 'Fucker'," Arthur said, then sighed. "Wendy didn't think it was that funny. When we got back to the apartment, she walked around the car as I got out and decked me. For a second, I'd thought she'd broken my jaw."

"You earned that," Andrea chuckled.

Nodding, "Yep, but I don't watch my mouth. I curtail it at times for fledgling ears, but I'm not limiting my vocabulary because others take offense to certain linguistic vitiations. They are only words; words that express unambiguous connotation and can relieve pent-up stress for the speaker which makes others that are around said speaker much happier because speaker isn't acting like a asshole," Arthur said and Shawn stopped laughing.

"Huh?" Shawn asked.

"Exactly," Arthur said.

"How can you go to church and talk like you do?" Andrea asked. "I hardly ever went, so I'm just asking."

"Andrea, language just conveys meaning. If it's the interpretation of that language that offends, don't interpret those words," Arthur said. "Am I religious? That depends. Do I believe in God? No, I *know* there is a God. I've seen too much in my life to even entertain that thought. Do I believe in the religions that are taught? No, what I believe is God is so much more than man's feeble mind can comprehend."

"But you went to church?" Shawn mumbled, trying to understand what Arthur was saying.

"Damn straight," Arthur nodded. "Church teaches something more than the Bible. It teaches morals and guess who goes there? Other people who believe in right and wrong, so we get along. But I'm selective on my churches. Wendy was raised Catholic but I'm sorry, they are a bit uptight for me. I like the structure, but we came to a compromise on Joseph; he was raised Baptist."

Shawn's mouth was hanging open as he gawked at Arthur. "Wow," Shawn mumbled.

Nodding, "Yeah, that sums it up rather nice," Andrea admitted.

The back door opened again and Kirk stuck his head out, "Breakfast is ready," he called out.

"That fast?" Arthur asked in mock surprise.

"You don't have any boxes so it takes a long time," Kirk huffed, ducking back inside.

"Why don't you have boxed food and stuff?" Shawn asked.

"Don't want the extra shit they put in," Arthur told him. "Many of the things that companies put in food here, other countries won't allow for human consumption. Besides, I would've had to buy those and that meant the government got money from me just because I wanted to eat. Wendy and I learned to do everything we could on our own. Hell, we make serious money selling stuff from here."

"Yeah, even a crop of marijuana," Shawn said, opening the door.

Stopping and giving a long sigh, "Shawn, I told you. That's hemp, not marijuana," Arthur groaned.

"It looks just like it," Shawn cried out. "Our neighbor grew it and I saw it."

"Why grow hemp?" Andrea asked, walking in and Arthur and Shawn followed to see everyone at the table waiting.

"Because I can make so much from it," Arthur chuckled, heading for his chair. "Fuel, paper, cloth, rope… Hell, it's a one plant shopping center."

"Clothes?" Andrea asked, putting Robin in her highchair.

"Hello?" Arthur said, sitting down. "Canvas is called 'canvas' because it first came from 'cannabis'."

Sitting down Andrea nodded, clearly impressed. "Now that is cool," she said. "And you do that?"

"Are you kidding?" Shawn chuckled. "They have silkworms."

Giving a remorseful sigh, "Yeah, that was Wendy's pride and joy, being able to produce silk," Arthur mumbled, rocking Nicole in his arm. "I only helped, but I guess I'm going to have to learn so I can teach all of you."

Leaning over, Andrea looked at Arthur's pants. "That's why the material for your clothes look so different, you made it," she gasped.

"Duh," Shawn sang out from across the table and Andrea cut her eyes toward him.

"But even you got boots the day we met," Andrea said.

Giving a regretful sigh, Arthur started loading his plate with his right hand as his left arm cradled Nicole. "That's one thing I've never done; shoemaking. I've got the books and tools, but never put the time into learning or doing it. Maybe one day."

Kirk and his brothers, along with Shawn stared at Arthur in shock. "But you can do everything!" Kirk cried out. "You sewed that sling up for Nicole to make it bulletproof and then showed us how to make boxes and wire those batteries up to those solar things and hundreds of other things."

"I wish I could do everything," Arthur said, trying to butter his biscuit with one hand. "What I know, I will and I am teaching all of you because you will need it now more than ever."

"Are we going to shoot guns?" Jim asked hopefully.

"If we get done early, we will," Arthur said and Jim pumped his fists in the air. "Jim, if you could recite the gun commandments from heart, I would be more willing to give you the chance to carry the AR I made for you."

Closing his eyes, Jim concentrated so hard his face was turning red. "One: Treat every gun as if it is loaded. Two: Always keep your gun pointed in a safe direction." Jim paused, squinting his eyes closed so hard his eyelids were turning white. "Three: Never point your gun at anything you don't intend to shoot. Four: Keep your finger off the trigger until you are ready to shoot. And five: Be aware of your targets foreground and background before you fire."

Jim opened his eyes and slumped sideways in his chair and his brother Pat reached out, catching Jim before he fell out of the chair. "My head hurts now," Jim mumbled as he rubbed his face.

Arthur just stared across the table at Jim. "Never seen that kind of effort in reciting anything," Arthur mumbled.

"Shit, I'm willing to let him carry my gun after watching that," Shawn chuckled.

"Jim, if you do good on the range today, you will get assigned your AR but it will be probationary," Arthur told him. Jim forgot about his head hurting as he bounced in his chair. "Jim, don't run from the lambs anymore."

Jim froze in midbounce, gasping at Arthur. "They attack me and try to eat my clothes to get to me!" Jim whined as the others turned away and snickered.

Looking up at the ceiling, "You can stop with the challenges any time now. I have learned humility," Arthur announced, then went back to eating.

Chapter Twenty Nine
You can't hide a road

After breakfast, the morning caravan of buggies descended the slope to the barn and tended to the animals. Pat drove Arthur and Nicole down in the lead with six buggies following behind. This was by Arthur's design, he wanted all the kids to know how to drive.

So far only Beth, Robin, and the babies hadn't driven. Beth had driven sitting in Shawn's lap a few times. The one time Robin had left her clothes on for half an hour, Arthur had tried to let her drive him around, but that stopped fast. Robin tried to run over the goats. The next trip into town, two electric kid cars came back to the farm, one for Beth and one for Robin.

Shawn moved to the milking area since they now milked four cows at a time. Shawn would empty the pumps as new cows were brought in. Now, they had twenty more dairy cows and that was when Shawn had learned what Kit and Kat were good at. He had thought they were just dogs and he heard Arthur talk about the dogs retrieving when they went hunting. What Shawn never expected was Kit and Kat could herd.

When they stopped at the farm with the trailers, Shawn actually felt a little fear about herding the cows into the trailer. All Arthur did was open one trailer and turned to Kit and Kat. "Load 'em," he commanded and the labs took off.

The labs made it look really easy until one bull decided he didn't want to go and charged the labs. That was when Donald and Daisy ran over and had words with the bull. It only took the bull a few seconds to figure out that leaving wasn't so bad.

Keeping an eye on the kids as they worked, Arthur moved over to the playpen that held the babies. The barn and hydroponic greenhouse had playpens he'd left there so the babies could be put down. But if worst came to worst, Arthur had a chest carrier he had sewn up that held Nicole and Lucas in slings on the side with Pam in a pack carrier in the middle.

Watching the kids with the sheared sheep, Arthur chuckled at remembering Vicki dragging a bag of wool. "They are going to get cold now," Vicki had pouted.

The sun was well up as they headed to the chicken coops. Even though the one they had moved from Jack's farm could automatically feed and water, Arthur had turned it off and they fed and watered the chickens.

With the chores done, everyone loaded up and headed to Jack's farm. This was where they parked all the vehicles and equipment now. Not to mention most of the stuff they had hauled back. There were mountains of stuff stacked in rows beside the barn.

As Shawn stopped in front of the barn, he looked at the long stack of chain link fence and a wall of pallets loaded with cinder blocks. Shawn didn't think there were any cinder blocks or bags of concrete left in a fifty-mile radius.

"Shawn, hook up the trailer with the plugs of grass," Arthur called out. "Andrea, hook up to the trailer with the trees. Kirk, you drive the tractor. Shelia, you take the tract steer. Pat, you drive the mini excavator."

Seeing the kids take off, Arthur headed for the Suburban and backed up to a trailer he'd had the kids help him on. It had solar panels mounted on one side and was loaded down with batteries and a large water pump.

After hooking up the trailer, Arthur did his walk around and counted heads. Checking the kids in the Suburban, Arthur picked Robin up and hugged her tight at seeing that she still had all her clothes on. Climbing in, he led the caravan down the valley at ten miles an hour. They were only going three and a half miles away, but it took a little bit to get there.

Vicki was sitting up front with Arthur and of course, Nicole riding in the crook of Arthur's arm. Beth and Jodi were in the back, singing to Lucas and Pam. Arthur was enjoying the sound of the kids as he slowly drove along, passing Tammy and Ted's house. Glancing over, Arthur saw the two graves they had dug and buried Nicole's parents in.

Turning south at the fork, Arthur couldn't help but think about how much Wendy would've loved having all these kids at the house.

"Is that the house?" Vicki asked, pointing ahead.

"Yep, Mike Kercher," Arthur said. "We call it the Kercher farm, but they don't farm anything."

"And we are going to hide this road?" Vicki asked with disbelief.

"You bet," Arthur grinned, pulling in front of the house. "Where do we set up the baby area?" he asked Vicki as he put the Suburban in park.

Looking around the area and giving the question very deep thought, Vicki finally pointed at the front yard. "I think the front yard. That way, it will be easier for everyone to switch out," Vicki answered.

"Then that's where it will be," Arthur said, climbing out.

Moving to the back of the Suburban, Arthur punched the fob to open the cargo door. Reaching in, he pulled out the playpen. Carrying it over to the shade of an oak tree in the front yard, Arthur grabbed one of the folded-up corners and jerked his hand back. He grinned as he watched the pen fold out, but not all the way. He placed Nicole in the bottom and then finished folding out the pen and locked the sides.

Turning around, he saw Vicki carrying Lucas and Betty carrying Pam over. Arthur watched as Betty placed Pam in the pen and then headed back to the Suburban. Nobody watched Vicki with the babies, that's who the kids went and talked to. To everyone, Vicki was considered, 'Little Momma'.

Carrying over three baby swings, Arthur grinned as the kids gathered around and Vicki told everyone the order that baby duty was going to go. It did hurt Beth's feelings because she was one of the ones that had to be watched. But Vicki told Beth it was her job to watch Robin, and the others would watch her. Beth always seemed to like that and didn't complain.

"Today by age, starting with the youngest and going to the oldest," Vicki called out and Jim groaned, since he was the youngest of the babysitters. "Unless Arthur says your job can't stop, you take your turn," Vicki said, looking around at the group with hard eyes.

She stopped when her eyes reached Andrea. "If the baby poops, you'd better change them and not leave it for the next person," Vicki told everyone but stared hard at Andrea.

"I only did that once," Andrea cried out and Vicki held up her hand.

"At feeding time, I'll come and help," Vicki said, dropping her hand.

"I would like to help," Andrea spoke up and Vicki gave a nod.

"Tony," Vicki snapped and Tony jumped. "Don't run with a baby in your arms."

Stomping his foot, "Robin was naked and wanted me to hold her," Tony whined.

Holding her hand up again, "No excuses," Vicki said and then turned to Arthur. "I'll try to feed Nicole, but she only likes her Arthur to feed her."

Putting the swings down, Arthur picked Vicki up in his arms and set her on his hip. "She needs to learn that others can feed her, but I'll do it if she won't eat. How about that?" Arthur asked and nuzzled his face into Vicki's neck, making her squeal.

"Okay," Vicki laughed out and he put her down.

Arthur turned to the kids. "I'm going to show you your jobs one at a time. Those of you on equipment, whose job is it to watch for others?"

"The operators," everyone answered.

"All machines are to be in low. Now, let's hide the road," Arthur said, leading the group to the creek that ran behind the house. "Pat, you will dig a hole here in the creek," Arthur said, walking out in the six-inch deep water. Grabbing rocks, Arthur outlined a circle. "You will dig it six-foot-deep, that's to the elbow of the arm."

Pat nodded and Arthur led them over to the tractor. "Now, that is a rotary tiller on the tractor and is very dangerous. Shawn will start off. We are tilling from here," Arthur said, pointing at a spot on the road. "All the way down the road to where that dirt track leads to the Kercher barn."

The kids looked back at the track to the barn that was across the dirt road. Going through an overgrown field, the track formed a circular drive that hit the dirt road just around a small curve a quarter of a mile away.

Walking around, Arthur continued laying out the jobs and then told the kids to get to work. He jumped up on the tractor and drove it to the road. Turning on the PTO shaft, Arthur lowered the tiller until the teeth were sunk in the packed dirt road.

Seeing Shawn understood, Arthur stopped and let him take over.

Arthur headed over to the trailer that had dozens of sapling trees with their roots bound up in burlap. Grabbing a bundle of orange flags, Arthur marked a line from the creek over the road Shawn was tilling up all the way to the hill that sat in front of the house.

After he did that, Andrea and several others started laying out metal fencing posts along the line Arthur had marked. Picking up a can of spray paint, Arthur moved past the line of flags and started painting Xs at random spots. Then, he had Shelia move over with the track steer that had an auger attachment on the front.

After the hole had been dug in the creek, Arthur pulled the trailer with the water pump over and unhooked it. Before he could go and check the work, Vicki called over the radio that Nicole refused to eat. Taking Nicole and the bottle, Arthur fed her as he walked around and watched over his kids.

Just before noon, they ate and then pulled over the forty-foot trailer that was carrying the pallets of sodded grass squares. Starting where the road was tilled up, they put the grass squares down over the road as Pat drove the truck very slowly, something Pat was very good at, down the tilled up road. They only had enough grass for several hundred yards.

As Arthur showed the kids how to use the seed spreaders, Shawn pulled the tractor over to the other trailer. Using the bucket, Shawn carried the trees to the holes that had been dug with the auger and dropped them in.

At two, they were putting up the barbed wire fence as Arthur pulled coils of water hoses from the trailer and laid them out. Kirk followed Arthur, carrying tripod water sprinklers that were five feet tall. When the sprinklers were set up, Arthur put a large hose in the hole that had been dug in the creek and turned a switch on the water pump.

The kids all turned as the sprinklers coughed and spit, then started sending out jets of water on the new trees and grass. "Holy shit, we hid a road," Shawn said, looking back from the front yard.

"I know where it was at," Shelia said, pointing at the very green grass.

"In a few weeks, you won't," Shawn said in amazement. "We can still use that dirt track to the barn but if anyone comes down this road, it will look like a dead end."

Walking over, Arthur patted Shawn's shoulder. "Now you're getting the idea. Work hard, but always work smart," Arthur told him. "We'll grab a 'Dead End' sign and put it on the road to finish the job."

"What about the north road?" Andrea asked.

"We will do the same where the road Ts off and crosses the north creek," Arthur said. "But that can wait. We have much more work to do; this was the road I was worried about."

"Guns now?" Jim asked, crossing his fingers.

"Not yet, we have work to do in the greenhouses and then we hit the gun range," Arthur said and Jim started jumping up and down cheering.

Pointing over at the pump trailer, Andrea asked. "What about that?"

"We'll leave it for a few weeks or so," Arthur said as the others started gathering up the stuff. "It's on a timer, so it will water the area for five hours every day. By then the grass should be set and if not, we'll leave it longer."

Everyone loaded up and took the new dirt track to pass a very dilapidated barn. Driving slow, Arthur felt like Pat as he glanced in the mirror to see the others following. Glancing to the backseat, Arthur saw Robin was passed out between the baby seats. "Holy shit, she's still wearing panties," Arthur mumbled. "And her boots."

"I wrestled her to get those panties on," Betty grunted from the back.

"It doesn't do any good," Vicki sang out. "Momma said she would grow out of it."

As soon as Vicki said 'Momma', Arthur heard a change in her tone and looked over. "Hey," he said and tapped the center of Vicki's chest. "As long as you're alive, she's right there with you, along with everyone you knew and know right now. We can only be sad now for short periods of time because each one of us is counting on the other very much."

"Do you get sad about Miss Wendy?" Vicki asked and Arthur swallowed a lump in his throat.

"Very much and I think about her every day," Arthur answered. "But I know she wants me to work hard and to be happy for this new family."

Looking over timidly, Vicki mumbled. "I feel bad sometimes when I'm happy."

"Baby girl, nobody would want you to feel bad about feeling happy. Especially after what's happened. We were once all separate but now, all of us are family. Not many in the world can say that now, so enjoy it," Arthur told her.

Looking ahead, Vicki nodded. "And you're the daddy who cusses and is super cool."

"Can I call you Poppa?" Jodi asked, climbing between the front seats.

Leaning over, Arthur kissed her on the cheek. "If you want to," Arthur said.

By the time they were finished in the hydroponic greenhouse, the greenhouse buried in the side of the hill, everyone was calling Arthur, Poppa.

All the kids were at the gun range on the other side of the knoll the greenhouse was buried in. Arthur had two 10/22s and two ARs with ten inch barrels for those who didn't have one to practice with. Each rifle had a suppressor. Jim was shooting the AR that Arthur had put together for him and was very proud.

Unlike Shawn and Andrea, everyone else was on probation with their guns. That meant they could carry them, but couldn't carry them with a round in the chamber. And Arthur always checked. Not only to see if a round was chambered, but if the weapon was on safe. To be honest, everyone was terrified if they were caught with a weapon off safe, so they checked constantly.

Watching the kids shooting, Andrea came over and stood beside Shawn and Arthur. "I never would've believed I would agree with giving a six-year-old an AR," Andrea said.

"He's almost seven," Shawn chuckled.

"End of this month, he'll be seven," Arthur said, watching Shelia change magazines on her AR.

"I know," Andrea huffed, rolling her eyes. "I was just saying I can't believe I agreed to it, not that I had a say."

Stepping over to Shelia, Arthur showed her how to change magazines by rocking the rifle to throw out the empty magazine. Walking back to Shawn and Andrea, Arthur nodded as Shelia did it. "I need all of you armed as fast as possible," Arthur said, never taking his eyes off the firing line.

"Yeah, it's dangerous out there," Shawn mumbled.

"We are way back in the woods," Andrea pointed out.

Shaking his head, Arthur headed back to the line to work with Tony. "I assure you, trouble will find us here and we will fight for our lives in this valley," Arthur said over his shoulder. The certainty in Arthur's voice startled them.

Both Shawn and Andrea jumped and fought not to look around. They knew the areas around the house and barn were monitored, but most of the cameras were set up for predators going after the farm animals. Not predators coming for them. Even the monitoring software that the cameras ran through was set up for animals. Until this morning, the only raccoon anyone had seen was on TV. And most of those were animated.

Arthur had it on his to do list and wasn't worried about it yet.

When Arthur came back, he stood between them. "You two will help enforce the probation by checking safeties and making sure a round isn't chambered," Arthur told both and both looked at him. Arthur's eyes roamed back and forth over the kids, watching their every move.

"How old were you when your dad taught you guns?" Andrea asked and Shawn groaned silently.

"Don't know who my dad is. My mom was a crack-smoking whore," Arthur said nonchalantly. "I shot my first gun at sixteen. In case you're wondering, I stole it from a federal building in Nashville. Still have it, but I keep it buried in a metal box. I'm sure you understand why. But, I'm thinking it will be safe for me to dig it up now."

Andrea's mouth fell open in shock as Shawn wanted to bow down and worship Arthur like a god. "Are you kidding?" Andrea gasped.

"Nope," Arthur chuckled. "Hope you don't think that's the only one I stole from the feds."

"You are so awesome," Shawn droned.

"Can I ask, when was the last time you stole?"

"Two days after my eighteenth birthday, October 23rd," Arthur answered. "Broke into an army depot in Kentucky and stole two M-16s with 203 grenade launchers. They're buried with the others. Before you ask, Wendy hadn't met me yet but I knew her. I knew if my luck ran out, I was an adult and I would be sent away for a long time, so I stopped. But I still kept up on the know-how."

"Poppa," Shawn said, making Arthur smile. "How many foster homes did you live in?"

"Sixteen," Arthur answered and then finally, Arthur glanced away from the firing line to Shawn. "Shawn, Wendy didn't take my last name when we married, I took hers. My birth name is Arthur Johnson, not Steele. I wasn't going to honor that skank by passing on her name."

As Arthur turned back to the firing line, Andrea mumbled, "Holy shit, sixteen."

"Guys," Arthur said as everyone on the firing line had stopped shooting and were listening, so Arthur glanced at them. "You know when I had my first real birthday party? You know, friends coming over, cake, and presents?" Arthur asked and then headed to the firing line to help pack up.

Grabbing the 10/22s, Arthur checked them and winked at those on the firing line and then looked up at Shawn and Andrea. "My son was ten years old and he and Wendy threw me a surprise birthday party down there in the office house. We lived there until

I finished this house. I have to say, it was worth the wait," Arthur smiled.

Seeing Jodi and Betty had their ARs, Arthur walked over and picked Nicole up from the playpen. "We are so throwing him a party," Shawn mumbled, watching Arthur walk away while surrounded by the kids.

"Okay, we need to find out when his birthday is," Andrea nodded as the group rounded the knoll.

Throwing up his hands, "He just told us," Shawn snapped. "October 21st."

"He remembers the day he chose to walk the line," Andrea said.

"Poppa also told me the reason he stopped doing the stupid shit was he was on a full academic scholarship," Shawn said, heading to the house. "He said colleges and corporations don't support people who resist them."

"The government better be glad Poppa decided to settle down. If he hadn't, I'm sure he would be rich and they would be poor," Andrea chuckled, heading to the house and heard a small splash.

"Robin!" Arthur shouted. "Take your boots off, not your panties before you jump in the swimming pool!" Arthur bellowed and Andrea heard a much bigger splash.

Chapter Thirty

A fear can be passed on

Hearing a giggle, Wendy opened her eyes as she sat up. Beside her on the blanket, Noah was playing with Ryan. Holding a stuffed toy, Noah would hold it over Ryan until it touched his face and jerk it back. Ryan would let out a giggle and then Noah would do it again.

"Did they wake you?" Jo Ann asked and Wendy turned to see Jo Ann sitting on the small trailer, looking out of the barn Wendy had pulled into last night.

Glancing at her watch and seeing she had slept for six hours, "I was supposed to be up two hours ago," Wendy said, pushing herself off the ground.

"Nah, you're driving, so Sally and I took watch," Jo Ann smiled. "Clouds are moving in."

Walking to the door, Wendy looked up at the dark clouds rolling in from the south. "Glad we left when we did," she said, feeling the fear building in her gut from storm clouds. Feeling Jo Ann step up beside her, Wendy looked down.

The only one actually wearing clothes was Noah. They were still wearing the wetsuits. The twins were wearing t-shirts over the wetsuits and Wendy saw Jo Ann had on a pair of tennis shoes they had picked up. "Pants didn't fit?" she asked and Jo Ann shook her head.

They were just north of Raleigh, Florida which was just a dot on a map. "How long until Sally gets up?" Wendy asked, moving to the trailer.

Looking at her watch, "Four o'clock," Jo Ann answered and moved over to help Wendy pull the gas tanks off. "How much gas did we use?"

"We have just over a quarter of a tank," Wendy told her, grabbing the funnel. "We were averaging twenty miles a gallon."

As Wendy put the funnel in the gas tank, she looked over and saw Jo Ann concentrating hard. "So, we need seventy-five gallons to get home," Jo Ann finally said.

"Very good," Wendy smiled. "We have six five-gallon cans, so how much is that?"

"Thirty gallons," Jo Ann answered quickly. "So, we won't have to get gas every time we stop?"

Pausing before she lifted up the first gas can, "No, if we stop and can fill the cans, we will," Wendy told her with a serious face. "We may have to change directions or any number of things. Always try to stay ahead of problems."

Nodding, Jo Ann moved over and helped Wendy lift the can up to the funnel. "It's heavy," Jo Ann grunted.

"Yes, it is," Wendy said and saw Noah come over while looking up at her and holding the stuffed animal up. "Can't play right now," Wendy told him, tilting the can back so the gas wouldn't overflow the funnel.

"Noah, sit with Ryan so he doesn't roll off the blanket," Jo Ann said liking the fact that the can was getting lighter. Noah took off back to the blanket and sat down.

It took three and a half cans to top off the Tahoe and both were panting as Wendy grabbed the hose from the Tahoe. She looked at the four cases of bottled water and two cases of sports drinks, hoping that would be enough to get them home.

"Wake Sally, so we can get some gas," Wendy said, picking up an empty can.

When Sally got up and saw Wendy at the door while holding the can, "Hold on, I saw something that will help," Sally said and ran into the barn. She came back rolling a red wagon.

"That's great," Wendy said, putting the can she was carrying in the wagon. She turned to see Jo Ann putting the baby pack carrier on and moved over and helped. When Wendy put Ryan in, she saw Ryan was almost half the length of the twins with his legs hanging down.

Checking her vest, Wendy grabbed the M4 off the dash since she didn't have to carry gas cans. Draping the single point sling over her head, Wendy checked the rifle and then let it hang under her right arm. "Let's get some gas," she said, picking Noah up and setting him on her left hip.

Feeling the magazines for the pistol under his butt, Noah kept wiggling as they walked out of the barn. "Did either of you hear or see anything?" Wendy asked.

"I saw an airplane," Sally said, pulling the wagon and Wendy jerked her head to look down at Sally.

"You did?" Wendy cried out. "When?"

"Just after eleven o'clock," Sally answered and then pointed over the field to the south before moving her arm to the east. "It flew over there, heading that way."

Liking the sound of that, Wendy squeezed Noah and lifted him up so he wasn't riding on the magazine carriers on her belt. "Anything else?"

"I heard engines," Jo Ann said, pointing to the east. "But they were really far off."

"No gunshots?" Wendy asked hopefully and both shook their heads and Wendy gave a thankful sigh.

They checked the farm truck, but it was diesel. Moving to the house, they saw two cars under the carport. When they'd arrived this morning, Wendy only opened the door of the house and smelled rotting flesh inside but she had called out. When nothing had come, she'd headed back to the barn.

"Let's see how much we get," Wendy said, putting Noah down. One was an old Lincoln and the other was a new Cadillac and had an anti-siphon valve. Reaching into the wagon, Wendy pulled out the oil drain pan and slid it under the back. Taking the M4 off and putting it on the trunk, Wendy grabbed the large screwdriver and hammer.

Crawling under the back, Wendy put the pan under the gas tank and took out the drainage plug in the pan. "Get a can ready," she said, putting the tip of the screwdriver against the tank. Arthur could do this with the heel of his hand, but Wendy needed a hammer. She tapped the screwdriver and punched the sheet metal that formed the fuel tank before yanking the screwdriver out.

A stream of gas shot out and Wendy centered it over the drainage pan, then scooted out. "It's peeing gas," Jo Ann laughed as Wendy laid the empty gas can down on its side.

"We need the pee," Wendy grinned, putting the hose from the oil pan drainage spout into the gas can.

The girls looked on as they heard the gas draining into the oil pan and then into the gas can. "Yes, Arthur taught me this. He said it was faster but you ruin the gas tank, but the cars he did it to, he didn't care," Wendy told them, seeing the fuel level in the gas can was nearing the opening.

Slowly, Wendy sat the gas can up while leaving the hose inside and the girls watched in wonder. "I think it's faster if you just suck it out," Sally said.

"Couldn't. New cars have a valve to stop just that," Wendy told them, grabbing another gas can.

When the gas stream finally stopped, the three empty cans were full. "Wow," Jo Ann said, bouncing Ryan in the carrier.

"Won't they have gas cans here?" Sally asked, looking around. "They have tractors and stuff, it's a farm."

"Good thinking," Wendy said, putting the stuff in the wagon. "Let's pull this back and look around real quick, then eat and get back on the road."

Sally went to grab the wagon and Wendy almost stopped her, but only said, "It's going to be heavy."

Grabbing the handle, Sally pulled hard to get the wagon to start rolling. It rolled fine on the cement carport but when the wheels of the trailer hit the grass, Sally had to pull hard and grunt for every inch. Bending over, Wendy pushed on the back and Sally gave a relieved smile.

Reaching the barn, Wendy put the cans on the trailer but let the twins strap them down. Sally assured them there weren't any gas cans in the barn, so they headed over to a shed. Inside, they found six yellow diesel fuel cans and one blue kerosene can. All of them held fuel. Then in the corner, Jo Ann found three red five-gallon cans. Two were empty and one was half full.

Letting Sally carry the empty cans, Wendy carried the half full can back and poured it into the half can that was strapped down. Putting the three cans on the wagon, they headed back to the carport. Shoving the siphon hose in the tank, Wendy blew and then sucked before yanking the end from her mouth and shoving it in the first can.

"I think this way is faster," Sally mumbled.

"I do too, but it tastes nasty," Wendy said, spitting out the gas taste.

When the three cans were full, Wendy pulled out the hose that was still pouring out gas. "Wish we could've taken all of it," she mumbled, putting the hose in the wagon. Again, she helped Sally get the wagon back to the barn but this time, Noah moved in front of Wendy to lean down and push the back of the wagon.

"Good boy," Wendy said, moving her right arm off the wagon and holding the M4 that was swinging under her arm, so it wouldn't hit Noah.

"With what we used last night, we have enough gas to get home!" Jo Ann announced as they strapped in the new cans.

"It would be cutting it close but remember, we will refill gas cans because I don't want to run out in the middle of nowhere," Wendy said, helping Jo Ann take the baby carrier off.

"I know, but it just feels good," Jo Ann smiled as Wendy took Ryan.

Reaching out, Wendy hugged Jo Ann. "Yes, it does," Wendy admitted, then moved over and hugged Sally. "We are doing pretty good."

Everyone sat down on the blanket and ate peanut butter and jelly sandwiches. Pulling out her pistol from the holster, Wendy started going over the commandments and how the gun functioned. Everyone was on their second sandwich and Ryan had finished his bottle when thunder rumbled across the sky.

Wendy glanced outside and her mouth went dry at seeing lightning flash to the south and the wind picking up. "Time to load up," she said, jumping to her feet. The twins looked on in shock as Wendy moved at hyper speed, loading up the last of the stuff.

Picking up Noah, Wendy put him in and then grabbed Jo Ann who was holding Ryan. Lifting them up, Wendy put them in the back and turned around to pick up Sally. Yanking her door open, Wendy put Sally in and pushed her until Sally stepped over the center console and dropped into the passenger seat.

Taking her M4 off, Wendy tossed it on the dash as she hopped in the seat. The engine was cranked before her door closed. "Ready?" Wendy asked, but didn't wait for an answer as she dropped the shifter in reverse.

Throwing up dirt as she backed up, Wendy tapped the brakes and threw the shifter into drive. Instead of pulling around the house and back to the road, Wendy took off across the grassy field. Barely slowing when she reached the ditch, Wendy guided the Tahoe back onto the road. Glancing back and seeing the trailer was fine, Wendy hit the accelerator.

The girls looked at Wendy in shock. Wendy was clearly scared and that upset their world to no end. "What's wrong?" Sally asked, glancing over at the speedometer and saw they were at fifty.

"A storm is coming," Wendy cried out very fast.

Sally turned to look at Jo Ann in the back who just shrugged. When Sally turned back to Wendy, thunder exploded outside and Wendy levitated out of the driver's seat and Sally felt the Tahoe speed up. Hearing the patter of rain, Sally saw large raindrops hitting the windows.

"It's just rain," Sally finally said.

"Sally," Wendy snapped as she started hyperventilating. "This is the south! Tornados drop out of the sky, destroy everything, and kill you! They like dropping from the sky in storms, not rain showers. That is a storm brewing outside!"

With wide eyes, Sally turned to Jo Ann and saw her face was pale. Having never given a thought about a storm before, the twins were now filled by Wendy's terror. Spinning in her seat, Sally looked around them. Not for people, but for funnel clouds; people be damned.

The rain picked up and Wendy had to slow down as lightning flashed outside and thunder exploded, making everyone squeal. Noah and Ryan latched onto Jo Ann as she too tried to see outside through the sheets of rain.

Almost missing a turn because she couldn't hear the GPS, Wendy slowed down to twenty. "Sally, turn the GPS up so we can hear it," Wendy said, having to raise her voice over the rain.

"Maybe we should've stayed in the barn," Jo Ann yelled from the back, trying to see funnel clouds even though it was dark outside now.

"No! Tornados love mobile homes and barns, you never stay in those!" Wendy shouted, gripping the steering wheel hard. With every flash of lightning, the twins scanned around as thunder shook the Tahoe.

Lightning forked through the sky, turning night into day and Sally cried out, "Tornado!" and Wendy buried her foot in the floorboard. Unable to see far up ahead of them, even with the lights on, Wendy turned to the GPS screen and followed the road using the car on the screen.

Jo Ann leaned over so she could see out the passenger windows as lightning flashed and she saw the shadow looming behind them. As she took a breath to scream, lightning flashed again and Jo Ann saw the shadow was a water tower. Not sure if that's what her sister had seen, Jo Ann kept looking around.

With her face pressed against the passenger door window, Sally tried to see where the shadow had gone but couldn't because trees were around them now. "I don't see it anymore," she finally said. Then, Sally realized they were hauling ass.

Turning around, Sally glanced over at the speedometer and saw the needle passing ninety. Looking at Wendy, Sally noticed Wendy would glance out the windshield but was keeping her eyes on the GPS screen. "Don't wreck or the tornado will catch us," Sally said with a dry mouth.

Nodding, Wendy tapped the brakes until she slowed to forty and she could see out of the windshield again as the wipers tried to keep the water off. Even tiny little Ryan could feel the fear that filled the Tahoe as he clutched Jo Ann tight.

It was an hour later when the rain slacked off and Wendy turned on the post light and aimed the powerful spotlight ahead. Now able to see really far, Wendy sped back up as the rain started coming down hard again. Having watched Wendy, Sally reached up and swiveled the post light in front of her until it pointed forward and turned it on.

With the two police spotlights shining, the Tahoe sped on until they crossed into Georgia. It was only then that Wendy slowed back to forty and turned the spotlights off. Everyone was panting hard like they had run the distance instead of ridden.

Climbing in the back, Sally grabbed bottles of sports drinks and handed a bottle of water to Jo Ann. Climbing back into the front seat, "Are there a bunch of storms like that near the house?" Sally asked and then handed Wendy a sports drink.

Bobbing her head side to side, "My husband built me a concrete house that a tornado can't knock down," Wendy sang out with a sassy tone.

"I love Arthur," Sally and Jo Ann said in unison.

Leaning over, Sally looked at the gas gauge. "The truck doesn't like going fast in the rain," Sally noted, seeing the needle at half a tank.

"I'll find more gas because I wanted out of that shit," Wendy said and turned up the bottle of sports drink and didn't stop until it was empty.

Rolling down her window, Wendy tossed the empty bottle out and then rolled her window back up. Looking in the rearview mirror, Wendy could see the flashes of lightning behind them as the rain finally stopped. "Girls, I want to stop and fill up, just in case we have to outrun the storm again," Wendy said.

"Okay," the girls said.

Not pulling over, Wendy stopped in the middle of the road. With both Noah and Ryan asleep, the three jumped out, acting like a NASCAR pit crew. The tank was topped off, all three peed and were back underway in five minutes.

When Wendy turned heading west, the twins kept their eyes scanning and looking for funnel-shaped shadows as Wendy's fear of storms was joined by new converts.

Chapter Thirty One

It's not wasted money, it's only taxpayer money

Feeling the ground shake, Sarah sat up and realized she had fallen asleep in her chair. She felt the room shake and even watched a pencil roll an inch on her desk. "What the hell?" she mumbled and grabbed the phone and pressed one of the speed dial buttons.

The phone rang and rang until Sarah finally hung up and pressed another number. Like before, the phone just rang and rang. Hanging up, Sarah tried two more numbers and felt more trembles, seeing it was the entire room shaking.

Her door busted open and Sutton barged in, "The bunker is under attack!" he gasped.

Hanging up the phone, Sarah jumped up. "By who?"

"Citizens," Sutton said out of breath, "seems this area wasn't as secret as the government hoped. I finally got one of the guards outside to answer the radio. He said it was thousands and they had heavy equipment and are using it to get inside."

"Bullshit! That door is ten feet of steel, if it's an inch," Sarah said, leaning over and tapping her keyboard.

"Sara, they aren't digging at the door. They are digging through the concrete around it," Sutton said as Sarah sat down, staring at her computer screens. Walking around and standing behind her, "Holy shit!" Sutton gasped.

One of the biggest bulldozers he had ever seen was rolling over the bunker, pushing up concrete as a dozen excavators dug into the concrete. A puff of smoke went off near the massive door and they felt the ground shake. "They are using explosives," Sarah said, tapping the screen and more images started flickering on.

"That's some of the ventilation stacks," Sutton said, pointing at people pouring drums of liquid down the broken pipes. He didn't need the camera to zoom in to see the red noses on many of those attacking.

"That motherfucker left us!" Sarah shouted and Sutton searched the subdivided screens until Sarah clicked and the image of Marine One lifting off the helipad filled one screen and then two identical choppers flew up beside it. The choppers turned and headed west. "Without this team, what can he do?"

"Live for a day," Sutton answered, feeling the room shake.

They both jumped as an alarm sounded and a voice came over the intercom. "West entrance has been breached. Please proceed past section doors."

"That's us," Sutton said as Sarah tapped the screen. "All that equipment was at the north entrance."

"No, they have some at the west entrance," Sarah said as fear gripped her. "What do we do?"

"I don't mean to sound funny, but we need to get the hell out of here," Sutton replied, then walked out of the room. He walked to the observation window and hit the intercom. "Move your asses, we have a mob breaking in," Sutton called out and the group ran for the decontamination chamber.

Walking back into Sarah's office, he saw her on the phone. "Who are you calling?" Sutton asked.

"Telling security not to close the doors into the central bunker until we get there," Sarah snapped, hanging up and pressing another number.

Walking around the desk, Sutton took the phone from her and hung it up. "We go there, we will get infected," Sutton told her. "You have the work backed up?"

"Yes," Sarah said, pointing at an external hard drive.

"Take it and come on," he said and left. Yanking the wires from the drive, Sarah took off after Sutton and found him in the changing room. "No, leave your suits on," he said, grabbing his off the wall and tossing one at Sara.

Everyone just stared as the ground shook again. When he was suited up, Sutton looked around the room at everyone in the blue hazmat suits. "Follow me and stay close," Sutton said, grabbing an emergency flashlight off the wall.

When he opened the door leading to the massive tunnel, everyone heard machine gun fire. Stepping out, Sutton glanced to his left that lead to the west entrance and saw soldiers in gas masks behind concrete barriers, shooting down the tunnel.

Running across the tunnel, Sutton opened the door to their quarters and ran in. Moving down the central hall, he glanced back and saw the last person close the door. "Are we going to hide under the beds? Because, I always got found there!" Sarah shouted inside her suit and only Sutton in front of her heard.

"Don't ever hide there," Sutton said, moving past a large common room. He turned into the men's room and walked into a large shower area.

"There's nowhere to hide," Sarah pointed out as Sutton moved over to a wall, grabbing the metal panel.

"I always had the best luck hiding under the stairs," Skannish said, walking up beside her.

They both jumped as the metal panel came off the wall with a snap. As Sutton moved to the side, they could see a rock wall but it was yards away. "Damn it, go through, we don't have all day," Sutton shouted and Sarah grabbed Skannish's hand and pulled him through the opening.

When she climbed through and turned around, it was then Sarah realized a hole had been carved out of the rock and a partitioned building had been put in the cavity. She turned around and watched Sutton back inout, holding the metal paneling. "Oh, dear Scott, my boy, you have some explaining to do," Skannish sang out.

They saw Sutton jerk his hands back as the metal slammed against the opening. "That took forever the last time," Sutton mumbled, but everyone heard because of the echo in his suit.

"Follow," Sutton said, walking past them and the gunfire retreated down the tunnel closer to them. When they neared the end of the building, everyone saw a dark gaping tunnel that led into the rock face.

When they followed Sutton into the tunnel, everyone stopped, gasping. It was just as big as the main tunnel leading to the central bunker. They all saw Sutton hadn't stopped and took off after him. The flashlight in Sutton's hand only sliced the darkness ahead without ending. Below their feet the floor was asphalt, but there were no overhead lights. When Sutton's flashlight shined around, they noticed the walls and roof overhead were exposed rock. In all the other tunnels and areas, the rock was covered with steel or concrete facing.

Hearing Skannish breathing hard, "Sutton, we have to slow down. Skannish can't keep this pace up," Sarah yelled, knowing they had traveled over a mile. Sutton stopped, shining the flashlight down the tunnel. When the beam hit the wall ahead, Sutton saw they were approaching a curve.

"We can walk now," Sutton told them.

"Now tell me, how did you know about this?" Skannish panted.

"After finding out about the security guards sneaking out and nobody figuring out how the flu got in the other bases, I asked the president if I could have a detailed plan of this bunker," Sutton explained. "I wanted to know if people could sneak in and the president sent me the plans."

He turned around and shined the light down the dark tunnel. "This is the way to the train station," Sutton told them.

"Are you joking?" Sarah asked and the group followed Sutton as he walked down the tunnel.

"Nope. One end of the train tunnel goes all the way to Camp David, the other end stops somewhere near the Pentagon," Sutton told them and then glanced back. "According to the plans, this part was stopped a year into the building of this bunker. But the train station area was completed."

"I can't believe you went off exploring like Indiana Jones and didn't invite me," Skannish chuckled. "My, I have to say, this is extraordinary."

Rounding another curve, they were met with a steel wall and Sutton walked up to a hatchway. Unlocking the wheel, Sutton spun the handle and then opened the door up. "That apartment building we were staying in was just placed in the opening of this tunnel, since they already had the space," he told them, stepping through the hatchway.

Everyone followed him in and were shocked to see Sutton taking off the suit. "Close the hatch. This area has its own filtration system down the tunnels. They aren't connected to the complex," Sutton told them.

Then everyone noticed there were lights around them, not many but light fixtures were overhead. "My word, look at this," Skannish said, kicking his suit off and looking down the tunnel and saw it opened up in a large area. "And to think I felt guilty, asking for a new desktop computer last year. How many billions did they just throw away with this?"

"I don't even want to know," Sutton laughed. "I've only been down here twice exploring, but found rooms stocked with all kinds of stuff."

"So that's why you stopped putting up a fight these last few days when I told you to go to sleep," Sarah snapped and everyone snickered.

"Well," Sutton cringed. "If I hadn't, we would be trapped in the lab."

"I wonder how many know of this?" Skannish mumbled as they stepped out into a cavernous opening. Train tracks ran through the center and the area could only be called a train station. "Reminds me of Grand Terminal in New York."

Raising his hand, Sutton pointed at buildings on the same side of the tracks they were on. "That first building was going to be a restaurant; a very fine dining restaurant. Those buildings past it are now just storage rooms. The one I checked out held hundreds of boxes of the old Nintendo entertainment systems," Sutton told them and then led them over.

"I hope there is food in that restaurant," Sarah said, finally letting Skannish's arm go and letting him walk on his own. Then she registered what Sutton had said. "Wait, the NES was put out in the eighties."

"I know. Me and my sister each had one," Sutton chuckled.

"How long do you think this area has been sealed off?" Sarah asked as Sutton opened the door to the restaurant.

"The last building on this side is packed with cases of MREs with a date of six years ago. So, I know someone has been in here in the last six years," Sutton answered and they all stopped to look around the opulent restaurant. At the far back corner, they saw a laptop set up on a corner table.

"That's mine," Sutton told them. "It's nice and quiet here."

"How many entrances into the complex lead here?" Sarah asked.

"Only the one we used," Sutton told her. "There are two maintenance tunnels that open up to the outside from here. I only had time to follow one and it was welded up and the outside opening was filled with cement."

"How do you know that?" Skannish asked, sitting down.

"It said so on the plan. The other one said the same," Sutton said, sitting down. "In each tunnel, according to the plans, there are entrances. The one that leads to Washington, you can see tire tracks. I'm not an expert, but they look old."

Slapping his thigh, "I feel like a kid, one of those Goonies," Skannish cackled. "I wonder if there is a pirate ship around here."

The others moved around, looking at the fine china and silverware sitting on the tables as Sarah sat down at the corner table with Sutton and Skannish. "Why is there power here?" Sarah asked.

"Well, you may not believe this, but they put in a nuclear power station," Sutton told her. "It's not a big one and it's only a mile from Camp David and supplies backup power there. It was put in to power the trains."

"What were those buildings on the other side for?" Sarah asked, seeing a bottle of water beside Sutton's laptop and grabbing it.

"Living areas, shops, a movie theater, a bowling alley and such, but most I looked in are just packed with supplies," Sutton told her. "This was going to be another living area around the train entrance, but they stopped and I don't know why."

Sarah looked up and saw the others leaving the restaurant to go explore. "Do you have any idea where the president is headed?" she asked.

"Yep, Denver," Sutton answered quickly. "If you think that complex we were in was big, it's nothing compared to that one."

Draining the bottle, Sarah looked over at him. "How do you know?"

Tapping the keyboard on the laptop, Sutton turned it around and showed her the screen. "Whoever the president told to send me the file, sent me the files on every top secret bunker the US has."

"How do you know it's all of them?"

Tapping the screen, "Sarah, that's seventy-nine bunkers in the US, linking tunnels connecting military bases and one bunker in Hawaii," Sutton told her. "I hope that's all because that would explain a lot of the debt."

With a huge grin, Skannish stood up. "Will you two accompany me so we can explore this?"

"What about the vaccine we were making?" Sarah asked, standing up.

"Well, my dear. I'm sorry to say, we will have to start over," Skannish said, walking slowly toward the doors. "Those that broke in sealed everyone's fate here. Atlanta only had several dozen chickens that were immune delivered to them."

Sutton walked past her, following Skannish. Putting the empty water bottle down and following, "I hope there is water," Sarah said.

"Oh, there is," Sutton told her, following Skannish out the doors. "Underground lake across the tracks that's filtered in a plant. It's a gravity based system and I don't think the filtration was necessary."

"So, we just explore while people die?" Sarah asked as Skannish headed into the first building.

"Sarah, we can't be exposed to the virus for several days at the soonest. Those people out there are just scared. We will figure out our next move later but now, let's see what our tax dollars have stored down here," Sutton told her, holding the door open. Inside, they could hear Skannish cackling up a storm.

"So, you played Nintendo?" Sarah asked walking in. "You think they have TVs and we could hook one up?"

"Oh, I'll kick your butt on Mario," Sutton boasted, following her inside.

"They have 'I Love Lucy," Skannish howled, holding up a VHS tape from a box he'd opened.

"Haven't seen one of those in a long time," Sutton admitted, looking at the tape.

"What is it?" Sarah asked, wrinkling her brow.

"Oh shit, do I feel old now," Sutton groaned. "Do you mean the tape or show?"

"Both! Who's Lucy and why is someone in love with her and why would others care?" Sarah asked with a shrug.

Skannish stopped opening the next box and turned around, not laughing anymore. "You were very abused as a child to even ask that," Skannish declared.

With her mouth gaping open, Sarah turned to Sutton who just shrugged. "Don't look at me because I know they have reruns on Nick at Night," Sutton said, moving down the room between stacks of boxes.

Chapter Thirty Two
The Caravan Man arrives

May 19

With his arm resting on the door, Shawn glanced over at Tony. They had pulled out after feeding the animals and he was driving the new Chevy 3500 quad cab and pulling a forty-foot trailer. In front of him was Andrea in the Dodge they had picked up on the day Andrea and her group had joined. But now, Andrea was pulling a forty-foot trailer like he was.

Only Arthur, driving the Suburban in the lead, was pulling the same trailer they had started out with. "Why doesn't Arthur let you drive one of those big trucks with him?" Tony asked. "I can drive this truck."

"Because we always go back to the shipping yard," Shawn answered and glanced over to see Tony was looking around, even glancing behind them. "If anyone is watching, they will see us coming back when Arthur loads those empty shipping containers."

The day after Andrea had joined them, after loading trailers from stores on the way home, they had set out to a trucking terminal. Arthur had climbed in one of the bobtail semis and had hooked up a tandem trailer. Even Shawn could tell Arthur had never driven a tandem trailer.

With Shelia driving the Suburban, the group had followed Arthur home as he'd driven the tandem trailers with shipping containers on them. Some days when they went out, Arthur would drive the truck back to the terminal and park it.

Then, Arthur would climb in the Suburban and they would head off into a nearby town and collect supplies. On the way back, Arthur would head back to the terminal, load two more containers, and lead them home. Behind Jack's barn now sat twelve of the containers. Yesterday, they had started moving stacks of plastic bins in the containers and it was then that Shawn realized Arthur wanted the stuff protected from the weather.

Of all the places they went for supplies, food stores were never on the list. Arthur avoided those like Satan was hiding at each one. More than once, Shawn had suggested it with all the mouths they had now to feed. It'd been only three days ago when he'd found out why.

They were pulling stuff from another hardware store and there had been a small grocery store across the street. When you added up both parking lots and the road the buildings were on, they'd been about three hundred yards from each other. But that hadn't stopped Vicki from spotting people running in and out of the grocery store.

Shawn remembered moving to the door and watching two men drag a woman out by the hair on her head. Someone did run to help, but one of the men had raised a pistol and shot them. When they had called Arthur over, he'd just told everyone to load up and opened the sliding doors.

Nobody moved as Arthur had slid the outer doors open and lifted his AR. Everyone jumped when his rifle coughed and those with rifles lifted them up, using the scopes to see what had happened. One of the men was on the ground holding his bloody side while the other held the woman's hair, spinning around and looking for the shooter.

When Arthur's rifle coughed again, the man let the woman go before grabbing his chest and stumbled around until he fell. The woman ran over and kicked him in the face and took off running.

Cool as a cucumber, Arthur had closed the outer door and walked back inside. "I said, load up," he'd snapped and then had picked Nicole up from the playpen.

"You think Arthur will let anyone else join us?" Tony asked as Shawn slowed, taking a sharp turn.

On instinct, Shawn looked back at the standup forklift strapped down on his trailer. Seeing it hadn't moved, Shawn glanced over at Tony. "I don't know," Shawn shrugged.

"I hope he doesn't," Tony said as the radio went off.

"People at the van ahead on the right," they heard Arthur's voice call out.

Trying to act calm, Tony pulled his AR up and turned to face the passenger window. They saw a nice conversion van parked in a large gravel area. Three people and a kid were standing around an outdoor grill. Shawn gave a sigh at seeing the group wave because he could see weapons on the adults.

"Tony, if Arthur didn't take risks on us, we wouldn't be with him," Shawn pointed out as Tony turned, keeping an eye on the group until they were out of sight. "He doesn't need us, that's for sure, and we are more of a drain than help, if you ask me."

"But we aren't scary," Tony said, turning around. "All those that have asked to come with us were freaky."

Remembering a sixteen-year-old boy they had met in Conway, Shawn couldn't help but shiver. Shawn was big for his age and was bigger than the boy that had strolled up, carrying an AK47 and two Glocks strapped to his hips. But the boy just gave him the creeps.

"We have to trust Arthur on who joins," Shawn finally said.

"But he asked you about that boy," Tony almost whined. "He never asked anyone about the others."

"That was the only kid so far that has asked to come. All the rest were adults," Shawn reminded Tony.

Looking over at Shawn, Tony was clearly worried. "I know, but I think Arthur would've let that boy come if you had said it was okay," Tony guessed. "We know now that he is running with that group in Morrilton."

Nodding, Shawn slowed as they turned onto another road. "Tony, I think it's you who's wrong," Shawn corrected. "I think Arthur didn't want the boy to come, but felt guilty because he was young. Arthur wanted to see if the boy freaked the rest of us out."

"I'm saying no if I'm asked," Tony admitted with no hesitation.

"What if we find a bunch like Vicki's again?"

Jerking his gaze over to Shawn, Tony slowly turned to look around them. "I was wrong," he mumbled. "We were shot at so many times trying to get out of Little Rock; I knew we were going to die."

"Placing camera," Arthur's voice said over the radio and Shawn saw the vehicles slow. When they stopped, Shawn saw Shelia dart out of the Suburban while carrying a small tripod with a game camera mounted on it.

Jumping a small ditch, Shelia put the camera next to a fence post and then ran back to the Suburban. "How that man thinks of stuff like that amazes me," Shawn mumbled. They had ransacked an outdoor store and Arthur had had them clear the shelves of all the game cameras. Nobody ever asked why they loaded up what they did. They always knew it was needed to keep them safe.

The next day, they had put out the first of the game cameras in Clarksville and the road leading to the farm. Every day they went out, they put cameras out and picked cameras up. Shawn was actually surprised at how many people they had taken pictures of.

Arthur loved to put cameras near intersections and there were dozens of cars moving around. Granted, they had only seen a few as they'd ridden around, but the cameras had caught a bunch. It was the camera they had placed in Morrilton that had caught the sixteen-year-old boy who had asked to join them, moving with a large heavily armed group.

And the group didn't look friendly. Even in the photos, Shawn could swear he felt a malevolence from them. Andrea had put forth that since they hadn't taken the boy, he'd joined someone else. Even as she'd said it, Shawn had known even Andrea hadn't believed it.

They had dozens of photos of the group and the boy moved with them too easy to have just joined them.

Getting back up to speed, Shawn glanced in the rearview mirror and saw the road was empty. "People at the house on the left," they heard Kirk call out over the radio.

Turning, Shawn saw a brick house well off the small road they were on. "You see them?" Shawn asked and turned to see Tony looking at the house with binoculars.

"Yeah, I see someone peeking out the front window near the bottom and hiding behind a curtain," Tony answered. "How in the hell did Kirk spot them?"

"The only one who's been with Poppa longer is Nicole," Shawn reminded him.

Lowering the binoculars, Tony kept his eyes on the house as they drove past. "Shawn, I don't want to mess up and get someone hurt," Tony mumbled in a breaking voice.

"Hey," Shawn said, looking over at him. "If Poppa thought that, you wouldn't be with us, so get that thought out of your head. You do what he says, like he says, and you don't have to worry about that."

Slowly, Tony started to smile. "Yeah, Poppa would know," Tony finally said, feeling much better.

Reaching over and patting Tony on the chest, Shawn pointed out a parking area near a small stream. "That's where you head for if you get separated," Shawn told him.

"Poppa called it a rally spot," Tony blurted out and Shawn just nodded with a grin.

Turning onto the road that would take them into Conway, Arthur called out to stop at the edge of town. They saw Shelia jump out and run over to a garbage can before pulling out a camera on a tripod. When she climbed back in, they pulled off.

They were heading back to one of the home improvement stores to get the stuff they had boxed up several days ago. The only place they'd visited repeatedly had been the truck terminal and Shawn really wanted to stop that. It was totally random to everyone, except to Arthur of when they would go back to get stuff they left behind.

"Truck ahead opposing lane," Arthur called over the radio and Tony pulled his AR up again.

"Remember to watch behind us," Shawn said, glancing at the mirrors.

"I am," Tony answered when Shawn saw a shiny truck heading toward them. Nobody slowed and Shawn saw people waving from the truck as it passed them. Behind the truck was a small trailer that was loaded down.

Watching the truck in his mirror, Shawn saw shopping bags in the bed of the truck. "Somebody's been shopping at Walmart," Shawn laughed.

"We won't go there because there's food," Tony said as they turned, heading into the home improvement center's parking lot.

"Like Poppa said, we will grow our own food," Shawn nodded, feeling his heart speed up. Arthur had always told them that when they revisited a place was the most dangerous. For the life of him, Shawn couldn't figure out why people would fight over this stuff when there was stuff to get all around here.

By no means was he stupid. Shawn knew that the man Arthur had shot hadn't been talking about Vicki's cat. Thinking that someone would do that to a little girl made Shawn's blood boil. Now, most in the group were armed and it just didn't make sense to attack a group that could shoot back.

They rounded the store and pulled past the loading dock to the drive-in door at the corner of the store. As Arthur slowed, Shawn couldn't help but be awed in his memory of Arthur. When they had added the new trucks and trailers, there wasn't going to be enough room for all three to pull in and face the front roll-up door.

Without telling anyone, Arthur just backed the Suburban with the trailer into the store and guided it down one of the aisles. The speed and ease with which he did it made everyone jealous, that Arthur could drive a trailer backwards better than they could forward.

Shawn came to a stop behind Andrea and saw Arthur get out and was thankful that Nicole wasn't in the baby sling. Arthur locked the door he had pried open and walked back to the Suburban. "Rally point, backup route," Arthur called over the radio. "Will feed the babies and then return tomorrow."

"Oh fuck," Tony gasped, hearing the code that someone hostile was around. Looking around with wide eyes, Tony begged. "Can I chamber a round?"

"Hell, no!" Shawn snapped, seeing the Suburban pull away. "You'll shoot one of us with as nervous as you are."

Nearing the door, Shawn saw the rock Arthur had placed there to keep it closed. "Oh, shit!" Shawn cried out, making Tony levitate out of his seat. Turning to the building, Tony saw Arthur squatting down beside a stack of shipping pallets behind the building with Donald and Daisy beside him.

"What the hell is he doing?" Tony gasped as they followed the Suburban out of the parking lot.

"Something I'm sure somebody won't like," Shawn said, picking up speed and heading back out of town.

Crouching down next to the pallets, Arthur scanned the trees behind the store slowly. Not seeing anything, he glanced at Donald and Daisy and saw they were looking at the door he had used to get in the store. "Yeah, I know someone's in there," he said softly.

Crouching over, Arthur moved back along the store to the loading docks and looked around for movement. Unless the ambushers were a big group or very lucky, the kids would make it to the rally spot. There were literally dozens of different roads that they could take.

Not seeing any movement, Arthur climbed up on the dock and eased over to the pedestrian door. This was their third visit to this store because it'd taken two trips just to get the big stuff he'd needed. All the stores he knew they were coming back to, Arthur had always left another door unlocked and if it wasn't unlocked, he could get inside easily.

With the dogs beside him, Arthur gently turned the knob and sighed as the door opened. Letting the dogs in first, Arthur eased in before closing the door. "Heel up," he said softly, passing the dogs and they moved along with him.

It was beyond dark as he moved into the store and stopped, letting his eyes adjust. When he could make out the aisles, Arthur pulled his AR to his shoulder and headed across the store to the door he had opened. That was the best ambush spot.

Halfway across he froze, hearing voices far off. Glancing down, he saw the shadowy forms of the dogs looking to the front of the store. Moving down the household aisle, Arthur weaved around some of the boxes they had packed, praying the kids hadn't left anything to trip over.

Reaching the first cross aisle, Arthur turned to head toward the voices that were getting louder. "I'm telling you, Chase, they knew we was here," Arthur heard and moved down the paint aisle, heading to the front of the store.

"How, Levi? We put the rock back and that little piece of paper," Chase barked.

"Hello, boys," Arthur mumbled to himself.

"You saw how fast they took off?" Levi asked. "I'm telling you, they knew we was in here."

"Bullshit, that Arthur ain't a ninja," Chase argued. "We've seen them check on buildings before and then come back. You watch, they will pull back and load up all these storage bins and boxes. Every time we watched, they always loaded big stuff first. They were just checking the area. We've seen them do that plenty."

Reaching the end of the aisle, Arthur eased out and looked toward the exit doors past the checkouts and saw two figures looking outside. With more than enough light now, Arthur eased closer to make sure they were alone.

"We should try to join them again," Levi said, looking out the door.

"Arthur knows he has a good thing and ain't going to let two hard legs join up," Chase shouted and punched Levi in the shoulder. "We take out Arthur and that husky kid, and we can take over that group. He's done taught them to drive, so we can just sit back and make them go out and get what we want."

"I want that redhead," Levi chuckled and Arthur fought not to pull out a knife. "I bet she's going to scream."

Moving past the return counter, Arthur eased past the checkouts while holding his AR on the two figures outlined in the light coming in through the door.

He saw Chase sneer at Levi. "You can have that little girl. I want that dirty blonde," Chase said and then turned to look outside. "She can't be twenty yet. I just hope Arthur hasn't put the stank on her yet. He don't seem the type, but you never know."

"If this don't work, let's join up with that group down near Morrilton," Levi suggested as Arthur was about to pull the trigger, but stopped.

"Fuck that," Chase snapped. "I ain't nobody's bitch. I join anyone, I'm joining up with that group in Mayflower. They don't have the size yet, so I can get in near the top."

"I'm just saying, if this don't work out because what people that are left, talk about Arthur just smoking folks who piss him off," Levi said. "Nobody wants to move around Clarksville."

"You can move around, dumbass. Just don't try running game on anyone if you see those trucks moving around," Chase said.

Levi turned to Chase and took a breath to speak when the other side of Chase's head exploded out and blood hit Levi's face. Before he could turn around, "Boy, you so much as twitch and the dogs will get supper early," Levi heard and knew that voice.

"Now, get on your knees and you might live through the day," Arthur told him, moving up and putting the suppressor on the back of Levi's head. As Levi knelt down, he saw the two Rottweilers move in front of him. Both had their teeth bared, giving off low growls.

When his knees touched the floor, Levi felt his AR pushed off his shoulder and heard it clatter on the floor. "We just wanted to join," Levi whimpered, feeling his legs get soaked. "There are crazies out there that just attack and people are staking out claims."

Patting Levi down, Arthur tossed a revolver and a pistol to the side and then stepped back, avoiding the growing pool of piss between Levi's knees. "Where is the group in Morrilton holding up?" Arthur asked.

"All I know is they are near the river," Levi answered, never taking his eyes off the dogs.

"The Mayflower group?"

"They ain't in the city. They are just north, set up in a building just off the interstate," Levi replied, closing his eyes and praying that Arthur would let him go.

Thinking for a minute, "What about the two groups here in Conway?" Arthur bluffed.

"I don't know about any groups here," Levi blurted out and felt the suppressor against the back of his head. "Look, man, people have seen your trucks and know to stay away. I only know of regular people around here. One guy shot at you last week and you shot up the store and then burned it down. Shit like that makes people leave you the hell alone."

Remembering the sniper that had taken a shot at him, Arthur nodded and pulled the suppressor off Levi's head. "I have an idea where they are," Arthur lied. "What about Russellville?"

"After you dropped those two in front of that grocery store, anyone that was in a group just up and left. Now I know a few crazies there, but not where they are," Levi answered and felt relieved. "Just so you know, there are people out there going gangster like it's the wild west. That's why we wanted to join up with ya."

Levi felt a sharp pain explode inside him as Arthur kicked him in the left kidney. When he hit the floor, Levi felt pain in each arm as the dogs latched on. "Cry out and the dogs start the attack," Arthur said calmly. "They are just holding you now."

Forcing his eyes open, Levi saw his wrists in the dogs' mouths as they pulled back, playing tug of war. "You wanted to kill me and hurt my kids," Arthur said, grabbing his radio. Pressing the transmit key, "Return, babies are fed, use alternate route," he called out.

"Returning," Andrea answered.

Putting the radio back on his belt, Arthur asked. "Why didn't Chase want to join Morrilton?"

"You do the shit work," Levi panted as the dogs kept the pressure constant. "They told us we would have to bring in two women each before we could join, and we couldn't have any women at the clubhouse until the next one joined."

"How many are they?"

"We ride around and stuff and only met them twice," Levi grunted, feeling Donald step back and pulling harder. "I know they have five, but we only talked to Skip and some kid-."

"Dean," Arthur finished and Levi nodded. Arthur snapped his fingers and the dogs let go of Levi's wrists and he cradled them to his chest.

"Please man, let me go and I swear, you'll never see me again," Levi begged.

"Oh, I am, don't worry," Arthur said, glancing out the front door. "I want you to tell everyone, this corridor of I-40 belongs to me."

"I will, but you should know that people already know about you. Not your name, but about the group of trucks riding around and call you the 'Caravan'. And you need to keep a lookout because there is still army at Fort Smith. We were there a week ago."

"Yeah, I heard them on the radio," Arthur said. "They have a bunch that are sick. That's why they didn't pick up these outposts around here. I have to ask, why haven't any of you got in those army vehicles like those Strykers?"

Stopping his grunting, Levi looked up at Arthur like he was stupid. "The army still has choppers up. I seen with my own eyes, someone take one of those wheeled tank things in Ozark. As they rode down I-40, it blew up and one of those Apaches flew over."

"Yeah, that would put a stop to that," Arthur nodded, seeing his group pull in.

"It happened in Little Rock also. We talked to a group that ran out of Little Rock. You touch the Army's stuff, they know."

Looking down at Levi, "Not if you unhook the transponder, dumbass," Arthur chuckled.

"People have tried," Levi winced as he moved his hands.

"Well, I took a five-ton and they never found me," Arthur grinned, seeing his group pull through the parking lot.

Levi looked up at Arthur in disbelief. "The truck at that checkpoint near Clarksville?" he asked and Arthur nodded. "We thought the army came back and got it, since most of the gear was gone."

"Nope, I took it," Arthur smiled and started walking off. He stopped and turned to Levi, "Sorry, forgot something," Arthur said, pulling the trigger and Levi jerked as the bullet hit him in the chest and Arthur moved his rifle, squeezing the trigger again and watching the bullet slam into Levi's face.

"Don't ever think about fucking with my kids," Arthur growled, spinning on his heel and broke into a jog. Bringing his AR to his chest, Arthur turned the mounted light on as he jogged to the back roll-up door.

When he rolled the door up, Arthur saw the vehicles parked outside and walked over as Andrea stuck her head out of her truck. "Was someone inside waiting?" she asked.

Turning to her as Shelia climbed out of the driver's seat to the passenger side, "Yeah, we knew them," Arthur called out as he opened the door. "It was Chase and Levi who wanted to join up with us."

Andrea gave a shudder as she pulled her head back in the truck and Arthur climbed in, putting the Suburban in gear. Pulling up, Arthur put the Suburban in reverse and backed inside while cranking the steering wheel and guided the trailer into the first cross aisle.

He looked up to watch Andrea drive past and then Shawn pulled inside as Arthur climbed out and looked back at Vicki. "You think we should watch the babies in the truck or breakout the playpens?" he asked.

"Did you shoot somebody?" Vicki asked.

"Two."

"Keep them in here, in case we have to leave fast," Vicki answered, shaking a bottle to mix the formula. At the house, the babies now drank goat's milk.

Nodding, "Call over the radio when it's time to change out," Arthur said, shutting his door and saw everyone was already out, turning on lights and setting them around the trailers.

"How did you know?" Shawn asked, walking over.

"Fishing string I had in the door jamb was gone, but the obvious markers were all put back," Arthur answered. "There are two bodies by the front door. I'll need your help with them before we leave."

"Just leave them," Shawn shrugged as Kirk and Pat drove the forklifts off the trailers.

Walking off, "Then nobody will see them," Arthur huffed. "Tell Kirk and Pat to load my trailer first. We are getting the stuff outside we were coming back for, but this is the last time we come to this store."

The group moved with practiced precision and soon, Arthur's trailer was stacked front to back with storage bins and boxes. Then they started filling Shawn's trailer as Shawn went to find Arthur. He found Arthur talking to Jim and Betty who were watching out the entrance door.

Walking past the registers, Shawn glanced over and saw Levi but couldn't remember the other one's name, but knew the face. "Knew you were trouble," Shawn mumbled and walked behind the return desk.

"Poppa," he called out over the desk. "Your trailer is full and mine shouldn't be more than a quarter full when the rest is loaded."

Patting Jim and Betty, Arthur turned and headed around the return desk and saw Shawn looking down at something. Climbing over the return desk, Arthur looked under the counter and found Shawn was staring at a safe. "Wonder what's in it?" Shawn asked with a grin.

Pulling a flashlight from his belt, Arthur knelt down and shined the light at the safe and then stood up and walked from behind the service desk. "I'll be back," Arthur called over his shoulder and Shawn turned back, looking at the safe and then back across the store and saw Arthur heading for some tools.

Ducking into the tool area for a second, Arthur stepped back in the front cross aisle, heading back. When Arthur got closer,

Shawn saw he was carrying something in each hand as the AR hung under his right arm.

Walking back in the return area, Shawn saw Arthur was carrying a ball-peen hammer and a huge metal punch. Kneeling down, Arthur put the tip of the punch at the two o'clock position on the combination dial and raised the hammer up, hitting the punch rod hard. A metal ring sounded out as the dial popped off the safe and skidded across the floor.

Putting the tip of the punch into the small hole left by the dial, Arthur aimed the punch to the right and hit it with the hammer one time very hard. Pulling the punch out, Arthur dropped the punch and the hammer before grabbing the handle and turned it.

Shawn jumped back when the handle turned and watched as Arthur opened the safe. "Just papers and a money bag," Arthur answered, standing up and patting Shawn on the chest as he walked off.

With his mouth hanging open, Shawn watched Arthur walk off and then turned back to the open safe. "I think you were more than a little misguided in your youth to be able to do that, Poppa," Shawn mumbled, snapping his mouth shut and walking out.

When the group left, there were two bodies hanging over the exit doors with a sign tied to their necks that read, 'Don't fuck with my kids or me'. It was signed, 'The Caravan Man'.

Chapter Thirty Three

A mind can only take so much before breaking

Lifting the full gas can back into the trailer, Wendy wanted to kick herself for leaving that wagon. Hearing small grunts, Wendy turned to see the twins carrying over another gas can between them. Running over, Wendy grabbed it. "I was coming back," she grinned as the twins let the can go.

"We still have two more," Jo Ann panted, throwing her hands up. She turned around, looking at the soft gray clouds overhead. "Is it going to storm again?"

"No, these clouds aren't dark enough," Wendy answered, putting the gas can in the trailer and turned around to see Noah and Ryan still sleeping on the blanket spread out beside the Tahoe. "It's going to rain, but not like last night."

When she turned back around, Wendy saw the twins looking up at the sky and memorizing the details. "I can't wait to tell Arthur that I'm not the only one terrified by storms," Wendy mumbled. Walking past the twins and heading back to the carport beside the house, Wendy did feel bad about using so much gas because she had hauled serious ass.

She had planned on keeping forty-five miles an hour and traveling eight hours a day, like they'd done the first day. That way, they could average around three hundred and fifty miles a day. Last night, they made it all the way into Georgia and were now only ten miles from Alabama. Wendy had made four hundred and sixty miles in six hours.

Now outside the moment, Wendy knew that had been stupid as shit. But at the time, it'd seemed very rational. There were abandoned cars and wrecks scattered all along the back roads she was taking. They had passed interstates and those were ten times worse and on interstate highways, they had seen a few cars moving.

It was after almost plowing into two wrecked cars last night, that had made Wendy finally pull over. The only saving grace was she'd been doing forty-five like she had planned.

Reaching the carport, Wendy looked at the two gas cans and gave a sigh. Not even entertaining the idea of grabbing both, Wendy picked up one and headed back to the barn, almost running over the twins who were behind her. "Thank you, girls," Wendy said, passing them.

After putting her gas can in the trailer, Wendy trotted back out and grabbed the last gas can from the twins who were halfway back. Even now, Wendy could tell she was still nowhere near her former strength and wouldn't be for some time.

Putting the gas can in, Wendy stepped back panting as the twins came over and strapped the cans down. "Can you hide under a bridge if a tornado comes?" Sally asked, ratcheting the strap down.

Catching her breath, "You can, but it's still dangerous because the debris can still get you and that's what's so deadly about tornados," Wendy explained, trying to slow her breathing down.

"So, you need a storm cellar?" Jo Ann asked, ratcheting the other strap down.

"I like my concrete house with metal shutters," Wendy huffed. "I sleep like a baby, no matter how bad a storm gets."

The twins turned to Wendy, "We love your house," they said in unison.

"Wait till you see it," Wendy said, finally getting her breathing under control.

Looking at her watch, "You sure you want to leave this early? It's not even three," Jo Ann said slowly, cutting her eyes up at the clouds.

"Guys, we can't cut the lights on tonight unless it rains hard," Wendy said, pushing off the trailer. "I'll probably have to use the night vision scope and will still have trouble staying at forty-five."

Walking around the trailer, Sally reached out to hold Wendy's hand. "But if it storms, we will turn on the lights and go really fast, right?" Sally asked.

Nodding hard, "Oh, yeah," Wendy sang out.

Loading up the boys and putting them in the backseat, Wendy was tempted to pull off the damn wetsuit and drive in the t-shirt that fit her. The only thing that had fit had been one pair of the boots and it'd been the six and half, not the worn-in sevens. The twins were in the same boat, only wearing the tennis shoes they had grabbed and t-shirts. At least their wetsuits didn't have arms like Wendy's did.

Taking the AR off, Wendy laid it on the dash and climbed in to see Jo Ann sitting up front. "We ready?" Wendy asked, looking around.

"Since we are leaving now, can we drive until morning?" Jo Ann asked with a pleading face.

"We are going to go as far as I can drive," Wendy said, cranking the Tahoe. What really pissed her off was that she knew how long it took to get from her house to Miami before the Rudolph flu. Her family had rented a beach house for the week and Arthur had driven her and Joseph down. He'd made it in eighteen hours and change. The only stops were pee breaks and to refuel.

A fight had almost broken out in Mississippi when Arthur had told Wendy that she had to hold her pee until he stopped for gas again. When Wendy had rolled down the passenger window and pulled down her pants to hang her ass out the window to piss, Arthur had sped off the interstate and stopped at the first store he'd seen.

"If both of you can stay up with me, I should be able to do it," Wendy offered, backing out.

Opening the center console, Jo Ann pulled out the small energy drink. "I know you had coffee, but I think these work better," Jo Ann told her.

"They make my head itch," Sally said, reaching from the backseat and taking the one in Jo Ann's hand.

"Only one every six hours," Wendy told them as she pulled around the house guiding the Tahoe back onto the road. They both nodded, turning up the small bottles.

Taking the top off one, Wendy turned it up. "I like coffee better," Wendy gagged out.

"I have the pot on my floorboard," Jo Ann said, tossing the bottles out. "I feel bad about littering."

"Baby, I've never littered either, but we aren't in normal times and I don't want Ryan or Noah getting ahold of the bottle caps," Wendy told her setting the cruise control.

Jo Ann opened the glove box and pulled out the binoculars she had found there when they'd stopped last night. Wendy had never checked the glove box, but remembered two pairs of binoculars that had been sitting on top of the gun safe. "I'm doing the best I can," Wendy breathed out.

"You're doing great," Sally said from the back seat.

"Yeah! You've fought bad guys, drove us through sharks, made sure there was food and water, saved Noah, outran a tornado..." Jo Ann stopped, throwing her hands up. "I can't even name all the stuff you've done, you're like Wonder Woman!"

Glancing over, Wendy sighed feeling rather bashful at the praise. "Thank you, guys."

They both smiled back and then Jo Ann lifted the binoculars up and looked ahead. It wasn't much longer before the boys woke up. Sally made peanut butter and jelly sandwiches for Noah as Jo Ann made up a bottle for Ryan.

"That's the last of the bread," Sally announced, wadding the plastic bag up. When Ryan reached to grab the bag, Sally rolled down the window and tossed it out. "We still have crackers, soup, and like a million of those trail bars."

"If we get a chance, we'll stop and look around," Wendy said, looking ahead. "We're in Alabama."

"I want another state that starts with 'A'," Jo Ann said, looking through the binoculars.

Reaching over, Wendy patted Jo Ann's leg. "Me too, baby."

Seeing a semitrailer blocking over half the road, Wendy moved over to the other lane and slowed because she couldn't see around it. Getting closer, Wendy slowed more at seeing the semi was jackknifed and had plowed into four other cars.

Glancing down at the ditch, Wendy slowed and drove into the ditch. "Why do those cars have holes in them?" Jo Ann asked.

"What?" Wendy gasped, steering the Tahoe back to the road and looking over at the wreck. A black sports car had bullet holes along the passenger side and Wendy could see two people up front. The next car she saw had a man hanging out the passenger side, holding a pistol in his dead hand.

"Those are bullet holes, girls," Wendy groaned, pulling away from the wreck. "That's why I stopped in Miami and shot those guys before they could get close."

"We can shoot out the windows and you can drive," Sally offered.

Laughing, "Girls, you just started learning guns and have only held the guns," Wendy said. "Tell you what though, tomorrow before we pull out, I'm going to let each of you shoot but we will have to load up and do it fast so we can leave after."

"Can you make the gun shoot quieter?" Jo Ann asked hopefully.

"When we get home, I can," Wendy winked at her.

Nodding, Jo Ann looked ahead with the binoculars. "Wendy, there's black clouds coming up from the ground. Does that mean a storm is forming?" Jo Ann asked.

Squinting her eyes, Wendy looked at the horizon. "Are you sure?"

Handing the binoculars over, "Yeah, and if it's a storm, we are going another way," Jo Ann informed everyone.

Slowing down again, Wendy lifted the binoculars up and zoomed in. "That's smoke," Wendy told them. "A lot of smoke from something burning."

Handing the binoculars back, "Grab the atlas and see what's ahead of us," Wendy told Jo Ann.

Opening the Atlas up, Jo Ann turned it in her lap. "We are on the road you have marked with a pink highlighter?" she asked.

"Yes, highway 84," Wendy said, glancing over.

"Dothan," Jo Ann said, pointing and gave a grin. "We don't go there, you have us on a road that circles it."

Getting closer, Wendy didn't need the binoculars to see the thick smoke billowing up in the air. "Girls, keep a sharp eye out," Wendy said, gripping the steering wheel tight with her left hand as her right pulled the Glock off the center console.

The closer they got to Dothan, the wider the billowing black smoke got. "The road can't be on fire," Wendy thought out loud.

"The road's still wet from the rain," Jo Ann cried out. "There's mud puddles everywhere."

Not having an answer, Wendy tried to come up with one and the smell of the fire hit them. "That's houses, not trees," Wendy said, wiggling her nose. When the GPS announced their turn two miles ahead, they passed a subdivision on their left and dozens of houses were on fire.

Turning ahead, they saw larger buildings on fire and the smoke started making it hazy around them. Making the right turn, they saw a big hospital across the street fully engulfed in flames. Afraid to speed up because the smoke got thick in places on the road, Wendy saw a huge factory burning but on the right side of the road, a small group of houses were smoldering.

When the smoke cleared off the road, they all turned to look in the loop they were driving around the city. They could see fires raging across subdivisions near them. Turning back to the road, Wendy saw a man running across the lanes in front of them and angling toward them.

"I see a man coming!" Jo Ann yelled out, pointing ahead.

"I see him," Wendy said. It was easy to tell he was a man because he was stark naked.

Wendy steered the Tahoe wider and saw the man adjust his run to intercept them. "Fuck this," Wendy said and punched the accelerator. The Tahoe lurched forward as Wendy dodged a stalled car. Now much closer, Wendy could tell the man was screaming with wild eyes, running to intercept them.

Still speeding up, Wendy couldn't move over anymore and just held the steering wheel. The man ran right into the back passenger door, on the driver's side. With the Tahoe doing sixty, the man was thrown back violently. Looking back, Wendy saw his head hit the pavement and literally bust open as the body skidded to a halt.

Jerking her eyes forward seeing the body never move after hitting the pavement, Wendy slowed down seeing businesses ahead. Most were already burned down, but some looked like they had just caught fire. Wendy jerked at seeing another naked person running at them, screaming. "Bullshit," Wendy growled, stomping the accelerator.

This time, they saw it was a woman angling to intercept them, but they had picked up too much speed. After they had passed the woman, Wendy slowed down and looked back in the mirror. The woman just ran across the highway and right into a burning building.

"That crazy woman just ran into the fire," Sally mumbled in disbelief.

Driving on, they saw several more people, but none charged at them. Off to their right, they saw a huge parking lot with a massive pile spread over it. When they were next to the parking lot, Wendy turned away. "Girls, look ahead," she snapped at them.

"Those were bodies," Jo Ann gasped, turning to look ahead.

"We've seen bodies," Sally pointed out.

Hearing the GPS telling her the turn was ahead, Wendy sighed with relief. "I know," Wendy said, not telling them even from that far away, she could see thousands of brass casings carpeting the parking lot.

Making the turn back onto eighty-four, Wendy groaned to see houses on both sides burning. They were two miles outside the city when a car shot onto the road in front of them and literally, took off like a bat out of hell. In seconds, it was gone.

"I want a car like that," Jo Ann mumbled as Wendy glanced in the mirror at the billowing black smoke.

"Baby, that was a Porsche. All of us couldn't fit in a Porsche," Wendy told her as she set the cruise control.

They rode in silence, trying to make sense of what they had witnessed as the afternoon sun started to set. Seeing a sign for another town coming up, everyone tensed up but they made the loop around Enterprise, seeing no fires and only a few people. None of which charged them butt-naked, screaming.

Spotting a wreck ahead, Wendy tapped the brakes and still no one had spoken forty miles later.

Getting closer to the wreck, Wendy saw the car had hit a light pole that had been in the road, but had been going so fast the light pole had shattered. Looking at the mangled car, Wendy gave a groan to see a mangled body ahead with a dog eating on it.

"That was the Porsche we saw," Jo Ann said, pointing at the mangled car.

"Yes, baby, he was going too fast," Wendy said as they passed the mangled and twisted body.

"That dog was eating the body," Sally pointed out.

"Their owners are dead, so they will eat anything they can," Wendy tried to explain, but just wanted this day to end already.

As darkness fell Wendy was thankful, just because it would cut down on the horrors they had to witness. Hearing Ryan cooing in the back brought a smile to Wendy's face. Then, she heard Sally groan in disgust just as the smell filled the Tahoe. "We aren't feeding him that crap anymore," Sally declared, trying not to breathe.

Noah crawled between the front seats onto Jo Ann's lap to get away from the stink. "Why don't you do this when it's Jo Ann's turn to change you?" Sally complained, grabbing a handful of wipes. Ryan wasn't helping as he kicked his legs and squealed.

"I really owe you, Sally," Jo Ann said as she hugged Noah, who was holding his nose.

When Sally tossed the diaper out, Wendy rolled down all the windows for a second to air out the inside. Rolling the windows back up, Wendy heard a water bottle sloshing and turned around to see Sally washing her hands over a towel. "It's like a booger you can't get off," she whined and Wendy fought not to laugh.

Jo Ann didn't feel that need to hold it and busted out laughing.

Hearing the back window roll down, Wendy turned to see Sally tossing the towel out. "I'll find another one," Sally said, seeing Wendy looking back.

"Sally, I would've thrown the towel out, so don't worry about it," Wendy chuckled.

"Those are car lights," Jo Ann said and Sally leaned over, looking ahead and saw lights in the distance.

"What do we do?" Sally asked, feeling her gut knot up.

"We can pull over and act like one of the hundred abandoned cars or just go right on. We don't have lights on, so he doesn't know we are here yet," Wendy offered.

"What do you think we should do?" Sally asked, poking her head between the seats.

Waving her hand at the road, "Just drive on," Wendy said. "And if that fucker turns around, I'll light his ass up."

The twins nodded and held their breath as they closed with the car. The car had on its bright lights and Wendy lifted her hand up, shielding her eyes so she could keep her night vision. When the car was near, everyone noticed when the lights turned to low, but Wendy kept her hand up until the car passed a few seconds later.

The twins turned around and Wendy glanced in the mirror as the car turned its bright lights back on and continued down the road. "They are just going," Sally called out, picking up Ryan and cuddling him to her chest.

With the sky overhead still cloudy, Wendy slowed until she felt safe that she wouldn't run into anything and then saw she was doing twenty. Stopping in the middle of the road, Wendy pulled out the monocular and put the headband on. Ten minutes later, Wendy pulled off and had to admit her left eye could see pretty well, but she felt like she was looking through a soda straw.

Leaning over and holding a sleeping Noah, Jo Ann saw the speedometer back at forty-five. "If you do the pedals, I'll drive," Jo Ann offered.

"When we get home, you and Sally are learning how to drive and shoot guns," Wendy chuckled.

"Can we listen to that dragon book you got?" Sally asked and saw Wendy nodding. The long black monocular sticking out from her face made Wendy look weird.

Jo Ann put the first of the nine disks in as a make-believe world was built in their minds with the story, taking them away from the hell around them.

Chapter Thirty Four
Please wear a pull-up

May 20

With Lucas in his arms, Shawn led the boys downstairs and found Andrea holding Pam and the other girls working in the kitchen. "I see you woke up," Andrea grinned.

"No. Actually, Tony did and fed Lucas the first time. He woke me the second," Shawn told her, walking in and Kirk looked at Shelia and Vicki in horror. They were making the dough without him and Pat.

"We have to learn how, Kirk," Vicki moaned.

"Okay," Kirk said, moving to the dishwasher and started putting away the dishes.

"Morning, guys," Arthur said, stepping out of his room and holding Nicole. "I can watch the babies, guys."

"Arthur, you're burning the candle at both ends," Andrea groaned and Shawn nodded.

"How can he burn a candle at both ends and why would you want to?" Vicki asked, looking up.

Walking over, Arthur kissed Vicki on the head. "I think you are the most innocent child I have ever met," Arthur declared.

The rapid clacking of heels on the floor announced Robin running out of Arthur's bedroom. Running past Arthur, Robin squealed when she saw the cats on the couch and headed for them. Seeing the toddler with boots and wearing a pull-up headed for them, the cats took off.

Laughing as Robin gave chase, Arthur headed over to the coffee pot and poured a cup. Walking to his office, Arthur headed back out carrying his laptop. When Arthur set it at his spot and went back for his coffee, Shawn ran over and sat down beside Arthur's chair.

Shawn really wanted to know computers, but his family had never bought one. When Shawn had seen the towers for the servers in the basement, Arthur's awesomeness had increased yet again in Shawn's eyes. "What are you going to do?" Shawn asked with a grin, setting Lucas's bottle down and started patting his back.

"Glance over the camera cards we pulled yesterday," Arthur said as he sat down. "I don't know the real facts about the flu, but its mortality has to be reported around ninety percent."

"My dad told me it was over ninety. He was a CEO at a hospital in Little Rock," Andrea said, moving Pam to the crook of her arm.

"That means ninety percent of people who caught the Rudolph flu will die?" Shawn asked. "I had it and got better, and Beth never got sick."

"Were you very sick?" Arthur asked, tapping his keyboard.

"No," Shawn said, leaning over and watching Arthur's hands and the screen. "The stomach flu I had two years ago was much worse."

"That's what I mean," Arthur said, taking a sip of coffee. "Clarksville should have around a thousand people, but I'll kiss your ass if there are two hundred there that are walking around. There may be a thousand, but six hundred are trying to cough up their lungs."

Setting his mug down, "Russellville is three times bigger and should have more survivors, but I'll wax my nipples if there are five hundred people left walking around in that town," Arthur snorted.

"It has the most crazies," Shawn noted, hearing a tiny burp from Lucas.

Unable to stop it, Arthur gave a visible shiver as it ran up his body. Being a nurse, he had seen mental disorders but very few true insane cases. The ones called crazy were truly insane and most looked like they'd never been sick with the flu. Some would just walk, others would charge anything, and then some would just stand and stare off. The one thing they all had were wide, gaping, wild-looking eyes that spoke of madness.

Anyone who looked at one wouldn't get close. More than once, they had seen survivors run from the crazies. One morning rolling into town, they'd passed one beating a car with a metal pipe that had a chunk of concrete on the end. When they drove out of town six hours later, he was still beating the car which was little more than scraps of metal and fiberglass by then.

Two day later when they went back, they saw dogs eating the body with the pipe still clutched in one hand, and the only things recognizable about the car were the engine and four tires.

Arthur had almost shot one when they'd been loading up stuff at a computer store. She had walked across the parking lot, but hadn't headed for the store. Instead, she'd just walked into the wall of the building and stumbled back before running into the wall again. She'd continued doing that when they'd left and for all Arthur knew she was still there, running into the building's wall.

Remembering all that, Arthur again shivered. "Yeah, they freak me the fuck out."

"You think those gangs are going to be a problem?" Shawn asked as Arthur hit a key and a slideshow started, showing pictures from the camera cards.

"In time, but they will have problems with each other and they won't come this far out into the sticks for some time," Arthur said, reaching over and taking a sip as he watched the screen. "I'm seeing kids, but not a lot of little ones," he mumbled.

"They can't survive without help," Andrea mumbled.

"I know, but I'm seeing people and when an adult sees a kid, their first impulse is to help," Arthur said, watching the screen.

"They hide," Shawn mumbled.

"Okay, that makes sense," Arthur said, staring at the screen.

"What are you trying to figure out?" Andrea asked, getting up.

"How much shit we are about to face," Arthur answered and the chatter died down instantly. "I really expected the shock of this to last a little longer before all of the bad elements started pulling together."

"You said those gangs wouldn't be a problem," Shawn reminded him.

"Shawn, they're bullies. Bullies are pussies at heart and if you stand up to them, they run away. People are going to stand up to them and group together doing it. Those are the ones I'm worried about. In time, some will see that it's easier to take than to make," Arthur said, tapping the keyboard. "That Dean is sure trying to find us."

Shawn leaned over and saw the teenager that he hadn't wanted to join them. "I see his ass again, I'm shooting his ass."

"Let me do it," Arthur suggested, tapping the keyboard and the slideshow resumed. "Killing someone isn't like TV and it affects everyone differently. I would prefer you to have a little more time to prepare for that."

"I'll kill anyone that tries to hurt us," Shawn declared.

Reaching over, Arthur patted Shawn's leg. "That is something else entirely. That isn't killing, it's protecting."

"Never thought about it like that," Andrea mumbled.

"How many more trips to town do we have?" Shawn asked.

"None for a few weeks," Arthur said. "It's time to start the fence around the house and then around the animals. I'm not worried about gangs finding us yet and animals shouldn't be a problem until winter. But crazies, I'm worried about," Arthur admitted. "They just wander around, so one could wander their ass through the woods."

"I've never seen one eat," Shawn said, pulling Lucas into the crook of his arm. "I've seen them drink water from puddles."

"They eat," Arthur said with no emotion and everyone looked at him. "Don't ask," he almost growled.

"Won't they climb over the fence?" Tony asked.

"When the fence is finished, they can try and die," Arthur told him.

"How big will the fence be?" Kirk asked sitting down at the table.

"Ten-foot-tall with barbed wire at the top and will enclose twenty-five acres," Arthur answered. "It will enclose all the greenhouses, the methane cubes, power plant and house."

"Methane cubes?" Shawn asked.

Looking over at Shawn, Arthur winked. "You'll see. We are going to build some more."

When breakfast was done, everyone sat down and the large table seemed really small.

It was after ten when Arthur led the group up from Jack's farm, driving various machines and trucks and trailers loaded with supplies. Parking them around the house, Arthur grabbed the baby sling and put Nicole in it. Heading to his shop, Arthur came out carrying his surveying equipment.

"You know how to use that?" Shawn cried out in wonder.

"Yeah, all of you will be learning today," Arthur said, putting the stuff in his buggy. "We are marking today and tomorrow, we start to clear."

Everyone ran for buggies as Pat climbed in Arthur's. "Where am I going, Poppa?" he asked.

Pointing northwest, "That way and I'll direct you," Arthur chuckled and then stopped. "Hold on," Arthur groaned, seeing Robin jumping in her pink Barbie Jeep. Climbing out, Arthur walked over and pulled Robin kicking and screaming out of the Jeep.

"Hey!" Arthur shouted and Robin stopped. "You wear clothes, I might let you drive your damn Jeep but walk around naked in cowboy boots, and you can forget that!"

Robin pouted as Arthur put her on his hip and walked back to his buggy. He could hear more than one kid snickering as he climbed back in the buggy. "Let's try this again," Arthur sighed as Robin leaned over to babble at Nicole and Nicole let out a squeal as she smiled at Robin.

"I'll give you money, Robin, if you keep your clothes on," Arthur tried bribing her.

"No," Robin snapped, lifting her chin and then turned and kissed Arthur's cheek. "Poppa," Robin said clearly and smiled.

Hugging her tight, Arthur grinned as Pat weaved around the trees. "Okay, you're a little cute, but would be much cuter with clothes. A pullup at the very least, please," Arthur tried and Robin just giggled. "Yeah, you're going to be my trying child," Arthur mumbled and Robin kissed his cheek again.

Chapter Thirty Five

Not everyone is evil or indifferent

"Wendy," Sally whispered, tapping Wendy's shoulder. Registering the voice and tapping as not a dream, Wendy opened her eyes to see Sally wasn't looking at her but at something else.

Sitting up, Wendy saw relief on Sally's face that she was awake now. "What?" Wendy asked in a low voice.

"I heard engines stop near us," Sally whispered.

Blinking her eyes, Wendy turned to the door of the large woodshed they were sleeping in. Then, she heard the unmistakable sound of a car door slamming. "Wake the others and try to keep the boys quiet," Wendy said, grabbing her M4 and moving to the side of the door.

They were outside of the small town of Meadville, Mississippi. Getting off the highway this morning, this was the first place Wendy had found that she could hide the Tahoe. It was parked under an awning on the right side of the shed. It wasn't completely hidden, but it was blocked from view from the road.

Glancing back, she saw the twins with the boys. "Move behind that tractor and be ready to run," Wendy whispered and the twins carried Noah and Ryan behind the ancient tractor. Hearing another motor coming, Wendy turned north where the noise was coming from.

The town of Meadville was half a mile away and she had thought the shed was far enough away, but now regretted her decision as a truck drove past. It was heading north toward the town, but slowed on the small road that ran past the house the shed sat behind. Hearing it stop, Wendy knew it was close and then she heard faint voices before doors closing.

"Crap," Wendy mumbled and glanced over at the Tahoe, thinking about just leaving. She knew it was more than one vehicle from hearing doors closing and from the voices, it was several people. Looking down at her rifle, Wendy checked it over as she took a deep breath to calm her nerves.

"Not everyone is an asshole," she reminded herself.

Leaving the doorway, Wendy moved over to a window beside the door with more cover. Keeping low, Wendy peered outside and heard the voices spreading out. Thinking that meant they were walking away from their vehicles, Wendy turned to the Tahoe again, thinking about getting the kids and just hauling ass.

"I saw a trailer with gas cans!" Wendy heard someone yell out and felt a pang in her chest. Rising up so only her eyes were above the window seal, Wendy looked out over the backyard to the house and road.

Two men carrying rifles were casually walking down the road toward them.

Letting the scenarios play out in her head, Wendy pulled the stock of the M4 to her shoulder. Watching the men walk off the road passing the house and heading for the shed, Wendy made her choice and then prayed that she could live with the results.

When the men were halfway to the shed, Wendy moved to the edge of the door, raising the M4 up and flipping the safety off. Aiming at the man carrying his rifle in his hands, Wendy shouted out. "You need to leave, that's our truck and gas!"

Both men stopped and saw her at the edge of the shed door fifty yards away, aiming at them. The man that had his rifle slung over his shoulder raised his hands. "We are just looking around," he called out as the other man let his rifle aim toward the ground.

"I'm here right now, so just back off. We will be leaving soon and only used the shed to sleep in, so you can have what's here when we leave," Wendy told him, keeping the crosshairs on the man holding his rifle low.

Wendy saw the one holding his gun low mumble something to the other and shifted his weight to move. "You move and I'll kill you," Wendy warned and the man stayed put. "Now back off."

"Lady, there are a lot more of us than you, so you need to relax," the man holding the rifle shouted out. Wendy realized the man was shouting to alert the others and moved her finger off the trigger housing to the trigger.

"We are heading home, so back off and let us leave and nobody gets hurt," Wendy told them.

"Lady, now you're just being a bitch," the man holding the rifle shouted. "Tell you what, why don't you just walk away now or we can work out something to let you keep your truck," the man sneered and the other chuckled.

Wendy's finger brushed the trigger twice and jerked her aim to the other as he started to dive to the ground. Moving her aim with the man, Wendy squeezed the trigger as she heard a gunshot and a bullet whiz past her. Seeing the man hit the ground grabbing his gut, Wendy squeezed the trigger two more times and felt a bullet slam into the door frame beside her.

Moving her aim, Wendy saw the first one she'd shot was on his side and aiming at the door as his rifle flashed. Squeezing the trigger four times, Wendy watched the man jerk with each hit, dropping his rifle. Moving back to the other man, Wendy saw him rolling around and shot him in the side of the head.

Glancing up the road, Wendy felt her blood turn cold, seeing nine figures coming.

"Girls, be ready to move," Wendy shouted out, ejecting the magazine and slamming in a fresh one. "If I say run and hide, you run and hide. I'll drive around to find you!" Wendy shouted, moving to the window.

She could hear Ryan crying over the ringing in her ears as she rested her M4 on the window. Letting out half her breath, Wendy aimed at a woman on the far right of the group. Not wanting the group to move around the house and get near the truck, Wendy held the crosshairs on the woman's chest and squeezed the trigger twice and watched the woman drop in mid-stride.

The woman hit the road with her face and her rifle clattered on the roadway. Moving her aim, Wendy centered on a man as he knelt down, aiming at her with a huge scope on a hunting rifle. Brushing the trigger twice, Wendy watched him twitch and the end of the rifle flashed.

Wendy felt the impact on the woodshed and splinters hit her arm, but ignored them as she moved her aim. Seeing a figure running hard across the back of the house and trying to get to the right side where large trees were, Wendy gave him a lead and pulled the trigger rapidly until she saw him crash down.

When she moved her aim back to the runner, Wendy heard bullets impacting all over the face of the shed. Ducking down, Wendy now heard the torrent of gunfire outside and bullets impacting over her head. Wondering why she wasn't hit, Wendy looked below the window and saw railroad ties stacked up along the front of the shed.

"Thank you for that," Wendy said and then tried to get up, but too many bullets were hitting the shed. When the gunfire slackened, Wendy popped up and pulled the trigger twice before she had a target. Resting her check on the stock, Wendy saw a man moving behind a lawnmower and pulled the trigger rapidly, watching the man fall short of the mower.

Moving her aim back to the right, Wendy saw the man she had hit in the leg had made it to the road and was leaving. Letting him go, Wendy moved back to the left when those outside had reloaded and another torrent of gunfire erupted, driving Wendy back down.

Ejecting the magazine, Wendy slammed in another while knowing some of the group would be closing in now. Waiting for a lull, Wendy braced herself to pop back up and then realized, the gunfire outside was still raging but no bullets were hitting the shed.

Popping up, Wendy saw four bodies down that she hadn't shot and watched a woman jerk and realized she'd been shot from the right side. Not questioning her luck, Wendy moved her aim to find the man she'd shot near the mower trying to aim to the right and squeezed the trigger, watching the man's head jerk and collapse to the ground.

Caught in a crossfire, the ones left outside tried to pull back but the unseen gunman was very good at shooting. Wendy watched the last one fall from behind a tree to the ground. Then, she watched as the unseen gunman started shooting those that were down.

Moving her aim, Wendy knew what they were doing and started shooting those on the ground, ensuring they were dead. Shifting to another body that was rolling around, Wendy heard a vehicle speed off, but continued shooting until there was no movement.

Ejecting her magazine, Wendy slapped in a new one. "Girls, get in the truck and lay down," Wendy said, but felt her voice more than heard it from the ringing in her ears.

With Ryan and Noah crying, Sally and Jo Ann carried them to the Tahoe and jumped in. Gathering her empty and partial magazines, Wendy shoved them in her mag holsters and moved over to the awning where the Tahoe was parked.

She stopped to see a man calmly walking out while supporting an AR in his hands. Knowing this was her savior, Wendy looked at the suppressor at the end of the man's AR with a little envy. "Thank you," Wendy called out when the man was twenty yards away.

Coming to a stop, the man released the pistol grip of his AR and gave a wave. "Knew that group was going to spot ya," the man said with a thick southern accent. He looked in his fifties with a gray beard and gray-streaked hair. "Word of advice; paint those red cans another color."

"Haven't had a chance, but I'll make time," Wendy said, stepping out from the awning. Hating to do it, Wendy asked. "You need a ride?"

"Nah, I live round here and if my kids lived through this Rudolph flu this is where they would come, so I'll wait on 'em," the man told her and let his rifle hang from the sling. Pulling out a chewing tobacco pouch, the man put a wad in his cheek. "Lady, I'm grateful for you askin', but you be wary of everybody. I seen stuff these last few weeks and people are just being downright mean. Even if they don't have to be mean, they are."

Nodding, "Yes, we've seen our share of that," Wendy said, relaxing and the more the man talked, the more she really wanted him to come.

"You need to git cause that fella that got away took off with purpose. I'm bettin' he's goin' for more," the man told her.

"Thank you again, I don't know how I would've gotten out of that without your help," Wendy said, walking over and held out her right hand. "My name's Wendy, Wendy Steele."

Taking her hand, the man shook it firmly. "Nice to meet ya, Wendy. Name's Logan Lancaster. Friends call me LL. If you are crossin' the Mississippi, be careful. There's a military checkpoint on the Louisiana side on the eastbound bridge. Two days ago, I only saw three soldiers still alive and they was coughing, but I've seen a few beat off that Rudolph flu even after coughin' up the blood."

"I'm one of them," Wendy said, glancing back and hearing the Tahoe crank up. "LL, if your kids don't show up and you are looking for a place, head to Clarksville, Arkansas and call out on CB channel six."

"I thank ya, ma'am, but that's why I'm watching that bridge in Natchez. Two of my kids would have to use it. I'd go with ya and keep ya covered, but I'm sure that yeller belly that got away will try makin' a call on ya. I'm going to stay around and see he don't," Logan told her with a wink, then spit a stream out.

"Thank you from my kids as well," Wendy said, holding out her hand again and Logan shook it.

"That's why I was so determined to give ya a hand," Logan said, tilting his head to the Tahoe. "They's good kids. Now, don't go anywhere near Shreveport cause the military is still there. Now some troops are helping, but others are still following those orders of keeping everyone in place and just shoot folks. My advice, avoid all of 'em. If those troops are still on the bridge, you need to just shoot 'em. I never got a chance on those on the Louisiana side. The checkpoint on this side on the westbound bridge is cleared out, unless some of those on the other side came over."

"I'll do that," Wendy said and heard the window roll down on the Tahoe.

"Come on, you know people can hear gunshots!" Sally cried out and rolled the window up.

"Smart kids," Logan said, raising his eyebrows. "You need to go cause I'm bettin' it won't be long 'fore more of that group will be showin' up."

"If your kids show up and you still want a place to head to, come see us," Wendy said and then turned and jogged back to the Tahoe. Taking her M4 off, Wendy saw the driver's door open up as she got close and Sally was climbing back over to the passenger seat.

Tossing her rifle on the dash, Wendy shut her door and backed out. By the time she was heading for the road, Logan was gone. "I wanted to tell him to be careful," Wendy mumbled, turning onto the highway.

"That man just walked into the trees and was gone," Jo Ann said behind her.

Gripping the steering wheel, Wendy watched the road ahead as Sally leaned over the console with wadded up napkins. "You have blood on your face," Sally said and wiped Wendy's left cheek and Wendy grimaced. "I see a splinter," Sally said, leaning over and almost blocking Wendy's view of the road.

Feeling a pinch on her cheek, Wendy gritted her teeth as Sally yanked her hand back. "It looks like a toothpick," Sally said, holding up the splinter that was several inches long and covered in blood.

With the splinter out, Wendy felt blood running down her cheek.

Sally tossed the splinter on the dashboard and held the wet napkins on the wound. In wonder, Wendy drove as Sally dabbed her cheek, tending to her wound. "Here's the first aid box," Jo Ann said, passing up a yellow plastic box.

Moving back to her seat, Sally grabbed some supplies and moved back over the center console. Feeling Sally spread ointment on her cheek, Wendy couldn't help but smile. "These are bad Band-Aids," Sally said, pulling out a two-inch Band-Aid. "They hurt coming off."

"It's okay," Wendy smiled at the warning as Sally put the Band-Aid on her cheek.

When she was done, Sally looked at the side of Wendy's neck and saw several abrasions and went to work on cleaning them. "None of these need Band-Aids," Sally told her.

"Okay, the rest will have to wait," Wendy told her. "Logan said there was a checkpoint on the bridge."

Climbing back into her seat, Sally put the kit up and grabbed the binoculars. "I'm tired of bad guys," Sally sighed.

"Hey, we had a good guy help us out," Wendy reminded her. "I was really getting worried there."

Looking ahead with the binoculars, "He looked like a nice Santa," Sally commented.

"There are mean Santas?" Wendy asked with a grin.

"Well, yeah," Sally huffed. "They don't let you tell them what to bring and only want the picture taken."

"Oh," Wendy said, reaching down and pulling the magazines she had used and passed them back to Jo Ann. "Reload those and hand me some more."

Reaching over the backseat, Jo Ann grabbed three loaded magazines and handed them to Wendy and then started reloading the ones Wendy had handed her. Loading magazines for the girls was tough and still a work in progress.

When Wendy reached the outskirts of Natchez, she didn't slow down from forty-five and the tires squealed as she drove the Tahoe around the few abandoned cars on the highway. Turning onto the highway that led to the bridge, Sally called out people and Wendy saw a small group near a store.

They all just turned and watched the Tahoe speeding down the road.

"Two people on the right," Jo Ann called out and Wendy turned to see a woman holding a rifle in one hand and a small child's hand in the other as they walked toward a group of houses.

"I see them," Wendy said, turning ahead. Seeing the bridge ahead, Wendy slowed as Sally turned forward with the binoculars. A sea of cars were parked on each side of the road and out into the grass, forming a funnel to the bridge.

"I don't see anyone moving," Sally said and Wendy reached over and Sally gave her the binoculars.

With the Tahoe slowly rolling forward, Wendy saw the sandbags in the outside lane with a HUMVEE parked and road barriers blocking the inside lane. The checkpoint sat under a railroad bridge that crossed over the highway. Turning, Wendy focused the binoculars on several tents that were set up in the median.

Handing the binoculars back, Wendy gripped the Glock from the center console. "Girls, stay low because we may have to shoot our way across."

"Those are army guys!" Sally cried out. "They are good guys."

"Baby, anyone that doesn't let us get home, are bad guys," Wendy told her in a hard tone. "We can't trust cops, army, or anyone, except us."

Sally leaned back in the seat and nodded, but Wendy never took her eyes off the checkpoint. Getting closer, Wendy rolled down her window to look for any movement and then looked at the sawhorse barricades and stopped right in front of them. She could see stop sticks placed on the ground under the barricades.

Looking around, Wendy cracked her door, "Don't get out, just run them over!" Sally cried out, grabbing her arm.

"See those things under the barriers? Those will give us flats if I run over them," Wendy said, opening her door. "Keep watch," she whispered back, stepping out.

Moving the Glock to her left hand, Wendy trotted up to the first barrier and moved it to the side, then pulled the stop sticks back. When she moved to the other barrier, Wendy stopped at seeing a soldier behind the sandbags with a bullet hole right between his eyes.

Looking past the soldier, Wendy saw two more with headshots and could tell they'd come from a rifle. "I have an idea who did that," she mumbled, pulling the barrier to the side. Wendy stopped and turned back to the soldiers. Seeing a black tube mounted to the helmet and flipped up, Wendy ran over behind the sandbags and took the helmet off the soldier.

Standing up, she saw the same on the others and took the helmets. Then she saw a bolt action sniper rifle with a tube attached in front of a massive scope. Knowing what that was, Wendy flipped the lever holding it on the rail system and pulled it off.

She ran back and just tossed the stuff inside and ran back behind the sandbags. Looking in the Hummer, Wendy saw a soldier behind the steering wheel with blood over his face and knew he'd died from flu. Stepping closer, Wendy saw a box in the soldier's lap that had binocular eyepieces at one end and a single lens at the other. Knowing it was something to observe with, Wendy grabbed it and yanked the helmet off the soldier.

Moving to the backseat, Wendy gave a sigh to see two boxes of MREs. Putting the stuff that she had on the boxes, Wendy carried the stuff back to the Tahoe. "Open your door, Jo Ann," Wendy called out and the back door opened and Wendy tossed the stuff in as Jo Ann got out of the way.

Shutting the door, Wendy jumped in and slammed the shifter in drive before hitting the gas. "Are you crazy?" Sally gasped. "They are army and bad guys and you took their stuff!"

"They were dead and didn't need it," Wendy said as the Tahoe picked up speed. "See if you see anything on the other bridge."

Picking up the binoculars Sally looked ahead, but they were almost over the bridge before she could see the other checkpoint. "Just an area like the one we just passed through. I don't see anyone moving," Sally told her.

"Get down," Wendy said, pushing the pedal hard and the engine roared. Like on the other side, there was a sea of cars pulled off the road on the eastbound side, but the lanes were clear. Speeding down westbound lanes, Wendy was thankful the road was cleared and then saw a crossroad ahead before a small town.

A field off to the side had a pile of bodies with a HUMVEE parked nearby and a gun mounted on the roof. Glancing down at the speedometer, Wendy saw she was passing sixty and let the needle climb. They saw nobody in the small town of Vidalia that sat at the foot of the bridge.

Fifteen miles down the road, Wendy slowed and they saw their first person in Louisiana, loading stuff in the back of a truck at a small store. The figure stopped and grabbed a rifle from the bed and then put it back, seeing the Tahoe speed past.

Tapping the cruise control for the first time today, Wendy glanced at the dashboard clock and saw it was only four eighteen p.m. "I feel like a week has happened just since we pulled into that shed," Wendy mumbled.

"What's in these boxes?" Jo Ann grunted, trying to move one box to the packed cargo area.

"Food, baby, food," Wendy smiled. "Open one and take out the packages so we can eat."

"Can we stop? I really need to pee," Sally asked in a low voice.

"Can you hold it for ten minutes? I want to get far enough away from the bridge, in case there were soldiers there. The farther we go, the more roads we pass and they won't know which one we took," Wendy explained.

"I can hold it," Sally assured her.

In the backseat, Jo Ann started reading off the menu choices. "Can I have the Chili-mac?" Sally asked and Jo Ann handed the package up.

"I want the stew, if you don't," Wendy said and Jo Ann passed it up.

"I'm eating the Ravioli with Noah," Jo Ann said with a smile.

Feeling it was safe enough, Wendy slowed to a stop in the road and let Sally jump out. Wendy climbed out and did a walk around and found a bullet hole in the wheel guard of the trailer, but nothing else. "They really wanted those cans," she mumbled, shaking her head. "There is shit everywhere, why risk it?"

"Done," Sally cried out and was already jumping in.

Not liking any answers her mind came up with, Wendy climbed inside and took off. The girls loved the MREs with all the stuff inside. Wendy thought they left a lot to be desired. "What's this?" Sally asked and Wendy glanced over at the binocular-looking box. "It's heavy."

"Don't know, but it's for observing and we need to observe, so I grabbed it," Wendy said, turning back to the road.

Turning the thing around in her lap, Sally took the covers off the lens and eyepieces and lifted it up, but couldn't see out. Putting it back in her lap, Sally continued her inspection and saw a switch and pressed it to hear the box whine. "I wonder if it's a game?" Sally said and lifted the box up and looked through it.

When it was at her eyes, Sally still couldn't see out and was about to put it down when color started coming on. "This thing only sees in black and white," Sally moaned, lowering the box.

Reaching over, Wendy took the box and used her legs to keep the steering wheel straight. The box was heavy enough that she needed both hands to hold it up. Looking through the eyepieces, Wendy grinned. "It's thermal binoculars."

"Are you sure?" Sally asked.

"Yeah. Arthur made a thermal camera a year ago and don't tell him, but this thing gives a much better image," Wendy said, looking around. Passing it back to Sally, "Take a look and then let Jo Ann, but we need to save the batteries until we know what kind it takes," Wendy said.

Nodding, Sally grabbed the thermal binocular and looked around, then passed it back to Jo Ann. Looking out the side of the Tahoe, "Holy crap, I see a person hiding near that house!" Jo Ann cried out. Dropping the thermal, Jo Ann looked at the house across the field and couldn't see the person hiding behind some bushes.

"Where?" Sally asked, looking with her binoculars.

Lifting the thermal back up to her eyes, "Behind those bushes in the front of the house," Jo Ann said. "I can see the outline of a person."

"Let me see," Sally said, swapping out with Jo Ann. "I see them," Sally gasped and then they rounded a curve and lost sight of the house.

"I couldn't see them with these," Jo Ann said, holding the binoculars and Sally looked ahead with the thermal.

"I like these. People can't hide," Sally told everyone.

"That's why we need to save the batteries," Wendy laughed at the girls' excitement. Then Ryan let everyone know, he was hungry.

Lowering the thermal, Sally looked at the box and saw a round cap. "Are the batteries in here?" She asked.

"Probably, but don't take them out until you turn it off," Wendy told her. "How about you let me do it?"

"You're driving," Sally said, turning off the thermal.

"Do we have to keep all these helmets?" Jo Ann asked.

"Those things on the front are night vision like I wore last night," Wendy said over her shoulder.

"All right! I want one," Jo Ann cheered, grabbing a bottle of water. "Is this another one you took off a helmet?"

Glancing in the rearview mirror, Wendy saw the clip-on thermal she'd taken off the sniper rifle. "No, that one is a thermal like the binocular," Wendy told her. "My husband bought one and I almost broke his legs."

"Why? They are cool." Sally asked.

"He paid two thousand dollars for something that cost almost thirty thousand dollars," Wendy told her.

"Wow, he can shop," Sally mumbled in awe.

"Sally, the person he bought it from stole it, that's why it was so cheap. Besides the fact that it has 'Property of US Government' on the side," Wendy said.

"Well, he didn't steal it," Jo Ann said, taking up for Arthur. "Just shows you he's smart and can really shop."

Turning to look out the window, Wendy couldn't help but laugh at the two taking up for Arthur. "In a way, I can see your side, but just having that is a crime. He already has enough shit buried that could have sent his ass to prison," Wendy told them as Sally got the battery compartment open.

"Hey, we have these," Sally cried out holding up a battery. "Jo Ann, hand me the batteries with two big As. It takes four."

"Double As," Wendy offered as Jo Ann passed up a package and picked Ryan up and put a bottle in his mouth. Instantly, Ryan was happy again.

"Next feeding, Ryan needs to eat some baby food," Wendy said, glancing back and saw Noah was caressing Ryan's head as he drank.

"I put that rice stuff in his bottle like you do," Jo Ann told her.

"Oh, you won't feed him that nasty green bean snot when you sit back there," Sally popped off as she fed in the new batteries.

"All right," Jo Ann moaned. "I'll feed him next time he's hungry."

Turning around and looking back at Jo Ann, "I'm feeding him the one that says chicken," Sally informed Jo Ann.

"I'll feed him the green snot!" Jo Ann shouted, making Ryan jerk and open his eyes but he never stopped drinking.

"Girls," Wendy called out and both just turned to her smiling.

With new batteries in, Sally turned the thermal back on and looked ahead. "I like having these," Sally said. "How long are we riding tonight?"

"If one of you girls can manage to stay awake and make sure I'm driving good, I don't want to stop until we get home," Wendy told them.

Putting the thermal down, Sally opened the center console and pulled out the energy drinks. "Jo Ann, when Ryan's finished eating, get that other pack of these from the back," Sally instructed, taking the top off and draining one down.

"You could wait till you're sleepy," Wendy laughed.

Holding her hands up as she shrugged, "But I'm already tired then," Sally whined.

Sally saw the smile drop off Wendy's face and jerked her head forward to see a large road that crossed over the road they were on. Grabbing the thermal, Sally lifted it up as she stood up on her knees in the seat. "I see cars on that bridge, but they aren't moving," Sally described. "Wait," she cried out, pointing to the right. "I just saw one drive past heading that way."

"What about under the interstate, can we drive through?" Wendy asked.

Staring ahead, slowly Sally nodded. "The road we are on we can, but that road beside us looks like it's blocked by a big truck."

Dropping her right hand down, Wendy picked up the Glock from the console. "Sally, I need you to sit down in the seat," Wendy told her.

Swiveling the thermal as she sat down, Sally pointed at a house off to the left. "People under the carport," Sally said and then turned away, scanning around.

Glancing over, Wendy saw two tall figures and several smaller ones standing around a truck pulled into the carport. "Another car just drove across the bridge, but it was going the other way," Sally reported.

Nearing the overpass, Wendy could see cars parked under the bridge in the opposite lanes. Turning right and left while looking down the interstate, Wendy saw a truck heading east and nothing moving on the other side heading west. Only a few abandoned cars dotted the interstate and then she lost sight as she drove under the overpass.

Coming out from under the overpass, Wendy glanced at the GPS and saw the small town ahead was Rayville. "That's a lot of big trucks," Sally mumbled and Wendy turned to her left where Sally was looking.

"Shit," Wendy gasped, seeing a truck stop but it and the field beside it were packed with parked trucks. There was a large business behind the truck stop and its parking lot was packed with semis.

"Did they have a sale and everyone got Rudolph there?" Sally asked as they passed the truck stop.

"No, baby. The government stopped all travel and truckers had to pull in. Most I think, would try for a truck stop that they knew," Wendy explained.

"Oh shit," Sally moaned and Wendy jerked her head over, looking at Sally. "There's a naked man walking near the road where it splits apart."

Turning away, Wendy saw the man just walking across the road, then he jerked his head around. Keeping her foot hovered over the pedal, Wendy watched the man but he just watched them pass by. Seeing the wild glaring eyes, Wendy gave a shiver.

Looking ahead, Wendy saw several dogs in a parking lot eating. Getting closer, Wendy saw it was a human body that had been dead for some time. Still on cruise control, Wendy just held her foot over the pedals.

The road led them into houses and Sally reported seeing several people and Wendy saw a truck cross over the street they were driving. When she reached the road that the truck had been on, Wendy turned and saw the truck driving away.

Ahead, Wendy saw railroad tracks and tapped the brake, knowing there would be a bump involved. In a business area,

Wendy slowed to twenty to cross the tracks and was glad she did after feeling the Tahoe lurch about.

"Push the gas, push the gas," Sally cried out and Wendy stomped the gas and the Tahoe took off. "Push it harder!"

"What is it?" Wendy yelled out, afraid to look back. She didn't have a long line of sight on the road and was afraid she would hit something as the Tahoe picked up speed quickly.

"Bad guys being mean to some people, but one pointed at us!" Sally cried out, looking behind them.

"Sally, look in front of us for threats," Wendy said, glancing down and seeing the needle pass seventy. She held it there, letting the Glock lay in her lap as she held the steering wheel tight. "I'll watch behind us but as fast as I'm going, I need eyes to the front."

"I'm looking straight, go faster!" Sally cried out, looking ahead and Wendy heard tears in Sally's voice.

Stomping her foot down, Wendy felt the big engine lurch forward as it let out a roar. Reaching the edge of town, the Tahoe was in triple digits as the road narrowed back down to two lanes. "I'm going fast, baby," Wendy said softly and cut her eyes over and saw the thermal pulled to Sally's face, but tears were running down her cheeks.

Keeping the pedal down, Wendy looked ahead and glanced in the mirror for any sign of pursuit. She could feel the tiny trailer almost floating behind them. "Cow in the road," Sally said.

Wendy was looking ahead and didn't see anything, but took her foot off the accelerator and then saw a dot in the distance. Tapping the brakes, Wendy was down to fifty by the time they'd reached the cow and she continued to slow down. More than once, one of her dumb ass cows had jumped out in front of her for no reason as she'd driven across the pasture.

Going past the cow, Wendy saw it was just standing in the road and chewing its cud.

Hitting 'Resume', Wendy let the Tahoe get back to forty-five. Seeing a sign for Oak Ridge, Wendy knew they had been hauling ass. They had covered ten miles in about four minutes. "We are a long way from them, Sally," Wendy assured her softly, but couldn't glance over as she turned onto another road.

"They were being mean to kids," Sally whimpered in a small voice, still looking ahead through the thermal.

Just hearing that made Wendy want to turn around. "You did a good job," Wendy told her and then reached over to squeeze Sally's leg. "You gave us warning and I was able to take off. They never had a chance to get close."

Finally, Sally lowered the thermal and wiped her eyes. "I'll stay awake until we get home," she sniffled.

Looking in the mirror, Wendy saw Jo Ann was holding a sleeping Ryan. "Can you put him down and come up here with your sister for a little bit?" Wendy asked.

"Noah's awake," Jo Ann said and put Ryan down on the pillows in the floorboard behind the passenger seat.

"Noah, come sit in my lap," Wendy called out and Noah bounced between the seats and over the center console and climbed into Wendy's lap. He tried to curl up, but the magazines on her vest kept digging into him. "Here," Wendy said, spinning him around and putting his hands on the steering wheel. "Hold it right there," Wendy said, tapping the brakes to slow down.

Jo Ann climbed in the front seat with Sally and held her hand as Sally laid her head on Jo Ann's shoulder. Sally pushed the thermal over into Jo Ann's lap and Jo Ann struggled to lift it up with one hand. Still holding Sally's hand, she moved her hand up and helped support the thermal as she looked ahead.

Undoing the side straps, Wendy folded the front of the vest over her head letting it rest over the headrest. "There we go," Wendy said, taking the steering wheel and Noah curled up against her chest.

"Momma," he said, snuggling into Wendy.

Tilting her head down, Wendy kissed the top of Noah's head. "Sally, if I knew you and the others would be okay, I would go back there and kill those bad guys for scaring you," Wendy admitted as she wrapped her arm around Noah.

With her head still on Jo Ann's shoulder, "I know," Sally said, wiping her nose with the back of her hand.

Lowering the thermal, Jo Ann looked down at her twin. "Wow, she really is," she said to Sally.

Wendy glanced over, never having heard Sally speak. "I know, but you're right," Jo Ann said and Wendy felt jealous that they could have a conversation without words.

"Can I ask what you guys were talking about?" Wendy asked, glad the sun was setting.

Lifting her head up, Sally stared at Jo Ann and then they both looked over at Wendy. "You're our momma now," they told Wendy and Wendy turned to the girls with a serious face.

"I'm sorry, but I've always looked at you two like my daughters," Wendy said with a sigh. "I always hoped you wouldn't get mad, but I see all of you as mine. I love you guys so much it hurts."

The twins climbed over the center console to cover Wendy's face with kisses and Wendy had to struggle to see the road until she could stop. Be damned if she was telling them to wait until she stopped. Finally stopped, Wendy held all three tight.

For several minutes, they just held a group hug. "Guys, let's do this at home," Wendy said regrettably. "I don't like stopping in plain sight."

"Okay," the twins said and Sally had a cheerful face again.

"You okay now?" Jo Ann asked and Sally nodded with her customary smile.

After Jo Ann climbed into the backseat, Wendy kissed Noah on the head and squeezed him tight. "Noah, I need you to get in the back, so we can get home," Wendy told him, pressing the accelerator.

After kissing Wendy on the cheek, Noah climbed in the back and Wendy reached over her head and pulled the vest back on. Tightening the side straps down, Wendy glanced over and saw Sally looking ahead. "Okay, the city of Bastrop is ahead and it is the biggest city we will go through. All the rest are very tiny," Wendy told them.

"Can we go fast?" Jo Ann asked.

"Not unless we have to, baby. We only went fast for like ten miles, but we used some gas to do it. Besides the fact that we could have a wreck really easy. I don't want to risk it unless we have to," Wendy explained.

They settled in and started looking around. When they reached the outskirts, they saw a truck pass them going the opposite way. Feeling something on her thigh, Wendy looked down and saw Sally had put the Glock in her lap. "It fell on your floorboard when we hugged you," Sally said, lifting the thermal up.

Even at forty-five, Wendy thought they were going too fast on the small streets, but kept going. Reaching the square, they saw a courthouse and several buildings looked burned down as the sun continued to drop below the horizon.

Hitting some railroad tracks that crossed the road, Wendy cursed for not slowing, feeling the tiny trailer yanking on them and throwing a fit. Seeing more tracks ahead, Wendy slowed.

"People on the right," Sally called out and Wendy looked over to see people loading stuff in trucks at a house. The group barely paused as they rode past.

By the time they reached the edge of town it was dark and Wendy put the harness on her head and turned the NVG on. "We only stop to pee and put gas in the truck," Wendy said, looking at the road ahead.

"Glad we filled the cans before going to sleep," Jo Ann said.

"It was hard going to sleep after drinking those little bottles," Sally admitted, looking ahead. "It's flat here."

"These are fields where crops are grown, baby," Wendy told her. "Give me a bottle of the good stuff."

Sally giggled and passed out the tiny bottles and all three turned them up, threw them outside, and settled in.

Chapter Thirty Six
That is your child

May 21

Taking the harness off her head, Wendy set it on the dash with the M4 as the sun reached over the horizon. Stretching her arms over her head Wendy let out a groan, making Jo Ann jerk beside her and glance over. "I don't like the roads here," Jo Ann announced as Wendy finished her stretch.

"Why?" Wendy asked, flexing her legs.

"They twist and turn, going up and down," Jo Ann said, lifting the thermal up. "You can't see far ahead of you."

"True, but that means people won't see us until we pass them by," Wendy answered.

Looking over at Wendy, "We've almost hit more stuff in the road in Arkansas than anywhere else," Jo Ann cried out in alarm. "Why do cows get in the road? There isn't any grass there!"

Laughing, Wendy glanced back and saw Sally holding Ryan and looking out the window. Noah had his head in Sally's lap and was sound asleep. "Baby, I have to tell you, cows are very stupid," Wendy chuckled.

"How much longer?" Sally asked.

Looking down at the gas gauge, "Let's stop and fill up the tank and stretch," Wendy told her. "I know these roads, but we are still seventy miles from home. We should be there around nine."

Stopping on a long stretch of road, Wendy put the Tahoe in park. Even Noah jumped out with them. Seeing Noah just run in a wide circle, Wendy grinned while undoing the straps over the cans. "That's it, Noah, get that energy out," Wendy said as Jo Ann opened the gas tank and put the funnel in.

With Ryan in her arms, Sally had to watch as Jo Ann helped Wendy lift the gas can up. "Will Arthur be mad if I take a nap before working on the farm?" Sally asked.

Lowering the empty can, Wendy looked over at Sally and laughed. "Baby, Arthur will rock you to sleep if you'll let him," Wendy bet, putting the empty can back on the trailer. "Our son is on a delayed timeline giving us grandkids, so you guys will have to fill that role."

Jo Ann gave a grunt as she pushed up on the next can to help Wendy pour it in. "Can we sleep with you and Arthur tonight, Momma?" Jo Ann asked as Wendy lowered the empty jug.

"Of course," Wendy said and then hugged Jo Ann.

When the tank was full, they only had one full gas can left, but Wendy wasn't stopping to fill up shit now. She walked around doing lunges on the road and turned to see Noah copying her. They all climbed back in with Sally and Jo Ann swapping seats.

After Jo Ann handed out MREs, they ate as Wendy set the cruise. Driving with the back of her hand, Wendy ate the cold meal with a grimace, "Last bottles of sport drinks," Jo Ann said, passing two up.

"We have little bottles of super drinks," Sally laughed out and Wendy glanced over and could almost see Sally vibrating in the seat.

"I told you, only one every six hours," Wendy chuckled, opening the package of dessert.

"I was getting sleepy," Sally whined, pausing her eating and lifting the thermal. "There are more cows in the road," Sally groaned, feeling Wendy tap the brake.

"That's a herd in the road," Wendy corrected, putting her MRE package down. Slowing to a crawl, Wendy had to use the push bumper to 'help' a cow out of their way.

Rolling down her window, Sally stuck her head out. "Move, stupid cows!" None of the cows moved, but several did turn and look.

"Our cows better be smarter," Sally grumbled, rolling the window back up.

It took them ten minutes of crawling before they reached the end of the herd of cows and Wendy resumed her speed. Hearing Velcro rip apart, a smell assaulted Wendy's nose. "Oh," she gasped and reached up to cover her nose.

"Ryan, don't move," Jo Ann whined in the backseat, but Ryan just laughed. "This is so gross."

"You have to do it fast or Ryan puts his hands in it," Sally instructed, cracking her window.

Taking her sister's advice, Jo Ann grabbed Ryan's ankles and held him up while using handfuls of baby wipes. "Roll my window down," Jo Ann gagged out. Sally hit the button and rolled down the window behind her.

Not even closing the diaper, Jo Ann just tossed it out along with the wipes she'd used. "Leave it down," Jo Ann gasped, taking deep breaths. She finished cleaning Ryan off and then grabbed a new diaper and put it on. "One box of wipes left," Jo Ann informed, grabbing a bottle of water and washing her hands over the towel she had changed Ryan on.

When she was done, the towel went out the window. Leaving the window down, Jo Ann picked Ryan up. "I should throw you out, but you are too cute," Jo Ann said and then blew a raspberry on Ryan's stomach, making him squeal.

Trying to keep her mind on the task of keeping alert, Wendy couldn't help but feel excited about being so close to home. "This is the Arkansas River, girls," Wendy told them. "That is the town of Ozark on the other side. Arthur and I bought some of our pigs there."

Crossing the bridge, the girls did glance at the water but turned, scanning around them. Reaching the other side, Wendy turned onto another road and everyone saw a man as he got out of a truck that was parked. With a pistol on his waist, the man put his hand on it as they drove past and then turned and headed inside a house.

"That man doesn't live there," Wendy told them. "The family that lives there buys quilts from me."

"We can come back later," Sally suggested.

"Nah, I'm sending Arthur," Wendy chuckled as they drove out of town.

Driving over Interstate 40, Wendy slowed on the overpass and looked to the east at a vehicle that had been blown up. "Did they have a war here?" Sally asked.

"I hope not, that's a Stryker," Wendy mumbled, easing the pedal down.

When the GPS told them to turn and Wendy didn't, Sally looked up as Wendy turned the GPS off. "I know where we are. I told the GPS to take us to Clarksville. In case we had to leave the Tahoe, I didn't want anyone to know where we were going," Wendy explained.

They rode on as the girls felt the excitement building and tried to keep an eye out. Then they felt Wendy slow and stop in front of a house. Sally looked at the mailbox. "Alicia Sutton, is this the Alicia that was with you on the ship?" Sally asked.

"Yeah, I was hoping she would be home, since she got off the ship a week before I did," Wendy said and then gave a long sigh. Turning around, Wendy left the dark house and continued on. The twins could tell Wendy knew where she was. The way Wendy turned from one dirt road to another and would weave around unseen bumps.

When she turned on a dirt road that headed for hills to the north, both girls felt like they were about to explode as trees closed in on both sides of the road.

"You really do live way out," Jo Ann said from the backseat with Noah and Ryan in her lap.

"Yeah, it took us forty-five minutes just to run to the closest real store, just over twenty minutes for a gas station," Wendy told them. "But I love it out here."

Rolling along the dirt road, the twins noticed a creek that ran along the side of the road. Coming around a curve, Wendy tapped the brakes and came to a stop. Sally saw her staring at a yellow sign that said, 'Dead End'. "What?" Sally asked.

"That sign has never been there," Wendy admitted, taking her foot off the brake and letting the Tahoe roll away under the idle. "This road leads into the valley," Wendy mumbled, trying to figure it out.

Not able to help, the girls just looked around at the thick trees and saw several deer. Driving for another few miles, they rounded a curve and saw a house on the left side of the road. "What the hell?!" Wendy shouted and stomped the brakes.

The road ahead stopped in front of the house and dark green grass seemed to form a road, but a fence ran across it. "Hey, those are water sprinklers," Sally said and then everyone noticed the half dozen water sprinklers watering the dark grass and trees.

"Are you sure you didn't miss a turn?" Jo Ann asked. "There are trees over there behind the fence. Not big ones, but trees older than I am."

Waving her hand at the house, "That's the Kercher house. They go to our church," Wendy cried out. "See that dark grass, that's where the road was."

"Um, there's a tree in the dark grass past the fence," Sally said, pointing ahead.

Looking around, Wendy saw a trailer near the creek that had solar panels and water hoses running to it. Turning, she saw the dirt track that led to the dilapidated barn. "I'll drive through the damn field," Wendy growled, stomping on the gas.

Driving past the dilapidated barn, the girls saw the track they were on continued past the barn and ended at a dirt road. Wendy stopped and looked back and saw someone had plowed up the road for a quarter of a mile, but the last few hundred yards only had small grass stems sticking out of the dirt.

"I knew I was on the right road," Wendy sighed with relief and turned back onto the dirt road that had disappeared.

When she reached Ted and Tammy's, Wendy gave a soft sob remembering sweet little Nicole and then saw two graves beside the house. "I bet Arthur did that," Wendy mumbled, taking her foot off the brake.

Looking ahead, Wendy's mouth fell open and her foot just slipped off the accelerator as she looked at Jack and Starlie's farm. "Holy crap, they must be rich! Look at all the stuff they have!" Sally cried out, rolling down her window.

Vehicles were parked in rows and most were new. "This isn't theirs," Wendy mumbled, looking around and finding it hard to believe this was the same valley she'd lived in.

Turning away from Jack's farm, Wendy saw the business house and there was more stuff stacked around in neat piles. Then to one side were two tanker trailers and a line of ATVs. "Arthur, you left the fucking farm?!" Wendy bellowed as the realization set in.

Gripping the steering wheel, Wendy stomped the accelerator.

***

Leading the kids, Arthur set his chainsaw down. "Okay, Shawn, your turn," Arthur said, looking down at Nicole asleep in the sling.

"You sure I'm ready?" Shawn asked nervously.

"You've seen me cut down ten trees and asked that on the last five. Tuck your dick in your boot and get your gear on," Arthur chuckled as the other kids stepped back.

Taking his AR off, Shawn adjusted his chaps and put his hard hat on before lowering the earmuffs. As Shawn knelt down to start the chainsaw, the dogs ran up to Arthur and looked out over the slope. All four gave soft growls and Arthur spun around, dropping to his right knee.

"Shawn, don't start the saw," Arthur snapped, pulling his AR up from under his arm.

Kirk ran up and tapped Shawn until Shawn looked back. Seeing Kirk scared, Shawn lifted his hardhat up. "Someone's coming," Kirk whispered, gripping his AR tight.

Turning and seeing Arthur looking down the slope, Shawn heard a vehicle approaching. "Shawn, get the kids behind trees. I don't know anyone that drives a Tahoe," Arthur called over his shoulder.

Only twenty feet from the gate, Arthur glanced down at the AR and then at Nicole. "Sorry, blue eyes, you'll have to ride this one out with me," Arthur said, looking up as the Tahoe stopped at the gate and the driver's door shot open. Arthur's mouth gaped and the AR fell from his numb hands.

Storming over to the keypad, Wendy punched in the code and the gate didn't open. "Arthur, you open this gate right now!" Wendy screamed. "I told you to stay at home! I swear, if you are sick I'm going to kick your ass!"

Hearing the dogs barking, Wendy turned to see Kit and Kat running at her full bore followed by Donald and Daisy. "Babies," Wendy cried out, loving on the dogs. "Is Arthur okay or does momma have to spank his ass?"

The kids all stepped out from behind the trees as Arthur slowly stood up. They knew it was Wendy because of the pictures around the house.

Lifting her head up from where the dogs had run from, Wendy felt her heart skip, seeing Arthur numbly walking through the trees to her. "Arthur!" Wendy cried out and took off running.

Instinctively, Arthur pulled Nicole under his left arm and holding his right out as Wendy jumped up, hitting him in the chest to wrap her arms and legs around him. "Baby," Arthur cried, hugging Wendy tight and Wendy kissed him and then leaned back.

"You shaved your beard," she noted and then realized Arthur was only holding her with one arm. Glancing down, Wendy gasped and released her legs to slide off. "I didn't hurt her, did I?" Wendy said, looking at the baby. Then Wendy reached out, moving the sling away from the face.

"Nicole?!" Wendy gasped and bent down to kiss Nicole.

Standing up from Nicole, Wendy felt Arthur pull her in and kissed her hard with tears rolling out of his eyes. "I thought you were dead," Arthur sobbed.

Wrapping her arms around him, "I thought I was too, baby. By the time I could move, there wasn't any way to let you know," Wendy said, crying into his neck.

Blinking the tears from her eyes, Wendy looked behind Arthur and gave a startle. Wendy's eyes grew big, seeing the mass of kids walking toward them. She pushed away from Arthur and looked at the kids, then back to Arthur. "Okay, I'm not that mad you left the farm," Wendy finally said.

"Now we have a big family," Arthur grinned, moving to hug Wendy, but she stopped him.

"It's not done yet," Wendy smiled and turned to the Tahoe. "Girls, bring the boys!"

Arthur and the kids watched two girls walk around the Tahoe. One carrying a baby and the other a toddler, "Twins!" Andrea said, behind them.

"Yeah, we have been through a lot, just as I'm sure you've been through a lot," Wendy said, turning around and noticed the kids behind Arthur were all looking at her with a reverence that was starting to bother her.

"Wendy, why are the twins looking at me like I walk on water?" Arthur asked, looking down at Sally and Jo Ann who were stopped at his feet.

"Guys, I'm Arthur's wife," Wendy told the group of kids.

"Oh, we know," Shawn said, stepping over in awe.

"Work's done today!" Arthur called out, putting an arm around Wendy and turned around. "Robin!" Arthur cried out. "I just put those damn clothes on you! You know how hard it was to find pink jeans and a shirt to fit your skinny ass?!"

Robin giggled and ran over in her pink boots and latched onto Arthur's leg. Looking up from Robin, Arthur looked Wendy in the eyes. "This one…. is your child," he said with a serious voice.

Bending down, Wendy picked up the naked, boot-wearing toddler. "Come on, girls. Let me show you our home," Wendy said, grabbing Arthur's hand. The entire group moved to the house and introductions were made. Then, everyone sat down in the living room. For the rest of the day, everyone told their stories of how they ended up in this new family.

Stay Connected with Thomas A Watson

Check out A-Poc Press Website at apocpress.com
Join the newsletter to get updates from Thomas & Tina Watson

Like Thomas A Watson Facebook Page
www.facebook.com/thomasawatson

Join the A-Poc Press Group Page
www.facebook.com/groups/apocpress

Follow Me on Twitter
www.twitter.com/1blueplague

Thank You for Reading, Please Remember to Leave a Review. Reviews are what helps pay the bills for indie authors.

We hope you have enjoyed our first book together.
Thomas & Tina Watson

47021097R00212

Made in the USA
Lexington, KY
04 August 2019